THE CHAINS OF FATE

THE AELFYN ARCHIVES
BOOK TWO

SAMANTHA AMSTUTZ

STARLIGHT FANTASY PUBLISHING LLC

The Chains of Fate

Copyright © 2024 by Samantha Amstutz

All rights reserved.

No part of this publication may be reproduced, distributed, or transmitted in any form or by any means, including photocopying, recording, or other electronic or mechanical methods, except for brief quotations in reviews, without the prior written permission of the publisher, except as permitted by U.S. copyright law. For permission requests, contact author.samantha.amstutz@gmail.com.

The story, all names, characters, and incidents portrayed in this production are a work of fiction. No identification with actual persons (living or deceased), places, buildings, and products is intended or should be inferred.

ISBN : 979-8-9897896-1-0

Editor: Hannah VanVels Ausbury

Cover Artist: Jeff Brown Graphics

*For those who've lost
some of their light to grief,
look up and see that even
the darkest sky fails to engulf the stars.*

CONTENTS

Reading Guidance	vii
Spice rack	ix
Guide & Summary	xiii
Chapter 1	1
Chapter 2	7
Chapter 3	20
Chapter 4	30
Chapter 5	47
Chapter 6	57
Chapter 7	63
Chapter 8	74
Chapter 9	89
Chapter 10	100
Chapter 11	106
Chapter 12	112
Chapter 13	116
Chapter 14	123
Chapter 15	136
Chapter 16	144
Chapter 17	155
Chapter 18	163
Chapter 19	169
Chapter 20	178
Chapter 21	186
Chapter 22	200
Chapter 23	211
Chapter 24	220
Chapter 25	227
Chapter 26	233
Chapter 27	237
Chapter 28	247
Chapter 29	263
Chapter 30	271

Chapter 31	280
Chapter 32	288
Chapter 33	300
Chapter 34	306
Chapter 35	318
Chapter 36	329
Chapter 37	337
Chapter 38	346
Chapter 39	355
Chapter 40	365
Chapter 41	370
Chapter 42	384
Chapter 43	396
Chapter 44	405
Chapter 45	413
Chapter 46	420
Chapter 47	432
Chapter 48	443
Chapter 49	456
Thank you for reading!	469
Acknowledgments	471
About the Author	473

READING GUIDANCE

This novel is intended for adults with darker themes some readers may find upsetting or disturbing. Please consider your mental health before diving into this story if you have any concerns about the following content warnings. This book ends on a brutal cliff-hanger.

Consensual sexual intimacy is on page. If you'd prefer to avoid or know when to expect intimate content, please refer to the "spice rack" for specific chapters on the following page.

This is by no means an exhaustive list or arranged in any particular order: panic attacks, death, graphic violence/gore, fire injury, eugenics, sexual encounters and suggestive themes, racism, adult language, DID, bullying, memories of substance abuse/addiction, alcohol use, choking, blood/bleeding, emotional/physical manipulation and abuse.

SPICE RACK

All of these chapters can be skipped without impacting the story beyond relationship building. Important plot points that may occur do come through in the following chapters.

Chapter 14- Full chapter intimate encounter

Chapter 19- Approximately the first 3/4 of the chapter is an intimate encounter

Chapter 45- Heavy sexual themes and environment, no intimate encounter between the main characters

Chapter 47- Full chapter intimate encounter

Cerulean Sea
Laendel
NYDORAEN
Timber Wilds
Frostvault Keep
Cerulean Basin
Kyansari
Aethyl
HALAEMA
Sapphire Basin
Hibernal Wastes
Cyan Mere
Centarya
Aetarryn
DOSYTHE
ALARI
ALLAENAR
Foothill Mines
Vaelyn
The Maelstrom

ACADEMY CENTARYA
Magus Quarters
Northern Dorms
Infirmary
Rending Field
Combat Yard
The Spire
Western Dorms
Portal Platform
Eastern Dorms
Axis Dorms
Shields and Portals
Force Yard
The Citadel
Southern Dorms

GUIDE & SUMMARY

The first few chapters of The Chains of Fate highlight significant events that took place in The Aspect of Essence and most of the information below comes through in narration. Refreshers and minor details about the characters and the known magic system can be found within the next few pages.

ESSENCE

The elves' magical source of power, thought to be drawn from the stars. Only pure-bloods have the potential to control all eight abilities (arch elves). The Elven-blooded (those with human and elf blood) have an easier time learning how to summon their talents by drawing on respective emotions tied to each ability. Talents are innate and cannot be learned.

Well- The source where magic is drawn from. Wells can be strengthened and expanded by continual use of magic. Strength is determined by the number of abilities, not the size of the Well. Magic must be regenerated by meditating (easier under starlight for most).

Rending - Destructive shadows that can either restrain a body, inflict perceived pain, or totally obliterate (known emotion to draw from: anger).

Mending - Healing powers that appear as red threads of light, cannot be used on the caster (known emotion to draw from: love/kindness).

Shielding - Violet crystalline wards that can serve as protective barriers on objects or a person (known emotion to draw on: fear).

Force - The caster can use weights of objects or the earth's gravity to push and pull, appears as blue light (known emotion to draw on: desire/determination).

Illumination - Any individual with elf blood possesses this ability. The user can create a variety of colorful lights or distribute a portion of their magical reserves to another to restore power (known emotion to draw on: happiness).

Portaling - Rifts can be opened only to known locations unless a bond is shared with another (corresponding emotion: trust and yearning).

Illusion - The ability to project realistic images, appears as turquoise light (corresponding emotion not yet revealed).

Telepathy - Mind to mind communication. Those without telepathy can still communicate so long as the person with the talent maintains the connection. Jassyn has discovered that telepathy is used in coercion. Compulsive magic is only able to be used by the king due to his strength in power. King Galaeryn can influence others into not speaking. Lykor's POV has revealed that the king can also control actions with coercive magic (corresponding emotion not yet revealed).

WRAITH ABILITIES

Warping - Can teleport from one location to another as long as the destination in view is visible and unobstructed.

Venom - Their fangs have paralytic qualities.
Cloaking - Can conceal and obscure themselves in shadows.

PROMINENT CHARACTERS

Serenna (Sir-REN-nah) **Vallende** (Val-LEND-e) - an elven-blooded and former princess of Allaenar, now an initiate at Centarya. Shares a bond with Prince Vesryn that spontaneously manifested but is not fully formed until they both accept the connection.
Essence abilities: rending, shielding, force, and mending (has yet to manifest illumination and portaling)
Jassyn (JAS-sin) **Raellyn** (Rae-ELL-in) - a mender and researcher at Centarya, half cousin to Vesryn
Essence abilities: mending, telepathy, shielding, illusion, illumination
Known shaman abilities: controlled plant life
Vesryn (VEZ-rin) **Falkyn** (FALL-kin) - prince of Alari, arch elf. Commander of Centarya and the rangers
Lykor (Lie-CORE) - wraith leader whose consciousness split from Aesar's (Vesryn's twin) at the hands of King Galaeryn during experiments with Essence. Aesar is thought to have perished during the first wraith appearance in an attack on Kyansari a century ago.
Essence abilities: shielding, rending, portaling, force (other talents were stripped away and not returned).

MINOR CHARACTERS

Kal (CAL) - A wraith and Lykor's captain.
Fenn (FEN) - A wraith, Kal's son, one of Lykor's lieutenants.
Elashor (e-LASH-or) **Vallende** (Val-LEND-e) - Serenna and Ayla's father and Alari's General, arch elf.

Velinya (Vel-LIN-ya) - Serenna's elven-blooded friend who was injured during the wraith attack on Centarya and taken to Kyansari with other wounded for healing.

Magister Thalaesyn (THAL-Aye-Sin) - Mender and researcher at Centarya, Jassyn's mentor and an arch elf

Galaeryn (ga-LARE-rin) **Falkyn** (FALL-kin) - Elven king of Alari, Vesryn's sire.

Ayla (EYE-la) Vallende - An initiate at Centarya, half niece to Jassyn, half sister to Serenna via Elashor. Engaged to Vesryn.

Lady Farine (Fa-REEN) **Vallende** - Elashor's mother and one of Jassyn's former contract holders.

Fynlas (FIN-las) **Kovaer** (COE-va-air) - an archivist who disappeared decades ago. Had a study in Farine Vallende's estate when he was one of her live-in companions. Tracked human shaman lines. Jassyn discovered both his and Serenna's family tree among many other elven bloodeds'.

Queen Maraelyn (Ma-REL-in) - Vesryn's mother who perished in the first wraith attack, half sister is Jassyn's mother.

Nelya (NEL-ya) - Jassyn's peer and research associate at Centarya.

Flight Captain Zaeryn (Zare-IN) - Vesryn's second in command of the rangers

RACES

Aelfyn (ALE-fin) - The elves' ancestors.
Elves - Ruling race, subjugated humans and elven-blooded.
Elven-blooded - Those with any amount of elf blood mixed with human blood.
Humans - Natives of the mortal shores, provide resources to Alari.
Wraith - Two groups of wraith have been speculated on: "mindless" wraith and "organized" wraith (Lykor's).

Druids - An extinct race who perished in the Great War with the Aelfyn, not much is known, but they were suspected to be shifters

Shamans - Ancient line of humans who had access to elemental power (fire, water, earth, wind, lightning).

PLACES

Centarya (Sen-TAR-e-ah) - The elven-blooded military academy.
Alari (a-LAR-e) - Elven realm
Kyansari (KEY-an-sar-e) - Elven capital
Frostvault Keep - Lykor's haven with the wraith, a dormant volcano thought to be an ancient druid capital.
Ranger Station - stables where the dracovae rides under Prince Vesryn are based out of, in the plains of northern Alari.

Human Realms
    Southern realm - **Allaenar** (Al-LAE-nar) Capital - **Vaelyn** (Vey-LIN), Serenna's former home
    Northern realm - **Nydoraen** (Nye-DOR-ain)
    Eastern realm - **Halaema** (Ha-LAE-ma)
    Western realm - **Dosythe** (Do-SITHE)

CHAPTER 1

JASSYN

Stars, am I seriously doing this?

Jassyn stalled in front of Vesryn's apartment. Resolve slowly leached out of his raised arm. He couldn't bring himself to knock on the looming oak doors.

Three harrowing days had elapsed since the wraith attack. In the wake of the destruction, a somber heaviness hovered above Centarya like a gathering storm. Based on gossip scavenged from other magus, Jassyn had gleaned that the prince had finally returned to campus that morning—presumably after spending days hunting the wraith that had fled.

After arguing with himself for the past hour, Jassyn had abandoned the safety of his chambers. He'd spent the entire ascent of the Spire—all five hundred stairs—fabricating countless excuses to turn around. Somewhere in the mire of his thoughts, he knew it was a futile attempt to convince himself that he didn't require his cousin's aid.

It would be better to go to the prince directly, he reluctantly reasoned, *and accept the consequences.* He didn't have anyone else.

Like the spiral stairs leading up the tower, Jassyn's thoughts circled back to the root of his problems—and the reason he desperately needed help sobering up. He'd nearly lost his ability to control Essence due to Stardust. If the wraith returned and he was useless during another assault...

Surely he could manage resisting the craving until his dependency no longer held his will hostage. But his determination to abstain from the drug eroded, like water weathering stone.

If someone like Vesryn can sober up, then so can I. Before Jassyn's birth, the prince's wild behavior had bordered on legendary debauchery in the courts. His cousin had somehow freed himself, overcoming his own addiction to Stardust decades prior.

Jassyn shook his head, wrestling with a festering madness. Tempted to return to his quarters, he warred with the urge to consume his remaining dust.

Initiates faced expulsion for possessing the drug on campus. On more than one occasion, the prince had ordered General Elashor to escort recruits off the island to stars knew where—most likely the human's war training camps. He could only imagine a magus like himself would face a harsher punishment. They were expected to set the example.

A zephyr of crisp air flowed through the sparse corridor, whirling Jassyn's awareness back to Vesryn's chambers. The furious breeze did nothing to alleviate his body's determination to scorch him with another wave of heat. He wiped a trickle of perspiration from his brow. Undoubtedly, his entire being would continue to revolt, wearing him down until he yielded and provided it with more of that condemning drug. *I still have some dust in my chambers. Just a pinch for relief—*

A pulse of Essence scattered Jassyn's thoughts. Servants scurried past him, rushing to close the arched windows with pulls of force before the thunderheads unleashed their fury above the floating island. Turning his attention back to Vesryn's doors, Jassyn's stomach churned alongside the brewing storm.

Why am I seeking Vesryn out as the person to help me? It would be more effective to receive aid from a child. Jassyn pivoted on the purple runner. Dodging the prince's staff, who were now igniting globes of illumination in the empty ivory sconces, he sped back down the corridor. *I can handle this on my own. I've already made it three days.*

Before descending the stairs, something Jassyn couldn't quite discern caught his attention outdoors. He halted by a window, focusing on the swaying willows below. Like the scattered leaves ripped away by the wind, he knew his actions were spiraling out of control.

Disappointment settled onto his shoulders, a bleak grief encompassing him like a cloak. The only person to blame was himself. His justifications for turning to the drug as an escape buried him under a mountain of guilt.

Farine Vallende purchasing one of the slots on his contracts had nearly broken him. Recalling his helplessness against the realm's laws, binding him to couple with Elashor's mother, bile surged in Jassyn's throat. He miserably failed at warding off the sporadic memories. All those faceless people Farine had imposed upon him for her entertainment. *I can't pretend what she forced me to do was about preserving the elven race.* Overwhelmed, he'd started obliterating his mind when summoned to her estate.

Vesryn had unexpectedly swooped in and intervened, exploiting a loophole by using his position on the council to claim exclusivity to Jassyn's bloodline, granting him freedom from the realm instead. Despite his liberation from contractually siring children, Farine's gluttonous hands still haunted Jassyn's dreams. *All of that is over, so why don't I have the strength to stop indulging?*

Remorse twisted Jassyn's gut. In his stupor after Vesryn had telepathically woken him the night of the assault, the only person he'd manage to save was one of their enemies.

Jassyn still tried denying that he'd summoned a foreign power, manipulating roots to halt that warrior's fall. He'd dared to hope that it was a hallucination, an effect of the drug. But he'd walked past the ruptured ground's glaring reminder at the base of the Spire. Touching his throat, Jassyn traced the scabs left behind from that soldier's gauntlet, providing more blatant evidence of the events.

Accompanying another bead of sweat, a residual fear slid down Jassyn's spine from the hazy memory. He wasn't entirely sure how that midnight-haired male with crimson eyes and flashing fangs looked more elf than wraith. More importantly, he wondered why that soldier was compelled and how he had Essence.

Tangling his fingers into his curls, Jassyn yanked his hair in frustration. If he'd had a clear head that night, he might've gotten answers. *The king must be involved with the compulsion, but that doesn't make any sense.* Nothing about that encounter made sense and the only answer Jassyn had received from that warrior was a snarl when he'd asked.

If the wraith return, I need to be ready. Determined, Jassyn whirled around and marched himself back down the hallway to Vesryn's rooms. He couldn't fix this predicament on his own. *I'll pay the price.*

Before changing his mind again, Jassyn knocked on the prince's door.

Too late, he realized that the withdrawal suspended him over a precipice of stupidity. Jassyn blanched at his error. His symptoms were simply confusing him. He could wean himself off the drug. *How hard could it be? Just a pinch would work...* Seized by the idea, Jassyn promptly spun on his heel, fleeing down the hallway.

Vesryn's voice boomed down the corridor, echoing a roll of thunder. "Jassyn!"

Jassyn skidded to a halt as a pounding agony lanced through

his skull. He considered how far he could dash down the stairs before the prince could catch up to him.

Shoulders slumping at the inevitable, Jassyn blew out a defeated sigh before turning. Hairs lifting as if in warning, a crack of lightning flashed while rain began pinging against the windows.

Seeing double, two copies of his cousin prowled toward him. Jassyn rapidly blinked Vesryn back into focus. Gaze sweeping over the prince, he surveyed Vesryn's sweaty bare chest and bootless feet. Jassyn pursed his lips. The prince's rumpled shorts were in danger of slipping indecently low—well past his excessively toned abdominals.

Vesryn's emerald eyes glittered with curiosity. "This is the first time you've *ever* come to my quarters, and you're going to leave after knocking?"

"I was here when you were bleeding out," Jassyn protested, clasping his hands behind his back to hide his quivering fingers. *That might've been the only time, come to think of it.*

As if reminded by Jassyn's prior visit, the prince idly traced the cluster of scars embedded in the center of his chest. An unexpected encounter with a band of organized wraith had resulted in the injury. Serenna had stitched Vesryn together to the best of her abilities, saving his life.

Jassyn started to angle back toward the stairs. "I'll...return later."

"Did you need something?" Vesryn arched a brow. "Or do you want to come in?" He slanted his head at his quarters. "Since you came all this way?"

Nose wrinkling at Vesryn's half-clad appearance, Jassyn studied his cousin's disarrayed topknot, barely restraining his silvery hair. "I—I didn't need anything." *My mind must still be affected if I thought coming to Vesryn was the solution. I'll simply consume the rest of my Stardust to erase the evidence of having it and sleep off any further urges. I can start fresh in the morning.* "I'd rather not interrupt…" Having no interest in the prince's current activities, Jassyn flapped a hand at what little disheveled garb Vesryn was wearing. "Whatever you were in the middle of."

Obviously humored, an irritating smirk tugged at Vesryn's mouth. "Trust me, I wouldn't answer the door—even for you—if you were interrupting anything *carnal*."

"And I'm already regretting knocking." Jassyn rubbed his temples, hoping that if the prince noticed the blown vessels webbed through his eyes, he'd assume it was from exhaustion.

Turning to his rooms, Vesryn beckoned over his shoulder. "Stars, I'll put on a fucking tunic if that'll make you stop twitching."

Jassyn scowled at his cousin's sculpted back. *It's not too late, I don't have to do this.*

But he knew his thoughts only disguised themselves as excuses. Guilt wrestled his reluctance into submission. Mustering his self-control, Jassyn resisted the impulse to sprint back to his quarters, his attention dancing around the box of Stardust waiting for his return. *I should've tossed the container off the island.* Deep down, he admitted that wouldn't have helped. He knew where to retrieve more.

With a stabilizing breath, Jassyn followed Vesryn into his chambers, unable to predict how the prince would react. Apprehension nipped at his heels as he imagined the likelihood of Vesryn banishing him from campus—or worse.

I'm going to regret this.

CHAPTER 2

JASSYN

Rain pummeled the expansive wall of windows in the prince's sitting room as Jassyn closed the door behind him. Much like quarters he'd expect at the palace, Vesryn's chambers were lavish, decorated with rich leather sofas complemented by ebony tables. He doubted the prince had a hand in furnishing the apartment, considering the impressive collection of books flanking one side of the room.

Loitering inside the apartment's threshold, Jassyn considered how to liven up the prince's suite—if only to distract himself from the reason for his visit. *I should bring Vesryn a plant.* Though he assumed a helpless life form would only be an additional responsibility for the staff.

"How's Serenna?" Vesryn asked before dropping to a padded exercise mat, extending his arms to brace himself. Unsurprisingly, the prince ignored his claim that he was going to cover himself up.

Jassyn tugged at the neck of his uniform, gripped by an insane notion to shed his leathers in the same fashion—anything to alleviate the heat erupting from his skin.

He fired back a response. "Why don't you ask her yourself?"

The prince emitted a humorless scoff. "I'm asking *you* since you're conveniently here in front of me."

Jassyn irritably drove his fingers through his curls, assuming his current state frayed his tolerance toward his cousin even more than usual. Hands itching, he searched for something to occupy himself with before Vesryn noticed his fidgeting.

Allowing himself to relax into the familiarity of their usual verbal sparring, Jassyn prodded, "You can't tell how she's been through the bond?"

"Right, I didn't think of that." Vesryn planted himself stiffly on his knuckles and toes, pushing his body up and down like a working bellows. "The last time I saw her, she was with you." He blew out a breath with his body's descent. "Since you haven't disclosed why you're here, I didn't think having a conversation in the meantime would kill you."

Now that he mentions it... Vesryn's punishment can't possibly be that severe, can it?

Eyes widening, Jassyn hastily shoved one of his golden blades back into his leathers, the knife's unintentional appearance splintering his composure. He warily inspected the pad of his thumb, not recalling his anxious fingers retrieving the dagger from his uniform's hidden seams. *I'm lucky I didn't cut myself.*

Jassyn's gaze darted to his cousin, but Vesryn was too engaged in pulverizing his body to notice the weapon. *I'm not going to stab him to stage my escape.* Jassyn quickly banished the coalescing thought before the temptation solidified.

He cleared his throat, providing the prince with his participation. "Serenna is unsettled, but who isn't?"

Legs becoming restless, Jassyn channeled his concentration into putting one foot in front of the other, walking a straight line as he veered to a wall of Vesryn's windows.

His attention snagged on the waterfall cascading from the permanent portal opened above the Spire, rushing down to saturate streams below. Stomach pitching from the dizzying height, Jassyn ripped his eyes away from the ground. Instead, he focused on the glistening rain, tracing the fascinating patterns of the drops rolling down the glass.

Realizing he should elaborate so the prince wouldn't detect anything unusual in the silence, Jassyn added over his shoulder, "Serenna has been helping move initiates into the other residence halls to make room for the capital's soldiers. Elashor took it upon himself to keep the recruits busy since you've been... absent."

"Of course he did," Vesryn muttered nearly to himself, their mutual dislike of the general a bizarre common ground.

To prepare for the wraith's potential return, the prince had permitted squadrons of Kyansari's elven-blooded warriors to occupy dwellings on campus under General Elashor's command. *The capital's presence would've been helpful during the assault. I'm told anyway.*

Guilt carved a path through Jassyn's chest like the flash of lightning cracking against the sky. *I came here for a reason.* Hauling himself away from the window, Jassyn steeled himself to face his cousin. *I need to get this over with. And then I can leave and get back to my chambers where I have—*

"You don't mind, do you?" Vesryn interjected as Jassyn opened his mouth. The prince lifted his feet to balance his weight over his hands, muscles flexing in waves. "I have a hundred left before I finish my set."

"Impressive." Jassyn's lip curled as he glanced sideways at the prince. *Why would anyone voluntarily decimate their body like he does?* "I'm surprised you can count that high. Don't let me interrupt."

Straying to the prince's bookshelves, a sudden tremor loosened Jassyn's legs, the shaking becoming more frequent and pronounced. Lurching forward, he caught himself before toppling over. After sparing a glance toward the prince as he straightened, Jassyn refocused on the books.

The last time he was here, he'd thieved a few texts concerning telepathy, not bothering to return them. He doubted Vesryn—

"You never brought my books back."

I guess he remembered. "I haven't finished reading them."

Vesryn only grunted in acknowledgment as he continued his ridiculous exercises.

Pursuit of more material on coercion was at the forefront of Jassyn's mind. Well, right behind regaining control over Essence —and the distracting fact that a sprinkle of Stardust was waiting in his chambers. Ruthlessly redirecting his thoughts, Jassyn mentally clasped onto the frail fibers of his clandestine academic interests. His research had always served as an adequate distraction before.

After he could think more clearly, Jassyn intended to uncover further information regarding the extinct elemental powers he'd stumbled upon while imprisoned in the Vallende estate. A shiver nearly unbalanced him as he imagined the worst possible punishment. *What if Vesryn sends me back to the Vallendes to make an example? He wouldn't. Would he?*

Jassyn shook the horrifying thought from his head, legs less steady than ever. He forced his mind back toward his studies, hoping the diversion would be enough fortification to rebalance him.

I wonder if Serenna has sensed anything strange in the earth yet. Fynlas, Elashor's sire and a former palace archivist who'd disappeared during a wraith attack decades ago, had traced her human lineage back to the shamans. Fynlas' research had tracked countless elven-blooded—Jassyn included. *I need to ask her soon. If the council found out the ancient magic was manifesting...*

Instead of dissecting his fears further, Jassyn sutured and

buried those worries before he descended into gloom. He scanned the vellum spines in front of him. Dismay nudged his brows together as he registered the texts weren't in any logical order. For whatever reason, Vesryn had an extensive collection ranging from Aelfyn history, the biology of dracovae, Essence mastery, and...*philosophy*.

Jassyn scoffed. One tome was a scandalous text recounting escapades of courtiers in the human realms when the races first mingled a century ago. *I'm sure that novel is the only book Vesryn would actually be interested in reading.* He could only assume it contained obscene illustrations.

Jassyn tilted his head and then winced when the motion aggravated a spike of vengeance, unleashing a rampage against his skull. The racing tempo of his pulse roaring in his ears drowned out a rumble of thunder. Muscles convulsing, he silently pleaded to the stars for the painful upheavals to subside.

Inhaling a shuddering breath as he recovered, Jassyn focused back on the prince's shelves, oddly appreciative for the distraction of Vesryn's chaotic disarray. *Does he simply shove his books in the most convenient places?* With a considering frown, Jassyn pinpointed the pattern—one he should've immediately detected. Of course, his cousin had arranged the volumes by size and color. *This is atrocious.*

"I...I'll see Serenna when I can," Vesryn said on an exhale, lowering to the ground. "After I take some time to...collect myself." Jassyn wondered if they'd been conversing and his mind wasn't keeping up with the discussion. The prince pushed himself back up, seemingly unaffected by the repetitive motion. "The past few days"—he blew out another breath—" have been trying."

"Serenna would probably appreciate seeing you before you leave the island again," Jassyn mentioned while perusing the shelves. *Am I encouraging them to spend more time together?*

After wiping his clammy palms on his leathers, Jassyn

plucked out an armful of books and rearranged them by title. *Or would it be better to order them by the archivist? Subject area?* It would take hours, but he considered indexing them for the prince. *Honestly, I could use the diversion.*

The familiar action of systematically cataloging his surroundings didn't ease Jassyn's throbbing head, but it almost prevented him from fixating on that blue powder shimmering with infused Essence. Almost.

"The bond with her," Vesryn grunted out, "Might be making me a little erratic since the attack."

Since the attack? He's been erratic his entire life. Balancing the stack of tomes on his hip, Jassyn reorganized one of the jumbled shelves. "What do you mean?"

"I just need to take a few days to get my head back on straight," Vesryn said, blowing out a breath. "That's all."

Jassyn sensed he wouldn't gather any more information concerning the prince's intentions with Serenna. Since Jassyn's assignment as her tutor in the human realms half a year prior, he'd become protective of her well-being. Especially once he'd realized Elashor's ambitions concerning her bloodline.

Genuinely curious how Vesryn had spent his time since the attack, Jassyn asked, "What happened with the wraith prisoners you transported to the dungeons? Did you get—"

"I'm not discussing that," Vesryn snapped, a sharp finality inoculating his words.

Rolling his eyes, Jassyn busied himself with filing the books onto the shelves. *He's the one who wanted to have a "conversation." If that's how he's going to be, I'll leave after I'm finished sorting these titles.* Assuming he could walk back across the room without falling on his face.

"What the bleeding stars are you doing?"

Jassyn spun to face the prince, snagging the top volume in his cradled stack before it slid off his pile. *Could he at least pretend to be winded?* Vesryn leaned back on his heels, studying him with an unnerving intensity. An uncomfortable silence loomed like thunderheads in the space between them. *Distract him so he doesn't notice anything is amiss.*

Jassyn cleared his throat. "I'm organizing your collection." Tearing free from the prince's gaze, he squeezed a book in at the end of a shelf. "I don't know how you find anything—if you even read. Who arranges by size and color?"

"I know where everything is." Vesryn raised both brows, like he thought Jassyn was the mad one. "You happen to be dismantling *my* bookcase."

Hands slippery, Jassyn nearly fumbled the stack of volumes. "Well, obviously, you've spent no time in a library if you believe that this is the appropriate way to file your collection."

"Fine, Magus *Meticulous*. Have it your way." Vesryn toweled off and tossed the cloth to a chair. "Are you going to tell me the reason for your visit? Or are you simply here to molest my tomes?"

Scowling, Jassyn evaded the question, rummaging for something else to say. He retrieved the texts from the next shelf, spreading them across an end table, determining how many he'd have to accommodate.

"I heard the magisters are crediting the training you required of us as the reason we survived." Mood turning bleak like the storm, Jassyn neglected acknowledging his absence during the assault. However, he believed Vesryn deserved recognition for how thoroughly he'd prepared the magus for a confrontation—not that anyone ever expected one to take place on their island.

First I'm pushing him toward Serenna, now I'm stroking his ego. Stars, something is seriously wrong with me.

Vesryn shouldered on a loose black tunic, his voice muffled before his head emerged. "Thirty percent of our recruits perished at the hands of those beasts." He brushed away the loose hair spilling across his face. "I failed to keep Centarya safe. Neither the rangers nor I have been able to locate the wraith."

Jassyn's thoughts skittered around the elven wraith he'd saved, having wondered more than once where he'd portaled to. *He's still out there. Somewhere.*

"There's fewer than a hundred dracovae riders," Jassyn said quietly, while he finished ordering the shelf. "The burden of responsibility isn't only yours to bear. I simply wanted to tell you that you have the magus' respect."

Vesryn wandered to the dining table. "We've spent the past three days scouring the realms," he nearly growled, pouring water from a silver pitcher. Half the liquid sloshed over the side of the glass. "We're no closer to finding the wraith now than we were eighty years ago when they broke free from the dungeons."

The prince clenched his jaw before draining the goblet. Jassyn jumped when Vesryn slammed the empty glass back on the table before filling another cup. Abruptly pivoting, the prince prowled in his direction before shoving the water at him.

"Am I supposed to guess why you're here?" Vesryn demanded. "I find it hard to believe that you came all this way to compliment me."

Jassyn's heart battered his ribs as the prince's gaze swept over him, calculating eyes narrowing, seeing far too much. Opting for silence, Jassyn snatched the offered glass, greedily downing the contents.

"You're sweating more than me and I have a feeling it isn't from your spectacular exertion of arranging my shelves." Vesryn crossed his arms, fingers drumming. "When was the last time?"

"I—" Betrayed by his body, a renewed wave of tremors pillaged control of Jassyn's muscles, rippling him like a sheet in the wind. He tightened his grip around the cup, his thoughts spiraling too quickly to snatch at an answer.

"You've consumed Stardust." It was more of a statement than a question. Vesryn frowned before realization flickered in his gaze. "Your mind was clouded the night of the attack when I telepathically linked with you." He released a disbelieving grunt. "I dismissed it as your typical way of shielding from me."

Jassyn leaned back as Vesryn raided his space, scrutinizing his face. The prince shook his head, tone tightening. "Judging from all those vessels blown in your eyes, you're getting close to hallucinating from the withdrawal."

Locking his knees, Jassyn carefully inched away from the prince. Before losing sensation in the rest of his extremities, he placed the cup on an end table. The empty glass rattled against the ebony wood.

Apprehension soaked Jassyn's leathers as he anticipated Vesryn's interrogation and eruption. He swallowed, the acknowledgment coming out as a hoarse whisper, his voice as unsteady as his limbs. "I—I need help."

The admission wasn't as freeing as he'd expected since Vesryn wasted no time restraining his shoulder, jutting his chin toward a chair. A command to sit.

No going back now. Jassyn crumbled onto a couch before his knees buckled. Pulling a throw pillow to his chest, he braced himself against an overwhelming surge of guilt.

Pouring another glass of water and setting it beside him, Vesryn drilled him with pointed questions about his habits, likely determining how severe the consequences should be.

"Initially, I took enough Stardust for memory loss," Jassyn admitted, running a hand through his curls, "but lately—"

"You've been blacking out?" Vesryn interjected, voice pitching high. His eyes bulged as he froze in the middle of sitting next to Jassyn on the sofa.

Gripping the armrest, Jassyn scooted to the edge when Vesryn resumed reclining, stealing most of the space. "I know it was foolish but—"

The prince interrupted him. "Stars, you're lucky you're not

dead." Vesryn untied the leather strap at the top of his head, shaking his hair free.

"I thought the dust would help…" Words abandoning him, Jassyn knew he had no excuse for indulging. "I only wanted to make my servitude to the Vallendes bearable. But if the wraith return…" Jassyn cleared his throat, regret killing the remaining words on his tongue.

"You don't need to justify your reasoning to me." Vesryn waved a hand disinterestedly, but something softened in his features. "If I would've intervened with your contracts sooner…" This time it was the prince who trailed off, avoiding his gaze.

Jassyn focused on lacing his quivering hands together, eyes welling with remorse. Growing somber, he gathered his decaying strength before the weight of his mistakes overwhelmed him. "I can't stop. I've tried." Chest constricting, Jassyn inhaled a stabilizing breath, a tight knot unraveling from sharing this much. "I want to—I know I *need* to."

The prince's jaw tightened before he muttered, "I would destroy every speck of Stardust if I could, having experienced how destructive it is. I don't know why my sire permits it." Vesryn blew out a heavy sigh. "Some part of you will always crave more, but the urge won't be unmanageable once it's out of your system."

Jassyn's relief was short-lived. Vesryn suddenly straightened, flashing his teeth. "You'll have to find something else to fill the void so you don't slip back into the habit." The prince reached over to shake Jassyn's shoulder. "Perhaps you'd like to take up sparring?" He squeezed Jassyn's bicep. "Maybe we could spend the evenings building some muscle on this delicate frame."

"I appreciate the offer," Jassyn said, ripping his arm out of his cousin's grip. "But sparring with you sounds less appealing than withdrawing from Stardust."

But still, Vesryn was unexpectedly calm. Jassyn had anticipated aggressive retribution, considering how ruthlessly he punished recruits for the same offense.

"You're not upset?" Jassyn ventured to ask, balancing on the cusp of surrendering his anxiety. "What about my position? Shouldn't you be banishing me from campus?" He swallowed. "Or—or worse?"

"If I continue to exile everyone who fucked up, the island would be empty." Vesryn threaded his fingers through his hair, retying the strands into a topknot. "If that were the case, I wouldn't even be here."

Unable to forgive himself, Jassyn felt like arguing simply for the sake of it, knowing his actions didn't deserve to be brushed aside so casually. Had he been in control of his abilities he could've made a difference, even if it was saving the life of just one initiate. "I don't know how many died because I wasn't able to mend them."

The prince's fingers drummed on the armrest. He stared out the window, watching the rain patter against the glass.

"Those deaths are on me," Vesryn said quietly.

"That's not true." Jassyn frowned. "You've spent nearly every waking moment hunting the wraith and—"

"And it hasn't been enough," Vesryn snarled. "If Serenna…" He buried his face in his hands, voice stifled with distress. "She almost died."

"But she didn't." Jassyn resisted the unnatural urge to reach out and comfort his cousin. "You can hardly blame yourself for the wraith attacking us. They've been harassing our realm for decades." Folding his arms, Jassyn fought to keep the jagged edge from his tone. "I don't know why we're even arguing about this."

"You're right," Vesryn said, uncovering his face. "We'll have plenty of time to debate our shortcomings over the next few days." He picked at a frayed thread on the sofa. "Though I suppose you won't recall much once the withdrawal fully kicks in." The prince rose and grabbed Jassyn's glass, refilled it and forced it back into his hands. "Stay hydrated. I imagine you'll start puking soon."

Jassyn stared at the water, unease pooling in his gut like the rain puddles forming on Vesryn's balcony. "How did you stop?" He glanced at his cousin for reassurance. They'd never discussed the prince's former vices, but his indulgence wasn't exactly a secret.

"I solicited help from my brother's dracovae handlers," Vesryn said, flopping back to the couch. "I ordered them to tether me and chain me in a stall." His mouth twisted. "I gave them instructions to leave me alone for a week, and to periodically shove food and water in through the door. They shielded the cell so they wouldn't have to hear my crazed screaming."

The prince sprawled across the sofa, hooking his ankles over an armrest. *Jassyn's* armrest. Pinching his lips, Jassyn debated how effective he'd be at displacing the prince's legs from his lap.

"It was far from pleasant sobering up only to realize I had spent days wallowing in my own filth." Vesryn rolled his eyes. "And you'll be pleased to know my flight captain has never let me forget it."

Jassyn emitted a disgusted scoff, sipping at the water, ready to curl into a ball and endure whatever the next few days would bring. "Lovely." Hand still shaking like reeds in the wind, he carefully placed the goblet on the end table beside him.

Vesryn lifted a palm. With a flare of force, an apple from the fruit basket on his dining table hovered through the air, landing on top of his waiting fingers. "I was under Stardust's influence for much longer than you, so I doubt you'll be reduced to that state." The prince gestured with his thumb to a door behind him. "In any case, you're staying with me." He grinned, a mischievous light flashing in his eyes. "I'll make sure you stay quite safe in my bed."

"What?" Jassyn heaved Vesryn's legs out of his lap. "That's unnecessary. I'll return to my chambers."

Vesryn swung his ankles back onto Jassyn's armrest. "Would you rather I settle into your apartment, poke around, and rearrange *your* books to my liking? I'll crack all the spines, stars help me." Jassyn flinched at the unsettling noise of Vesryn biting into the apple. "You're going to be incapacitated. You'll need someone to watch over you so you don't try anything stupid."

Jassyn leaned his head against the couch, staring at the ceiling. "And what makes you the perfect guardian for that?"

Vesryn nudged Jassyn's shoulder with his bare toes. "You came to me."

Thwarted, Jassyn scowled, conceding to suffer through spending time with the prince. *What was I expecting?*

"You can change out of your leathers and get into something more comfortable." Vesryn bounced the half-eaten apple in his palm. "I have some of that cashmere you're so fond of."

Jassyn's eye twitched when Vesryn pronounced it as "cazzmere."

"You have no idea how much I'm looking forward to spending this quality time together," the prince said, ruffling his curls. "You really should visit more often, you know."

Jassyn didn't have any remaining fight left to fend Vesryn off. *I brought this on myself.* He wilted like a trampled flower, melting deeper into the sofa.

Submitting to resignation and exhaustion, Jassyn covered his face in a fit of despair, begging the pounding in his head to subside. He felt like weeping in both relief for the help and in defeat when Vesryn started rubbing his shoulder in what he interpreted as compassionate amusement.

Jassyn swallowed to stave off a renewed lurching in his gut. *Oh stars.* That was one of his final coherent thoughts before dashing to the bathing chambers to empty the contents of his stomach.

CHAPTER 3

LYKOR

Lykor lurked, still like a shadow, silent as the night. Clouds obscured the moons, threatening to smother the mountains with a late spring snow. Tapping into one of his wraith abilities, he concealed himself in a shroud of darkness—invisible to prying eyes.

At the rim of a frosty vale surrounded by pine trees, Lykor lingered fifty paces away from a lone dracovae rider's camp. A fire pressed back the gloom against the starless sky. Tongues of flame reflected in each of the dracovae's slatey scales as it lay curled around the elf nestled against its feathered shoulder. The beast huffed in its sleep, the heavy exhale unfurling from its beak as a plume of steam.

Lykor had detected the dracovae's silhouette against the horizon that morning, soaring above the glacial edge of the continental shelf. He'd opened a portal hundreds of leagues away from the safety of the wraith's stronghold for his people to tend their fishing nets along the frigid coast.

If he believed in such a thing, Lykor would've said that the stars had aligned, positioning him in the same location as this elf. He'd been tracking the rider the entire day while she made sweeping flights across the northwestern border of the Timber Wilds.

Lykor doubted the dracovae would survive a journey to their hidden fortress without freezing to death, but this elven patrol was still too close to the Hibernal Wastes for his liking. Judging from the sheathed weapons and the scaled armor bundled under her cloak, Lykor suspected the riders were now warriors—a shift from when Aesar had simply managed curation of the beasts' population a century ago.

Now apparently involved in the elven military, Lykor anticipated this rider had orders or information he could extract. Today marked three days after their failed assault and her proximity was a threat to his people—especially since she was inching closer to their remote borders. Hunting. Intruding.

The wraith's scouting parties had already discovered camps of assembled humans spanning across every realm. An alarming number of mortals had gathered along the fringes of the Wastes. It was only a matter of time before they fanned out, scouring for the wraith under King Galaeryn's tyranny. Lykor knew that their time sheltering in the secluded stronghold was coming to an end—if the presence of this rider and the human war bands were any sign.

He knew the king wouldn't simply forget about the wraith. Now that Galaeryn had assembled his pawns, Lykor presumed the king would set his sights on the Aelfyn homeland, to claim whatever their ancestors had left behind beyond the sea. But only after tying up his loose end on this side of the world—eliminating the wraith. In the prisons, Galaeryn had boasted to Lykor about his ambitions. But what hope did the wraith have of stopping him?

Reminded of those half-elves the king had bred for a gruesome purpose, Lykor's awareness brushed the bond-holder, who'd obviously surviving the attack. Essence leashed this nuisance to him—one he deduced was some half-elf spawn.

He contemplated using the connection to locate, abduct, and haul them to the wraith's fortress. If he could force their acceptance of the bond, he could manipulate their magic and control their power. Then he finally wouldn't be stretched so fucking thin all the time as the only one among the wraith with magic.

Sensing Aesar stirring, like one rolling over in sleep, Lykor's hackles rose. He assumed Aesar had perceived his intentions and disagreed. As usual. Lykor shoved his other half into a recess in their mind. Perhaps he could keep that meddling presence locked away indefinitely.

In some pathetic attempt at heroism, Aesar had unforgivably sabotaged Lykor's carefully staged assault against the half-elf army. He'd seized control of their body, sounded the retreat, and then jumped from the highest peak of a tower. As if his martyrdom would've solved anything.

Lykor clamped down on his fury, grinding his fangs. *I DIDN'T ENDURE TWENTY YEARS IN THE ELVEN DUNGEONS TO BE CAST ASIDE.*

Lykor hadn't ripped away control of their body from Aesar in time as they'd plunged to the ground, but he'd survived. Or rather, someone had somehow halted his fall.

WHY DIDN'T THAT ELF KILL ME? Thoughts twisting with conflict, contorting like vines, Lykor dredged up memories invaded by a pair of striking amber eyes—one of the king's half-elves.

Lykor's mind tilled up an echo of that raven-haired male's scoffed words. *I saved you.*

WHY? AND WHY DID I NOT EVISCERATE HIM?

Perhaps he'd hesitated when crushing that elf's throat after seeing the despondency settling over in his face. The fear. Then the acceptance. Something inexplicable had doused the murderous fire in Lykor's veins. Perhaps it was the way that elf had bitterly laughed in the face of death like Lykor had done so many times to spurn the king.

Muttering to himself, Lykor steered his disconcerting thoughts away from the elf who'd scattered his common sense like ashes on the wind. That hadn't been the only unexpected incident that night.

WHY WAS VESRYN THERE?

Lykor fled from the witless thought as soon as it emerged. His spine spasmed in anticipation, expecting the king's compulsive magic to invade his awareness, reducing him to a bystander in his mind. The coercion demanded the death of the prince, lest Vesryn wander into the wraith's prison a century ago and uncover Galaeryn's plans.

Acsar's twin never did.

Once Lykor had emerged, splitting from Aesar's consciousness to shield him from his sire, the king had flaunted why he hadn't tortured Vesryn in the same fashion—the torment that had reduced Lykor to a wraith.

Instead of harming the other prince, Galaeryn had maintained the convenience of an heir and boasted about molding another type of monster—someone star-bent on vengeance to hunt down the wraith he continued to create. What better way to exert control over the realms than by fabricating a conflict, crafting a convenient excuse to corral the mortals and frighten the elves into compliance?

Lykor trembled, breath rattling in his lungs. Waiting for the coercion's dominance. Thoughts brushing Aesar's twin always triggered the destructive magic harnessed to Lykor's mind. Against his will, rending would uncontrollably whip out of him, as if seeking Vesryn out.

Except...

Nothing happened.

WHAT?

Blinking, Lykor frowned, tangled in a web of confusion, unable to comprehend why the oppressive magic hadn't overpowered him like it had every other time his thoughts touched...Vesryn.

The realization chilled Lykor's blood like the wind's frigid bite. *THAT AMBER-EYED ELF FIDDLED WITH MY MIND.*

The male had known of the coercion—he'd even asked, offered to help. Frowning, Lykor tunneled inward, still sensing the dark magic latched onto his awareness like a parasite. He released a breath. Perhaps the compulsion was degrading. Surely Galaeryn's power couldn't endure until the end of time.

COULD THAT ELF ACTUALLY HELP ME LIKE HE'D CLAIMED? Lykor idly stroked the silver hilt at his waist, the metallic leaves and vines framing the golden blade. Lykor couldn't say why he'd pilfered the dagger like it was some trophy, but its presence kindled a spark of foolish hope.

The tentative promise of freedom from the king's coercion lured Lykor down a treacherous path that would surely lead to disappointment.

He flinched, recalling how the monarch had honed his coercive magic, shredding Lykor's mind. Destroying any natural defenses he'd previously possessed, stealing his ability to barricade his awareness. Leaving him vulnerable.

If the king had discovered how to control Lykor absolutely, that would've been the end of what little resistance Lykor had maintained over the years. He could only assume that was Galaeryn's eventual intent.

Absolute dominance.

Giving himself a shake, Lykor dispelled the suppressed memories, shoving them back behind an obsidian door where he kept those horrific thoughts.

He grounded himself to the present, snapping his clawed gauntlet into a fist. The metal articulated with a squeal, the grating sound splitting the tranquility of the night. Realizing the mistake, his attention flew to the rider, ensuring she and the dracovae still slept.

This elven scout was obviously on the hunt for something. But so was he.

Unsheathing the stolen blade, Lykor dipped into his Well, hauling out a stream of Essence. He clenched the dagger. His wrath and hatred toward the elves had only intensified after the failed raid—his greatest desire was to keep his people safe. Like a serpent coiling around a branch, he spun a blue tendril of force along the length of the silver hilt.

Lykor snarled at the sleeping rider, flaring his magic to expel his fury. The dagger lifted from his palm, hovering in the air, turning as he aimed the golden tip at the slumbering warrior. Releasing power in a streaking volley, he sent the knife flying on wings of force.

Impaled in the shoulder, the rider startled awake with a cry of alarm, magic tethered—stifled. She clawed at the hilt. Lykor tossed a hand up, punching out a swarm of force, anchoring the blade to bone.

Shrugging off his invisibility, Lykor focused his awareness to his chest, taking advantage of his partial-wraith form. Building a pressure near the point of fracturing pain, he folded in on himself and warped across the clearing.

Reappearing in front of the warrior, Lykor snagged her leathers, hauling her away from the rousing dracovae. Unwilling to slay the innocent beast, he tore open a portal and shoved the rider through before the dracovae could aid its master with slicing talons and its razor-sharp bill.

On the other side of the gateway, in the bowels of the Frostvault Keep, Lykor pitched the elf forward into a darkened tunnel, steering her toward a set of stairs. He would've portaled to the interrogation chamber directly, but the extinct druids— the former masters of the wraith's volcano fortress—had enough foresight to lace the brig's stonework with gold. Traveling in or out by rifts was impossible. An inconvenience now.

Essence unraveled wherever gold touched—one of the

curses the druids condemned on the Aelfyn before their downfall. But the wraith's gold-firing crossbows hadn't been a tide-turning advantage during the assault like Lykor had hoped, despite piercing through the elves' magical shields. But if the wraith had a power like the druids—

The rider charged at Lykor with daggers flashing, yanking his attention back to the hallway. The silver blades reflected flames from the spiked iron sconces. Spurred by irritation, Lykor flicked his gauntlet, a blast of force spinning the knives out of her fingers. The weapons struck the stone walls, clattering to the floor. Fueled by retribution, he shoved her down the winding earthen steps with a burst of power.

The warrior went tumbling. Her screech morphed into a piercing scream as she crashed to the bottom of the stairwell. Lykor strolled unhurriedly, descending with heavy, booted footsteps that echoed against the stark surroundings.

Strangled by heat collected from the Slag and spewed through the labyrinth of vents, he yanked off his fur cloak, discarding it on a step.

When Lykor reached the dimmed halls of the dungeon, the warrior struggled to stand, stifling a whimper of pain. Twisted unnaturally, one of her legs bowed out like a broken branch, incapable of supporting weight. One of the rider's blood-soaked arms dangled uselessly, white bone jutting through flesh.

After all these years, Lykor had finally captured an elven prisoner, and he was ravenous for revenge. He'd balance the scales, destroying one elf's life at a time, repaying the debt for what the king had inflicted upon him. To purge one of the king's soldiers before her power could harm the wraith, to extinguish her Essence before the king could siphon it and augment his own. Lykor would pry words from her lips and uncover the elves' immediate plans.

Baring his fangs, Lykor stalked to the elf sprawled on the ground. The warrior's boots scraped against the stone floor in her meager attempt to shuffle away, her mangled leg preventing escape.

Reaching down, Lykor seized her auburn hair, the darker color leading him to believe she was one of those half-elf spawn. Not that the difference in blood mattered—they were all elves to him and would bleed all the same.

Leaving the cell-lined hallway, Lykor dragged her to an empty chamber set up for questioning captives. He'd collected a plethora of tools for this purpose, lining the chamber with every variety of weapon the wraith could craft, plated with gold. All for show and intimidation—he wouldn't need them.

With an eruption of force, he slammed the elf against a wall. She sucked in a labored breath as her back collided with stone.

Lykor snatched the golden chains swinging from the ceiling, shoving the warrior's broken arm into a manacle, drawing out a hiss. Shackling her wrists and neck, Lykor left the knife tethering her power in her shoulder.

He prowled to the center of the chamber, pivoting on his heel to study her. To think. Swept away in capturing the elf, he'd put no thought into what questions he'd ask of a prisoner. Lykor supposed he should begin by gouging out her knowledge of the king's intentions, to bridge the gaps a century had hollowed in his.

He had no doubts the elves were doing the same to those Aesar had abandoned on the island. Lykor's fangs drew blood from his gums, dwelling on the wraith left behind. All those lives lost. Deserted. His people would break under torture. Reveal the location of their fortress. Lykor's objective became clear—he needed to learn how much time remained until the elves confronted them in force.

"What do you know of the wraith?" Lykor demanded.

The warrior dragged in breath through her nose before spitting at him, the spittle hardly landing halfway across the room.

Lykor's lip curled away from his teeth. In one step, he

warped, materializing in front of her. With his gauntlet, he snatched the elf by the throat, lifting her to her toes. He wrenched her neck to make the restraints cut into her collarbones, flashing his fangs at her insolence.

"I will ask one more time," Lykor clipped, rage boiling beneath his ribs. Shadows whipped around him in a tempest, fury evoking rending. "Answer unsatisfactorily and I won't hesitate to plait your entrails after I peel the flesh from your bones."

The warrior whimpered, eyes rolling with fear, but remained silent.

Lykor struck out with a sliver of darkness. Cutting like a blade, he channeled the rending, splitting the female's skin under his gauntlet. She swore as he withdrew the metal from her throat. The flesh from her neck sloughed away, stuck to the steel like sap dripping off a pine.

The way she stubbornly set her jaw had Lykor snarling. Eyes flicking to her broken arm, he detected the next key to try to unlock her secrets. He grabbed the exposed bone, twisting it farther in the wrong direction.

The female shrieked through her teeth as she panted. Eyes glazing over, she slumped in the chains, passing out.

Lykor growled in disgust. With a flick of force, he wiped away the sticky mess sullying his armor. He crushed his claw into a fist, letting the squeal of the steel soothe him as he started pacing the room.

Like a bolt of lightning, a violent thought collided with him. His head whipped back to the elf. During his imprisonment, he'd learned of dark magic that the king and his general had meddled with. Lykor had no reservations about exploiting those same techniques against their own.

He could take her power.

Like the king had done to him—to all the wraith—pilfering Essence from the elves they used to be. Not anticipating an escape, Galaeryn had returned a handful of talents to Lykor to see if he'd retain strength over his abilities. The wraith wouldn't have survived this long without the Essence Lykor possessed, but he was far from the arch elf that Aesar used to be.

Ripping off his gauntlet and flinging it aside, Lykor exposed his dominant right hand, the claw that belonged to some beast. Skin to skin contact worked best. How many times had Galaeryn extracted and inserted abilities while experimenting on him? Hundreds? Half hadn't survived the siphoning process, perishing from the unbearable agony of talents cleaved from the Well.

Dissolving the horrors of the past, Lykor prowled forward as shadows spilled from his claw like noxious fog. He yanked the golden blade out of the elf's shoulder, sheathing it back at his side before shredding her leathers with a slash of rending. Lykor plunged his talons into the slumped warrior's chest.

And pillaged everything.

CHAPTER 4

JASSYN

Jassyn shifted his feet at the edge of an outdoor training yard a quarter mile from the massive dracovae stables. The midmorning sun glinted off various weapons arranged on multiple racks. Perched in a mountainous plateau near Alari's northern border, the Ranger Station towered over the far end of the practice fields.

"This isn't necessary," Jassyn said. One last attempt at a futile protest.

Standing in the center of one of the sandy circles, Vesryn tied back his hair with a leather strap. "My face begs to differ." The prince gestured to his unmarred jaw, where an hour ago, Jassyn had healed the bruises he'd apparently bestowed upon Vesryn in his previous incapacitated state. "I need to teach you to throw a punch properly so you don't fuck up your hand again."

Jassyn had awakened that morning feeling resurrected. Most of the Stardust had vacated his system after two long days locked away in the prince's chambers.

Wary of Vesryn's notorious lack of skill, Jassyn rubbed his bruised knuckles, unwilling to allow the prince to mend him in return. Scattered bits and pieces were all that Jassyn could remember—yielding his stomach, attempting to escape, and even *brawling* with his cousin.

"And I'm not forgetting that you stabbed me!" Voice pitched high with scandalization, Vesryn pointed to his shoulder's unblemished skin, another spot Jassyn had healed. "Seven concealed daggers is rather excessive, but if you insist on carrying so many, then you're going to learn how to use them."

"Shredding my leathers to recover the blades was completely uncalled for," Jassyn grumbled. "I had that armor broken in."

He vaguely recalled the confrontation that had occurred in the middle of the first night when he'd attempted to sneak out of Vesryn's chambers, intending to retrieve his supply of Stardust. Instead of slipping out of the prince's apartment undetected, Jassyn had tripped over his cousin, who'd been sleeping on the floor like a guard dog.

While in his deranged state, knifing the prince had been the only reasonable course of action. In a mad dash toward freedom, Jassyn had made it halfway down the hallway before Vesryn had tackled him, dragging him back into his lair.

Enduring his crazed assaults, the prince had dutifully played caretaker. Vesryn's dedication tilled up a twinge of guilt. *I suppose I should be thanking him.*

As he inhaled the crisp mountain air, a breath of relief cleansed Jassyn's lungs. Now freed from the clutches of Stardust, the world sharpened around him.

Jassyn studied the stable hands in the distance, too busy seeing to their morning chores to bother looking over at the practice yards. No one else remained at the Ranger Station—the warriors had departed at dawn to patrol on their dracovae, hunting for signs of the wraith. Jassyn surveyed the scattered clouds, but nothing more than an empty sky stared back.

"Relax," Vesryn said, shaking out his wrists. "Nobody is

watching. I knew you wouldn't want an audience—that's why I brought us here instead of staying on campus."

Jassyn readjusted his white magus leathers, dismayed that it would take weeks to get this new set pliable. But if a destroyed uniform and spending more time with the prince was the price of losing dependence on the dust, the bill came in much lower than he'd expected. Though Vesryn undoubtedly would collect interest on the debt with whatever "training" he had in store.

The sun skimmed the mountain peaks, warming Jassyn's skin and frying his nerves. He took one hesitant step from the grass into the training field before obstinacy claimed him. "I was throwing up yesterday." He crossed his arms. "I'm not sure this is the best idea."

"You'll be fine," Vesryn said, waving off his concern, obviously determined to outmatch his stubbornness. The prince pulled an arm tight across his chest, stretching. "Sweating out the residual Stardust hardly compares to what you've already been through." Tugging off his ragged boots and socks, the prince sent them sailing to the edge of the ring with a tendril of force. "Take off your shoes."

Shoulders slumping in defeat, Jassyn let the argument drop. Bickering would only prolong the inevitable and he might as well get this over with. Judging from what he'd heard of Serenna's "lessons" with the prince, he expected that his cousin would have something ludicrous planned.

Like a wolf greedily defending a kill, Vesryn wasn't likely to slacken his hold now that Jassyn had consented to participating. *How did I let him talk me into this?*

After peeling off his footwear, Jassyn joined the prince in the ring, feet sinking into the gritty sand. *Vesryn will probably throw me around and say it's for my own good.*

He hadn't made a habit of setting foot in the practice yards at Centarya beyond the required magus training that Vesryn had implemented at the start of the spring term. Exercise wasn't at the forefront of his mind—he was more comfortable diving into research.

Logically, Jassyn could recognize the practicality of honing skills and training for combat. He reflexively touched the scabs scored in his flesh by that elven wraith's gauntlet. *I was useless when I was pinned by my throat.* Perhaps that was why he'd agreed —he'd had enough of being at the mercy of others.

"Since you're not carrying any bulk around, I imagine you'll be quick on your feet," Vesryn said, stretching out his other arm behind his head. "But you'll need to develop coordination for that. Find your balance," he commanded, demonstrating by standing on one foot, kicking his other knee in front of him at an angle.

Jassyn copied the prince, wobbling shortly after holding the position. Teetering and shifting his weight, he found maintaining the pose only became more difficult as the seconds ticked by. Before Jassyn knew it, sweat plastered his curls to his forehead.

"How long are we going to do this?" Jassyn gritted out, muscles trembling in earnest.

Vesryn's arched brow suggested his protest was dramatic.

The next half hour didn't offer any respite while the prince ran him through a series of contorting stretches that appeared much simpler when performed by his cousin. Frustration spiked through Jassyn as he tried to copy the forms, his new set of stiff armor hindering his movements. *If I would've changed into that cashmere he was waving around, my best leathers wouldn't be dismantled.* Anchoring his feet in the sand, Jassyn brought himself back to the moment, tracking time with his heartbeats.

"Summon your power and connect your magic to your body's motion," Vesryn instructed, circling him. He used his toes to nudge Jassyn's foot back, correcting his stance. "Make your pretty lights dance or something."

Legs shaking in protest from balancing, Jassyn channeled his awareness to his Well—replenished by the prince that morning. Tonight, he'd be able to regenerate on his own when the stars bloomed. For the first time in weeks, Jassyn effortlessly seized Essence while Vesryn drifted a few paces away.

A current of magic raced through his veins, saturating him with a clarity and harmony that he hadn't realized Stardust had deprived him of while he'd spent the past few weeks living in a haze. Thoughts abruptly lurching back to the drug, Jassyn wrestled with his mind, dragging in a slow breath and releasing his desire for it on the exhale.

Refocusing on his magic and recentering his swaying body, Jassyn raised his palms. Power fountained from his Well, spinning as a glittering stream of Essence around his fingertips. Bending the power into his illumination talent, he summoned a dozen hovering orbs of white light. Flicking his wrist, the shimmering globes went whirling over Vesryn's shoulder.

A shift in the breeze stirred his curls, offering some relief from his body heating with exertion. Senses tingling as his skin pebbled, Jassyn jerked his attention away from the wind. He blinked against the sunlight cresting the mountains, pointedly ignoring the unusual sensation.

I need to determine what that earthen power was before I accidentally call roots out of the ground again. Or do something worse that I can't control.

The prince looped back in front of him. "Can you believe that even after the attack, the council is still insisting on holding that ridiculous tournament?"

Jassyn swayed, the question dragging him out of his thoughts. The burning in his legs rushed back to the forefront of his awareness. Stumbling, he caught himself before toppling over, abandoning the balancing stance by planting both feet on the ground. Vesryn didn't correct him, seeming too absorbed as he tilted his head, waiting for Jassyn's reply.

"Of course they are," Jassyn scoffed, yanking in air to even out his breathing. It was no surprise that the realm still expected the recruits to bloody each other for the capital's entertainment. "Like that's where our priorities should be."

"I was the only vote against the competition—it was the majority of the council's idea, not mine," Vesryn said almost defensively, kicking at a clump of sand. "You mentioned the magus...respected me." The prince considered him while fiddling with a frayed thread on his armor's dragon sigil. "Where do you think their loyalties lie?"

Jassyn's response was automatic, a conditioned response for preservation. "To the council." He narrowed his eyes on the prince, suddenly unsure of what Vesryn wanted from him. "What other choice is there?"

Vesryn seemingly agreed with a grunt but didn't offer any further words. Crossing his arms, the prince drummed his fingers. His attention flicked to one of Jassyn's drifting globes, as if recalling their training.

A pressure vibrated through the ring as Vesryn's magic ignited. Shadows rose around the prince like fog. He sliced through a few of Jassyn's shining orbs with a tendril of rending, extinguishing their light.

Jassyn wiped away the sweat beading on his forehead. Drawing in a steadying breath, he flexed his hands, concentrating on keeping the illumination out of the prince's reach.

Feet stirring sand, Vesryn started pacing as his shadows spiraled around them. "Do you think the magus would stand with me if the council attempted to put someone else in command?"

Jassyn's brows shot up as he studied the prince, who'd apparently overlooked the fact that his position in the realm was second only to the king. "Why would they appoint anyone else? Who would even fill the role?" His quivering legs threatened to collapse at his conclusion, dread pitching his tone higher. "*Elashor?*"

Vesryn didn't answer, the silence expanding like his cloud of magic. He formed a fist, punching out a wave of darkness, engulfing one of Jassyn's spinning lights.

Unease prickled Jassyn's scalp. "You don't think it'll come to bloodshed between us and the capital, do you?"

Vesryn's gaze unfocused toward the mountains in Centarya's direction. "I won't let that happen."

An unexpected blade of fear punctured Jassyn's chest, stealing his breath as he imagined someone aside from the prince in command. He inhaled sharply at the possibility of the council having direct control over Centarya. Vesryn had been the only pure-blood and the only member of the higher political circles to lift a finger during the attack.

He's different from the rest of them. The prince had taken an interest in the welfare of the elven-blooded and perhaps that was in part to the bond that had formed between him and Serenna. Rebalancing himself, Jassyn buried his toes in the sand. *Scorching stars, it's not even a decision. I'd rather stand with Vesryn if it comes to that.*

Jassyn's tongue stuck to the roof of his mouth as he swallowed. Straightening, he cleared his throat. "I can gather an idea of where the magus' loyalties would lie. If given a choice, I can't imagine it's with the council." Directing his illumination, Jassyn's remaining spheres of light dodged the prince's pursuing magic. "I've kept to the fringes of the magus community though because of…" He faltered when Vesryn's eyes flicked to his forehead, where the Vallende's had tattooed their sigil, displaying Jassyn's servitude to their family before he'd had it erased. The prince averted his gaze and Jassyn didn't feel the need to explain further. Instead he asked, "Where is this coming from?"

Vesryn studied his palm as shadows twined across his fingertips. "Something happened in the dungeons with our wraith prisoners." A glower flashed across his face. "Elashor was there."

Jassyn tensed at the admission. The prince normally annihilated the creatures without taking prisoners and no one had questioned them before. Everyone believed they were mindless beasts, so what was the point?

"I thought the capital couldn't care less about what you do with the wraith," Jassyn said. He flared new droplets of light to replace the magic Vesryn had extinguished, scattering the illumination around the yard like a burst of rain.

"Exactly." Vesryn punctuated the word by a jabbing finger. "Elashor was too interested in the interrogation for my liking. The council has never been involved before—that's why I'm concerned now." The prince frowned off into the distance. The pressure of his magic coalesced, the whirlwind of shadows twisting around the training ring. "I told Elashor to leave. I commanded his soldiers to leave, but they..." Vesryn blew a breath out of his nose. "They disregarded my orders when they should've complied, no questions asked."

Despite the warm sun, Jassyn shivered, alarm binding his stomach into a knot. "The differences between the organized attack on campus and the mindless wraith you hunt across the realms probably sparked the council's interest."

But Elashor would go unchecked if he acquired more power, bypassing the prince and taking a step closer to the king. If Vesryn was removed, Centarya would be at the general's mercy. Lungs seized by fear, Jassyn's breath came faster, heartbeat rampant. *Vesryn's protection won't mean anything if the council strips him of command.* If Elashor had his way, Jassyn would undoubtedly be sent back to Farine, forced to participate in the twisted ways she found pleasure.

In a battle for breath, Jassyn wrestled every thought away from that likely, horrifying reality. He yanked his awareness back to the coarse sand embracing his feet. Clutching his magic like a lifeline, he channeled his focus on the charge of power rushing through him, spinning the globes of illumination faster around them.

Surfacing from the tide of panic, Jassyn returned to the prince's concerns, voicing his assumptions before his mind caught up. "I'm sure Elashor didn't want you alone with the prisoners and gathering answers without his knowledge."

The prince clenched his jaw, fingers twitching. "The general's behavior in the dungeons was a blatant disregard for my authority." A pulse of rending engulfed a smattering of Jassyn's lights that didn't scurry out of reach fast enough. "And Kyansari's soldiers didn't acknowledge my presence. Their eyes were..." Vesryn shook his head. "I don't know. Dull. Not bloodshot like yours were from Stardust. Just...blank."

"Do you think they've been compelled?" Jassyn blurted, his tongue recklessly loosened.

Vesryn frowned, taken aback. "My sire only used that magic on those in the delegations sent to the mortal realms, but that practice shouldn't be occurring anymore since our world is open to the humans."

As far as we know, the king is the only one with the strength to fabricate compulsion. But the only flimsy proof Jassyn had of the king's direct involvement was a snarl from an elven wraith that could've been interpreted as anything when he asked if the monarch was the one who'd compelled him.

Flaring a burst of force at a weapons rack positioned on the perimeter of the yard, Vesryn yanked two staffs toward him. He extended both palms, catching one in each. "Why would you think there's compulsion on the soldiers?" he prompted, tossing Jassyn a sparring stick.

Somehow, Jassyn caught the staff, even though his entire body felt ready to fray like Vesryn's boots. Following the prince's lead, he rallied his strength and released his magic. Running his fingers along the smooth grains, Jassyn clutched the middle, the width nearly the size of his wrist.

"I think I've detected coercion on campus." Unwilling to divulge his encounter with the wraith, Jassyn kept to himself that he'd sensed similar telepathic magic on the warrior's mind.

Silence thickened between them, broken by a dracovae's piercing screech in the distance. Vesryn tilted his head, silver hair mirroring the sunlight. "What do you mean?"

Uncertainty tangled in Jassyn's chest, coiling into a knot of hesitation. Unsure how far he could trust the prince, Jassyn held his tongue. He hadn't disclosed his discovery of the telepathic web on Magister Thalaesyn to anyone. Not even his peer Nelya, who he'd worked closely with for decades. For weeks, he'd secretly inspected the compulsive magic snared across his mentor's mind. But he needed to trust someone eventually and Vesryn was starting to look like the only option.

Squaring his stance, Jassyn moored his feet in the sand and ventured to ask, "Would there be any motive for the king to compel Magister Thalaesyn?"

As soon as the words rushed out of his mouth, Jassyn's fingers tensed on the weapon. The prince went still. His question bordered on an accusation. Vesryn didn't exactly have a close affiliation with his sire, but that didn't mean he had any reason to share in Jassyn's suspicions.

With no warning, the prince rushed him. Jassyn locked his knees, bracing for impact. Recalling training from a time in his youth that seemed more like a dream rather than a memory, Jassyn pivoted on the ball of his foot. Whipping the staff, he met the prince in a concussive *clunk* of wood. The jolt rattled his elbows, shuddered through his arms, and vibrated straight to his teeth.

"I can't think of any reason why Thalaesyn would be compelled," Vesryn said, retreating a step and giving Jassyn an approving nod. "How did you find out?"

"I found him incapacitated one afternoon." Relaxing his shoulders, Jassyn wiped his sweaty palms against his leathers. "I assessed him—intending to mend him—and perceived a magic that I assumed was coercion."

Feet shuffling, Jassyn readjusted his grip on the sparring staff, orbiting the prince as Vesryn looped around him. "That's where I discovered the Stardust," Jassyn admitted, unintentionally revealing Thalaesyn's vices with his loose tongue.

Vesryn pursed his lips. "I've always had a blind spot with Thalaesyn, but considering recent events, that'll need to change." The prince whirled his staff low, like he aimed to sweep Jassyn off his feet.

Leaping back, the deep sand slowed Jassyn's movement. "Blind spot?" he asked, his voice strained from the effort. Anticipating another hit, Jassyn clenched his teeth before he slapped Vesryn's staff in a deflecting blow. "Not meddling in someone else's business doesn't sound like you at all." He spun, using his momentum to drive the prince's weapon away.

Jassyn was aware of the discord between the magister and the king, coinciding around the appearance of the wraith. King Galaeryn had banished Thalaesyn to Centarya after the elves had completed the academy's construction. Perhaps Vesryn knew more of the strife between them.

"Do you have a history with the magister?" Jassyn gritted out, twisting his wrists to meet Vesryn's staff in a crash that jolted up his arms. Jassyn didn't bother attempting an offensive move. It was all he could do to parry every thrust his cousin sent whistling in his direction.

Vesryn denied him any reprieve. "Thalaesyn and my mother…worked closely together when the infertility crisis began," he said, lunging again.

The prince's staff cleaved the air—this time nearly clipping Jassyn's head. Rearing back, Jassyn reeled to halt the slash with a sloppy counter.

"Thalaesyn hasn't allowed Stardust to interfere with his duties to any notable degree before," Vesryn said as their staffs met three times in a series of wooden *clacks*. "I should've anticipated his habits affecting someone else." The prince frowned at his staff before adjusting his feet under his shoulders. He twirled the weapon, sending it blurring in front of him like a windmill. "After you're feeling more like yourself, you'll show me this coercion. In the meantime, I'll figure out how to address the magister's *recreation*."

Jassyn faltered, regretting that he'd exposed the start of his addiction. He never intended to cause trouble for his mentor. But Vesryn setting his jaw had him reconsidering any protest.

"I suppose I can show you the magic on Thalaesyn's mind—if he agrees." Jassyn yanked in breaths before Vesryn's next assault, his thoughts wheeling back to their previous conversation. "What did you find out from the wraith?"

"Nothing," Vesryn said, dashing forward. Their staffs collided in a crash of wood. Once. Twice. Three times, a relentless bombardment of blows. Vesryn spun. Jassyn leaped away as the butt end of the prince's weapon nearly punched him in the gut. "I killed them."

Jassyn fumbled, snatching the staff before it clattered to the ground. "*What?*"

Vesryn straightened from the onslaught, blinking rapidly. "One of them said my name." The prince's voice lowered, suspended on the brink of disbelief and bitterness. "I don't know if it's more unsettling that those beasts can speak or the fact that it seemed to want *mercy*."

Reclaiming his rebelling lungs, Jassyn's eyes widened in stunned silence even though he'd already discovered that wraith could converse. *The wraith probably heard someone address the prince and learned his name.*

The tendons in Vesryn's neck strained before he slammed the staff into the sand, leaning against it. "I lost control. I rended every single one before I extracted any answers."

Anger disintegrating, the prince scrubbed a hand over his

face. "The attack...dredged up memories I've kept buried for so long." His fingers tightened on the staff, grinding the wood further into the earth. "I couldn't lose Serenna like I did my brother. Even if we haven't accepted our bond yet, I don't think I'd survive another connection breaking or failing another person." Vesryn slumped as he shook his head, staring at the ground. "I ruined the only chance we had of discovering where those beasts came from." His words dwindled to a whisper, nearly dusted away by the breeze. "I'm so tired of fucking up."

Jassyn's chest splintered in response, fracturing under the weight of his own guilt. He almost confessed his encounter with the elven wraith, informing his cousin that one of their number could wield Essence. But Jassyn wavered, the scab of his shame still too fresh to rip back open. It wouldn't be any consolation to the prince anyway.

Jassyn hardly heard Vesryn as he spoke to the ground. "The night the wraith killed my mother and brother... I wasn't at the palace. I should've been, but I wasn't." The prince swallowed. "I was at the Vallende estate...out of my mind..." Vesryn cleared his throat, voice breaking as he traced a whorl on the staff. "The only thing I remember was feeling split apart when the bond shattered. I blacked out after it happened. I don't know for how long." He blew out an unsteady sigh. "When I woke...Aesar was...just gone."

Jassyn's heart stopped at the admission and then twisted painfully as he watched Vesryn's features contort, haunted by the pain of the past. An overwhelming urge had him wanting to provide some measure of reassurance that the prince wasn't alone. Unsure of what to do, Jassyn hesitantly stepped forward, reaching out to clasp his cousin's shoulder.

"I'm sorry," he said, knowing words were an empty comfort while the prince drowned in regret. "I never knew the details of that night."

Vesryn's shoulders caved in. "If I didn't foul myself with

Stardust for years, Aesar wouldn't be dead." He drew in a shuddering breath. "My mother wouldn't be dead. Along with so many others. The wraith left nothing behind but shredded corpses. My sire didn't even allow me to say goodbye." The prince released a bitter laugh. "All I have to remember my brother are a shelf of his books, his glaives, and his boots."

Sadness devoured Jassyn whole as he glanced at Vesryn's shoes at the edge of the yard—that offensive, tattered pair he'd always detested. He blinked back an uncomfortable sting in his eyes, realizing why the prince clung to the unsightly footwear. After decades, the leather was falling apart—most likely only held intact by magic. *We're all broken in our own ways and sometimes it's only frayed threads holding our seams together.*

"Thank you for helping me the last few days," Jassyn said, squeezing his cousin's shoulder before pulling away. He wiped at a stray tear, suddenly finding the distant mountains interesting to look at. *We've both failed those around us. Maybe we're not so different after all.*

Wingbeats thundered through the air. The prince tossed his staff to the sand and rolled his shoulders. "Take a break and get some water. I need to speak with Zaeryn."

The weight of the moment dissipated. Jassyn turned, following Vesryn's gaze over his head toward the sky. The earth trembled, the vibrations rippling up his legs as the rangers' flight captain landed her chestnut dracovae in a sprawling meadow.

Vesryn strode off while Jassyn stumbled to the watering rifts located in the grass outside the ring, beyond grateful for the interruption. Two horizontal portals spanning a pace in the air suspended an undulating column of water, presumably drawn from a nearby mountain stream. Seeing no other way to drink, Jassyn cupped his hands to catch the flow, splashing water over his face.

Eyes unfocusing, he stared at the gushing fountain, dwelling on the long road ahead—especially considering Vesryn's star-bent notion to personally oversee his fitness. *But if outright war with the wraith is approaching, I need to prepare.*

As his body relaxed, Jassyn's senses suddenly buzzed, his skin pinching tight with his lifting hairs. Everything lurched into a vivid, crisp focus. The wind sighed as it shifted. The grass thrummed under his toes. A stream of water from the portal's cascade began rippling toward him like a flower turning with the sun.

Jassyn frantically squeezed his eyes shut, ruthlessly yanking his awareness inward, away from the earth. The handful of times he'd allowed his mind to drift recently, the surrounding world had seemed to beckon to him. He hadn't yet determined how to prevent it from spontaneously happening. *How am I supposed to tune out this magic when it's always around me?*

Not having the head space to deal with how he channeled a power that was supposed to be extinct, Jassyn shoved the thought away to dwell on at another time. Instead, he focused on recovering his body, quenching his thirst, and slowing his heartbeats along with his breaths.

Jassyn jumped when the prince's voice sounded next to him. "Slow down." Vesryn swatted him away from catching the column's water. "You'll throw up again at the rate you're going. And I've had a lifetime's worth of hearing you retch."

Gut sloshing as he wiped his hands on his leathers, Jassyn sighed. The prince probably had a point.

Vesryn helped himself to the draft, shoving his face into the flow with the manners of an animal at a watering hole. "I think you should come to the sparring ring in the evenings," Vesryn said after he finished drinking, wiping his arm across his mouth.

Jassyn released a humorless laugh. "I can hardly stand on one leg without falling over, let alone be of any consequence to anyone who wants to practice."

"You have to start somewhere." Vesryn shrugged. "Why not train with the best?"

Too exhausted to fire back a retort, Jassyn settled on rolling his eyes.

The prince's attention wandered over his shoulder. Twisting around, Jassyn saw Flight Captain Zaeryn sitting in the grass, sharpening a knife while her dracovae stretched out, brown scales absorbing the sun. She waved across the field.

Vesryn nodded in her direction, raising a hand back. "She asked if I'd be bringing you around more."

Jassyn studied the prince's second in command. "I have no interest in joining the rangers." He glared at his cousin. "You ruined the whole flying experience for me."

"You missed my meaning." Vesryn smirked, apparently unrepentant for inducing Jassyn's fear of heights by shoving him off a dracovae in flight decades ago. "She's curious about you." The prince caught water with his hands this time, before guzzling from his palms. "Like...she'd be interested in getting to *know* you."

Jassyn's lip curled in disgust at the stream of liquid leaking from the corner of Vesryn's mouth. He blinked, registering the prince's insinuation. "I don't think so."

"Why not? She's a formidable fighter and has put me on my back more times than I can count." Vesryn elbowed him. "Those thighs of hers could snap a dracovae's rib. You should see how —"

"I'm not ready for something like that," Jassyn snapped, his chest constricting with discomfort. "And I doubt I'll ever be."

Vesryn's mirth morphed to understanding before he brushed loose fringes of hair away from his face, averting his eyes. "Right. Of course. I'll fend her off for you if it comes to that." Clearing his throat, he quickly backtracked topics. "But you should still consider training. I think working your body to exhaustion in the evenings will be an excellent distraction from the dust—to break your former routines." The prince broke into a grin, sidling closer to shake Jassyn's shoulder. "In any case, I'll be tucking you in every night, ensuring you don't slip up."

If we keep this up, I'm sure Vesryn will think we're friends. Jassyn rubbed his temples, mouth pinching into a line. "Fine," he breathed out in reluctant agreement.

The prince's eyes lit up, glinting with a wretched delight. "Really?"

"Don't make me regret it." Jassyn jabbed a finger at Vesryn's chest, pushing him back out of his space. "I'm sure your influence will be more destructive than Stardust."

Vesryn clapped Jassyn on the back, nearly sending him sprawling. "Oh, I guarantee it."

CHAPTER 5

SERENNA

"Shield!" A female magus bellowed at Serenna from the side of the Combat Yard.

Serenna didn't shield.

A brutal blast of force smacked Serenna upside the head, flashing a torrent of stars behind her eyes. She'd had no time to practice fabricating wards after Vesryn had snapped her into the ability a little over a week ago.

Blinking, Serenna found herself staring at the ground, hands sinking into sand. Shaking her head to dislodge the ringing in her ears, she swayed to her feet. A violent rush of shadows veiled Serenna in a gale of darkness.

"No rending!" the magus shouted.

Serenna scowled at the interfering menace before whipping her attention back to Ayla, twenty paces across from her. Wiping away perspiration trickling down her forehead, Serenna ignored the bursts of magic flaring around the other initiates scattered out in pairs.

The rules of the duel were completely unfair, stifling any advantage Serenna had with her aptitude in rending. She wasn't going to obliterate Alari's soon-to-be princess—she just wanted to bring that snake to her belly.

Serenna wouldn't have been in such a fury if Ayla hadn't taunted her with her impending engagement to the prince before their match, a vicious reminder that their sire had deemed Ayla a more suitable consort for the realm. Serenna's mood hadn't improved once her sister had started hurling her around the ring. *Half-sister*, she corrected, detesting even that close of an association.

Wrestling her emotions back behind iron bars in her mind, Serenna smothered her shadows before the magus reprimanded her again. Catching her breath, she twisted glimmering Essence around her hands, readying herself for another round that she was now seriously dreading.

The instructors had organized this "pre-tournament" practice, and Serenna thought the extra training would be prudent preparation—especially if the wraith returned. She wouldn't have bothered if she'd known that the conniving magus intended to pair her against Ayla. Intentionally, she had no doubts.

The odds were stacked against her. Fanning the flames of her self-pity, Serenna checked off her sister's advantages in her head. *Ayla has more abilities than me so she's automatically stronger, and she's obviously had more practice so she has more magic in her Well to draw from.*

Vesryn had suspended formal classes for two weeks while workers restored the battle-scarred campus. In the meantime, Jassyn had promised Serenna that he'd escort her to Kyansari to visit Velinya, who'd been transported to the capital's healing grounds after the attack.

Between the absence of the prince and her friends, restlessness had Serenna seeking a diversion. *I wouldn't have wasted my time if I knew this was going to turn into a public beating.* But it was too late to back down. The stubborn fragments of Serenna's pride prevented her from yielding even though she had no grand illusions that she'd be the victor.

Ayla flicked her flame-colored braid over her shoulder before folding her arms, tapping her boot in the sand, apparently already bored with tossing Serenna around. Rolling her eyes, Ayla called out to the hovering instructor, "Could you at least match me against someone who'll present half a challenge?"

Grinding her teeth, Serenna snatched her force talent from her Well, the unformed Essence in her hands morphing into a cerulean orb of light. *Only an arch elf with all eight abilities would best her. And Ayla knows it.*

Mending wouldn't be useful, and Serenna couldn't weave a shield even if her life depended on it. She had yet to manifest illumination and portaling—not that the remainder of her abilities would've been effective against her sister.

Ignoring Ayla's question, the magus blazed a burst of light between her and Serenna, signaling the start of their next round. A riptide of Essence crackled from Ayla's extended fingers.

Serenna's eyes widened as four portals cleaved the surrounding air, boxing her in a prison. She didn't have any warning before Ayla catapulted blows of force through each rift, aiming to pummel her from every direction.

Diving to the ground to escape the onslaught, Serenna scuttled through the sand on her hands and knees, fleeing through the closest gateway. On the other side, she realized the idiocy of the tactic. The portal had dumped her out nearly on top of her sister.

Serenna clambered to her feet, much closer to Ayla than she wanted to be. Unlike her sister, she hadn't had years of extensive training in hand-to-hand combat. Serenna staggered back, creating more space. Her attention darted to the other pairs of recruits, calculating how far she could scurry to put more distance between them.

Portals unraveling, Ayla punched out a shock wave of force. Flailing with her power, Serenna returned the attack, casting a blue blast toward Ayla. Their magic collided, splitting the air with a *crack* like thunder.

The clash of magic swelled between them, shoving them apart. Serenna locked her teeth, boots skidding backward, digging trenches into the ring. In a frantic attempt to try something different, she slapped a wave of power against the earth.

A purple lattice ignited around Ayla, slamming into a solid shield, leaving her unscathed. A cloud of dust sailed in the sunlight while sand settled back to the ground. Waving a hand in front of her face, Serenna spluttered a series of coughs from the stirred debris. She flinched as an unexpected presence coiled around her mind, voice trickling into her awareness.

Come on, Harpy, you throw better magic than that when you're facing me.

Focus fracturing, Serenna's heart tripped and then raced. Her pulse jumped when she followed the subtle tug of the bond, detecting the prince near the yard's perimeter trees. The spectating initiates eyed him warily, inching away. Vesryn arched a questioning brow at her, rolling a loose thread on his stitched dragon.

It took Serenna an annoying amount of effort to rip her attention away from the prince's untimely presence. She silently seethed to herself, returning her focus to the match. *Now he conveniently appears when I'm getting flung across the ring!*

Serenna had sensed that the prince had returned to campus a few days prior. Assuming he had a hundred demands taking up his time, she hadn't ascended the Spire like a moon-eyed girl to seek him out.

Using the telepathic link the prince still had latched onto her mind, Serenna sent him a snippy thought. *You let me practice with rending, these horrid magus don't. I've hardly—*

The world turned upside down when a barrage of power launched Serenna into the air. Essence slipped out of her grip from the sudden shock. She crashed onto her back, colliding with the sand.

What air Serenna had left abandoned her lungs when Ayla rammed into her. They grappled in a tangle of arms and fingers until Ayla wrenched Serenna's hands next to her head, staking her to the ground like a pinned beetle on display.

"Do you honestly think a half-breed from the human realms can compete with me?" Ayla hissed, straddling Serenna's hips. "You have no place among the elves."

Unable to combat the insecurity that her sister's vicious words had induced, something in Serenna's chest iced over, fracturing with the truth. She had yet to set foot in Kyansari. *I'll never be a pure-blood and belong.* And Serenna wanted to scream at Ayla that neither would she, a fact that her sister always conveniently forgot.

Serenna bucked and squirmed under Ayla like a worm writhing in water. She yanked in air past the sting of her sister's flaying words and the fact that the realm had reduced her to nothing more than fodder for the wraith.

Ayla's perfectly painted lips peeled back from her teeth when Serenna didn't respond. "Why do you think our sire selected *me* as the prince's consort instead of you?"

Serenna steered her mind away from the half-formed bond with the prince—the twin silver cords connecting them. It wasn't like Vesryn had chosen her either. Essence had randomly linked their Wells. She knew he wouldn't have looked at her twice if the magic hadn't forced his attention.

He said he wanted to figure out what this power between us means before we fully accept the bond, but why would he bind himself more completely to someone who can't even fight off another recruit?

Embarrassment seared Serenna's cheeks. The prince was witnessing Ayla defeat her. She hadn't forgotten that his intervention—using their connection and summoning her power for her—was the only reason she'd survived the wraith's assault.

Simmering frustration with Ayla's constant advantage had Serenna spitting words. "Tell me," she goaded, despite being helpless on her back, "how does it feel being sold to the highest bidder?"

"There is no greater bloodline than Falkyns'." Ayla's sapphire eyes flashed as she dug her nails into Serenna's arms. Scarlet braid spilling over her shoulder, she leaned closer, words malicious with her disdain. "You will not ruin this for me."

As if Serenna had any hope of altering the will of the realm. *I can't even get up!* A disbelieving, bitter laugh burst from Serenna's lips. *Ayla is dragging this out on purpose, proving she's better and doesn't need magic to subdue me. Stars scorch her!*

"I'm sure our sire will be *so* proud when you spread your legs to produce a litter for his line," Serenna bit back, scraping her heels in the sand. She pointlessly tried hooking Ayla's legs, straining to knock her sister off. "Will the king pay him extra once you prove your worth? Or will you get a pat on the head? Enlighten me, I always get confused with your elven customs."

Ayla's fingers cinched tighter around Serenna's wrists, grinding her further into the sand. "I heard you failed to bed that half-breed our sire wrapped up in a bow and delivered to your miserable human court." Ayla sneered, hovering above Serenna's face. "Why would he waste opportunities on you when you couldn't even manage to fuck a whore?"

Serenna sucked in a sharp breath. Jassyn was Ayla's family after a fashion—a half uncle or something. Not that blood relations meant anything to the elves. It didn't surprise her that this vile viper regarded him in such a way.

Hands balling into fists next to her head, Serenna's loathing of this...this detestable *creature* incubated under her rage, threatening to hatch with the heat of her fury. Serenna's revulsion erupted, snapping out its wings. Her vision went red.

Ayla emitted a satisfying gasp when shadows burst from Serenna, tombing them in a pocket of darkness. Magic twisted around them, a blurred obsidian cloud, shading the sun. Serenna brought Ayla to her knees before with rending. *I'll do it again!*

Vesryn's corrective intervention brushed against her mind. *Serenna, play nice.*

Erupting with frustration from the prince denying her retribution, Serenna swatted his presence out of her mind. Stomach jolting, her eyes widened when Ayla pulled back her arm. Shocked dismay broke through Serenna's rage as she registered that her sister intended to punch her in the face.

Time slowed to a distorted crawl. Serenna scrambled to use a different talent, floundering to haul up another ability from her Well. A tingle rushed to her fingertips, her perception towed toward something else lurking at the edge of her awareness.

A window opened in her mind, like peering through glass, grasping at a fleeting reflection. A sudden breeze stirred, the gust rolling strands of hair across her face. Something peculiar whispered in the wind, a dormant heartbeat reviving, rousing from a long slumber.

Vesryn battered Serenna with commands that she didn't decipher as Ayla's fist inched closer. Shadows dispersing, her hold on Essence waned.

Gazing inward, Serenna's vision unfocused as she perceived a strange, silent breath of energy beyond the magic in her Well. There was a shift in the earth, a puzzle piece clicking into place.

A puff of dust kicked up in a whirl of air, gently spiraling across the yard. She saw them. Dancing currents—streams of power waiting to be called.

Reaching out with her mind, Serenna snatched at a draft. Her senses flared like feathers, blazing to life. Foreign sensations, separate from the rush of Essence, snapped the world into a crystal focus, somehow synchronizing her with the breeze.

She twisted the gale, warping it to her will.

Ayla screeched, flying off Serenna's body like a sail yanked taut, wrenched away by an invisible force. Her sister tumbled and rolled across the yard.

Panting from the effort, Serenna didn't have time to dwell on what she did with her power. She clambered to her feet, dashing toward Ayla while tossing out a hand to lash her sister to the sand with coils of force.

Vesryn probably sent magic through the bond like he did during the attack. Helping me. Again.

Jumping on Ayla, Serenna faltered as soon as she raised her fist.

Obviously reading Serenna's desire to beat her sister to a pulp, Vesryn's humor spiked. *Like this,* he said, seeding a vision into her mind, showing her the correct way to position her thumb.

Serenna's chest heaved with indecision while she caught her breath. She lowered her arm over Ayla's immobilized body, knowing she only had moments before her sister countered her magic and freed herself from the hold.

I won't brawl over the prince.

Why not?

Serenna scowled at Vesryn across the ring—she hadn't meant to send him that scattered thought. He smirked, unsheathing a dagger to idly flip.

Your arrogance concerns me, she snapped. *Don't you have—*

Ayla headbutted her.

Serenna shrieked, reeling back as her teeth impaled her lip. The sharp pain in her mouth sliced through her foolish hesitation.

Flinging out a hand, Serenna launched a wave of force at the prince. She snatched Vesryn's knife out of the air with a whip of power. Yanking her magic, the weapon soared across the ring like an arrow. Breath hitching, Serenna begged the stars that she'd catch the dagger by the hilt instead of the blade.

Miraculously, the leather grip smacked into her waiting palm. Serenna shoved the blade against Ayla's throat. Baring her teeth, Serenna's lip burned as it split further.

"Yield," she seethed.

Ayla's nostrils flared. Her eyes dashed to the magus monitoring the duels, but they didn't intervene—likely deferring to the prince, allowing him to decide when to stop the escalation.

Serenna knew he wouldn't.

A pulse of Ayla's power hummed in response, poised to retaliate. Serenna jammed the knife into her sister's ivory skin, drawing a stream of blood.

"I yield," Ayla hissed through her teeth.

"Louder," Serenna ordered with hideous satisfaction, drunk on victory. "I don't think the prince heard."

After forcing Ayla to squeal her surrender, Serenna wiped Vesryn's dagger on her sister's tunic and lurched to her feet. Releasing her magic, Serenna thumbed the streak of blood off her mouth, wincing at the stinging cut.

Eyes swinging toward the prince, her chest heated when Vesryn grinned his approval. He jerked his head for her to join him.

Recapturing her breath, Serenna lifted her chin. She glided out of the ring, her throat too dry to swallow as every onlooker watched her approach the prince. *Nothing is unusual about us talking—he's my trainer for the tournament.* Attention riveted on her, Vesryn's emerald eyes hypnotically reeled her in.

Serenna's stomach fluttered when the prince opened a portal. She sensed Vesryn's emotions warring through the bond —concern, fury, agitation. She withdrew her attempts at deciphering him, her own alarm compounding as she worried she was somehow responsible for his irritable mood.

"I have a special activity planned," Vesryn said as she joined him. He glanced at the looming gateway. "Some extracurricular practice before...the tournament."

Serenna's attention hooked on his fingers tapping against his thigh. Sweat trickled down her neck as she handed Vesryn his dagger, her hands nearly shaking with mirrored unease. Recalling her forced participation in the prince's other unconventional "training," the cogs of Serenna's mind churned through every guess of where he could be taking her.

She didn't come up with an answer before following Vesryn through the rift, leaving Centarya behind her.

CHAPTER 6

SERENNA

The portal's compressing chill rippled over Serenna as a roaring silence rushed through her ears. Stepping out on the other side of the rift, she blinked into darkness, smothered by stagnant air. An eerie sense of foreboding percolated from the void's surroundings. She tensed, every nerve firing as her heartbeat ricocheted against her ribs.

"Vesryn?" Serenna whispered, her hushed voice swallowed by shadows.

A vibration of Essence answered. Azure illumination flared to life in the corridor, the orbs whirling around them. The prince's hand clamped over hers like a fetter, the tension in his fingers feeling more controlling than comforting.

Serenna tripped over her boots as Vesryn practically dragged her down a hallway lined with iron-barred cells. Unable to see within the brig's depths, the grim stillness had her imagining the area was devoid of inhabitants.

She tightened her grip against the prince's palm, glancing up at him. The contact of his skin against hers had Essence nearly jumping through her veins, straining to twine with his magic through the bond.

"Where are we?" Her quiet question still sounded too loud, the pressure of silence too ominous to disturb.

The hovering illumination highlighted a tendon flexing in Vesryn's neck as he clenched his jaw. "Kyansari's dungeons."

His curt answer had the hairs on Serenna's arms lifting. "Why?" Waiting for a reply that didn't come, she peered into the black cells, sifting for a reason. Shoulders weighed down by the oppressive gloom, she suppressed a shudder, attempting to inquire again. "What are we doing here?"

Vesryn remained silent, tugging on her arm when she balked, steering her around a corner that spilled toward a stairwell. Serenna's legs became leaden with fear, but the prince gave her no choice but to quicken her stride, driving her down the steps, deeper into the suffocating prison.

On the lower level, stone doors lined the hallway, concealing what lay on the other side. Vesryn stalked halfway down the corridor before finally releasing her. Apprehension slid down Serenna's spine as she rubbed feeling back into her twinging fingers.

The prince jerked his chin toward the smooth door indented into the rockwork, his command clipped. "Untangle the shield."

Pulse thundering in her ears, Serenna braced herself, wiping her clammy palms on her chestnut leathers. The prince's face held less expression than the surrounding stones, resigning her to the fact that asking more questions would yield no answers.

Floundering in a sea of uncertainty, Serenna searched the bond for reassurance. Her shoulders jerked tight when she angled her awareness toward the prince. Vesryn wasn't barricading himself—she doubted he could, with that volcano's worth of wrath ready to erupt.

Serenna jumped when the prince snapped at her, his words reverberating off the stones. "Stop reading me and open the stars-cursed door." His fingers twitched at his sides like he was restraining himself from wringing her neck.

Heart hammering—more so with fear of him now than anything else—Serenna raised a feeble confession, words breathless with nervousness. "I—I don't know how to untangle wards."

I'll show you. Vesryn's growl was a violent jab in her head as he telepathically unfolded images of a shield's lattice in her mind.

Confusion twisted through her from the rapid shift in his mood since they'd left Centarya. For the first time, Serenna sensed he was at the end of whatever scant tolerance he currently possessed.

Chest tightening with an uneven breath, Serenna's fingers trembled when she raised her hand to the door. The cool rock scraped against her palm as she wrestled to clear her thoughts. Vesryn's impatience, crashing into her in waves, only engulfed her further in unease. Abandoning the futile attempt of calming her mind to summon Essence, Serenna resorted to channeling her fear to haul the corresponding talent from her Well.

Violet light fountained under her fingertips, lacing along the rock like a spider's web. The invisible woven ward silently hummed in response, igniting to reveal a crystalline grid. Threads of power slithered against the stone as Serenna twined Essence around the shield's knots, unraveling the magic locking the door.

She spared a quick glance at Vesryn, about to ask if it was possible to sever the ward with a slash of rending, but she sensed that he wasn't in the mood to suffer a conversation. *I wish he'd explain what this is about.*

Serenna retreated a step when the shield's remaining fibers disintegrated, crumbling like ash. Waiting for further instruction, her Essence shimmered around them.

Flicking his wrist, Vesryn shoved the rock inward with a pulse of force. Serenna cringed, stone grating against stone as his magic drove the slab away from the opening, sliding against the ground. A sudden burst of light radiating from the chamber made her squint.

Serenna's stomach clenched when Vesryn seized her wrist, his fingertips stronger than steel. He dragged her inside the cell. After several moments of blinking against the blazing brightness, her eyes focused on a hulking figure across the room.

A wraith.

Serenna gasped, terror stripping the breath from her lungs. The monster went wild, snarling and gnashing its fangs. Fear impaled her like a javelin of ice, freezing her mind, shattering any thoughts. Essence deserted her as the sight of those blood-red eyes had her instinctively dashing to flee.

Before Serenna could scamper a pace, Vesryn nearly ripped her arm out of its socket, hauling her back to his side. Panic speared her as she frantically flailed against the prince's unrelenting grip.

"Calm down!" Vesryn shouted, spinning her around to face the wraith. "Stars, it's secured."

Unable to draw in enough air, Serenna panicked as the prince forced her to stare at the creature. His fingers gouged into her shoulders, anchoring her in place. Upon seeing coils of rending shackling the wraith to the opposite end of the stark cell, Serenna slowly reclaimed control of her breathing.

The chained wraith's bared fangs dripped saliva, as if desperate to shred them with its teeth. Dirty from the squalor of the prison, tattered clothing hung from its gaunt form, clinging to indigo skin. Its crimson eyes rolled, savage and feral, a mindless beast in humanoid form. This wasn't one of the wraith from the attack.

Vesryn turned Serenna back around, jade gaze boring into hers. "You lost control of your power." His hands tightened against her. "That can't happen. Even if you're terrified." Serenna flinched, the prince's sharp words cutting like a blade. "You need to stay in control."

Shame scalded Serenna's cheeks, her ineptitude on display once again. She swallowed, her words broken. "Why am I here?"

Vesryn seized the front of her leathers, drawing her up to her toes. "Because," he snarled in her face, more vicious than the monster in the chamber. "You need to master your power to protect yourself. You almost died," he raged, shaking her. "I *felt* it!" The prince's word ricocheted off the stone walls, slamming against her. "And there wasn't anything I could do!"

The heat of his fury scorched Serenna through their connection, stinging her worse than a slap. He'd never raised his voice like that—so inflamed. The intensity of his ranting had her blinking back startled tears, helpless against the crash of his anger surging through the bond.

"I couldn't portal without risking a horde of wraith coming through with me, and I couldn't rend them all fast enough to reach you." Vesryn's fists trembled against her leathers. He yanked in ragged breaths, eyes unhinged. "Thank the stars you managed to defend yourself."

Releasing her, the prince crossed his arms, staring up at the ceiling. Serenna sensed him collecting himself, leashing his emotions, but the rapid rise and fall of his shoulders didn't abate.

He drew a hand over his face, shaking his head. "I can't afford to have you be my weakness." Vesryn sounded like he was talking more to himself than her.

Serenna flinched, his words rattling her like thunder. Her heart skidded to a halt. *So he's finally figured out what this connection between us means—a weakness because of my incompetence.* Imagining the likely possibility of him rejecting the bond instead of accepting it fully, disappointment cleaved her chest. *He's giving me one more chance to prove myself, and all I've done is demonstrate that he shouldn't have wasted his time.*

Restraining her hands from reaching out, Serenna folded them across her middle. The reassurance of touch would've only been for her benefit anyway. She knew she wouldn't find any until she honed her abilities to the prince's standards.

Her voice cracked, on the verge of breaking. "What do I have to do?"

Vesryn gathered his power. The radiance of his magic shimmered around them like the sun glinting off of the ocean's waves. Flicking a hand, the stone door screeched against the floor, ramming shut. Locking them in with the wraith.

The prince jerked his head toward the snarling monster. "You've killed them before." It wasn't a question, but Serenna nodded anyway. "You need to do it again. Every time."

"What?" Serenna's brows jumped up her face. She glanced at the defenseless wraith thrashing against its magical restraints. Her horrified revelation came out as a whisper. "You want me to kill it?"

"No, I don't want you to kill it," Vesryn snapped. "Yet." He scowled at the creature. "I have another use for it. Gather your power," he ordered, implying she didn't have any choice.

He grabbed her arm. Serenna tensed, tracking a splinter of darkness spinning from the prince's palm, aimed at the wraith. When the rending restraining the creature unraveled, Vesryn shoved her in the monster's direction.

Serenna didn't even have time to scream before the wraith charged her.

CHAPTER 7

LYKOR

"Stop!"

A taloned claw seized Lykor's wrist, wrenching him away from the prisoner slumped in chains.

Concentration disrupted, Lykor staggered back from the intoxicating rush of magic, blinking rapidly to reorient himself in the interrogation chamber. His eyes slowly came into focus in the dim torchlight.

Essence boiled under his skin, scalding his Well. His senses crackled like a lightning-charged tempest, chest pounding with an ocean's worth of power. He sucked in a breath against the overwhelming surge of magic threatening to burst through his ribs.

Baring his teeth at the intrusion, Lykor ripped his arm out of Kal's grasp. Lykor's power ignited alongside his rage. Shadows blasted around the room, the darkness disintegrating where the magic touched the gold woven into the walls.

Fenn, one of Kal's brood—and one of Lykor's lieutenants—drew Lykor's attention with his colossal height as he shifted nervously behind his father's shoulder. Claws shoved into his cloak pockets, Fenn's crimson eyes volleyed between them. The pair must've heard the screams when the elf roused in the middle of the siphoning.

Ice clung to their fur overcoats. Lykor presumed they'd recently finished a patrol shift on the tundra's surface. Favoring the customs of the wraith's younger generation—those born in their fortress—Fenn wore his frivolously long hair tied back, decorated with intermittent strands of thin obsidian braids. Rings and studs trimmed the points of his ears, designating his rank. As Fenn's eyes widened, Lykor followed the lieutenant's gaze.

The female rider was dead.

And she was no longer an elf. The warrior hadn't survived the transformation to wraith.

Dispelling his shadows, displeasure churned through Lykor. Reaping her power too hastily, he'd squandered the opportunity to harvest information.

Kal's voice dropped to a shaken whisper. "What have you done?"

Ignoring his captain, Lykor swiped disheveled hair out of his eyes. Torchlight glinted off the silver strands. Lykor stilled. Silver instead of black. Back to Aesar's original hue.

Mind ablaze with curiosity, Lykor tried to elongate his fangs. Nothing happened. He ran his tongue along even teeth, detecting no trace of his sharpened canines.

Assessing the power in his Well, Lykor inhaled sharply, snared by surprise. His only intention had been to siphon the elf's magic, augmenting his current abilities in the process. He didn't consider that she might possess the innate talents that the king had severed from Aesar.

With all eight abilities returned, they were an arch elf. No longer reduced, their form unchained from the suspension between elf and wraith. Lykor glanced up at his captain, now standing a head shorter than Kal and Fenn—restored to Aesar's elven height.

Lykor idly wondered if he'd have to maintain an illusion to distort his appearance in front of mirrors. If he saw Vesryn looking back, he could only guess that the coercion would trigger him to kill himself. *I DOUBT THE KING ANTICIPATED THIS.*

Inspecting his fingers, Lykor released a disgusted scoff. Despite reversing to an arch elf's body, the skeletal claw stubbornly refused to shift back into an elven hand. He'd somehow known he'd never escape the reminders of the dungeon's horrors.

Kal's talons clacked as his claws clenched at his sides. "This isn't the way."

Lykor barked out a laugh, an expulsion of air at the useless objection. "The wraith have no advantages." Yanking a burst of force from his Well, he snatched his gauntlet from the ground and shoved the armor back onto his fucking claw. "I won't hesitate to drain Essence from every stars-cursed elf."

"You'd be turning innocents into wraith." Kal's scarlet glare blazed with fury. "That crime would make you no better than the king."

"And what gave you the impression that I care? Perhaps I'll redistribute power like Galaeryn always spoke about." Lykor took an aggressive step closer to his captain, driving a gauntleted finger into Kal's chest. "Except I'll give the elves' magic *back* to the wraith."

Before Kal could argue, Lykor diverted him with a sarcastic taunt. "Don't you prefer gazing upon this elven form, anyway?" Sneering, Lykor gestured to his moonbeam complexion, plucking at his hair, silver like frosted starlight. "Isn't this how you remember Aesar?"

Kal retreated a step, landing next to Fenn. "*Aesar* would never steal power."

Fenn placed a claw on his father's shoulder, talons tensing

against Kal's cloak. A warning. Possessing more sense than the captain, the young lieutenant averted his gaze, keeping silent.

"Perhaps Aesar's weakness was why he fractured in the dungeons." Lykor rolled his shoulders, haunted by the impression of those golden spikes Galaeryn had impaled into his spine so long ago. "None of us would be here if I didn't suffer all that fucking torture on his behalf."

Glancing around the interrogation chamber, irritatingly dim now due to loss of his wraith sight, Lykor seized Essence. Angling his awareness toward Aesar's sleeping presence, he tapped into Aesar's knowledge. Rummaging through his memories, Lykor flicked his wrist, igniting the room with white illumination, a talent he hadn't had at his disposal before. Fenn cringed, shielding his eyes from the sudden wave of blinding light.

"Let me talk to him," Kal demanded, his pupils swallowed by his crimson glower.

Shadows combusted from Lykor, answering his fury. They all wanted their prince. Even the elders, Kyansari's citizens who Lykor had delivered from the prisons after the king had reduced them all to wraith. No one wanted *him*, the one who'd survived for them. Protected them. Endured all the torments for them.

A chain of darkness lashed out, wrapping around Kal. Lykor yanked his captain to him, reaching up to snatch Kal's throat.

"Do you know where your precious Aesar is?" Lykor hissed in Kal's face, dragging him down to eye level. "He's drifting. Thinking he's still plunging to his death. Taking the coward's way out." Lykor squeezed, the metal joints in his gauntlet squealing. Shadows mobbed like ravens, spinning in a gale. "He won't be coming back."

Lykor's eyes flicked to Fenn, who was nervously chewing on a lip ring in the same aggravating habit as his father. He eyed the rending but didn't retreat, scaled boots scraping against the stone floor as he shifted his weight.

Kal gritted his teeth, fangs elongating. "Aesar was trying to save us from *you*," he gasped in a strangled breath.

"About time you've finally accepted that I'm not Aesar." Lykor flung Kal away, sending him stumbling. "It only took a fucking century."

Disappearing, Kal warped before he fell. He reappeared next to Fenn, lurching on his feet to regain his balance, the intricate braids in his midnight hair swinging.

Lykor jerked his head in command toward the wraith in chains. "Lieutenant, make yourself useful and clean up this mess." With a pull of force, Lykor yanked an iron key off the wall, hurling it at Fenn with his power.

Fenn plucked the key from the air. Always eager to prove himself, he obediently busied himself with freeing the chained prisoner.

"How can you bring yourself to steal Essence from another?" Kal questioned, catching his breath and rubbing the indents in his throat. His eyes darted to his son and then to the dead rider. "After the king plundered from all of us? And from you, how many times?"

"I won't hesitate to return Galaeryn's terror tenfold." Lykor pivoted on his heel to leave. "Better that we pillage Essence from these half-elves he's bred before he can amass more power," he growled over his shoulder.

Lykor stomped through the cell-lined hallway and back up the stairs, footsteps echoing against the stone. Even if it meant succumbing to the consequences—turning into a monster like the king—Lykor had no reservations about embracing the same darkness to be the protector the wraith needed.

Obviously never predicting their escape, Galaeryn had boasted his ambitions while Lykor had been at his mercy.

Powerless to stop the king, Lykor steered his thoughts away from what he knew of Galaeryn's plans.

He envisioned the obsidian door to the chamber Galaeryn had tortured him in. In the safety of his mind, Lykor had stowed all of those horrific memories, concealing them to shield Aesar. Vacating his thoughts of the king, Lykor shoved everything back into that harrowing room.

"What happened to the male who led us from the prisons?" Kal asked, storming up the stairs behind him. Lykor didn't waste his breath on a reply. "This vengeance against the king is polluting your judgment." When he caught up on the landing, Kal snatched Lykor's arm. "How many deaths will it take before you see that?"

Lykor rounded on him, erupting. "Aesar is the reason so many died!" His voice crashed around the stairwell. "He meddled by sounding the retreat. Those deaths are on him." Lykor ripped his arm out of Kal's claw. "By now, they've extracted our location from the people *he* abandoned!"

Frustration immolating like a dry stack of kindling, Lykor twisted, smashing his gauntlet into the wall instead of Kal's face. The stone cracked and shattered. Splintered rock chips tumbled down the stairs in a spray of dust. "Aesar's intervention compromised the safety of our fortress." Lykor's chest heaved with the cataclysm of his fury. "He's ruined everything."

Kal's eyes shied away from Lykor's face before he bit out his words. "What's your plan then, Lykor? *You* put everything at risk by insisting on that attack in the first place!"

"The elves forced my hand!" Lykor snarled, flinging out an arm. "You're supposed to be our military expert. Why else would they gather a human army on top of constructing that island? They're coming for us."

Kal's nostrils flared as he folded his arms across his armor. "You don't know that."

Snatching his previously discarded cloak, Lykor shouldered

it on. He stalked forward to where the gold veins of the dungeon tapered off, no longer hindering his portals. The tunnel's maw opened up to a cavernous chamber where offshoots spidered toward various areas of the keep.

Wrenching Essence, Lykor split a fissure in the air. "I'll prove it to you, since you refuse to believe me." He tore a portal open to a mountaintop on the edge of the Hibernal Wastes, where snow yielded to grass-covered hills.

Barging through the rift's consuming darkness, Lykor knew Kal would follow. His captain never missed an opportunity to infringe on Aesar's behalf.

Surrounded by rocky peaks, Lykor blinked against the sun's sudden glare. He veered to an overlook, boots churning through crusted snow.

Kal swore at his back when he emerged through the portal. Swiping Aesar's knowledge of Essence again, Lykor twined an illusion. Turquoise light surged from his palms, shrouding them to appear as the mountainous backdrop, obscured from any wandering eyes below.

"You knew the king wouldn't tolerate our escape indefinitely," Lykor growled. He prowled toward the rim of the precipice, slicing through the frigid breeze. "He's sending the mortals after us like we're an inconvenience. A loose end. He didn't bother sending his arch elves to pursue us—their lives are too *valuable*." He jutted his chin toward the edge of the cliff, a demand for Kal to see for himself. "Our demise ensures his plans remain veiled. As if any elf would believe us—we're monsters in their eyes. Galaeryn will never cease stealing power, and now he has a continuous source of magic with those half-elves."

Kal blew out a breath, his gaze swinging over the expanse before them, a mile below. He studied the human camps scattered like waves in a sea. "We can't stand against so many."

"What an astounding deduction, *Captain*. Observations like that have me questioning your rank." Lykor jammed a silver strand of wind-whipped hair behind his pointed ear. "The humans will try to drive us out of hiding. Why else would they be on our doorstep?" Lykor grunted his disbelief at the thousands spread out before them. "We'll leave the realms and take the wraith somewhere safe—to the west, across the Hibernal Wastes. There's no other option."

Kal frowned, spinning a ring in his brow. "We have no idea if anything is beyond these frozen mountains. It could be the world's edge or an icy sea." He drew his billowing cloak closer. "Galaeryn would've already made the trek if he believed that direction to be a viable choice. The west is impassable. I'm sure you know Aesar once tried to cross the expanse with his brother. They attempted portal jumping with the dracovae but never found the other side."

Lykor sensed Aesar finally stirring, as if the repeated mention of his name had roused him. Lykor's voice was an irritated growl through fused teeth as he willed Aesar to remain deep in slumber. "Then you also know *Aesar's* dusty books indicate that it's possible the druids had lands on the other side of the world. The Aelfyn obviously came from somewhere when their ships crashed on the mortal shores."

"Crossing the Wastes would be insanity. You'd lead our people to more death." Kal shook his head, braids swinging in the gale whipping around the mountainside. "The wraith are restless, especially our younger warriors, those 'reavers.' They won't stand for something like this—they've been questioning your judgment."

"I'll do it alone. Just like I've done everything else," Lykor raged, battling the inflamed tide of shadows threatening to torrent from his skin. "I'll portal jump from horizon to horizon, across that fucking snowscape, no matter how many days or weeks it takes until I reach the other side. When I'm done, I'll drop a gateway back on your doorstep."

To his credit, Kal didn't flinch or raise his voice. The projected calm only boiled Lykor's agitation.

"What would kill you first, the exposure to the elements or your dangerous habit of exhausting your power?" Kal demanded, a tendon rippling along his neck as his face settled into a furious glare. "Some things are beyond the capabilities of Essence—even for arch elves. What happens when you push yourself too far, as you always do?" He emitted a laugh, bitter like the wind. "How many times has your recklessness nearly cost you your life? How many times has Aesar regenerated for you and dragged you back to the fortress on the verge of collapse?" The red glow in Kal's eyes dimmed as he searched Lykor's face. "Your plan is madness."

Lykor crossed his arms. "I'm willing to take that risk. You and I both know Aesar believes the druids may have left something behind—something the wraith could use. If our stronghold is any evidence, that ancient race could have more weapons or technologies that the elves don't." Lykor paced the edge of the cliff, casting a scowl at the mortal camps below. "If anything remains, we need to seize it before the king. Leaving our fortress and heading west is our only option."

"And do you think a thousand years have left the other side of the world unscathed?" Kal dug the toe of his boot into the snow. "We don't know if anything survived their war. What if the Aelfyn still rule?"

"And what if those lands are empty and ripe for the taking?" Lykor snarled. The metal of his gauntlet screeched when he clenched his fist. "We could argue about unknowns all day. It's only a matter of time until Galaeryn's forces discover us. We need to find a new haven."

Kal heaved a frustrated sigh. "There could be another way." His eyes slowly lifted, meeting Lykor's stare. "Aesar's brother needs to know the truth. I could warn him, tell him what happened to us. I know he'd help."

"No." Lykor scoffed, turning back to study the camps below, unwilling to take the risk. "One person won't make a difference."

"But he's involved in their military. What if he could combine forces with us? We've been hiding long enough." Kal's voice grew desperate. "All you have to do is open a portal to that island. Get me close. Now that you have illusion again, you could disguise my wraith form." Kal clutched his shoulder. "I could even appear how I used to and—"

Lykor slapped his claw away. "I said *no*."

"If you would let me—"

"Are you deaf?" Lykor bared his teeth, regretting the loss of his fangs. "Which word didn't you understand? No one can stand against the king or his growing power."

"But Vesryn—"

The coercion seized control of Lykor's body, gripping his mind and ransacking his magic. A bystander behind his own eyes, Lykor was helpless as his Essence automatically reacted, triggered by the prince's spoken name. His spine went rigid, sundering the air in his lungs. Ice flooded his veins, freezing his bones as solidly as the surrounding snowdrifts.

Even realms away, Galaeryn's influence still shackled him. No matter how far Lykor fled, he knew he'd never be able to escape. Even if the wraith made it to the other side of the world.

Fingers twitching, confined in his own body, Lykor feverishly tried to resist the magic. *IF ANYONE GETS TO KILL KAL, IT'S GOING TO BE ME AND NOT THIS FUCKING COMPULSION.*

He didn't know why he bothered. Any attempt to oppose the king's relentless hold was as futile as grasping the wind. The corners of his vision spotted—he only had moments until darkness extinguished his awareness.

Losing himself to the chaos, a fragile thought surfaced, a tiny glimmer of hope that perhaps the amber-eyed elf could dismantle the coercion on his mind. *HE ALREADY LOOSENED THE MAGIC.* Lykor ruthlessly crushed the delusional notion of freedom. *LIKE I TOLD HIM, NO ONE CAN SAVE ME.*

A funnel of midnight streaked toward Kal's throat. This compulsory reaction was completely avoidable—both of them had worked around the king's magic for decades. But Lykor had known that his captain's flapping tongue would inevitably lead to his demise.

A cloud of rending converged like a tempest. Surely, if there were Essence wielders overseeing the mortals below, they'd sense the might of his power. Lykor's vision faded, submerging him into a sea of black.

Kal had no defense against the shadows. Eyes widening, he warped away.

But he wasn't fast enough.

CHAPTER 8

SERENNA

The wraith crashed into Serenna, knocking her flat on the dungeon floor. Head bouncing against the stone, black flecks exploded behind her eyes. She screamed as fangs snapped in her face and talons sliced at her leathers.

The monster's stifling weight vanished as suddenly as it had rammed into her. A pulse of Vesryn's power flared behind her, throwing the creature back across the cell with a strike of force. Arms flailing, it snarled against the magic, grotesquely long canines extended. Restraining shadows coiled around the wraith, securing it back against a wall.

Serenna hauled in sharp breaths, a storm of renewed terror dredging up memories from the night of the assault. She pushed herself up to a sitting position, clutching her panic-closed throat. Air burned her lungs as she warily watched the red-eyed beast, expecting it to charge across the room again. Shaking, Serenna relived what she'd thought were her final moments—both the resurrected memory from the attack and the previous few seconds.

"You would've been dead," the prince said behind her, yanking Serenna out of the fear-induced trance.

Serenna swiveled to face him. Vesryn loomed like a thundercloud at the edge of the stark chamber, fingers tapping against his folded arms.

"No thanks to you!" Serenna's voice was shrill with disbelief. "Scorching stars, what the—"

Cutting her off, Vesryn snarled like the wraith across the chamber. "Shut up and get back on your feet."

"Why?" Serenna battled his glare with her own, stubbornly staying where she was on the floor. "So you have a better view of that monster tearing me to shreds?"

Vesryn's mouth thinned, agitation blazing through the bond. "Summon your magic and fight."

Dread flooded Serenna's entire body. *He intends to make me train until I'm not a burden anymore.* Her fingers went numb, splayed on the cold stone. *Why doesn't he reject this connection between us and just be done with me?*

Vesryn clenched his jaw before flicking his wrist. Serenna's neck pinched from swinging too quickly to face the wraith. The creature shot toward her like an arrow. Serenna scrambled to her feet, reeling backward.

"Vesryn!" she pleaded, a strangled squeal as the monster reached her, claws slashing, smashing her to the ground.

The prince hauled the wraith back to the wall again with a push of force. "Dead," he drawled.

Serenna scurried to stand, legs kicking under her as she steadied herself. Her eyes widened, assessing the flaps of lacerated skin on her arms. Dark blood welled from the deep cuts, dripping down her fingertips, splashing on the floor.

She didn't feel it.

Gaping at the prince, Serenna realized he rendered her impervious to the pain, absorbing the feeling of her injuries through the bond.

Guilt flickered in Vesryn's face before he erased his features, becoming as expressionless as stone. He bared his teeth, biting out his words. "Fight. Back."

Serenna drew herself up, quivering with unease, betraying her attempt at confidence. Overwhelmed by the beast's attack, her heart mauled the confines of her ribs. Serenna dashed a glance at the wraith, ensuring Vesryn still had it secured.

She faced the prince, digging her nails into her palms. "I can't—"

The wraith crashed into her.

Anger replaced Serenna's terror as Vesryn hauled the creature back to the wall with another magical punch. *He's doing this until I'm desensitized to these monsters like he is.*

Serenna wobbled to her feet, livid at the prince and with herself for being unable to fend off one mindless wraith on her own. Ironically, her magic finally roared to life—rending summoned by fury.

Vesryn shot her an exasperated look, clicking his tongue as her shadows raced along the floor. "You're not using rending."

With a surprised gasp, Serenna staggered. A tide of Essence engulfed her through the bond. Every muscle locked in bewilderment, a rope drawn taught. Her access to rending vanished, snuffed out like a flame.

"That's *my* power!" Serenna grappled with Vesryn through the nexus linking them, straining to reclaim her ability, wrestling him in a battle of wills. *I should've known he could do something like this since he summoned my magic for me during the assault.*

Conceding that she wouldn't outmaneuver him, Serenna sucked in air at the loss. Her skin prickled with alarm that the prince had this much control over her—even without fully accepting their bond. *Yet another aspect of Essence that he's withheld from me. What more can be done with the bond that I'm not aware of?*

"What am I supposed to do?" Serenna seethed, indignation eroding her dismay. "Let that wraith assault me until I bleed to death?" Vesryn's silence only incensed her further.

The stress of the week was catching up to her, unraveling her like a spool of thread. She'd spent the previous days fretting over Velinya's absence and anxious that the wraith would return in force. Ayla's taunting—giving voice to Serenna's trepidation that she wasn't worthy enough for a place in the realm—had only frayed her to the point of snapping.

Bitterness welled inside of her, flooding out in a deluge of words. "Would you—for once—just tell me what you want?" Serenna's jaw clicked shut before she carelessly unleashed anything else.

Vesryn's unblinking gaze bored into hers. "You're going to learn how to summon your magic without tapping into your emotions."

"Like you're so in control of yours at the moment!" Serenna assumed his unbridled irritation was only feeding hers.

A muscle in Vesryn's jaw jumped as he squared his stance. "Use force or shielding."

"You can't be bothered to teach me *how* to use my power without my feelings?" Serenna glared at the prince, pointing a bloody finger at him. "You're the one who's been twisting my emotions this entire time to pry my abilities out!"

A pulse of magic directed across the room was Vesryn's only response. Spinning around, Serenna gritted her teeth as the wraith sprinted toward her. Its victorious snarl at freedom echoed in the chambers, colliding into her from every direction.

Time ticked by with each of its footsteps, red eyes burning, bare feet slapping stone. Serenna breathed in deeply, then exhaled her frustration and severed her thoughts. Blocking her awareness of the prince, she slammed iron gates over her mind, caging every emotion.

Serenna snatched at her magic. A spark of Essence blazed to life, gleaming as it spiraled around her hands like starlight. She heaved her force talent out of her Well.

Striking out, blue tendrils thrashed from her fingertips. Serenna trussed the wraith in a vice-like grip, halting its crazed charge. The monster's limbs twitched as it combatted her power, but it didn't gain any ground.

With a shriek, Serenna swung her other hand toward the prince. Releasing a shock wave of force, pressure exploded from her palm, reverberating against the stone walls. Shards of rock clattered to the floor, sending debris ricocheting across the chamber in a thin layer of dust.

Unsurprisingly, Vesryn had tossed a shield around himself. An aggravating smirk tugged at his lips when he unraveled his barrier. "I'm nearly impressed that you wielded two channels of power at once, despite directing one at me." Unsheathing his belt knife, the prince idly began flipping and catching the dagger.

His nonchalance only stoked Serenna's ire. She glared at him while her body shook from the effort of battling the wraith. Fangs bared, it strained against her magic.

"Now use your power to shove that fiend back to the wall and release it again," Vesryn said, kicking a boot behind him to lean against the stone.

Serenna's lungs fought to expand as she panted from the exertion of restraining the beast. "I am *not* doing that."

Vesryn shrugged, snatching the blade's hilt out of the air. "No matter." He waved his dagger. "I will." Blue force magic warped around the prince as he wrenched the wraith from her power's grip, steering it across the room. "Now that you're more angry than afraid, let it get closer and use a shield instead."

Leaving her no time to react, Vesryn released the wraith. Heart hammering in her ears, Serenna frantically fabricated a sloppy ward, copying the lattice the prince unfolded in her mind while the creature charged her. She barely solidified the barrier in time before the monster collided with her power.

Serenna's eyes bulged when her ward's threads unraveled from the onslaught. Throwing out a hand, she blasted the wraith away with a punch of force.

Vesryn chuckled, casting shadows to bind the monster back to the opposite wall.

"I'm glad you find this so entertaining," Serenna bristled, swaying on her feet as Vesryn continued to flip that stupid dagger, indifferent to her annoyance and exhaustion. "How much longer will you insist on this torture?"

"Until you drain your Well." Vesryn caught his knife without looking while holding her scowl. "Then I'll infuse you with my power and you'll keep practicing until you deplete your magic again."

Serenna's jaw went slack at what he was demanding of her, and without allowing her to recover from her duel with Ayla. He might as well have ordered her to run around Centarya a hundred times.

"You—you can't be serious," she spluttered.

"We're going to do this every day until I'm satisfied with your abilities." He balanced the tip of the blade on his finger. "Lucky for you, there's no short supply of wraith to corral."

Serenna's spine stiffened in protest, incredulity ringing in her tone. "Don't act like you're not punishing me for—"

"I'm not punishing you," Vesryn interrupted, almost defensively, snatching his dagger as it tumbled from his finger. "I'm *training* you."

Serenna scoffed. "We clearly have different opinions on the definition of 'training.'" She folded her bloody arms, still unaffected by the injuries scored into her skin. "You could learn a thing or two from Jassyn. He would *never*—"

Vesryn threw his knife directly at her face.

With a yelp, Serenna lurched backward, horror paralyzing her mind. Steered by instinct, she snatched the speeding weapon with a whip of force.

Serenna yanked in a sharp breath, released from shock. Grabbing the suspended dagger out of the air, she clenched the leather hilt. *How dare he!* Fury sharper than the steel in her palm, she lunged across the dungeon for the prince, punching forward with the blade.

Letting her reach him, Vesryn struck faster than a viper's strike. He seized her wrist in a smack of skin, halting the knife before it bit into the center of his chest.

Bracing her boots against the stone, Serenna wrestled against him, every fiber intent on thrusting the weapon through his leathers. She snatched the prince's other forearm, digging nails into flesh, fighting to pull herself closer. Muscles straining from the exertion, Serenna screeched in frustration that her physical strength was no match for a warrior.

Vesryn gripped a fistful of her hair, prying her neck back. Serenna gasped when he pushed her arm, forcing the dagger against her throat.

She went still, her pulse helplessly hammering against the icy steel. Serenna's chest held her breath hostage when the prince lowered his mouth. A flash of desire—that most certainly belonged to *him*—irrationally overrode her anger, quelling any remaining resistance.

Blood heating, every nerve in her body fired when Vesryn's lips skimmed the edge of her ear, sweeping down in a caress from the uppermost point to the lobe. Serenna drew in a rough inhale through her teeth, lashes fluttering against her will when the prince's mouth brushed the sensitive skin along her neck beside the knife. A wave of flame rippled down her spine, straight to her toes.

Drawing back, Vesryn's face hovered above hers. He smirked. "You forgot about the wraith."

Snapped out of the moment, Serenna's eyes flew wide, locking with his. "You're joking."

The creature's footfalls echoed through the chamber as it bolted toward them. Vesryn's iron grip prevented her from moving. A heartbeat passed before Serenna flared her magic, encompassing them in a violet dome. She flinched when the wraith's body crashed against the barrier.

Vesryn's fingers relaxed their tangled hold in her hair, moving to brush against the base of her neck with feather-light strokes. Serenna's traitorous magic reacted to the scrape of his calluses in a chaotic frenzy, desperate to intertwine with his power. Shoulders slacking, her common sense wavered alongside the tentative control she had on the ward.

Something bloomed in the space between them. Hauled into the orbit of the prince's gaze, Serenna's mind emptied as she fell into the depths of his emerald eyes. Vesryn's chest collided with hers with every shared breath as they stared at each other, disregarding the wraith smacking against the shield, breaking the silence.

A circular heat looped through Serenna's chest as she sensed through the bond that the prince's wants mirrored her own. So close to his mouth, Serenna's pulse skipped when her thoughts sauntered back to their first frantic kiss days ago. Obviously reading what she was feeling, Vesryn's lips curved in response.

Any logical thought Serenna had left sailed out of her head, replaced with a reckless need to reach the prince's mouth. Vesryn inhaled an erratic breath when she leaned into the blade. A warm trickle of blood rolled down Serenna's neck, but she didn't feel her skin splitting.

Vesryn's nostrils flared, indicating that he did, but he silently refused to relent. "Careful," he warned. "I keep my daggers sharp."

"Now you're concerned for my well-being?" Serenna gritted out as she pushed harder against the knife.

Yanking the dagger out of her hand and away from her throat, Vesryn sheathed the weapon back at his hip. "I'm not kissing you in a dungeon with a wraith," he hissed, releasing her. "How long can you hold this shield?"

Serenna clutched the front of Vesryn's leathers, expecting her knees to buckle when her power faltered. "Not much longer." She swallowed, assessing her magic, sensing the emptiness floating in her chest. "My Well is nearly drained."

Vesryn's eyes glittered in the hovering illumination. "I'll wait."

The surrounding barrier unraveled when the dregs of Serenna's magic fizzled out moments later. The prince flicked a hand to fling the wraith back, anchoring it to a wall with rending.

Collapsing from the loss of power and *not* as an excuse to melt further into Vesryn's arms, Serenna sagged into him as he lowered her to the floor. Exhaustion flooded into the void left behind by her magic, towing her back to the dungeon as the vestiges of their heated moment evaporated.

Serenna studied the snarling monster, voicing her earlier observation as the prince settled beside her. "This isn't the same type of wraith that attacked us. Why is it mindless when the others weren't?"

Vesryn drummed his fingers on his knee. "I don't know." Eyes flicking to the creature across the chamber, a crease dented his brow. "I found this one roaming the wilds a few days ago." He glared at the wraith. "Instead of rending it on sight, I decided to bring it here so you could practice and overcome your fear."

Serenna folded her legs under herself. "That's a little cruel." An unsettling feeling roosted in the back of her mind as she noticed the disturbing familiarity of its pointed ears. "It's mindless, but it's not like it's a rabbit to feed Naru."

Vesryn shrugged, obviously uninterested in the topic or her opinion on his methods. He changed the subject. "From now on, you're going to drain your magic completely and regenerate afterward—every day." He extracted a radiant orb of white light from his chest, offering it to her. Shaking his head, Vesryn stared at the globe hovering above his palm. "I should've had you increasing the depth of your Well weeks ago."

Serenna reminded herself how furious she was with the prince—and herself—before he'd distracted her. She scowled at the replenishing Essence flickering between them.

"I'll regenerate tonight." Serenna tilted her chin, refusing to accept the offered magic. "I can manage that much. I don't need you doing it for me."

Ignoring her objection, Vesryn grabbed her shoulder, eyes narrowing with an intensity that nearly made her shy away. "Don't give me that look, you harpy," he growled.

Before Serenna's annoyance had time to smolder into a flame, Vesryn shoved the Essence into her chest. She gasped as the charge of energy crackled like sparks bursting from a log, spiraling into every pore as her magic regenerated, replenishing her empty Well. The vessels around her heart flared and glowed as her body absorbed the prince's magic.

Catching her breath from the rush of power, Serenna wiped the drying blood on her arms against her leathers. "Why do you call me a harpy?"

Vesryn's smirk gave the impression that he'd been waiting for her to ask. "Harpies," he enunciated dramatically, "were thought to be female druids who shifted to either a dragon or a bird of prey—the details are a little unclear. Aesar and I found an enlightening text depicting harpies in all manners of…erotic positions." The way he ran his thumb along his bottom lip had Serenna's attention latched straight back to his mouth. He shrugged before giving her a roguish grin. "My interest in books might've stayed piqued if every tome contained images with such fascinating and informative detail."

Shifting on the uncomfortable cell floor, Serenna rolled her eyes. "That really explains nothing beyond your depravity." Her heart betrayed her dismissiveness by slamming into her stomach when Vesryn slipped his fingers over her leg.

The prince looked at her through a curtain of hooded lashes. "I was more interested in looking at their bared breasts. But apparently, harpies had a habit of ripping the hearts out of those who didn't satisfy their insatiable appetites." Leaning closer, he braced his other palm on the floor next to her hip.

Serenna's breath came in a rapid rush, parting her lips as the prince's hand glided up her leg, sending a flush of heat straight between her thighs.

Vesryn's eyes traveled a slow journey, drifting up her body from where his fingertips rested in the crease of her waist to meet her gaze. "When I realized Essence linked us with this bond, I knew it would only be a matter of time until you sank your claws into me and yanked the beating heart out of my chest."

A swell of warmth jumped to Serenna's spine when Vesryn's fingers tightened around her leg. Dangerously close to where an ache was starting to throb. His eyes didn't stray from hers. Forcing herself to blink free, Serenna's scattered mind reassembled his words.

Her question came out breathless as Vesryn lowered his mouth—the wraith across the room forgotten as the prince consumed her vision. "Are you saying that you won't satisfy me?"

Hooking a finger under her chin, Vesryn angled her face up to his, so close that scents of crisp wind and leather pushed back the stifling earthen odor of the dungeon. "I suppose I'll risk you tearing out my heart if that's the case." His thumb brushed her bottom lip. "But I think you'll discover I can be quite thorough."

Serenna threw her arms around the prince's neck as their mouths collided. She kissed him desperately, met with the same urgency as their lips fused together between gasps for breath. Weaving her fingers through his silvery hair, Serenna greedily pressed into him.

Vesryn's mouth muffled her moan as he pinned her to the cell floor, settling between her thighs. Serenna inhaled a hiss of pain when his teeth grazed her split lip. Apparently he wanted her to feel it, not absorbing the sting through the bond. The prince deepened the kiss, his tongue soothing over the sharp twinge with a tingle of pleasure before diving further into her mouth.

The bond's magic writhed under Serenna's skin, blurring all sense of who the frenzied need belonged to. She combusted with an explosion of desire when Vesryn rolled his hips rhythmically against hers, driving her into the ground. Tongues intertwining, Serenna arched into him, losing all capacity for thought. Their bodies clashed, frantically moving faster and faster.

The leathers between them were too much. She needed more. Snaking her fingers between them, Serenna grappled with the ties of his trousers.

One of Vesryn's hands shot down and circled both of her wrists. He wrenched her arms above her head. Cheeks stained with a flush, the prince was just as out of breath as she was when he pulled away.

"Not here with a wraith," he said.

As if he wasn't the one pounding their bodies into the floor. "Then toss it through a portal," Serenna protested, hooking her legs around his waist, fighting to pull him closer.

"Your training session isn't over." Untangling himself from her, Vesryn retreated with a chuckle. He pushed Serenna's eager hands away when she tried to haul him back on top of her.

"Of course it isn't." Serenna released a disgusted sigh, sitting back up.

With an irritated huff, she retied the laces to her bodice, unsurprised that the prince had loosened them without her knowledge. *What am I doing?* She paused on a knot. *On a dungeon floor, no less.* She glanced at the wraith, still mindlessly flailing against Vesryn's restrictive magic.

He's promised to Ayla, she sharply reminded herself. That thought extinguished any lingering kindling of lust. *I want to be something more than his plaything.* Serenna's heart twisted at the distance the realm had established between her and the prince, even if no one would bat an eye if they were involved. *I just want to feel like I belong somewhere.*

Serenna pulled her legs to her chest, lacing her fingers around her knees. Working up the courage to put her unease into words, she cleared her throat, unsure how to voice her concerns without succumbing to envy. "About this bond and your engagement..." The scowl on the prince's face made her falter.

"We're here for your training," Vesryn said, his irritation flashing through their connection. Flaring Essence, he tugged a water flask to his hand that she hadn't noticed resting against a wall. "I'm in no mood to discuss my royal responsibilities."

Conveniently, he never seemed to be in the mood for *that*. Serenna opened her mouth to press on with a question about Ayla, but bit her tongue when Vesryn clenched his jaw, shoving the canteen at her.

"You need to be ready if the wraith return." A command. His tone suggested that now wasn't the time for the conversation she wanted—needed—to have.

Serenna didn't feel like she was asking for a lot. *I just want some assurance of what will happen to us once he's married off.*

She drank from the offered flask while her heart battled with shame and dejection, sinking her with doubts. Resentment of her failures sent her in a downward spiral. *I don't deserve to be his champion, let alone anything more. I'm a liability to him, not an asset.* Defeat pricked at the corners of her vision.

Unable to meet Vesryn's eyes, Serenna absorbed herself with twisting the cap back on the canteen as she assembled her thoughts. "I'm sorry my incompetence distracted you during the attack." Despair needled an ache in her chest. She swallowed, making a poor attempt at furiously blinking away a stream of tears. Her voice broke without her permission under the strain of her inadequacies. "I understand if you want to reject the bond—"

"What?" Vesryn interrupted her. He cupped her face, turning her head to meet his gaze, eyes searching hers.

Serenna barely heard her words. "You were so angry when you brought me here." She hastily swiped at a stray tear before it spilled down her face.

"I'm not angry with you." Vesryn's eyes softened as his thumb brushed her cheek. "I'm angry at the wraith. And furious that I wasn't able to protect you. That's why we're doing this." He dropped his hand, his brow forming a severe ridge. "I want to ensure you can defend yourself in case…I can't be there." His voice lowered, and she sensed regret rolling through him. "Again."

Serenna rapidly blinked, processing his words. "Oh."

Relief unwound the tension in her shoulders. *He couldn't have said that when we portaled here?* Serenna studied the snarling wraith, talons clacking as it clenched its claws, still mindlessly fighting the shadowy restraints. Regardless of the prince's motive, he wasn't wrong. *I need to be able to fend for myself. I can't always count on being rescued.*

They sank into a swelling silence. Vesryn unfolded from the ground, offering a hand to help her rise.

"Wraith can fade into shadows unless they're in bright light." Vesryn suddenly dispelled the illumination, plunging the cell into darkness. "We'll level the playing field." His voice echoed from every direction as he left Serenna's side. "If you can detect their life force in the dark, their invisibility won't be a match for you."

Serenna slumped with a weary sigh, hearing the wraith charge across the chambers. "I really hate you," she muttered.

CHAPTER 9

JASSYN

The sun melted below the island's horizon while Jassyn spent the quiet evening sitting at the table on his private balcony—the first night back at his quarters since his time with the prince. The floral scents from the Infirmary's lavender hedges fluttered up to the magus' residence hall on a breeze.

Brushing the stirred curls away from his eyes, Jassyn flipped through the ancient volume Farine had granted him the final time she'd summoned him to her estate. He'd scoured the tome multiple times. For all its tattered pages, the amount of useful information from Fynlas' research was scant. Archivists hadn't documented shaman powers—the control of fire, water, earth, wind, and lightning—since the extinction of both the shamans and the druids a millennium ago.

Farine intentionally provided a single book from Fynlas' study to whet my curiosity and have me crawling back for more. An incident at her estate where she'd forced him to grovel at her jeweled slippers skirted the fringes of Jassyn's mind before he took a shuddering breath, forcibly shoving the thought away.

She knows something I don't and would be delighted if I begged for what she's withholding. Dread lanced and then twisted though Jassyn's gut as he considered returning to the Vallende manor willingly to obtain answers. *There's knowledge in that estate, but I don't have the strength to pay the price she's set.*

Squeezing his eyes shut, Jassyn steered his mind away from the horrors he'd endured at Farine's hands, suppressing a sudden urge to bury the memories in Stardust. Steadying himself, Jassyn opened his eyes and directed his attention toward the screen of wisteria vines sheltering his balcony from the neighboring magus.

Perception coasting like clouds on the wind, he stretched his awareness out to the plants. The veins of the leaves hummed with energy, like they had a heartbeat of their own. Jassyn tugged on the droning power and a cluster of blooming flowers drifted to his extended palm.

I need to learn how to control this new magic. As the vines coiled around his hands, Jassyn clenched the plants as a sobering thought flitted across his mind. Regardless of the prince's exclusive claim to his bloodline, the elves would undoubtedly force him back into servitude if they discovered that the elemental magic had awakened in him. Aside from the Vallendes, some of the higher members of Alari's society must've known that the council had deliberately intermingled human lineages bearing the ancient powers with prominent elven lines.

Jassyn wrestled for control of his breathing before fear compressed his chest. *I've hardly had two weeks of freedom.* The last thing he wanted to do was fall back into the council's clutches.

I'm not alone though, Jassyn reminded himself. Many at Centarya had the ancestral ties—including Serenna. Her name was inked at the bottom of one of the family trees hidden away in Fynlas' study.

He doubted that Elashor had informed Serenna about the shaman roots in her mortal bloodline, considering she thought shamans were simply human folklore. *I have to tell her.* She needed to be aware of the danger if her powers suddenly manifested too.

Thoughts shattering, Jassyn's muscles spasmed like he'd been struck by a wave of lightning. He flinched, his control on the earth fracturing. The vine wilted and drooped, no longer prodded by power. Jassyn tensed, sensing a groping presence cling to his mind. Cringing, he knew the incessant touch could only belong to the prince.

Come to my quarters, Vesryn commanded through the telepathic link, confirming Jassyn's suspicion.

I think we've spent quite enough time together lately, Jassyn clipped. Assembling his mental barricades, he swiped the prince out of his head with all the attention he would've afforded brushing dust off a shelf. Having only retired to his chambers mere hours ago after joining the prince at the Ranger Station, he wasn't about to drag himself back to Vesryn's rooms.

The prince redoubled his efforts, latching onto Jassyn's mind like a leech. Irritation compounding, Jassyn rolled his shoulders, hoping his cousin would grow bored and relent.

Moments passed while Vesryn persistently battered against his barrier. Exhaustion from the previous few days had Jassyn dropping his face into his hands in defeat.

What could you possibly need? Jassyn snapped, abandoning his mental shield. He scowled toward the peak of the Spire when the prince's telepathic presence flooded back into his awareness.

I took Serenna training and she came out with a few scrapes and bruises. I thought you could heal her.

Seriously? Jassyn stretched in his seat, massaging one of his aching calves, loosening a knotted muscle. *Why can't you handle mending something so minor?*

Do you really want me healing her on my own?

You're right. Jassyn's nose wrinkled in disgust, smelling his cousin's manipulation radiating from the top of the tower. *I had to straighten that last mess after you "mended" her finger into a useless hook.* Blowing out a sigh, Jassyn rose and gathered Fynlas' research, returning indoors. His watery legs already dreaded ascending the Spire. *I'm on my way.* Driving his hands through his curls, he shoved the prince out of his mind.

Tucking the tome away in a bookcase, Jassyn wondered how he'd manage to clandestinely exercise his new power. Since Vesryn was intent on ensuring he didn't relapse, Jassyn could only assume that his cousin wouldn't permit him to have any significant time alone.

A wave shimmered in the middle of Jassyn's sitting room, unfolding into a portal. He rolled his eyes to the ceiling, pleading to the stars for strength. *I see Vesryn made himself familiar enough with my living quarters.* At some point in the past few days, the prince had taken it upon himself to root around in Jassyn's belongings and dispose of his Stardust supply.

Lips thinning, Jassyn stomped through the rift. He could concede that the gateway was a convenience, but he didn't have to tolerate Vesryn's unsolicited intrusion into his chambers whenever he pleased.

Half blinded by the glaring angle of the descending sun in the prince's apartment, Jassyn detected his cousin outside on his balcony, his silhouette framed by the flowing waterfall. Vesryn wandered into the sitting room, leaving the sliding glass door open to permit the evening breeze.

Unwilling to cultivate the prince's gesture into a habit, Jassyn withheld his gratitude for the portal that'd spared him the daunting climb. "I don't appreciate you slithering through my mind or helping yourself to my quarters," he announced as the rift disappeared. Jassyn surveyed the apartment. "Where's Serenna?"

As if summoned, the bathing chamber door banged open. Freshly showered, mahogany hair hanging loose and damp down her back, Serenna glided into the opulent sitting room. Nose in the air, she clearly was making it a point to ignore the prince as she weaved around the couches, avoiding him.

Instead of her leathers, she wore loungewear of that cashmere material Vesryn favored. Jassyn frowned between her and his cousin, disregarding the unsettling fact that she had a set of nightwear in the prince's rooms.

After he processed Serenna's outfit, Jassyn's eyes darted across her, assessing her split lip and the trenches gouged down her arms. He blinked. Discolored skin peeked out from under her clothes, concealing further injuries.

"Scrapes and bruises?" Turning to the prince, Jassyn's question came out strangled. *"Scrapes and bruises?"* He flung an arm out toward her. "She's more mangled now than she was after the assault!"

Jassyn whirled back to Serenna, gently tapping into her mind. *What happened? Did Vesryn do this?* He kept half of his attention on his cousin as they silently had a conversation before Vesryn noticed.

The prince, Serenna scathingly replied, glacial eyes flashing toward Vesryn, *insisted on training in the dungeons. He unleashed one of those mindless wraith on me!*

Jassyn gaped like a fish nicked from water. *He what?*

She silently displayed her arms. *But I can't feel anything—he's absorbing the pain through the bond.*

That doesn't excuse him. Jassyn clenched his fists as something furious seared him like a hot iron, stoking his ire. *Can you bind him with rending?*

Serenna startled through the telepathic link. *Why?*

Just help me. This behavior of his ends now.

Jassyn launched in Vesryn's direction, rolling one of his daggers to his fingers as soon as he moved. Shadows raced across the floor, twisting around the prince. For half a heartbeat, Jassyn feared the magic would strike him until he sensed that the pulse of Essence emanated behind him from Serenna. He jammed the golden blade against his cousin's throat before Vesryn's eyes finished widening.

Serenna sucked in a sharp breath. Looking back at her, Jassyn saw her wincing before she glanced at him for guidance. She cradled her arm, continuing to spin her rending across the room. Since he'd negated their bond by tethering the prince, it was obvious she could now feel her wounds. He hadn't considered that.

Vesryn's gaze volleyed between them, eyes glinting with a sadistic delight. "Well, this evening is proving to be more interesting than I expected." Unphased by the blood welling around the dagger's edge, he arched a brow. "I can't say I've ever been magically restrained *and* tethered before. You've outdone yourself with this added touch of knife play—"

Fuming at his cousin, Jassyn shoved his knife further into Vesryn's neck, if only to shut him up and get his attention. And maybe because it was a little satisfying to dominate the prince for once.

"You said you would keep her safe," Jassyn hissed, leaning into Vesryn's face, recalling the prince's words when he'd disclosed the bond with Serenna.

Vesryn tossed what little part of his head he could move, shaking silvery fringes of hair out of his eyes. "Compared to a day in the Combat Yard, she isn't any worse for wear."

Serenna scoffed her disagreement. "The magus don't release wraith on us!"

"Maybe I'll have them start." Vesryn didn't bother muzzling his unapologetic smirk. "How else are you going to master your fear?"

"I'm sure Jassyn would've had a better solution." With a dismissive sniff, Serenna crossed her shredded arms, grimaced, and then unfolded them. "*He* would've shown me how to protect myself instead of throwing a wraith at me until I figured it out."

Why am I not surprised by this? A braid of exhaustion and irritation had Jassyn rubbing his forehead with his free hand. He was amazed that a headache hadn't rallied in his skull while they started to bicker.

Interrupting their argument before they got carried away, Jassyn addressed the prince with a savage stillness. "You do not get to summon me every time Serenna gets hurt and expect me to clean up *your* mess."

"I'm not doing anything wrong," Vesryn fired back, his humor ebbing slightly. "She couldn't even feel her injuries until you intervened."

"That's not an excuse." Glancing back at Serenna, Jassyn's eyes pinned on the cut across her neck that appeared to be caused by a blade, not talons. Her cheeks flushed before she averted her gaze, clearing her throat. Jassyn turned back to the prince, his eroding patience with his cousin transmuting to determination. "I won't allow this to continue."

"You won't...allow..." Voice pitched low, Vesryn's jaw worked as if he was slowly comprehending the word. "You won't *allow* Serenna's training to continue?"

"No, I won't allow you to exploit me for magic while you're a capable arch elf." Jassyn applied more pressure at the end of his knife, marrow boiling with a newfound resolve. "What if I'm not there to heal her every time you snap your fingers?" He snapped in front of Vesryn's face to drive the point. A tendon strained in the prince's neck. "If you're putting Serenna in situations where she's getting hurt, then it's going to be *you* healing her. I can't fathom why you think this is acceptable."

Vesryn's muscles trembled as he fought against Serenna's shadows. "You don't get to—"

"Since you want everyone to train so badly," Jassyn interrupted, silencing the prince. "It's your turn to practice."

Throat tensing, looking to be on the verge of arguing further, Vesryn's nostrils flared as they wrestled each other with their stares. Heartbeats passed in the expanding silence, shrinking the room.

Displeasure simmering in the air, Jassyn gritted teeth, his voice deadly quiet. He punctuated his next word like a hammer hitting a nail. "*Now.*"

"Fine," the prince snapped, his conceding growl cutting the thickening tension. "Since you're obviously taking lessons in defiance from Serenna now." Vesryn's gaze flicked to her. His words came out rough, sounding like someone forcibly pried them out. "Show me how."

Relaxing at the surrender, Jassyn withdrew his dagger and wiped the blade on Vesryn's leathers. Sparked by petty triumph, he impulsively took advantage of the body bind and patted his cousin on the cheek. Serenna snorted a laugh as Vesryn's mouth went slack. Stepping back, Jassyn nodded at her, bidding her to free him from the rending.

"Are you sure?" Serenna's eyes darted to the prince, likely gauging if he'd retaliate.

Jassyn shrugged. He twirled the knife across his fingertips, offering her the hilt. "Unless you want to stab him a few times first to make it even."

Vesryn released a low chuckle wrapped in darkness. "While you're at it, you can slap me around because I must be dreaming. I think I'm falling in love with this new Jassyn."

Not dignifying the prince with a response, Jassyn rolled his eyes. He shoved past Vesryn, clipping his shoulder. Serenna's shadows receded when she extinguished her power.

Jassyn tucked his blade back into a hidden seam, gesturing to one of the leather couches. "Serenna, you might as well get comfortable." He glanced out the windows to the stars blossoming across the darkening sky. "I have a feeling this will take a while."

Serenna complied, stiff-backed, with a hand braced on the armrest. Jassyn didn't fault her unease. Vesryn wielded his magic with brutal blows rather than a refined weaving. It was no surprise that the prince's historical attempts at mending did more harm than good.

Pursing his lips, Jassyn studied the single bruise next to the cut on Serenna's throat. Vesryn's obnoxious mouth had obviously wrought that one. A question nearly scorched his tongue, demanding to know what exactly had happened in the dungeons before he concluded that he didn't really want to know.

Instead, Jassyn shot his cousin a disapproving scowl. As if sensing his attention, Vesryn ripped his eyes away from the points of Serenna's ears. Jassyn had half a mind to cuff the prince upside the head but resisted the urge, unsure how much further his luck would hold if he continued pushing the prince.

"I'll form a telepathic link to show you the healing lattices," Jassyn said. He reluctantly cast out a wave of telepathy toward the prince, skin crawling at the disturbing way their minds seamlessly fused. He blew out a breath, releasing the tension pinching his shoulders. "Unfolding my knowledge into that thick skull of yours will be the fastest way for you to learn."

Vesryn smirked as Essence streamed from his fingertips. Pulling from his Well, Jassyn's own power sprang to life, surrounding him in a shimmering wave. Summoning his mending talent, a ruby ray of magic cascaded down his arms, pooling into his palms.

"Are you ready?" Jassyn asked Serenna. Vesryn joined him at her side. Picking at one of her nails, she divided a glance between them before nodding.

Touch her shoulder, Jassyn instructed. *It's easier for novices if there's physical contact.*

The prince shot him a look at the slight but complied, resting a glowing hand on Serenna, fingers skimming the bare skin of her neckline. Jassyn considered slapping him away when he noted the way Vesryn's mouth quirked as she shuddered.

Jassyn speared a thought at the prince. *If you're quite finished fondling her, can we get on with it?*

Vesryn's protest was scandalized. *You told me to.*

Wasting a withering look on his cousin, Jassyn directed the prince's attention toward Serenna's less serious injuries. He fabricated the most efficient mending lattices in Vesryn's mind to demonstrate how to heal her split lip and shallow scrapes. He hoped the prince would catch on.

Vesryn didn't.

Their progress slowed to a crawl while the moons rose in the sky. *Stars, you're going to give her a scar if you knit her vessels backward like that.* Jassyn hurriedly sent out a thread of mending to correct Vesryn's attempt before the prince caused permanent damage.

Take away the swelling with this simple lattice I keep showing you. It's not that hard. Jassyn cast out the same wisp of power for the third time. *And I don't even want to know about this knife wound.*

She tried to kiss me, Vesryn sent back, a pathetic attempt to defend himself. *Your annoyance is completely unjustified. I couldn't let her take advantage of me in the dungeons in front of a wraith. You really should reprimand* her *instead.*

I'm sure it's still your fault, Jassyn snapped. *Focus. Could you stop rubbing her shoulder like that for a scorching second?*

Vesryn halted the motion of his fingers, muttering several curses under his breath. He wiped the sweat away from his brow with the back of his arm.

Are you this relentless with the recruits? Vesryn snarled when Jassyn corrected him once again.

Aren't you? The initiates show more promise, anyway. You should've learned these skills a century ago.

Finally, after Vesryn bumbled enough with his magic, Jassyn was satisfied with the way they'd stitched Serenna back together. He couldn't sever the telepathic link fast enough as they each released the hold on their power.

"Thank you," Serenna said to him.

Vesryn scoffed. "I'm the one who healed you."

Serenna sniffed and crossed her legs, angling away from the prince.

Jassyn wondered if they'd ensnare him in the crossfire of their squabbling if he lingered. While he considered if he could shuffle to the door without either of them noticing, Vesryn opened a portal, motioning him through. An obvious dismissal, but convenient nonetheless. Jassyn's eagerness to remove himself from Vesryn's apartments nearly had him dashing through the rift. *But I don't want to leave Serenna alone with him if she's still upset.*

Turning toward her, Jassyn assumed she'd appreciate an escape. "I'll walk you back to your quarters if you're ready to go." His gaze flicked to Vesryn, but he wasn't about to ask for permission he didn't require. "There are a few things I think we should discuss."

Serenna leaped from the sofa and was out the door before Jassyn could blink. Apparently she wasn't concerned about walking across campus in sleepwear.

Jassyn quickly organized his thoughts, assembling the best way to disclose their shaman bloodlines. He'd at least inform Serenna of what he'd discovered at the Vallende estate. He wasn't quite ready to confess that the elemental magic had manifested in him. Not yet. While he trusted her, he wasn't ready to risk the capital finding out if the knowledge became more widespread.

The dejection in Vesryn's face as he stared after Serenna disappearing down the corridor almost had Jassyn sympathizing with him. Almost.

Jassyn patted his cousin's shoulder before departing. "We really need to work on your lesson planning."

CHAPTER 10

LYKOR

Propped against the headboard, Lykor's body jerked, his consciousness hauled out of sleep. He inhaled a sharp breath through his teeth, blinking at the tome clamped between his hand and claw. The dream of amber irises hovering above him dissipated like fog. Digging his fists into his eyes, Lykor drove out the face he saw every time he let his mind wander.

Hearing papers rustle, Lykor swiveled toward the sound and blew out a disgusted sigh. Kal's back was to him as he sorted through reports at his desk. The last memory Lykor recalled as rending extinguished his awareness was a fountain of obsidian blood erupting from his captain's neck.

How poetic that Aesar roused in time to deliver Kal from his own stupidity. Now it seemed like an inconvenience—not an oversight on the king's part—that Aesar wasn't coerced.

A muffled whistle emitted from the vents circulating heated air around the chambers. Flickering flames from pronged sconces glinted off the maces, swords, and knives festooning the walls. Kal would've been just as comfortable holed up in the armory, considering his dwelling contained nearly as many weapons.

These appalling rooms were becoming horridly familiar, a constant reminder of both Aesar's relentless presence and his insistence on spending Lykor's unconscious evenings with Kal.

Frustration had Lykor hurtling the book clutched in his claw across the bed, almost rending his captain of his own volition. Shoving a strand of silver hair away from his eyes, Lykor irritably growled, cursing Aesar for not bothering to return their body to their own quarters. He presumed it was near dawn and sensed that Aesar was slumbering—and would be for the next few hours if left undisturbed.

Afflicted with his captain's presence, it appeared that he and Kal would only continue this all too predictable routine, shuffling between indifference and intolerance. Like the shell Lykor was trapped in—forced to share with another—was any fault of his own.

Suspecting that Kal intended to ignore him while he dressed and left, Lykor ripped the covers off. He snatched his stack of clothes that Aesar had folded neatly on the nightstand, shoving his legs into his trousers and fastening his belt.

Before Lykor could open a portal, Kal spoke over his shoulder, not bothering to face him. "Aesar found something in that tome you should look into today."

Lykor muttered a string of dark words about where Kal could fuck himself with said tome.

"Why should I concern myself with Aesar's antiquated books?" Lykor snapped, seized with the temptation to leave before they fully engaged in a conversation. Or rather another vexing, circular argument. Lykor couldn't comprehend why Aesar's pedantic pursuits affected him. But Kal insisted on clinging to the past, pathetically attempting to shove Lykor into Aesar's mold.

Kal tensed before rising to face him. Braids unraveled, black hair grazed his shoulders in waves—a modest elven style he'd maintained throughout the years, despite adapting to the younger wraith custom of infesting his face with rings. Lykor assumed they'd portaled to the secluded hot springs that Aesar favored judging from his own damp hair and the assault of piney soap.

Kal's features remained impassive, all evidence of his mangled throat healed. His tongue dug into the back side of his lip ring—a nervous habit. His burning stare regarded Lykor, eyes swirling a storm of disapproval in the torchlight.

Talons digging into his palm, Lykor clenched his claw at his side, if only to keep his fingers away from strangling that resentment off of his captain's face. Kal had wildly misplaced his annoyance. *I WASN'T THE LACKWIT WHO TRIGGERED THE COERCION.*

Kal's silence and searing gaze only infuriated him further as they faced each other in a standoff. "Tell me," Lykor snarled, instinctively baring fangs he no longer had. "I'm already at the end of my finite tolerance and have no desire to spend another second in this fucking room."

Jaw ticking, Kal relented before Lykor resorted to thrashing the answer out of him with rending. "As you know, Aesar assumes this fortress was one of the druid capitals." A rattle of breath escaped through Kal's clenched teeth. "If his translation is correct, he believes our stronghold may harbor a Heart of Stars. You need to start looking for it instead of disappearing every day."

"Don't tell me what I need to do," Lykor growled.

Uninterested in prolonging the conversation by asking what a Heart of Stars was, Lykor tunneled his awareness inward to Aesar's mind. Using the phrase as a lodestone to search, he rummaged through the relevant knowledge. Retrieving what he needed, Lykor blinked the room into focus, glaring back at Kal's scowling face.

Lykor scoffed, incredulity running his mouth. "And what use would a Heart of Stars be to the wraith?"

Kal's lips twisted before he wandered to his armor stands. "Aesar believes the Hearts may have functions other than unveiling talents."

"They're Aelfyn trinkets." Lykor barked out a disbelieving laugh as Kal shouldered on his leathers. "The elves' ancestors only brought one Heart to these shores *and* it's in the king's possession—you've conveniently overlooked that obvious fact." Burrowing his fingers across his scalp, Lykor tied his hair into a knot.

"Would you discuss it with Aesar when he wakes?" Kal gritted out, adjusting his spiked shoulder pads. "If you'd bother to look further into his thoughts, you'll see that he believes the druids may have hidden a Heart in our fortress—and possibly others in scattered locations."

Lykor scrubbed a hand down his face as his frustration boiled to exasperation. He was so tired. So tired of worrying about the wraith's future. So tired of wondering what the elves had extracted from those Aesar had abandoned on that floating isle. So wearied from waking in Kal's chambers, forced to interact with him like this arrangement was something he'd agreed to. Normally, Lykor could never get his captain to shut up. But of course, now that he wanted information, Kal was stubbornly reticent like he was making some point.

Irritation curled in Lykor's gut, morphing into anger. Restraining himself from ripping Kal in half, Lykor lashed out with a whip of shadows instead. Grunting, Kal's spine went rigid, immobilized in the twisting darkness.

Stalking toward the captain, Lykor used his claw to snatch Kal's chin. "Enlighten me as to why I should give a fuck about these Hearts. If I have to ask one more time, I'll splatter you across the wall." Lykor scored Kal's midnight skin with his talons. "I doubt Aesar could reassemble your putrid innards after that."

Kal's nostrils flared, a muscle feathering in his jaw. "You know of the Great War between the Aelfyn and the druids." Kal didn't wait for his acknowledgement. His eyes flicked toward the tome Lykor had discarded. "That text indicates they fought over possession of the Hearts. Aesar doesn't know how many there were, but he believes the relics may have some importance."

Lykor's grip tightened as Kal glowered with fire in his eyes. Unraveling the shadows, Lykor tore his claw away from his captain's face. Locating his boots near the door, Lykor flung out a strand of force, yanking them to his hand.

Kal was intentionally withholding information to pressure him into working with Aesar, who'd become increasingly irksome, insisting the same. Aesar had been content with letting Lykor handle the impossible decisions this past century but now felt the need to be involved. They probably collaborated to coordinate their efforts, intending to collectively wear him down.

Lykor stomped on his shoes, remaining silent with nothing to say. What he needed to do was start portal jumping across the Wastes to discover a new haven for the wraith, not delve through their fortress on a hunch because a dusty tome had information a thousand years gone. It was past time for Aesar to do something useful for once instead of plaiting Kal's hair.

Lykor drove his thoughts away from his other reckless idea —returning to the floating isle in search of the amber-eyed elf. The thought taunted him. If there was some way to free himself from the coercion, the risk would be worth it.

Feeling the weight of Kal's attention had Lykor snarling. "You handle this, *Captain*. I have better things to do than run around as your fucking page boy."

Kal rolled his shoulders before retrieving a holstered crossbow, slinging the weapon over his back, now incessantly rambling on. "Aesar thinks the Hearts could be tied to dragons —if any remain." His voice lowered along with his eyes, cast to the floor. "Weren't they important to you?"

Lykor stiffened, drawing to a halt before opening a rift to his quarters. His scalp prickled at the memory. He hadn't dwelled on it since the king had chuckled at the name he'd claimed as his own—the name of the first dragon who'd sacrificed himself in the battle against the Aelfyn. Long ago, Aesar had read of the creature, who'd attempted to buy the druids and shamans time to flee.

It hadn't been enough.

"Talk to Aesar when he wakes or look through his memories —in the library, before…" Heartbeats passed before Kal met his gaze, shaking his head with a sigh. "Before all of this began."

Lykor's chest tightened, constricted by a remnant of fear that Aesar had experienced that day. Cracking his neck, he released a breath. In his mindspace, Lykor locked everything away out of sight, shoving Aesar's residual panic behind the dungeon's obsidian doors.

Unable to resist the urge now that Kal had brought it up, Lykor sifted through Aesar's thoughts, living the past through his eyes.

As Kal's rooms vanished around him, Lykor's physical body tensed, seeing Vesryn across from him in Kyansari's library, a century ago. But the coercion's demands didn't extend through time like this, moments passed and gone.

His awareness faded into Aesar's memory—the day that started the beginning of the end.

CHAPTER 11

AESAR

A CENTURY AGO

Eyes sliding toward the hushed debate, Aesar glanced at his mother and Thalaesyn sequestered in a corner of the library. Framed by an expansive wall of windows that stretched the height of the research tower, their table overlooked Kyansari's glass spires.

Attendants bustled around the queen, categorizing what she and Thalaesyn had determined to be helpful as they researched what had caused the infertility of their entire race. The pair had been studying for decades, organizing the archivists and investigating the affliction that evidently ran rampant across their realm.

Shamelessly sparing a glance toward the library's atrium, Aesar briefly locked eyes with Kallyn. Heart abruptly banging against his ribs, he ripped his gaze away, clearing his throat.

The youngest in their guard, Kal—as he preferred—was hardly a quarter century older than Aesar and his twin. Despite his youth, Kal had advanced through the warrior's ranks.

Considering the shadow Kal's older half-brother, Elashor,

cast in the court, their captain's ambition came at no surprise. But Elashor's influence with the king hadn't secured Kal his position. Kal had set himself apart, training to be a weapons master on his own.

Aesar found the presence of their guards in the library more than a little excessive with the capital's peace. Even the uncivilized humans didn't risk crossing Alari's closed borders.

Regardless, their presence was entirely Vesryn's fault. The queen had assembled a contingent of their personal wardens years prior, thanks to his twin.

Vesryn had plucked every scorching pigeon from Kyansari's skies with nets of force, shooing the entire corralled population of birds through a portal. Needless to say, the palace's Winter Lunar Solstice that year was one the nobles weren't likely to forget. The servants were still cleaning up feathers nearly a decade later.

Vesryn's exaggerated sigh across from him had Aesar glancing at his twin, who was picking at his nails with a jeweled belt knife. Fully aware that Vesryn deliberately tried to elicit a response, Aesar ignored him.

His brother had yet another new pair of polished boots sprawled on the table, his life's ambition seeming to be never wearing the same clothing twice. As if noticing his masked irritation, Vesryn's eyes flicked to him.

Aesar's attention inadvertently sauntered over his brother's shoulder to their captain again. Arching a brow, Vesryn twisted around, glancing at Kal.

If you need a private corner to slip off to, Vesryn said through the bond, turning to face him with rowdy delight tugging at his mouth, *the tenth level has an excellent alcove tucked away in that labyrinth of bookcases. You wouldn't believe how effective those heavy curtains are at muffling sounds.* He ran the blade's edge under a nail, amusement rippling off of him. *There's a shelf at the perfect height for bending someone over. I discovered—*

Aesar scowled and battled his mortification, his harsh retort cutting his brother off as he fired back his own response. *That's hardly appropriate for his position.*

Are you implying you're the one who'd rather be bent over? Vesryn chuckled when Aesar rolled his eyes. *If you're too shy, I'll ask him on your behalf. I can't handle these flirtatious looks for much longer. The tension between you two is so thick, it's making my—*

Throwing out a hand, Aesar punched out a pulse of force. He knocked Vesryn backward, sending him toppling over his chair.

Vesryn growled, picking himself up from the floor. "Are you finished nosing through your books yet?" He sheathed his blade irritably with a rasp of leather against steel. "I thought we were flying today."

Aesar pointed at the tome open before him, tapping the picture.

Vesryn's annoyance vanished, eyes lighting up before he rushed to his side. "Did you find more pictures of harpies?"

Aesar swatted Vesryn's wandering hands away from volume. He switched to communicating through the bond, not wanting to attract attention from his twin's lack of modesty. *I'm not showing you drawings like that again since you can't stop jerking off to those books.*

I'm offended that you think I require books to help with that. Vesryn's attention darted back to Kal. *It's your fault, anyway. Your insistence to maintain this stubborn celibacy simply because he's our guard is driving me—*

Aesar rubbed his forehead, speaking out loud to interrupt his twin. "This is more interesting than your concerning fixation on harpies."

Aesar glanced at his mother and Thalaesyn, who were still preoccupied with their quiet conversation. He lowered his voice anyway, directing his brother's attention back to the volume. "This tome has me questioning the myth of dragons—I've never seen anything like it before."

His twin retained his excitement despite the absence of those fabled female shapeshifters. Leaning forward, Vesryn trailed his fingers over the faded picture of a black dragon that appeared to be chained to the ground.

Vesryn tilted his head. "What's wrong with it?"

Aesar pointed to depicted waves of glimmering light. "I'm not sure, but it looks shackled by some type of magic." He assumed it was Essence connecting the dragon to the Aelfyn female holding a glowing prism above her head.

As his twin peered closer, Aesar sensed Vesryn's puzzlement through the bond. "Does the crystal she's holding look like the Heart of Stars to you?"

A thrum of energy had Aesar's attention whipping to the library's entrance. In radiant white robes outlined by silver threads, King Galaeryn swept into the atrium, conversing with General Elashor. Aesar could only assume they were discussing the pressures from the council, as they always did. Divided by the prospect of diluting elven blood, discussions of intermingling with the humans to preserve their race had been the only topic in the palace for decades.

Aesar nudged his twin. "Let's ask our sire about this—he knows everything."

Pushing back from the table, Aesar nearly dropped the tome in his enthusiasm to discover what the king knew about dragons. Following closely, Vesryn's boots clipped his heels.

Essence-infused gems studded in the king's ears splashed rings of light as he turned from his exchange with Elashor. Their sire's brows rose as they approached him, a beam of sun glancing off of his silver hair. "I had hoped you two wouldn't follow in your mother's footsteps. Surely there's a better use for your time than lurking among the shelves."

Before Aesar could voice a defensive response about how the elves' survival could very well depend on the queen's research, Vesryn interjected. "As soon as you can answer Aesar's question about dragons, we're flying." Vesryn shot him a glower. "Naru and Trella have been restless since they fledged."

The king's jade eyes hooked on the open volume in Aesar's hands before darting to Elashor.

After that, Aesar's memories were a blur. He didn't even register the lash of magic ripping the tome from his fingertips before darkness erupted from his sire.

Shadows engulfed the library, blocking out the sun spilling in through the windows as rending cleaved the air. Launched back with a blast of force, Aesar landed halfway across the atrium, punched to the ground. Air whooshed out of Vesryn, crashing to the marbled floor beside him.

A wave of pressure pinned them to the ground. Aesar's panicked thoughts collided with his twin's as the library attendants screamed, the room crumbling around them.

The darkness receded nearly as fast as it had appeared. Light reentered the chambers as scattered papers fluttered like falling leaves. Vesryn had thrown himself nearly on top of him, acting like an anchor in a storm. They both were bound to the floor, prisoners to the king's shadows.

Blade unsheathed—something Aesar had never witnessed before outside of sparring—Kal had somehow reacted to position himself in front of them. As if he could challenge both Elashor and the king. If Kal had fabricated a shield, the king's rending had sliced through the ward, claiming him as a hostage too.

Aesar's mind darted to Vesryn's. His brother's fear clashed against his through the bond. *Kal drew his sword on the king.* A frantic terror bludgeoned his chest. Aesar's hearing droned to a muted buzz as he tried and failed to summon his power. Essence sputtered like a guttering flame as he struggled uselessly in the rending bind, unable to stand.

Galaeryn's wild eyes rampaged around the atrium. He sneered, dividing a look between the queen and Thalaesyn, now on their feet, surrounded by their own shields. Their mother's eyes blazed with wrath as her gaze landed on them incapacitated on the ground.

The king had spared nothing, tearing apart the entire library. Shelves lay broken on the floor, along with countless books ripped off the walls. Aesar's eyes popped, his stomach pooling with dread. His sire had even shattered the windows, scattering glass everywhere.

Why did he do this? he asked Vesryn as silence encased the room.

The snowstorm of papers didn't have time to settle before the king spun on his heel, stalking out of the library with Elashor trailing behind, clinging like a shadow.

CHAPTER 12

LYKOR

Freed from the memory, Lykor shuddered a rough exhale. The storm of his heartbeat vibrated with a charge, his entire being poised to protect Aesar from the king. Stifling the wild urge provoked by the vision, Lykor detached his mind from the buried past.

Focusing on the chambers in front of him, Lykor watched Kal tense, eyeing the rending billowing through the room. Dispelling Aesar's lingering fear, Lykor cracked his neck and surrendered the hold on his magic. Feeling flooded back into his limbs in a prickling rush as he comprehended the significance of possessing a Heart of Stars.

They were the key to freeing the dragons the Aelfyn had chained in the war. Galaeryn had one Heart in his possession, and it was possible he'd already located more.

There was a reason the king had targeted Aesar during that first staged "wraith attack." Aesar had learned too much of what Galaeryn and Elashor attempted to conceal—though Lykor had yet to discover what the dragons could offer.

WHAT WOULD IT MEAN FOR THE WRAITH IF WE COULD FREE THOSE BEASTS FIRST? Lykor nearly shook

Aesar out of sleep to question him, but realized the answers didn't matter.

If the king's reaction to Aesar's curiosity of the dragons was any sign, then the creatures and the relics were important. With loathing engraved in his bones, Lykor would retaliate and snatch away anything that Galaeryn desired—just as the king had ruthlessly stolen everything from the wraith.

If his people could somehow ally themselves with the dragons—if any were still alive—they might have a chance at survival. First, they'd have to collect the Hearts if the king didn't already possess them all and uncover wherever the Aelfyn had chained those beasts.

Lykor had no doubts that any remaining dragons were somewhere on the other side of the world. Surely they would've been discovered long ago if they dwelled in the mortal realms.

Lykor veered his attention back to Kal. He'd never voice it, but he grudgingly acknowledged the benefits of Aesar's intervention—at least Kal was still present to manage the trivialities.

"Set Mara on organizing the search for the Heart that Aesar thinks we might be sitting on," Lykor ordered, rolling his shoulders to banish Aesar's lingering wave of dread. "Have her double the crews excavating the collapsed chambers around the Slag."

Trapped in a whirlpool of responsibilities, Lykor considered what to do if the restless generation discovered his plans. He didn't have time to sacrifice by addressing the various factions sowing seeds of dissent.

"I don't want those 'reavers' on the Heart's trail," he told Kal, clenching his claw like he could prevent the wraith's former unity from slipping through his fingers. "Busy them with patrols and keep knowledge of the Hearts between us. If the warriors are losing respect for me, perhaps they'll be more inclined to listen to you."

Kal grunted, turning to leave without a parting word.

"Wait," Lykor said, seized by an impulse.

Stalking to his captain, Lykor flared Essence and began ripping talents out of his own chest, severing abilities from his Well. Unlike the king siphoning magic against his will, offering power freely had no agonizing effects. Pooling his magic, Lykor started to assemble a globe containing illumination, telepathy, and illusion—those talents he could live without. He couldn't conceive why having all eight talents mattered—he'd never been an arch elf like Aesar.

So drained from shouldering the burden of caring for his people alone, Lykor hardly cared if his physical form balanced between elf and wraith as he shifted from his arch elf appearance. Galaeryn had broken and remade him too many times to count. Even after becoming whole again, his wraith claw had still persisted. Lykor accepted the irreparable damage to his body.

Kal's jaw went slack, eyes widening in alarm. He scrambled backward toward the door when a radiant orb of light hovered above Lykor's palm.

Kal held his claws up as if to fend Lykor off. "I already told Aesar I didn't want—"

Ignoring his protest, Lykor shoved the abilities into his captain's chest. Kal collapsed to his hands and knees as the invasion of light fractured through his veins like fissures cracking through ice.

"Stars scorch you," Kal swore, lurching back to his feet. He swayed, his hair shifting to a bronze hue. "You never should've stolen Essence from that elf. I've come to terms with the loss." Igniting his magic, Kal clutched his chest, wresting the power from his Well.

Snatching his wrist, Lykor yanked away Kal's arm, halting his efforts at withdrawing the talents.

"You will keep those abilities and make yourself useful," Lykor growled, his claw tightening around Kal's now-elven hand, all traces of the wraith talons eradicated. "Surely you see the advantages of both of us having Essence."

Kal's crimson eyes blazed into his from a face reminiscent of the elf that Aesar remembered—his body like Lykor's now, in the middle of the transformation between elf and wraith.

Skin crawling where they touched, Lykor flung Kal's arm away. "Do I need to spell out the benefits for you?" Frustration gnawed on his nerves. Everything he did for the wraith was met by Kal's combativeness and scorn. "You can communicate with the warriors telepathically and illusions can conceal us in daylight if the humans continue pushing closer to our patrols. And then there's whatever fucking use you can find for illumination."

"Fine." Kal's glare burned a hole through him as he yanked on his boots and crouched to lace the leather ties.

"I'll leave a portal open near the surface lifts for today's rotation," Lykor said, catching his reflection in a dressing mirror. Familiar scarlet eyes framed by midnight hair scowled back at him before he turned his attention to his captain. "I'm taking the wraithlings out to forage their goats. It might be the final time we can do it safely with those humans encroaching. I want Fenn's squadron with us patrolling our mountain pastures. Have him organize the scouts to hunt on the outskirts. There should still be migrating elk."

Ignoring him, Kal strapped knives next to the crossbow on his back. Sheathing his longsword at his hip, he pivoted, leaving Lykor alone in the silent room.

CHAPTER 13

SERENNA

Serenna entered her dim sleeping chamber after spending the fourth afternoon in a row with the prince, forced to fend off the mindless wraith in the dungeons. She wandered through the room to open a curtain. *I need to manifest illumination since Velinya isn't here to brighten our apartment with magic.*

Her friend's extended absence reminded her that Jassyn had planned to escort her to Kyansari's healing district. Now that a week had passed since the attack, he wasn't the only mender who found it unusual that the injured hadn't returned from the capital. Worried whispers had begun to circulate around campus, settling into a layer of unease.

As Serenna reached for a drape, her door slammed shut. Before she could spin around, a hand wrapped over her mouth. Panic consumed her in a wildfire. Serenna's mind exploded in terror, every nerve blazing to fight for her life.

Flailing, she sent her fists and feet striking out at the sudden restriction. Palm suffocating her scream, Serenna went wild, shrieking and kicking to free herself. Stronger than steel, her assailant's arm clamped over her middle, yanking her back into their chest.

"Stars, relax. It's me," Vesryn said, close enough that the air from his words skittered over the edge of her ear.

Serenna stilled, panting through her nose. Vesryn's iron-clad muscles slackened in response but he kept her spine locked against him. Serenna considered blasting the prince away with her power or biting his hand if he continued to smother her face.

Why don't I sense him? There was only that faint silver cord—what she assumed to be the unformed part of the bond—that drifted alongside the bright light she'd come to recognize as Vesryn's presence. But it was gone, like he wasn't even there—like when Jassyn had tethered him earlier in the week.

Vesryn released her. Serenna whirled to face him, racing heartbeat slowing to a dull thunder in her ears. Speechless from fright, her mind teetered between confusion and alarm.

Grinning, the prince wiggled his fingers in front of her face. A ring flashed in a shard of sunlight slipping in through the curtains. "I masked my presence using Jassyn's trick with gold." Vesryn's triumphant smirk only proved he lacked any remorse for nearly arresting her heart.

"Maybe I should whip a blade from my leathers and use one of 'Jassyn's tricks' on you too," Serenna seethed. "No wonder he stabs you." She'd watch the pair spar more than once in the evenings. And *not* because Vesryn went shirtless in the late spring's warmth.

"That was only once." Vesryn's glee slipped. "And it wasn't my fault. A lucky breeze unbalanced me. That was completely unnatural."

"You deserved it." Serenna noted the sore spot and tucked away the information, intending to jab him with it again later. She irritably tossed her disheveled braid over her shoulder. "Just because you know my chambers well enough to portal doesn't mean you have permission to sneak around."

While she couldn't deny the convenience of avoiding the Spire's ascent whenever the prince felt the need to summon her for training, Serenna should've known that no good would've come from asking the prince to attune himself to her sitting room. And now she was paying for her lapse in judgment.

Vesryn tugged the ring off. With a catapult of his thumb, he flung it into the air, catching it as it fell. His presence zipped in and out of Serenna's awareness during the brief moments the gold wasn't touching his skin.

"Your first instinct wasn't even to respond with your power," he said, like his theatrics were justification for scaring her. He sent the ring twirling up again. "You obviously need more practice."

"What do you want me to do?" Serenna slapped the ring out of the air. "Splatter anyone who startles me?" The jewelry sailed across the room, clattering to the floor with a satisfying *clink* before rolling to hide under one of her dressers. "I don't think a wraith is going to be lurking in my chambers. Unlike *you*."

"Maybe not," Vesryn agreed, tracking the path of the ring before glancing back at her. "Regardless, using the advantage of your power should be your first reaction."

Serenna rolled her eyes, stalking to her bed. "Is there a reason you're here beyond conditioning me with terror?" She dropped to the mattress to unlace her boots. "Haven't you had your fill of that this week?"

The grin Vesryn gave her was all shades of amusement. Raising a hand to ignite orbs of whirling illumination, he cast her chambers in a dim glow. "I have a different activity in mind for tomorrow instead of training in the dungeons." The prince lifted the side of her dresser to retrieve the ring. He bounced the jewelry in his palm while she ground her teeth. "I figured you've made enough progress and earned a break from fending off the wraith."

"How generous," Serenna said, unweaving the braid in her hair. "Considering you so admirably proved that I need more experience."

Attempting to predict what the prince had planned, Serenna imagined the worst scenarios. Through flashes of the bond between Vesryn tossing and snatching the ring, she sensed him buzzing with anticipation, impatient for her to ask.

Cheeks puffing with a blown out breath, Serenna's question was resigned. "What did you have in mind?"

Vesryn cocked his head. "Do you want to visit Naru and fly with me?"

"Fly?" Serenna's hands froze in the middle of unraveling her hair. She blinked, taking a moment to determine if he was joking. "As in, *ride* Naru…in the air?"

"That would be the definition of 'flying.'" Pursing his lips, Vesryn's humor faded. "I received word that one of the human settlements spotted a group of three wraith skulking in the western realm." He glanced at the sliver of light spilling in through the curtains. "It'll be dark soon, so we'll hunt at dawn." Finally bored with the ring, Vesryn tucked the band into a pocket. He shrugged. "But if you don't want to go, I understand."

Serenna dropped her freed hair and scowled. "Of course I want to go." Excitement spun through her at the prospect of soaring the skies, slightly dampened by the thought of tracking down the wraith.

"In the meantime, there's something we haven't finished," Vesryn said. His attention flicked over her shoulder to the bed before he took a predatory step forward.

Heart bolting, ready to combust from that heated look in his eyes, Serenna scrambled to stand. Likely reading the effect he had on her, the prince grinned. Serenna's pulse pounded into a gallop as the bond flared like a beacon, flashing his desire.

What little common sense Serenna possessed had her side-stepping toward the closed door leading to the sitting room. Even though all she wanted to do was grab Vesryn and finish what they'd mindlessly started on the dungeon floor earlier in the week, Serenna was hesitant to encourage him further. It didn't matter what she wanted, she had to be realistic about what could be between them. *I'm not interested in being cast in Ayla's shadow as the prince's courtesan.*

Vesryn hadn't mentioned the invitation he'd offered to the Summer Lunar Solstice again, where—ironically—the king would announce the prince's engagement to Ayla. Serenna couldn't say why she'd expected to go, considering Vesryn was half dead and delirious when he'd brought it up. Holding onto the last scrap of hope that she had a place in Kyansari was foolish.

Jassyn had informed Serenna of her shaman ancestry and she had yet to wrap her head around her ties to those ancient elementalists. With him divulging the secret, it seemed her usefulness to the realm only existed in her blood—and furthering the population like her sire had been so adamant about. She didn't know if she wanted to belong in that world anymore. Not that she really had a choice.

Serenna retreated to the threshold of the room, facing the prince across the bed chamber. "I—I'm not sure this is proper," she stammered before she lost her nerve in denying his advances.

Vesryn arched his brow, glancing at her bed. "And when have I ever given you the impression that my intention is to be proper?"

The calculation in his tone sent Serenna's pulse lurching as she directed her thoughts away from being tangled in her sheets with him. Steadying herself, she gripped the door handle. She didn't want an argument, but she had to be honest with herself

—and him. *Though trying to reason with Vesryn is as pointless as sparring with the wind.*

"You're engaged." An acidic question rolled off of Serenna's tongue before she could bite back the remark. "How many times do I have to ask what that means for us and this bond?"

The prince's eyes flashed with a look that could only be called dangerous, making her reckless heart skip in her chest. Courage splintering, Serenna opened the door, fleeing to the sitting room. Where it was brighter and more appropriate for a conversation that would likely turn heated if she didn't leash her erratic emotions.

Vesryn's boots struck the hardwood floor, sounding furious. Serenna spun around in time for him to seize her shoulders. He dragged her back into her bed chamber, shoving her against the wall. She squeaked as the swift motion pinned her beside the door. Snatching her chin, Vesryn angled her face to meet his eyes.

"You know that engagement means nothing to me." The rumble from the prince's cadence reverberated through her chest, low and sensual, flushing her with a wave of heat. His other hand trailed up her arm, palms rough, but fingers gentle. Serenna's magic shivered in response as static built where their bodies touched.

Her protest was feeble. "That doesn't mean you have the option of ignoring your duty."

"I'm handling it," Vesryn growled, his hands tensing against her.

Struggling between the weight of the prince's combative glare and her established unworthiness of him, Serenna whispered, "I want to belong somewhere, but I don't have a place in the realm." Blinking back a sting of disappointment, she glanced away after the confession.

"Fuck the realm," Vesryn snarled, his fury scorching her through the bond.

Serenna tensed in his grip when he slammed the door shut. Her heart rattled along with the wood shaking on its hinges.

The prince's jaw tightened before he gently cupped the sides of her face. Lowering his mouth to hers, he growled, "I'll show you exactly how much more you matter to me."

CHAPTER 14

SERENNA

Serenna's heart stopped as the prince's mouth hovered a whisper away from hers. The pressure of his fingertips on her face and the simmer in his eyes fractured her concerns about his duty. Serenna's chest bumped against his while the offer floated between them. She swallowed, struggling to see beyond the haze of desire obscuring her thoughts.

"But what does this mean for us?" Serenna asked, searching the prince's face.

I know I'm powerless against what the realm requires of him, but I want to have a place somewhere in all of this. "What about this bond?" Seeking reassurance, she clutched his forearms. "We haven't discussed completing it. Can we talk—"

Vesryn's mouth crashed into hers. The prince's tongue swept past Serenna's parted lips, swallowing her startled gasp, silencing her worries. Shattered air rushed out of her lungs from the intensity of the kiss. Her hands tightened around him, all resistance vaporizing completely.

Cradling her face, Vesryn angled Serenna's mouth into his, shoving her further into the wall. She explored his corded muscles, palms skimming over his tanned skin, winding up his shoulders to thread through his hair.

Vesryn's hands slid torturously slowly from her neck to her hips. His fingers cinched against her leathers, digging into her curves in a possessive way that sent Serenna's heart thundering.

The prince must've sensed her desire rising because his mouth abruptly turned feverish, a wild clash of tongues and teeth as he battled to kiss her senseless.

A moan slipped past Serenna's lips when he ground the evidence of his hardened body against her stomach with a savage thrust. Vesryn growled into her mouth in return as she eagerly rolled her hips against his, knotting her fingers against his scalp, dragging him closer.

"Vesryn," Serenna pleaded in a voice pitched embarrassingly high, hoping she didn't need to say anything else. Their bodies writhed together against the wall as a throbbing ache for more built urgently between her thighs.

The prince pulled away and Serenna caught her ragged breath with him. Head spinning, she untangled her fingers from his hair, counting her heartbeats as she anxiously waited for him to make the next move.

The prince studied her through hooded lashes, lust pitching his voice low. "I don't want my *duty* to the realm—that absurd engagement—to taint this magic between us." Vesryn cupped her face, thumbs sweeping over cheeks. His gaze shifted to rake a trail over her body, heating Serenna's skin like he dragged her over coals. "I don't deserve another bond, but if the stars gave me a second chance, I'm not denying this power."

Serenna's heart clenched against a sliver of confusion, questioning if he only wanted her for the bond. The desire she sensed from him ignited something in her chest, even if she couldn't decipher if his feelings extended further.

But in this moment, perhaps there was an irrational part of her that didn't care. She had him to herself and the realm couldn't snatch that away. *We all might be dead if the wraith return, so what does the future really matter?*

Serenna squeaked when Vesryn suddenly hoisted her in the air, fingers squeezing the backs of her thighs. She wrapped her legs around his waist as he walked them toward the bed. The prince tossed her in the middle of the mattress and she bounced with a squawk. Kicking off his boots, Vesryn smirked before joining her on the covers, prowling over her.

Hooking her arms around the prince's neck and her ankles over his legs, Serenna yanked his body on top of hers. Demanding everything he'd denied her in the dungeons, she arched up to him, crushing her body into his.

"So greedy," Vesryn chuckled. His mouth pursued hers as he settled in the cradle of her thighs.

A sweeping wave of his hips thrust Serenna deeper into the bed. The rigid length straining against his trousers drove into her, the fires of the prince's hunger incinerating her mind. Riding every roll of his hips with mirrored urgency, Serenna writhed against him, desperate to feel every honed inch of muscle.

Her pulse scattered when Vesryn slid a hand between them, squeezing her waist with a tantalizing grip. Warm and firm, his fingers spanned across her leathers, gliding down her body with a purpose.

Serenna's breath came in rapid bursts, requiring more air than his mouth allowed. Clinging to his arms, she whimpered as he circled dangerously close to her core.

Finally reaching where she wanted him, the prince cupped her center, swirling his fingers. The pressure from his palm built an exquisite riot of sensations, flooding her with heat from the inside out. As he rubbed the outside of her leathers, a delicious ache began to pulse. Serenna rocked her hips against him, chasing the offered friction.

Needing more of him, Serenna quested lower, seeking the

hard ridge concealed by his trousers. When she reached him, Vesryn's body jerked as he cursed. Serenna shuddered at the primal way he grunted approvingly against her mouth. Running her hand down his solid length, her core clenched when he bucked into her palm, urging her on.

Curling her fingers around what his leathers permitted, Serenna squeezed with a slight pressure as she stroked. The prince growling into her throat sent her into a lust-fueled frenzy. She mindlessly grabbed at the clasps and laces of his trousers, her teeth scraping into his as she furiously sparred his tongue with her own.

"Easy," Vesryn rumbled against her.

Serenna huffed a laugh against his lips at his ridiculous warning but didn't slow her efforts in untangling the ties. A pulse of magic drew her short.

She couldn't move.

Serenna's eyes flew to the prince's face as he pulled away.

Tendrils of shadows streamed from Vesryn, spiraling around them to halt her progress. For a terrible moment Serenna wondered if he wanted her to stop. Her flash of fear quickly rearranged, sensing the pacing beast of his caged desire.

Propping himself on his elbows, Vesryn hovered above her. The heat in his gaze and the hunger echoing through the bond kindled the flames he'd already stoked low in her belly.

"Let me go," Serenna demanded, squirming against the torrent of darkness, only able to shift her head. "I want..." She swallowed, catching her breath. "I want more."

"I can tell," Vesryn said, breaking into an aggravating grin. "Just tell me to stop and I'll release you." Serenna stilled, ceasing her efforts with struggling as he sat up, shifting to straddle her thighs. "But if you want to play..." His gaze suggestively drifted down her body and then back up to her eyes.

"I don't want to *play*," Serenna hissed with as much dignity as she could muster, helpless and bewildered under his magic. The prince slowly unweaved the ties to her bodice. She refused to whine. But if he wanted her to beg, she was halfway there. "I want you to keep kissing me."

Serenna gasped, squeezing her eyes shut when Vesryn did just that, pushing her clothes out of the way to drag his mouth along her stomach. His teasing tongue swirled around her navel as he finished freeing her from her tunic. The prince hauled her shadow-shackled body up to tear the remaining chemise layer over her head.

Sitting back up, Vesryn flexed his fingers. "And what I want," he said as darkness danced across his knuckles, "is for you to break out of this body lock." Wisps of shadows coiled around Serenna's wrists, steering her arms up to the headboard, completely exposing her bare chest to him.

Serenna glared at the restraining magic looping around her, caressing her breasts, furious with herself for giving Vesryn the satisfaction of trembling in the bindings. Her blood surged under the rending's unexpected tingle—a pleasure with an alarming, silent threat of pain. But she knew the prince wouldn't harm her, even if she refused to participate.

Like a vile bird, Vesryn tilted his head. As if perching across her lap was exactly where he wanted to be. Leaning forward, strands of silvery hair spilled over his shoulders. "It's time you learn how to channel your power regardless of the...*distractions*."

Serenna's voice came out more shrill than she would've liked. "I can hardly summon Essence without my emotions and now you're expecting me to harness my magic with *distractions?*"

"You mastered breaking out of a body lock weeks ago in class." The prince skimmed a callused palm up her stomach, tormenting fingers lazily winding up to her chest.

Serenna shivered in anticipation, her skin pebbling under his touch. She flailed in the shadowy bindings as he circled a finger closer and closer around the peak of her breast.

"Vesryn." Serenna battled for breath in frantic bursts, every fiber of her awareness honed in on the prince's fingers skating over her naked flesh. "I can't even *think* about my power with you on top of me!"

Chuckling, Vesryn rolled her nipple in between his fingers before dropping his mouth to her chest. Serenna released a ruptured moan when his tongue flicked out, lips clamping around the bud, shooting a flood of heat straight to her core.

After dispensing the same attention to her other breast, Vesryn's voice was husky and low. "We haven't even begun, Princess."

Serenna blinked as the prince tucked his fingers into the waist of her leathers, balling the material into a fist. Grazing her hips, the bond's current zipped under his touch.

Aroused alarm had Serenna's voice half strangled. "What are you doing?"

"Summon your power," Vesryn instructed, his other hand gripping her thigh.

Power? Serenna's thoughts dispersed the closer the prince's fingers roved in between her legs. She trembled when he unraveled the ties cinching her leathers together.

"I guarantee if you don't call your magic now, it won't get any easier." Angling out of the way, Vesryn ripped her trousers off with an impressive fluid motion, discarding her pants on the floor. His lips quirked. "I'll make sure of it."

Serenna whimpered from her crippled position, panicked excitement stealing her words as the prince kneed her legs apart.

"Summon your power," he repeated, face drifting down between her thighs.

Serenna sucked in a breath, pulse jumping when he lowered to kiss the inside of her bared leg. She ineffectively tugged against the shadows, trying to arch her body toward the sensation of his mouth skimming across her skin.

All she could manage was releasing a frustrated breath, unable to even perceive her Well. "I can't."

"Then try harder," the prince said, his teeth scraping against her, traveling closer to her thin undergarments.

The rending spiraling around Serenna's wrists pulsed like a heartbeat. A sudden surge of pleasure undulated from the tips of her ears to the ends of her toes.

Squeezing her eyes shut only sharpened her focus on Vesryn's lips skimming up her thigh. A tide of warmth pooled in anticipation of him reaching his destination. After several half-hearted attempts of tunneling inward to sense her magic, Serenna admitted defeat. "I can't do it."

The prince's fingers lazily rotated a feather-light graze against the remaining garment. "Why not?" Pulling on the fabric, he rubbed the material against the seam of her entrance.

Serenna stifled whatever pathetic noise tried to flee from her throat by grinding her teeth, unable to conceal the evidence of how he'd effectively coiled her into a jumbled knot. "You know *why*," she snapped. The pressure from the prince's teasing hand had her flesh throbbing with need, drenching the material between them. "Your face between my legs is hindering any progress I can make."

Vesryn preened at the praise. "I'll take that as a compliment." Gripping the sides of her hips, he yanked her undergarments down with his teeth. Slices of rending slashed the fabric into ribbons. The prince lobbed the tattered remains dismissively behind him.

Serenna's mind went blank when Vesryn tossed her legs over his shoulders before lowering his face. His emerald eyes shackled her to the bed as effectively as the shadows enveloping her. The prince had the audacity to smirk before diving between her thighs.

Serenna sucked in a hiss through her teeth as the warmth from Vesryn's mouth merged with the dampness between her legs, blasting her with a bolt of pleasure. When his tongue stroked wickedly down her center, she threw her head back, blinded by stars.

All semblance of sense abandoned her as the prince's tongue plunged into her core, curving inside of her. Retreating, he sucked that sensitive area, coaxing her body toward a euphoric peak. His ferocity had Serenna dissolving into eager moans, body throbbing in time with the stroke of his tongue.

Serenna's eyes flew open when Vesryn suddenly paused, the pounding pressure he'd built fading in the worst way. Completely bared to him, her cheeks flushed as his gaze locked on hers. It wasn't her first time with a lover, but it was her first time with someone...like him.

Despite knowing what she felt through the bond, the prince studied her. As if waiting for any sign that she wanted him to continue or stop. The consuming way he looked at her only made Serenna redden further. If she could've moved, she would've been covering herself up.

"You don't have to be shy," Vesryn said, brushing the inside of her leg, his rough fingers kindling flames in their path. His cruel shadows furled, stroking the peaks of her breasts, shooting tingles of pleasure straight to her spine. "I've been wanting to do this since the first day you talked back to me."

Serenna couldn't help but laugh, her embarrassment evaporating. "You're lying."

"You know I'm not. I've always been curious how intimacy would feel with a bond." One side of Vesryn's mouth lifted. "Though I doubt my advances would've been welcome at that time."

"And whose fault was—" Serenna gasped, clicking her teeth shut as the prince's lips returned, clamping down on that bundle of nerves. He flicked and swirled his tongue around her entrance, rebuilding the tightness in her core.

Serenna sensed that his focus was entirely on her reactions.

A coil of bliss knotted as he drew out her pleasure, release slowly gathering like an afternoon storm.

"Vesryn," Serenna panted as he wound her tighter and higher, needing rougher friction than his current touch. The shadows restricting her from grabbing the prince or shoving herself further into him was an unforeseen torture. "Please."

Vesryn emerged from between her legs. Loose strands of hair tumbled in front of his face, brushing his ruddy cheeks. His voice was hoarse with amusement when he answered. "I'm not letting you finish until you break out of this hold."

Serenna's jaw dropped along with her stomach. "*What?*"

Vesryn didn't allow her any further protest. Arms hooked around her legs, he lifted her hips higher to plunge his tongue deeper, proceeding to devour her.

The prince's mouth moved as he read how she reacted. Serenna now realized that he was reading the bond to use her body's responses *against* her. As soon as he built pressure close to a devastating crescendo, he either slowed down, applied his tongue to the wrong places, or simply grinned at her, intentionally dissolving her release by withholding.

The stars-cursed bastard *knew*.

Frantic, Serenna knew she'd have no hope of blocking herself from the bond so she battered at her power, demanding that Essence answer her. Vesryn had previously used desire to pry out her force talent, but that emotion would be useless in shattering this rending hold.

Mouth working, tongue flicking along the center of her body, the prince drove Serenna to the cusp of release, again and again. Pressure spiraling low inside of her, she whimpered as he pushed her to the highest peak, anticipating that he'd let her vault over the edge.

Instead, Vesryn retreated, clicking his tongue. "Come on, Harpy," he growled, shadows dancing around her. "You're not even trying."

Serenna's pulse leaped as a sliver of darkness stroked down her slit with a sensation that she could only process as torturously pleasant. Desperate for a release, she trembled, twitching within the confines of her skin, fighting to push her body into his.

Serenna yanked in air, her core pounding with unsatiated arousal. It took her more than one attempt to speak. "How do I summon my power while you're doing *that* to me?"

The prince dipped a finger inside of her. Serenna emitted something between a shriek and a moan when he curled his hand to reach her innermost wall. Her eyes rolled back into her head as the prince worked his fingers, stroking and teasing, his thumb joining to caress that sensitive peak of nerves.

Serenna shuddered with waves of pleasure before Vesryn settled her legs back to the bed. The prince inched up her body, trailing a wake of kisses over her chest.

"Separate your mind from your environment," Vesryn whispered into her ear, his teeth grazing the point. "Like you do when assembling your mental barricades."

Completely at his mercy, unwilling to slam a door against the pleasure he offered, Serenna's words were a pathetic whine this time. "But I don't want to."

Moaning, she arched as much as the rending allowed when the prince stretched her with a second rough finger, the friction of his calluses crafting another round of bliss. Serenna's knees shook, overwhelmed by the collective sensations of the prince's shadows skimming over her body, his mouth sucking at her neck, and the friction of his fingers rhythmically pumping inside of her.

Vesryn's lips swept over hers. Serenna released a shocked gasp against their tangling tongues when his shadows joined his hand, the combined pleasure fracturing her sight. As soon as her core started to flutter, the prince withdrew, reclaiming his fingers and magic.

Serenna ripped her lips away from his, screeching in frustration as he yanked her back from careening over the edge.

"You're not going to win this," Vesryn said, chuckling with more smugness than anyone had a right to possess. "Not when I can tell what you're feeling through the bond."

"Stars scorch you," Serenna seethed, squeezing her eyes shut, attempting to sever her mind from her body. She sensed the prince fully intended to force her into obedience by swinging her pleasure out of reach.

Behind her eyelids, she felt Vesryn shift his weight lower. Blood jerking in every direction, the return of his mouth between her thighs brought a renewed wave of warmth. Serenna emitted a discouraged sob at the way his tongue flattened against her aching center, delivering only half the pressure she needed to chase a release.

Serenna spent what had to be years straining to block out every sensation, forcibly steering her awareness away from the pleasure the prince was wringing out of her body. Since he intended to continue torturing her forever, she stubbornly refused to break first and demand that he stop.

Against all odds, Serenna distanced her mind enough to reach the intangible space where Essence lay waiting. She recklessly snatched at her magic, desperately hauling rending from her Well.

It took multiple tries.

Power igniting, shadows thrashing, Serenna hurtled her entire strength against the prince's restrictive magic, severing his rending with a vicious slice of her own. Her body bolted up as she disintegrated his grip.

Grinning, Vesryn peeked up from between her legs. Serenna seized his hair and shoved his face back down, grinding against his mouth before collapsing back to the bed.

Vesryn laughed against her, the rumbling from his lips burying a rapturous tide of vibrations deep into her core. The prince doubled his efforts, fingers pumping, tongue flicking. Serenna locked him in with her thighs, savagely moving with him. Chasing pleasure, she rode against his mouth, building her release.

Serenna whimpered, mind unraveling, lightheaded, so close to the brink. This time, Vesryn let her tumble over the edge—shoving her off when he did something inexplicable with his shadows.

Magic ricocheted against her from the inside out, sending Serenna's spine arching off the mattress. She fissured and shattered, her climax shuddering, barreling through her body in crashing waves. Serenna went limp, collapsing onto her pillows.

"Scorching stars," Vesryn panted against her, hauling himself up to her face. He smoothed her hair away from her eyes. "That felt..." He didn't finish the thought before his ravenous lips collided with hers.

Serenna didn't have time to catch her breath as their mouths kindled against each other, stoking coals in the fire. No longer willing to be the only one unclothed, Serenna tackled the half-tied laces of Vesryn's trousers. *I'll die if he stops me again.*

"As much as I want to," the prince said, halting her hands.

Serenna's wordless objection began flying off her tongue before he interrupted her.

"Jassyn has been badgering me telepathically for the past fifteen minutes." Vesryn's voice was tight with annoyance. "Apparently, he requires my assistance at this *exact* moment and refuses to take no for an answer."

If it was anyone but Jassyn, Serenna would've protested. She propped herself up. "Well, you deserve it for all the times you've harassed *him*."

Rising, Vesryn tied the laces of his trousers and slipped back into his boots. Serenna's mouth twitched with amusement from his disarray. The prince yanked his leathers straight, shoving stray strands of hair out of his eyes.

"I plan to continue this later." Leaning down, the prince brushed his lips against hers. "I'll see you in the morning."

Muttering to himself about Jassyn's atrocious timing, Vesryn opened a portal. Serenna leaned back into her pillows, watching him disappear. As the cloud of lust cleared from her mind, she frowned, realizing they'd never truly talked.

CHAPTER 15

JASSYN

Sensing a surge of power, Jassyn jerked his head up from the tome he was reading at the dining table. *About time.* He'd only been persistent in bothering his cousin since Vesryn was stubbornly balking. *Let's see how he likes being the one pestered.*

As expected, the prince's portal tore open in the middle of his sitting room. Readjusting his plated ear cuffs from the sudden jarring, Jassyn pushed away the remnants of his dinner.

Vesryn stalked through the portal, snarling. "This had better be life threatening or I'm opening a rift to the Hibernal Wastes and tossing you through."

Folding his arms, Jassyn leaned back in his chair. He returned the prince's scowl, sweeping his attention over his cousin's disheveled state. Silver hair half out of his topknot, rumpled tunic, and—

Jassyn yanked his gaze up, clashing with his cousin's eyes. His mouth pinched further into a glower upon noticing that Vesryn's excessively tight leathers only highlighted his blatant erection.

"That's not a bad idea," Jassyn grated out through his

clenched jaw, thinking his teeth might crack. "You obviously need to cool off in a snowdrift before we go anywhere."

The prince's nostrils flared as he released his magic, the rift fading behind him. "I don't know which part of 'I'm giving Serenna the most mind-blowing clim—'"

Jassyn slammed the book in front of him shut, cutting his cousin off. "It was my mistake to assume you were simply being lewd." His cheeks heated with discomfort that he hoped the prince interpreted as anger. "I assure you, it won't happen again."

Uttering something incoherent to himself, Vesryn ran his fingers through his hair. Apparently noticing the sorry state, he untangled the dangling leather strap, rebinding the top portion.

The prince's lips twitched. "You said I needed to work on my lesson planning. That delightful body lock trick sparked the idea of drawing Serenna's power out with a more...enjoyable approach."

"Excuse me?" Jassyn could only express his disbelief through a scoff, unable to form a response. He couldn't begin to decipher how the prince had been *inspired* when they'd had him tethered with a knife against his throat.

Vesryn smirked. "Serenna struggled spectacularly."

"I didn't ask." Jassyn's ears singed. Regret assaulted him, making him wish that he hadn't bothered reaching out to his cousin this evening. "If you're quite finished informing me of"— he pointedly kept his eyes fastened on the prince's—"whatever you did with Serenna, can we discuss why I asked you to come?"

"Thanks to you, I actually didn't, but—"

"Scorching stars, I'm referring to the coercion on the magister," Jassyn all but pleaded, shoving his palms into his eyes.

"Why do you need my help with Thalaesyn?" Blessedly redirected, Vesryn joined him at the table. The prince unceremoniously readjusting himself had Jassyn rolling his eyes. "This really could've waited another day." Vesryn gripped the back of a chair, releasing a humored grunt. "Or another minute. What I felt through the bond nearly had me—"

"Again, I didn't ask," Jassyn said, driving a hand through his curls. "And quite frankly, I really don't want to know." Vesryn opened his mouth and Jassyn silenced him by holding up a finger. "You're the commander—I figured the authority of your presence would be helpful in the event of any...reactions on Thalaesyn's part if I inquired about the compulsion."

Vesryn snatched a slice of beef from the discarded dinner plate. Jassyn's lip curled as the prince shoved it into his mouth. With the hand he just had in his trousers.

"Since you mentioned it," Vesryn said around the mouthful, "I've been trying to determine why there'd even be coercion on Thalaesyn. It's possible he might know something from the first time the wraith attacked the capital." A muscle jumped in the prince's jaw before he grabbed Jassyn's glass of water and guzzled the contents. "He somehow survived that night when so many others in the palace didn't." Shaking his head, the prince dropped into the chair across from Jassyn, evidently intending to finish the leftovers. "My sire banished him to the dungeons until the completion of Centarya, but I never thought to ask why."

Jassyn traced the binding on the tome, studying the way the prince's brows contorted as his eyes unfocused on the cold plate of food. "You have a theory," he prompted, hoping to guide Vesryn out of the canyon of his thoughts.

The prince blinked out of his contemplation. "It's more of a pattern I've noticed with the wraith," he said, rolling up a slice of cured veal. "I doubt it's related to the coercion on Thalaesyn, but it might be worth mentioning." Vesryn dipped the meat into a saucer of ground mustard. He paused, seeming to realize that he was thieving the remnants of Jassyn's dinner. "You don't mind, do you?" he asked, shoving the veal into his mouth.

Jassyn flapped his hand, urging him to continue.

"I've realized that the wraith have only targeted the elven-blooded in recent decades. Those beasts haven't attacked pure-bloods since the first few raids on the city—before we even had the elven-blooded population." Vesryn tugged the plate closer to him, elbows mantling on the table like a hawk hovering over a hare. "That alone is probably why everyone in the capital has dismissed the threat."

"But the wraith didn't abduct anyone from campus like they do in Kyansari," Jassyn brought up. "They killed us indiscriminately." Skin pebbling, he stopped himself from feeling the memory of the warrior's gauntlet crushing his throat. *Except I was spared.* "Why would they drag off citizens from the capital but not here?"

"I don't have an answer for that, but it doesn't sit well with me." Vesryn moved on to a crusty edge of bread, stacking slices of meat on the flat surface. "The assault on Centarya only strengthens our theory that there are two distinct groups of wraith. The repetitive raids on the capital and the sporadic attacks in human realms have nothing in common with the intelligent wraith who came here—or those organized wraith who nearly killed me in the wilds." As if reminded of that confrontation, the prince rubbed the scars on the center of his chest.

"The disparities might point toward different levels of thinking—or maybe motivation." A disquieting feeling had Jassyn suddenly restless. He rose, shelving the tomes behind him in one of his bookcases. "If the wraith are after the elven-blooded specifically, it logically makes sense for them to target Centarya."

The prince's eyes followed him, flashing with residual anger. "That Essence wielder working with the wraith has obviously been on campus before since they opened portals for the army." Vesryn stood, finished with scarfing down the rest of the meal. "I can only assume they're someone disgruntled from the capital and star-bent on purging the elven-blooded." He crossed his arms. "Even after a century, there are still those vocally opposed to mixing elf and human blood."

Jassyn averted his guilty gaze. *I'll have to tell Vesryn about that encounter I had with the elven wraith so he's not scouring the capital for someone to blame.* But the knowledge of that warrior using Essence wouldn't change anything beyond the prince's theories, as the campus was already preparing for a potential return. *But the coercion on that wraith might connect all of our questions.*

Vesryn's nomadic attention wandering around his sitting room towed Jassyn from drifting into a sea of thoughts. "Let's get this over with," Jassyn said, seizing the prince's elbow before his cousin could fiddle with his books. "And let me do the talking. Magister Thalaesyn doesn't know I've been assessing him and I'd rather be the one to tell him." He steered the prince out of his chambers before Vesryn shook him off in the hallway.

"How familiar are you with coercion?" Jassyn asked while they descended the stairs, leading the way to the Infirmary.

The prince shrugged, picking something unsavory out of his teeth. "I know my sire is the only one strong enough to wield it. I haven't tried to replicate that magic and wouldn't even know where to start."

Skimming his hand over the cool marble railing of the staircase, Jassyn mentally organized his thoughts to settle the worry weighing on his shoulders. "Do you think the king would know if we manipulated his power?"

"You described the coercion like a shield made of telepathy and I'm assuming my sire tied off the magic." Vesryn nodded to a magus who held an entrance door open for them. "I know his power is tremendous, but I can't imagine he can perceive every elf he's placed under compulsion."

At some point, Jassyn wanted to ask if the prince found anything peculiar with the king's increasing strength in Essence —something that shouldn't be possible. Regardless how expansive a Well to draw from was, strength was determined by the number of abilities. *One thing at a time.*

Entering the magus' courtyard, both rising moons hung as dim crescents amid the scattering of stars. A warbling of birds roosting in the willows ushered them along the cobbled walkway. The tranquil melody of their evening songs warred with Jassyn's nervousness for the coming conversation with his mentor.

Vesryn suddenly skidded to a halt, his boots scuffing over the pathway's stones. His face went slack, horror widening his eyes. "What if I'm compelled?" The prince touched his head, as if feeling for the strands of magic. "Stars, do you think there's coercion on my mind and I don't know it?"

"There's not." Jassyn strode ahead, anticipating what his mentor's reaction would be with both him and Vesryn showing up unannounced. "At least there wasn't a little over a week ago."

The prince's fingers started twitching as he worked himself up. "How can you be—"

"I've already checked." Jassyn waved for Vesryn to follow.

His attention hooked on a patrol of Kyansari's soldiers, white plated armor clinking. In his sweep of the warriors, Jassyn registered the blank look in their faces that Vesryn had mentioned. They didn't even acknowledge or salute the prince.

Holding his breath, Jassyn couldn't shake the unsettled feeling stirring in his gut while they passed. He'd have to relay this to Nelya—at the prince's request, they'd begun organizing a ring of trusted magus to track anything unusual.

"What do you mean you've 'already checked?'" Vesryn asked, ignoring the squadron and lengthening his stride to return to Jassyn's side.

"I assessed you after that *excitement* in your bathing chambers." Rounding the empty Rending Field, a soft breeze whispered through the Infirmary's line of lavender hedges. "If you don't remember, it's probably because you were busy going stupid staring at Serenna."

"I was impaled. Multiple times," Vesryn bristled, shooting him a scowl. "And don't you find that a little invasive?" Igniting his power, the prince blasted the Infirmary doors with a pulse of force rather than bothering to push on the handle.

"Like you're someone who has any right to speak about personal space," Jassyn hissed, lowering his voice so as to not to disturb the few menders closing the healing wing for the evening.

Winding through the Infirmary's alcoves, Jassyn skated in front of the prince when they arrived at the magister's office. He intended to knock on Thalaesyn's door to give his mentor some type of warning, but Vesryn shouldered past him, charging through.

The room revealed its chaotic state—scattered research amid a jungle of clutter. Jassyn's attention darted toward his cousin. *Vesryn isn't going to know what to rummage through first with all the debris in here.*

Surprisingly, the prince remained focused on Thalaesyn, sitting behind his desk. Vesryn plowed around precarious stacks of books on the verge of teetering over, waded over the crumpled scrolls bunched into waves of paper on the floor, and avoided an overflowing wastebasket ringed by a puddle of ink stained into the tile.

The magister rose and saluted the prince with a hand over his heart. Out of his typical robes, his loose tunic hung over a pair of soft breeches. Jassyn assumed their arrival had disrupted his evening routine. His attention drifted to the sofa, unable to comprehend why Thalaesyn preferred to spend his nights on the tattered couch rather than in the Spire's comfortable apartments.

Thalaesyn's gray eyes sharpened on them. "Prince Vesryn."

Jassyn noted his mentor's bloodshot gaze as he closed the

door, hesitantly joining his cousin. He began clearing off the tomes and papers drowning the chairs across from the magister's desk.

"We have some questions," Vesryn said. Flicking a hand, a wave of Essence shimmered, unfolding into a portal in the only empty space.

"We can have our discussion here," Jassyn protested, stacking the volumes on the floor. Wincing at his mentor, he wanted to avoid giving the impression that this was an interrogation. He suspected going to Vesryn's office might put Thalaesyn on the defensive before they had a chance to gather any information.

"I'm not risking any of the menders walking in." Vesryn slanted his head to the rift, commanding the magister to go through.

Igniting his magic, Jassyn tossed a hand toward the exit, hastily shielding the door. "Now we have privacy."

Thalaesyn's eyes volleyed between them before he drew himself up, tucking a strand of golden hair behind a pointed ear. Vesryn blew out a breath before scruffing Thalaesyn by the back of his shirt, steering him through the portal.

Jassyn blinked as they disappeared. *Did he seriously* abduct *the magister?*

CHAPTER 16

JASSYN

Jassyn rushed through the gateway, gasping as icy rain pelted him from every direction. Sheltering his face, he wiped the pouring water out of his eyes. Having expected Vesryn's portal to transport them to the Spire, Jassyn spun around, orienting himself with the surroundings.

Lightning flashed over an endless expanse of churning waters, momentarily stealing his sight. The gateway behind him faded as his focus landed on the prince.

Standing under an overhang dangling from a husk of a building, Vesryn clutched the magister's arm as if expecting Thalaesyn to open his own rift and flee. Desperate to curb the prince's rash behavior before another reckless impulse struck him, Jassyn darted across what looked to be the ruins of a deteriorating stone dock.

Waves from the surrounding black ocean crashed over the ledge, surging around his boots. Dashing toward the prince, Jassyn reined in his confusion as he slid over the algae clinging to the slippery surface.

He raised his voice to be heard over the thunder warring with the wind. "Why didn't you portal us to your office?"

Every frantic heartbeat doubled his questions and dismay. To combat the darkness, Jassyn flared globes of illumination, the wisps of light nearly swallowed by the night. He flinched as another charge of energy gathered in the air. Toppled towers flashed through the hazy mist, outlined by a spinning barrage of rain. Thunder rattled the crumbled stones, the proximity of the storm rippling a shiver across his spine. The lip of the ancient tiled roof hardly offered any shelter from the ocean's raging spray.

"You can't abduct the magister," Jassyn protested when Vesryn just shrugged, despite knowing that no one regulated the prince. Every hair on his neck lifted in alarm before a strike of lightning blasted into the sea, the explosion of crashing waves drowned out by the thunder's roar. "Where in the bleeding stars are we?"

Vesryn swept away water dripping down his face and released his hold on the Thalaesyn. He vaguely waved a hand around the ruins, ignoring the magister's tight-lipped fury. "What's left of this isle is the remains of Halaema's first capital. It collapsed into the sea during a quake centuries ago. No one will find us here. Although..." Vesryn studied the brewing tempest. "We have little time. The Maelstrom seems to hunt Essence wielders on its waters. You have until the storm gets closer to evaluate Thalaesyn."

"Evaluate?" Thalaesyn fumed, yanking his tunic straight from the prince's jostling.

"*Closer?*" Jassyn sputtered at the same time. He frantically scanned the blackened horizon. "It's already too close!"

An apprehensive chill drenched Jassyn's chest like the deluge sluicing over his skin. That crackling blue and purple lightning whipping through the cloudy currents couldn't be natural. Serenna had told him stories of spring typhoons that periodically battered Vaelyn's castle walls—a few in her memory had even destroyed buildings that weren't stone. The monstrous whirlwind in the distance must've been hundreds of times the strength of those storms.

Reading the question in Thalaesyn's eyes, Jassyn swallowed down the anxiety climbing up his throat. His attention bounced back to the prince. "There's no reason to be somewhere so dangerous. We shouldn't be doing it this way."

Jassyn's muscles locked as a charged buzz shuddered over his skin, another wave of lightning forming in the air. Assessing Thalaesyn with the added pressure of the storm threatened to fracture his focus. Wrestling his nerves into submission, Jassyn slowed his breathing, counting the seconds between the lightning and thunder.

Vesryn folded his arms, tipping his chin at the magister. "What can you tell us of the coercion the king placed on you?"

Jassyn held his breath at the blunt force of the blow. *I suppose with the Maelstrom approaching, there's no time to dance around subtly.* Though he honestly hadn't expected much tact from the prince.

Thalaesyn wrung out his damp tunic, jaw silently working. "I'm aware that the compulsive magic exists." His eyes narrowed first on Vesryn and then on Jassyn, as if processing their unusual dynamic. "How do you two know about it?"

Jassyn readied a response, brimming with eagerness to release the truth that he'd secretly been assessing his mentor's mind for weeks. Vesryn cut in before Jassyn could get a word out, his tone sharp. "And why have you said nothing about my sire's compulsion for a century? What did you do to warrant it?"

"If I could even speak of what the magic prevents me from saying, who would I have told? And who would've believed me? *You?*" Thalaesyn bared his teeth. "The council's hound who tracks down the wraith without asking questions, not thinking twice about slaughtering those innocents?"

Jassyn tensed while Thalaesyn glared at Vesryn in a way that suggested they shared more of a history than he'd assumed—aside from the magister simply being present as one of the palace researchers. Eyes bouncing back to the prince, Jassyn braced for Vesryn's reaction.

Vesryn went still, a predator honed in on prey. His words were dangerously quiet, unsettlingly calm like the eye of a storm. "Innocents?" The prince suddenly lunged, driving a finger into Thalaesyn's chest. "Has the coercion degraded your mind so much over these years that you've forgotten how many those beasts have stolen from us?"

"That's where you're mistaken." Thalaesyn's face contorted with anger, but his voice didn't rise to meet Vesryn's outburst. "I know what the coercion is concealing, but Galaeryn saw to it that I can't discuss it."

Jassyn shoved his trepidation aside. He hesitantly placed a hand on Vesryn's arm, hoping to temper the prince's erratic behavior before he harmed the magister.

"You wanted me to examine the magic," Jassyn gently reminded him. Vesryn's muscles strained beneath his fingers. "It's possible that I might be able to untangle the power and Magister Thalaesyn can tell us what the king has concealed." The island shuddered under Jassyn's boots, drawing his attention back to their dwindling time as the Maelstrom pursued them.

Vesryn's fists quivered at his sides before his shoulders relaxed. The prince retreated a step, jerking his head at Thalaesyn, a muscle jumping in his clenched jaw.

"May I assess the coercion on your mind?" Jassyn asked, ruthlessly ripping his awareness away from the storm's alarming energy. "If I can do so safely, I'll try to unravel the magic."

At Thalaesyn's nod, Jassyn hovered a hand by his mentor's head. While thunder rumbled, he hauled on his Well, spinning a wave of telepathic power through Thalaesyn's veins, channeling raw Essence toward the magister's mind.

Unable to take the lingering silence as his imagination cycled through the countless horrific consequences they'd face if the king discovered they were meddling with his magic, Jassyn asked, "Why were you banished?" He'd never had the courage to inquire before, and occupying himself with a conversation while he worked would also keep his attention off of the impending danger stalking the coast.

"I discovered—" Thalaesyn's brows collided with what looked like a flash of pain before he cleared his throat. With a heavy exhale, he tried again. "The king wouldn't have known—" Thalaesyn seized, yanking in a sharp breath, his words cut off.

The magister twisted a silver ring that glittered with Essence around his finger before focusing on the prince. "Your anger and pain are justified, but you've been misguided. You're not the only one with regrets from that night." Vesryn flinched at Thalaesyn's words, likely reminded of his absence from the palace during the attack. "Your mother and brother wouldn't have perished if I hadn't meddled in magic that I had no business manipulating." Thalaesyn's voice was hoarse with remorse. "It's all my fault. The only reason Galaeryn hasn't killed me—or worse—is because I might still be *useful* in furthering his dark plans." His gaze unfocused on the roiling sea, bitter regret lingering in his words. "I don't know why he didn't leave me rotting in the palace dungeons."

"Your imprisonment disturbed too many in court," Vesryn said, the war in his eyes subsiding as he calmed. "Especially those loyal to my mother." His fingers started tapping across his arms while Jassyn directed his attention into Thalaesyn's skull. "The opening of Centarya allowed for a more...acceptable exile."

Jassyn jerked when Vesryn's presence suddenly slipped into

his head. *Could you not?* Jassyn asked. *Your hovering is bound to be distracting.*

Show me what you're doing, Vesryn insisted.

Resigned that the prince would only harass him until he relented, Jassyn released a weary sigh. *As long as you simply observe and don't interrupt me,* he conceded, permitting the telepathic link to coil around his mind. Jassyn embarked on an explanation, detailing everything he knew about the knotted network of telepathy. *I'll attempt to unravel a knot of coercion—I'm not sure what to expect.*

What Jassyn didn't divulge was how he'd accidentally untangled some measure of compulsion before. Though the magic on the elven wraith warrior wasn't as extensive as the power snaring Thalaesyn—at least from the muddled details Jassyn recalled.

I shouldn't have attempted to use Essence while under the influence of Stardust, he thought to himself. Guilt percolated into his bones like the chilly rain seeping into his skin. *Any mishaps could've caused irreparable damage.*

Jassyn targeted one of the countless snarls of coercion. He picked at the magic like he was attempting to unravel a single thread from a long rope, careful to not jumble the fibers in the other strands. Using his own telepathy talent like a magnet to draw out and counter the weaves, he loosened a cord of power.

The storm is getting closer, Vesryn warned.

Why did you bring us here? Jassyn wiped the beading mist and nervous perspiration off his face. *We could've worked in Thalaesyn's office. You're rushing me and this isn't something to be hurried.*

Jassyn sensed Vesryn's fingers twitching through their telepathic link, likely wanting to try untwining the knot of coercion himself. The progress of untangling a single strand of magic was painfully slow—unlike the Maelstrom's impending approach.

Jassyn glanced at the turbid waters and the windstorm barreling toward them.

What would happen if you cut the clump off? Vesryn asked, drawing Jassyn's attention back to the magister under his hands.

I don't know what damage we could cause by simply unraveling the magic, Jassyn said, continuing to pluck at the coercion. *By doing it this way, I can monitor Thalaesyn and make sure there aren't any adverse—*

A streak of rending penetrated the magister's skull, slicing the coiled telepathy in half.

Jassyn's pulse skidded to a halt. He sucked in a shocked breath when the cluster of coercion he was working on disintegrated like a wick burned by a flame.

Thalaesyn staggered backward.

"Stop!" Jassyn shouted at his cousin, rushing to catch the magister before he collapsed. "You have no idea what you're doing." He helped steady Thalaesyn on his feet before rounding on the prince. "Stars, you can hardly heal a scorching bruise! You have no business trying to free his mind."

"But did it work?" Vesryn asked, eyes bright with curiosity as his shadows receded.

"I doubt it!" Jassyn said, grabbing fistfuls of his soaking curls. "There are a hundred knots in that web." Dueling waves of incredulity and disbelief at Vesryn's idiocy had Jassyn's heart furiously flinging itself against his ribs. "Don't do that again. We can't even begin to guess what effect untangling the coercion might have on his mind."

Thalaesyn's hand trembled as he touched his head. "The wraith are my fault." He flinched at the admission, eyes darting between Vesryn and Jassyn. Thalaesyn focused on the prince, his words spilling out in a rush. "You need to stop killing them. They're not the enemy—"

Shadows erupted from Vesryn, the black cloud around him

mirroring the Maelstrom's wrath. Darkness seized Thalaesyn in a violent hold.

Without even thinking, Jassyn grabbed the prince. To do what, he had no idea, but Vesryn shoved him off.

The prince snatched the front of the immobilized magister's tunic. "How can you say that?" he snarled, eyes blazing with outrage. "Those monsters took everything from me!" Chest heaving, he shook Thalaesyn. "They took everything from you!"

Apparently, Thalaesyn finally had enough of the prince and ignited his own Essence in response. His rending hacked at the prince's shadows but Vesryn's magic exploded, a hundred straps lashing to bind the magister completely.

Using all his strength, Jassyn hauled Vesryn away. Sensing the prince's power flare in response, Jassyn tossed his hands up, frantically slamming a shield around himself to avoid the restrictive hold.

"We need to *listen* to what Magister Thalaesyn has to say," Jassyn gritted out as Vesryn's rending battered his ward. "He knows something. That's why we're doing this—to get answers."

A tendon in Vesryn's neck strained as his shadows roiled like the waves slapping the stones. The prince rounded on Thalaesyn. "Where were you the night of the attack? How did *you* survive?"

"Galaeryn already had me tethered in the dungeons," Thalaesyn snapped. "I couldn't even warn Maraelyn of what I'd done through our bond."

Jassyn blinked. *He was bonded to the queen?*

Releasing his hold on Thalaesyn, Vesryn started pacing, brow dented in a furrow. The prince cut his hand over to Jassyn, pointing at the magister. "Keep working."

"We've had enough for one night." Jassyn glanced at Thalaesyn before studying the raging ocean as another echo of thunder crashed above them. "The storm is nearly here. Let's return to Centarya and we can figure out how to proceed."

"Now!" Vesryn barked at him.

Jassyn shook his head, struggling to keep calm, but urgency laced his tone. "Vesryn, we need to leave." The wind sped up, whipping curls in his face. Visibly closer, the Maelstrom's eerie lightning crackled and flashed, ripping at the sea.

"He's had enough," Jassyn repeated, scalp prickling.

"I'll do it myself," Vesryn growled. He stalked toward the magister, shadows angry, swirling in his wake.

Jassyn threw himself between them, realizing that his cousin intended to sever the knots of coercion with the brutal force of rending. "You could damage his mind. Irrevocably." Jassyn's stomach pitched in a sea of dread, keenly aware of his inability to stop the prince. "We could lose everything the king tried to conceal, not to mention Magister Thalaesyn's sanity."

Vesryn shoved past Jassyn's shoulder, shadows coiling around his hands as he grabbed for the magister. Jassyn had heartbeats to consider snatching one of his golden daggers to tether his cousin. If he could have his mentor restrain Vesryn like Serenna had with rending, they might jointly buy enough time to settle the prince.

Before he could roll a blade to his fingers, Jassyn's body seized, a numbness zipping through his veins. An electrifying charge coalesced under his skin, shooting down his arms. Vesryn's eyes widened with his.

Lightning had hurtled from the clouds, straight into Jassyn's fists.

Staggering away from Thalaesyn and the prince, Jassyn wrenched his arms closer to his body. Horror crystalized in his chest as the wave of sparks danced between his fingertips. *This isn't happening.*

Jassyn's gaze whipped to Vesryn, then to Thalaesyn, and then to the light striking between his trembling hands.

"I—" The power flared, expanding to an orb the size of his head. Jassyn stumbled out from the roof's shelter, panic compressing his ribs. Every muscle tensing from the effort of dragging in labored breaths, he frantically considered what to do with the lightning twisting in his palms.

His eyes flitted to the sky, blinking back rain, like there would be an answer in the storm. *The earth's magic left me when I released my hold on the ground, but I have no idea how to dispel lightning!*

"You need to get out of here," Jassyn said, backing away further, shaking water out of his face. "I—I don't know what's happening."

Neither the prince nor Thalaesyn moved, both wide-eyed and staring at the electric web.

Panting now, Jassyn extended his arms, the clash of magic surging through his bones. Purple and blue sparks spilled out in waves instead of dissipating like he desperately willed. If anything, the sizzling globe of power surged in response.

"You need to portal out of here," Jassyn pleaded, alarm rising in his throat. "I don't want to hurt you."

Vesryn opened a gateway and unceremoniously shoved Thalaesyn through. Closing the rift, he approached Jassyn, joining him in the rain. "This is...unexpected." The prince tilted his head, attention riveted on the spinning sparks. "Care to explain?"

Stinging sweat and sea spray dripped into Jassyn's eyes, but he didn't move for fear of this foreign magic spiraling even more out of control. Terror had him blurting a confession.

"I channeled something in the earth." Jassyn swallowed past his panic. "During the wraith attack. I don't know what I did, but I felt something. A different power. I called roots from the ground. That's—that's what happened in front of the Spire." His chest constricted, waiting for Vesryn's reaction. "I...I think I can access elemental magic."

Vesryn's brows drew together, a sign of his intensive thinking. "Is it like Essence?" As if charmed, the prince lifted a hand to touch the magic bouncing around his palms.

"Don't!" Jassyn yelled, jerking his arms away from his cousin. His mind raced to process the question, fear sundering his lungs. "I think it's actually lightning."

Vesryn's eyes lit up with manic excitement, reflecting the blue glow from Jassyn's fists. The prince grinned, clearly not frightened like he was. "Then wield it."

CHAPTER 17

SERENNA

In the dracovae's valley, the sun crested over the mountaintops, quickly burning off a faint layer of fog. Despite how occupied he seemed, Serenna kept a wary eye trained on Naru's razor-sharp bill. Settled on the ground with his raptor-taloned feet tucked under his body, he idly picked at the remaining scraps of rabbit. Serenna wrinkled her nose as his rubbery tongue flicked over the grass, licking every drop of gore.

Vesryn swung a saddle over Naru's feathered shoulders. When the dracovae rose, the prince ruffled his obsidian neck, stirring out a puff of dust from beneath his plumes. Even someone as tall as Jassyn could walk under the beast's chest without stooping. Beyond his front legs, Naru's feathers morphed into leathery scales, his fin-like lizard tail trailing on the earth.

Serenna joined the prince at his side, watching him expertly cinch the multitude of straps, fasten the buckles, and tighten the clasps on the intricate contraption. She voiced her concerns about falling off, but Vesryn assured her that if she slipped, he'd halt her descent before she splattered on the ground. Which really did nothing to ease any of her anxious nerves.

"How do you steer Naru while you're flying?" Serenna asked, noting the absence of any type of halter or bridle.

"I ask him," Vesryn said, tugging on a group of knotted ropes as if ensuring their reliability. "By sending telepathic images."

Serenna's brows rose as Naru blinked his double eyelid, white iris scanning her and the prince. "Does he listen?"

Vesryn released an amused snort. "When it suits him."

"Sounds like you're perfect for each other," Serenna muttered. She reached out to stroke the soft plumes on Naru's neck. "What about rangers who don't have telepathy?"

"The dracovae are trained to respond to the pressure of your feet on their sides and the way you shift your weight." Vesryn adjusted loop lengths on the stirrup ladder, running down from the peak of Naru's back. "They're also intelligent enough to understand and follow a variety of verbal commands."

As the prince continued talking about whatever else the rangers did to pilot the flying beasts, Serenna's attention wandered. His nimble fingers raced distractingly over the saddle's straps, deftly tying the leather. Her pulse skipped, recalling how rough his palms felt gliding against her body last night and—

Vesryn's hands halted, twitching over a buckle. He angled toward her, an incredulous question scrawled across his forehead. Forgetting herself and the inconvenient fact that the prince could read her reactions through the bond, Serenna's cheeks blazed with embarrassment.

She cleared her throat, struggling to recall Vesryn's last few words. "What was that?" Shifting her weight did nothing to alleviate the sudden ache hammering between her thighs.

"Should I be concerned about your self-control?" Vesryn emitted a self-satisfied chuckle, obviously detecting her feelings since she didn't have her mental barricades in place. "Perhaps you'd rather..." he trailed off, amusement settling into his features as he glanced over her shoulder, "...spend the day *romping* in the valley?" The prince's attention veered back to linger on her lips.

"Is—is that an option?" Serenna stammered, the flush now racing to the tips of her ears for voicing the brazen question.

One side of Vesryn's mouth quirked, drawing her awareness straight to his dimple. Taking a predatory step closer, his eyes glittered like sea glass in the sun. A shiver spiraled down Serenna's spine when the prince curled a finger under her chin. "Oh, I think you could persuade me," he breathed, hovering his lips above hers.

As Serenna rose on her toes to meet his mouth, the prince tapped the end of her nose. "It is rather tragic that we have work to do first."

Serenna crossed her arms with an irritated huff, forcefully expelling the suggested images of her and the prince tangled in the meadow. *Of course he's all business.*

"Anyway," Vesryn said, returning to finish fussing over the saddle straps, cinching a girth over the scales behind Naru's front legs. "The Aelfyn intentionally bred the dracovae to fly with us, but ultimately these featherbrains are the ones deciding who they'll permit as riders." Naru wrapped his neck back to watch the prince, clacking his beak as if interpreting the slight. "Luckily for you, Naru appreciated the rabbit treat you prepared for him, so he doesn't mind if you ride along with me." After securing a final knot, Vesryn gave him a pat, turning toward Serenna.

The prince slid his hands over her hips, tightening his fingers across her waist as he reeled her closer to him. A swell crested and tumbled in Serenna's stomach, capsizing all coherent thought.

Vesryn's eyes traveled over her face. "I can give you the best chance at a fledged dracovae choosing you as its rider."

Breaking free from the spell in his gaze, Serenna registered what he was implying. It wasn't like she had any better options, but she hadn't yet decided if she wanted to join the rangers or if that was just what the prince desired.

Stubbornly shaking her head, Serenna said, "I'd rather earn a position."

Vesryn's hands dropped away as she retreated a step, separating herself from the bias he freely offered. A muscle flexed in his jaw, his silent disapproval sparking a prickle of worry.

More words spilled from Serenna's mouth to explain. "I imagine the rangers who worked for their rank would object if I'm shown any favor or given special privileges." She glanced away, staring at Naru's mate, Trella, in the distance. The morning sun drenched her vibrant plumes as she preened her white feathers. "You've already done more than you should've by choosing me as your champion for the tournament. I've done nothing to deserve it besides having random chance form this bond."

Sensing the prince's annoyance and displeasure twisting together, Serenna hesitantly met his gaze. Vesryn held her stare for an uncomfortable moment before his irritation spiked. Her breath snagged in a startled gasp when he seized her arms, dragging her back toward him.

"This is the last time I hear you say that you're unworthy." The prince's words were a fierce growl, imbued with annoyance. "The stars chose to link us."

Serenna swallowed, scorched by his ire. *Does he want me or this bond?* Her heart whipped into a whirlwind of confused emotions as he leaned closer.

Vesryn's hands tightened around her forearms. "Just because you haven't had the luxury of time to manifest your full power doesn't make you any less deserving."

Letting go, the prince retreated, tapping on one of Naru's legs. The dracovae snapped his beak but lifted a clawed foot. Ending their conversation as if he'd settled the matter, Vesryn focused his attention on casting a sliver of rending to trim back Naru's talons.

A small part of Serenna nearly asked if he ever intended to complete the bond—or if he wanted to. But the last thing she wanted to do was pressure him if he was hesitant to accept a bond for a second time. It didn't seem like a conversation to have while the prince needed to focus on corralling the rogue wraith. *It's obvious I need more training, so a deeper magical connection between us would only be a risk for him.*

Serenna glanced back across the vale, letting the weight of the moment reign until she couldn't stew in the silence any longer. "What will Trella do while we're gone?" The female dracovae had wandered closer than the first time they'd visited the pair. Rousing her feathers and scales in a clatter, she tilted her eagle-like head, watching them with curious eyes.

"I'll leave the portal open for as long as I can in case she wants to follow." Vesryn released Naru's clawed foot. "She normally does."

"Portal?" Fidgeting, Serenna readjusted the sleeves on her uniform, pulling the material down to her wrists. Despite the comfortable weather from the late spring day, they wore a full set of leathers to protect themselves from the cooler elements in the skies. "Why do we need to portal?"

"We'll save flight time moving by gateway. I've traveled enough with Naru that I can get us closer to the wraith's reported location without having to fly across the realms." Vesryn secured his hair in a topknot, binding it out of his face with a leather strap. "The hunts are going to become more difficult if someone with magic is working with those beasts, but we should be able to handle three wraith."

"We?" Serenna followed the prince's lead, wrapping her braid into a tight coil on the top of her head.

"Why do you think we've been training in the dungeons all week?" Vesryn's attention finally flicked back to her, disintegrating Serenna's previous apprehension. "I wouldn't put you in danger if I thought you couldn't handle yourself." The prince kneeled to tighten the laces on his boots, glancing up at her. "And besides, I remember you demanding that I not hunt the wraith alone."

Serenna sniffed dismissively. "It's about time you decided to be sensible for your safety."

Lunging forward, Vesryn snatched the backs of her legs. Serenna squeaked, stumbling into his chest. The prince's hands glided down her calves before refastening the laces on her boots.

"You don't want any loose ends tangled up in the saddle," he said, grinning up at her, knowing exactly what he was doing to her pulse.

Serenna frowned as he knotted the leather into intricate loops, nearly tight enough to cause discomfort. "How am I supposed to untie those?"

"You broke out of the rending binds last night, so I'm sure you'll figure it out." Rising to his full height, the prince smirked. "But considering how much you struggled, I imagine we'll have to practice again."

Serenna's wordless bluster was lost as Vesryn turned and placed a boot in one of the stirrup loops. Ascending the ladder, he climbed up the side of Naru. At the top of the dracovae's back, he settled into the saddle.

"Ready?" Vesryn asked, patting his thigh.

Serenna pinched her lips. "I'm not sitting in your lap."

She stroked Naru's neck, receiving a trilling chirp. Copying the prince's motion, she hooked her boot into a looped ring and pulled herself up.

Serenna unsuccessfully swatted Vesryn's hands away when he snatched her at the top. Seizing her waist, he squeezed her hips while dragging her down in front of him.

"I'm helping," he said defensively while Serenna's blood jerked in enough directions to give her whiplash. Crouching over her, the mountain of his chest stacked against her spine. The prince suggestively ran his hands down the tops of her thighs, steering her feet into a higher set of stirrups, adjusting the loops over her boots. "Just guiding you in," he said in a voice that could only mean trouble.

To reinstate some shred of control, Serenna elbowed Vesryn's abdomen when his lips brushed against the point of her ear. "I can handle myself." He didn't seem to notice her feeble protest through that wall of solid muscle.

Vesryn's thighs clamped around hers, wedging them even closer. Not giving him the satisfaction of melting into his chest, Serenna sat up straight, putting more distance between them even though they both had ample room.

Ignoring the gesture, the prince curved his arm across her middle, hauling her back into the cradle of his lap. Sighing, Serenna let Vesryn win this round and folded into him, not quite relaxing.

Naru tossed his head and stretched his wings, ruffling his feathers. Trella emitted a screech, flapping in response. The female dracovae boldly approached, seemingly not keen on being left behind.

Violet light flared as the prince fabricated a shield in front of them. "This will dampen the wind enough so that the breeze won't tear out our eyes," he explained, twining an inverse wave of illumination into the ward to render it invisible.

He then extended a hand, opening a massive portal. Tossing his head, Naru started prancing toward the rift. Lurching with his motion, Serenna grabbed the swell of the saddle. She steadied herself, adjusting to the dracovae's foreign gait that dipped and swayed from side to side.

The last thing she registered before entering the portal's embrace was Vesryn's lips skimming across the side of her throat. "Hang on," he said, mouth skating over the shell of her ear.

Serenna shivered as the inky portal swallowed the surrounding mountain valley in darkness.

CHAPTER 18

SERENNA

It took Serenna a disorienting moment to realize they were falling. Fast. Plummeting from the sky.

Going rigid, every muscle in her legs locked against the saddle. Seizing the prince's arm, Serenna's shriek ripped through the terror wedged in her throat. Wind screamed past her ears as they plunged straight for the scattered clouds below.

Naru tucked his wings in tight, streaking down toward the fluffy sea, faster than a crashing comet. The steep plunge launched Serenna's heart into her mouth. Vesryn crouched over her, leaning into the dive. His unrestrained, wild laughter thundered against her back.

A blur of mist drenched them, shading the rising sun when they dipped into the clouds. Cool water droplets beaded on Serenna's face and clung to her leathers. Naru sliced through the wisps, rapidly cutting the air as they descended to the earth.

A sudden break in the white haze loosened the fear in Serenna's chest, releasing her lungs so she could take her first full breath. Vast grassy plains stretched out over the landscape, thousands of feet below.

Serenna's stomach slapped against her spine when Naru's

wings snapped out, yanking their fall to a halt. Feathers flaring, the dracovae's body twisted underneath her legs as he tipped to one side, sawing through the atmosphere in a sweeping loop.

Panting, Serenna reclaimed her breathing. Her heart slowed its steady trampling of her ribs as her pulse settled back into place.

"I should have known you'd make a gateway to another realm in the *sky*," she shrilled to the prince over the whistle of the wind. Serenna could feel him grinning behind her.

Trella suddenly burst through the layer of clouds. The female dracovae streaked past them in a blinding white blur, legs folded close to her body. Fanning her wings hundreds of feet lower, she screeched, a wild and piercing sound that only a behemoth raptor could make. Trella leveled out, gliding in looping circles.

"Can you keep yourself balanced in the saddle?" Vesryn asked.

"I think so." Serenna loosened her shoulders, settling into the steady rhythm of Naru's flapping. Each thunderous stroke of his wings had them dipping and rising, like a ship's deck bobbing at sea. "As long as this buzzard doesn't dive again."

"In that case…" Vesryn reached forward and fastened a strap across her lap and over each thigh, binding her to the contraption. "Don't pull his feathers." The prince gave the dracovae's neck an affectionate pat, running a plume through his fingertips. "If you do, I'm not responsible if he decides to roll you off."

As if agreeing with the prince, Naru peered back at them before emitting a chorus of clacks. Vesryn shifted, bumping into her. Serenna twisted around at the prince's jostling to see him flinging his legs together over Naru's side.

Alarm pitched her question high. "What are you doing?"

Vesryn fabricated a shield across his face. "Flying, of course." He smirked as if it was the most obvious answer. "It's the best part." And with that stupid grin, he jumped.

Serenna gasped, jerking forward to stare past Naru's shoulder. She watched in stunned horror as the prince free fell to the earth, descending with his limbs thrown out like a starfish, catching the wind.

Frantically, Serenna looked back at Naru. He tracked the prince, pearly eyes pinned on Vesryn's back. Frolicking with a shake of his head, the dracovae released an ear-splitting screech, answered by Trella below.

Naru's body coiled and tightened under Serenna's legs, ready to spring. *Oh no.* Wings snapping shut, he launched into a dive.

Swallowing another scream, Serenna lunged forward to seize the front of the saddle. Knees clamping against the dracovae's sides, her fingers slipped with fear. Her hands shook from the effort of hanging on, knuckled locked around the cantle. Despite the shield Vesryn had tied off, wind whipped against her face, stinging her cheeks as strands of her braid loosened, thrashing behind her.

They soared past Trella, overtaking the prince, winning the race toward the earth. The air howled in Serenna's ears as they shot to the ground faster than she'd imagined was possible.

A surge of the prince's exhilaration bolted through the bond, crowding out Serenna's worry. Assuming that this was a practiced event between Vesryn and his dracovae, she caught snatches of her breath, hesitantly trusting Naru's turbulent flight.

Serenna's stomach abruptly flew into her throat as Naru's wings unfolded, legs jerking against the straps anchoring her to the saddle. Eyes pinned above, the dracovae tracked Vesryn's fall through the air, as if calculating his descent.

Serenna's head swam when she braved a look to find the prince—no more than a dark speck in the sky. Feathers flaring, Naru banked, gliding on a warm current as he slowed their plunge. Wings oscillating to the left and right, he angled them below the prince.

The blurred world sharpened as the landscape's mosaic came into focus. Streaks of color transformed into more detailed grassy plains as they sailed above the earth.

Swallowing her fear, Serenna hesitantly peeled her aching fingers off of the cantle, now having a moment to experience soaring through the sky without having to hang on for her life. Sunbeams flooding through gaps in the clouds warmed her leathers.

Skin tingling, a peculiar sensation swept over her. Tendrils lit up in Serenna's vision, a thousand ribbons igniting with light. There were streamers everywhere, like endless waves rippling in the ocean. The sky above, the earth below—an eternal sea of twisting currents.

Fascination and confusion left Serenna breathless. *Am I seeing...wind?*

Caught somewhere between disbelief and wonder, she tentatively reached out a hand. A whirl of air curved around her, like a seedling leaning toward the sun.

Naru's piercing screech wrenched Serenna's attention back to her body. The strands disintegrated like smoke. Shaking her head, she sensed the prince and turned around as Vesryn's boots touched the base of Naru's tail. In a fluid motion, he raced along the dracovae's croup and up his spine, returning to the saddle.

"You're absolutely mad," Serenna said while the prince settled behind her, a rush of exhilaration still radiating through the bond.

After the prince resecured his boots in the stirrups, Naru banked and climbed in the sky. His wings strummed the air until he reached the same elevation as Trella, trilling as he arced around his mate.

"Do you want a turn?" Vesryn asked as the grasslands rushed

by below. Half of his wind-ravaged hair had become unbound, whipping in a silver halo around them. "I promise I'll catch you."

Before Serenna could consider partaking in the same brainless activity, the prince tensed behind her. She spotted the group of wraith on a collision course with a village in the distance.

Only now considering the implications of their hunt, a nervous sweat drenched the back of her neck. The prince would expect her to rend the creatures, but Serenna hadn't sorted through her feelings on killing the mindless monsters when she wasn't fighting for survival.

We'll restrain the beasts and portal them to the Ranger Station, Vesryn said telepathically, rather than yelling over the wind.

Startled, she glanced back at him. *Restrain them? We're not killing them?*

No. Vesryn's fury simmered, the sharp edge to his thoughts stirring her unease.

Serenna sensed there was something he wasn't sharing that sparked this abrupt shift in how he handled the wraith. Curiosity stormed through her, a whirlwind of questions that she kept to herself.

There have been...developments, the prince seemed to add as an afterthought, the dark tension of his mood clashing against her. Vesryn didn't elaborate further as his fingers tapped an agitated tempo where his hand rested on her thigh.

This isn't a joyride anymore, Princess, the prince said as he urged Naru lower. *Secure the one on the right when we land.*

Relieved that she wouldn't have to obliterate the wraith, a tangle of unease unraveled. She leaned forward with a sense of purpose, knowing Vesryn could effortlessly restrained all three. Eager to prove that the last week of fending off the creatures had sufficiently prepared her for binding one wraith, Serenna reached for her Well. Essence surged with a crackle of energy in her veins, surrounding her with a shimmering glow.

Anticipating Naru's landing as the plains rushed up to meet them, Serenna's stomach pitched. Taloned feet striking the earth, the shock jarred Serenna's teeth, rattling her spine. The ground thundered as the dracovae charged across the grasslands, kicking up a swirl of dust. She clung to the saddle as they galloped in a rolling, loping run.

Bending Essence, Serenna sought the silent space in her mind. With a ruthless focus, she hauled rending out of her Well. Raising her hand, shadows twisted around her fingertips. Wisps of darkness streaked out from her and the prince, hurtling forward fifty paces to wrap around the group of wraith.

Naru slowed, orbiting the monsters like a wolf on the hunt. His tail periodically thrashed against the ground, seeming to mirror the prince's agitation she felt through the bond. Immobilized in their bindings, the wraith snarled and flashed their fangs.

Serenna studied their crazed behavior with a frown—they were just as rabid as the monsters Vesryn had brought to the dungeons. Upon closer inspection, a cold sliver of dread seeped into her marrow. She noticed one of the wraith with matted, curly hair wore tattered leathers from Centarya.

CHAPTER 19

SERENNA

A quick trip to the dracovae stables with their feral prisoners had the wraith entrusted to the rangers. The warriors had modified a section of stalls into makeshift holding cells, closing the doors and slats leading to the hallway.

Flight Captain Zaeryn wove a shield around the walls to stifle the sounds of the snarling and thrashing. She jabbed at the prince, saying that it reminded her of when they'd locked *him* up. Serenna could only imagine why, but didn't have time to ask —or dwell on where that mindless wraith had stolen an academy uniform from.

After the whirlwind of activity at the stables, Vesryn portaled them back to his chambers. No sooner than Serenna stepped on the other side of the rift, he grabbed her.

She sucked in a breath against the unexpected shock of his mouth against hers, hot and demanding. Tongue sweeping past her teeth, a wildfire roared through the bond, incinerating her every sense and thought. The past few hours of hunting and retrieving the wraith flew out of her head—nothing else existed while the prince's lips were on hers.

"We started something last night," Vesryn nearly growled into her throat, snatching the base of her braid to angle her face further up to his. "And I want to finish it."

Toes curling in her boots, Serenna clutched the front of his leathers, yanking him closer. "No interruptions this time?" she breathlessly asked around the frenzied way their mouths met.

"I'm done waiting." Vesryn's teeth grazed her bottom lip. "I have obligations in the capital tonight," he said, nipping gently. "But I intend to have you first."

The desire woven into the prince's words sent a wave of heat flooding between Serenna's thighs. Strong hands bracketing her hips, Vesryn's fingers tightened as he reclaimed her mouth, the pressure of his lips hazing her mind. Before Serenna had time to conjure a coherent response, he steered her through his sitting room.

Laced with ferocious want, their kiss turned frantic, searing her from the inside out. Each of Serenna's inhales became sharper, more urgent as she dragged in serrated breaths against the prince's mouth. Heart fluttering, she walked backward as Vesryn herded her to his sleeping chambers.

Serenna's pulse jolted when her back collided with a solid surface. Her eyes flew open as the prince broke their kiss. She reoriented herself—still in Vesryn's sitting room, pressed against the balcony door. His hand snaked around her waist, unlatching the sliding glass behind her.

Slightly puzzled about the location, Serenna swallowed, her head obviously not keeping pace with her body. Looking up at the prince, she saw the question in his eyes, felt his hunger devouring her through the bond.

"Don't stop," she breathed, breaking through the wordless chaos of her thoughts.

That was all the acknowledgement Vesryn required. Ripping the sliding door open, he steered Serenna out onto the patio.

A curtain of water roared from the portal opened above the

peak of the Spire. The flow cascaded past the balcony, captured by channels and pools below. Serenna's middle lurched from the height but settled back into place when the prince's mouth crashed back into hers.

His hands circled her waist, their tongues returning to dance in the space between their breaths. Fingers roving over Vesryn's leathers in return, Serenna cursed the concealing material, desperate for the touch of skin.

The fading sun splashed warmth over her already heated body, the breeze winding around the tower doing nothing to cool her off. Serenna's heart battered against the confines of her ribs, every beat pounding with a strange mix of nervousness and excitement.

The prince suddenly spun her around. Gasping in surprise, Serenna caught herself on the stone parapet, eyes flying open to the horizon.

Driving his hips into hers, Vesryn pinned her to the ledge. Demand fueling her desire, Serenna arched against him, their leathers too restricting as they slid together.

Chest pressing against her back, fingers locking around the front of her throat, Vesryn dragged his mouth up the curve of her neck to the point of her ear. Lashes fluttering, Serenna squirmed against the prince as his teasing lips swept back down to that sensitive spot where her shoulder dipped.

They were doing this. At the peak of the Spire. Overlooking campus. Serenna's head spun at the thought of them exposed at the top of the island, but was relieved that the waterfall and height obscured them from any potential observers.

Closing out the world hundreds of feet below, Serenna leaned into the prince, angling her neck to give better access to her throat. She shuddered when Vesryn's hands began mapping her body, skimming down to her curves, sliding across her stomach, drifting up to land on her chest.

A wildness reared its head as Serenna felt the swelling

outline of his arousal pressing into the base of her spine. Their leathers created a dreadful distance, taunting the needy ache throbbing between her thighs. Keenly aware that Vesryn was riveted on her reactions, Serenna silently begged for more, tugging on the bond.

The prince must've registered her near-frantic desire, because his hands roved lower, quickly unraveling the laces of her trousers. He was nothing but efficient. Before Serenna knew it, Vesryn had her leathers and undergarments shoved down to her ankles. Skin bared, curls of mist from the crashing waterfall beaded on her thighs.

Not wasting any time, the rustle of leather behind her signaled that the prince had freed himself in the same way. He prodded her legs apart with a knee. Core tightening from the silent command, Serenna opened for him, as far as the restricting uniform allowed.

Vesryn's breath was uneven and rough against her neck as he planted his boots next to hers. "That's it," he panted, wrapping his callused hands around her hips.

Wishing the prince would've sacrificed seconds to shed the rest of her clothing, Serenna nearly unlaced her bodice herself—until a deep groan reverberated from his throat.

Her priorities quickly rearranged when Vesryn slid the rigid length of his arousal between them. Serenna sucked in air through her teeth as their hot flesh merged, the unyielding hardness of him gliding along the slickness of her.

"Fuck," the prince growled, the word butchered along its journey from deep in his throat.

Rocking back and forth against her center, the tip of his length teasingly sank into exactly where she needed him. The tantalizing pressure he swirled around her entrance before retreating promised more.

Driven by a mirrored desire, Serenna rolled her hips with a whimper. A wordless demand. Like the prince, she wasn't interested in waiting and reached for him behind her back. Wrapping her fingers around his solid length drew out a satisfying shudder and a hiss against her neck.

Vesryn breathed a husky laugh. "I can feel how much you want me."

Senseless now, Serenna pumped him from root to tip, guiding him closer. She wasn't the only one gasping and trembling when she pushed herself on her toes to line him up.

The prince needed no further encouragement. One hand braced against her waist, digging in his fingers, he seized a fistful of her hair, arching her spine. His hips stroked forward, sliding into her a fraction. Serenna released a moan as the first inch of him stretched her in all the right ways. Still teasing. Still not enough.

She cried out in protest when Vesryn withdrew. He rubbed the length of his shaft against the seam of her body. Back and forth. Sliding a palm to her core, the pads of his fingertips circled that pulsing bundle of aching nerves.

Tightening his grip in her hair with the slightest sting prickling her scalp, Vesryn's voice was a rasp in her ear. "The stars made you for me."

Serenna's breath hitched as she writhed under his hand, smothered by the flames of passion scalding her through the bond. The prince's lips clamped around the point of her ear and Serenna grabbed the parapet before she collapsed, nearly undone.

Fingers strumming against her center, Vesryn delivered the pressure she needed, cresting her pleasure alarmingly fast. Indecision had Serenna snagged somewhere between seating herself fully on that length he was tormenting her with or greedily leaning forward to grind into his palm.

Mouth returning to her throat, the prince's arousal nudged her entrance again, the tip dragging through her drenched flesh before diving further. This time, he didn't hold back.

Vesryn rammed his hips into hers, claiming her with one savage thrust.

The blissful stretch had Serenna's head falling back into his chest when he released her hair. Her body melted around him, absorbing every offered inch.

Breath shuddering against Serenna's neck, the prince grunted as he plunged deeper, pinning her against the balcony's ledge until he buried himself to the hilt. For a few fleeting heartbeats, they both stilled, gasping for air.

Vesryn suddenly retreated and then snapped his hips forward, sheathing himself again with a vicious lunge. Catching herself on the parapet's ledge, Serenna's fingers splayed as she braced herself against the stone. Fractured whimpers escaped her as the prince set a demanding pace. He bucked, driving into her again and again, each brutal slap of their bodies coming together harder and faster than the last.

Vesryn's hand cinched against Serenna's hip, crushing her body further into his while the other continued to coil that sensitive spot between her thighs into a blissful knot. Heartbeat racing nearly to the point of detonating, her world faded into oblivion under his expert strokes.

Somehow, the prince plunged even deeper, dragging out a sound between a shriek and a moan from Serenna's throat. The noise only seemed to encourage his punishing rhythm, delivering blow after blow.

"Come with me," Vesryn growled in Serenna's ear, his hand continuing to build that knotted bliss between her thighs.

While sooner than expected, the order still made her core clench. The prince's fingers swirled and strummed, dragging out spine-tingling rapture. Knees trembling, Serenna ground herself against his palm, meeting every one of his erratic thrusts.

A collision of sensations exploded through the bond. The prince barreled over the edge, his arousal jerking and throbbing, spilling himself inside of her. Vesryn swore against her neck, delivering one last wicked stroke with a guttural groan.

Something about the prince finding his release crested Serenna over the final swells, losing control of her movements as she climbed the same peak. A tremor shuddered from her toes straight to her core as Vesryn's hand drove her body to the brink.

Serenna's inner walls fluttered, clamping down. Climax crashing over her, light streaked across her vision, sending her spiraling into a free fall. Despite the wind whirling around them, she couldn't catch enough air as she finished panting the prince's name.

Vesyrn's fingers found Serenna's face, tilting her head back toward him. Lips meeting hers, this time he delivered a softer kiss, long and slow. Heartbeat calming, she settled back down somewhere between the clouds and the Spire.

Serenna gasped against the prince's mouth, severing the kiss when he suddenly pulled out, the absence of him evoking a different kind of ache. Turning back to gaze across the island, she peeled her fingers away from the ledge.

I suppose there's no graceful way to do this. She clumsily hauled up her leathers, hearing the rustle of Vesryn doing the same. Thinking about how she was going to clean herself up, a nervousness began to root until the prince spoke behind her.

"You can help yourself to the bathing chambers."

Twisting around, Serenna met his satisfied smirk. The expected awkwardness from the moment vanished. "I can't say you're a poor host."

Vesryn grabbed the sides of her face, hauling her mouth back to his. "Oh, there's more to my hospitality that I have yet to show you." His lips swept over hers. "But that'll unfortunately have to wait for another day." His eyes darted into his apartments. "I am rather...late."

Hearing the dismissal, Serenna stiffened as he released her. *Well, he did say he has business in the capital even if this feels abrupt.*

Serenna tried to walk normally rather than shuffling to Vesryn's bathing chambers. Since the prince was in a rush to leave, she swiftly tidied herself up and rebraided her wind and passion-mussed hair.

Returning to the sitting room, she found Vesryn staring out of his balcony windows, hands clasped behind his back. The setting sun descended under the island's horizon, throwing splashes of reds and golds across his silver strands.

"Thank you," Serenna said, hurriedly adding, "For taking me flying today." Cheeks heating, she didn't draw attention to what they just did.

Vesryn turned toward her, one side of his mouth tugging up. "We'll make a ranger out of you yet."

Sensing the prince barricading his emotions from the bond to close himself off, Serenna froze. He absently thumbed his bottom lip, his focus seeming to drift.

Worried that something had shifted between them, an anxious feeling claimed Serenna's mind. Silently chiding herself, she shook out the tension in her shoulders. *He obviously enjoyed himself and must be preoccupied with his obligations tonight.*

"I'll…see you later," she said as the unusual silence constricted the air.

Vesryn straightened and gathered his power. "I can portal you to your rooms." Essence unfurled, wending around him in a rush.

"No need." Serenna said weakly, clearing her throat. "I'll head down to the mess hall. Dinner should start soon."

The prince simply nodded, his attention wandering back to the campus grounds. To assuage her mind, Serenna almost asked what was bothering him. Instead, she swallowed her concern and left his chambers. *I'm sure he needs to inform the council about the wraith prisoners and doesn't want me sharing in his fretting.*

Lost in thought and turning over the last few minutes, Serenna picked at every word. She wove her way through the corridors, heading to the stairs to begin her descent. An overwhelming haze of cloying perfume accosted her nose as she rounded a corner.

Serenna staggered in her tracks, nearly running straight into Ayla.

CHAPTER 20

SERENNA

"What are you doing up here?" Serenna blurted, the words slipping out as she skidded to a halt. She'd never observed anyone aside from the prince's staff and Jassyn at the top level of the Spire.

Ayla's manicured brows rose. "I don't need to explain my presence. But, if you must know..." she trailed off, flashing her teeth. "I'm expected."

Registering that her sister wasn't in uniform, Serenna's eyes popped. A silky emerald gown cinched her slim waist, clinging to her generous curves. Serenna's mouth went slack at the plunging neckline. The dress was more fitting for a night carousing around court than traipsing through the hallways of the Spire.

Jewels glittering with Essence garnished Ayla's creamy skin. Her striking, flame-colored hair somehow both contrasted and complemented her regal gown. Ruby locks coiled around a silver diadem studded with matching magic-infused gems. Ayla looked more magnificent than the gathered nobles that Serenna had seen at the start of the term—like she belonged among the aristocrats in Kyansari's courts.

Like their princess.

The thought plummeted her heart straight to the floor. A monstrous weight of despair settled on her chest as she processed Ayla's statement. *She's going to Vesryn's chambers.*

"Getting an eyeful?" Ayla sneered, the question snapping Serenna's attention back to her face. "I know this might be taxing for someone like you to imagine," she said, venom dripping from her words, "but believe it or not, some of us receive invitations to royal functions."

Their sire's eyes—the color of the sea that Serenna now despised sharing—impaled her like a glacial shard of ice. Ayla pointedly sniffed, her ruby lip curling as her gaze roved over Serenna's sleeved riding leathers.

"I see you're adopting the same disgusting habits as the prince and spending time around those flying beasts." Serenna flinched when Ayla reached out and swiped a finger across the shoulder of her uniform, like a disgruntled tavern owner inspecting the level of grime on the bar. "I thought I smelled that reptilian rank from five floors below. I have no intention of satisfying the prince's every depraved desire if he prefers riding his females like he does those creatures." Ayla crossed her arms, the motion nearly toppling the rest of her cleavage from her dress. "But I suppose someone of your standing is suited for tending to those perverted needs."

A sting of heat flushed the tips of Serenna's ears as Ayla so graphically described the activity she'd engaged in hardly minutes ago. Unsuccessfully masking her dismay, Serenna silently convinced herself that what was between her and the prince went beyond physical desires. *He told me what's between us is more than a bond.*

Ayla traced the delicate gems nuzzled against her chest. "I suppose our sire gave you the same advice about getting close to the royal line." She emitted a breathy laugh, adjusting the jewels.

"I have no qualms about sharing, so long as you remember that your place *isn't* in court."

Serenna couldn't say that the admission even felt like a threat. Ayla didn't so much as bat those excessively darkened lashes upon seeing her departing the prince's dwelling level. Serenna was well-informed of her place, considering Vesryn had escorted her to the dungeons instead of to a ball. Her nails dug into her palms as she swallowed her disgust. *I suppose his "obligations in the capital" include entertaining his betrothed.*

Serenna finally found her voice, unfurling her fingers before she broke any bones. "I have no intention of partaking in any *sharing* of the prince." She wished she didn't splutter like she was in the wrong, but the impact of jealousy collided with her disbelief.

"That doesn't surprise me." Ayla flicked an ironed curl away from her eyes. "From what I've gathered, your human upbringing interferes with embracing our culture." She picked at one of her lacquered nails. "A shame really, since all our sire drones on about is how you're squandering your bloodline's potential."

Serenna blinked, wondering if her sister knew about her shaman heritage. But she didn't have time to worry about it as Ayla relentlessly railed on.

"I'll suppose we'll be seeing more of each other up here." Ayla's slippered foot toed the purple runner, nose wrinkling as if the rug offended her. "Since you're not involved in Kyansari's inner circles, I'm sure you have yet to hear that the prince and I will be wed at the Winter Lunar Solstice. The king demands the stability of the Falkyn line by producing heirs for the realm— especially now with the prince star-bent on leading this silly war."

A ringing started to mute Serenna's ears as Ayla expectantly peered at her from under a curtain of lashes, unblinking like a viper poised to strike.

"It would be a shame, really, if the prince perished before we produced offspring. In fact"—Ayla tapped her painted lips—"after our dinner tonight, I plan to have him." She released a girlish giggle, lowering her voice conspiratorially. "Is he as thorough of a lover as everyone in the capital claims?"

Every sentence was a blow, every word a punch to Serenna's gut. Ayla patiently waited for her answer. As if Serenna had any hope of recovering from that verbal assault. *Vesryn warmed himself up with me so he could go all night with her. Is this his way of "handling" the engagement?* Serenna flushed further, the rushed moments on the balcony now aggressively ambushing her with regret.

Breaking Serenna's silence, Ayla's laugh chimed through the hallway. "Well, no matter." She dismissively waved. "I'll find out for myself." Ayla fussed with her gems again before glancing back at Serenna, her eyes widening with mock worry. "You know what?" She gasped. "While I'm thinking about it, we might not be able to produce heirs since I'm nearly a pureblood." Ayla closed the distance between them with a single step, crowding over Serenna with her height. She lifted Serenna's limp braid, turning over the mahogany plait in her palm, as if inspecting the darker *human* coloring. "Perhaps you'd like the honor of stepping in as a surrogate."

Serenna nearly released a bitter laugh, her inability to speak carrying the weight of a thousand unsaid words. Ayla acted as if the likelihood of Serenna conceiving was any greater than her own. She had to assume they both shared a similar cycle as the other elven-blooded—twice a year.

The reminder of Elashor's degrading expectations doused Serenna with ice, freezing a lump of anger in her throat. *Has my worth to the realm really been reduced to bearing spawn for Ayla? I refuse to live in her shadow.*

"Anyway, I must be going," Ayla said, glancing out through the arched windows. "I'll inquire with our sire if he'd like to consider you as a candidate to carry the prince's offspring if we're unable to reproduce—I figure you have enough human blood in your veins." Ayla slipped past her, escorted by her mantle of fragrances as she glided away. "Enjoy your night," she said, flashing a vicious grin over her shoulder. "I know I will."

Serenna stared after Ayla's swaying hips, incapable of processing their interaction. *Vesryn rushed me out of his chambers because she was on the way?* Serenna forgot how to breathe as hot, anguished tears welled in her eyes.

The joy from the most wonderful day dissipated faster than a plume of smoke. She knew better than to assume that happiness was anything more than a breeze—temporary and fleeting.

Serenna didn't remember descending the stairs of the Spire, the steps below her feet blurring. Her body gave an involuntary jerk when Vesryn's presence faded in the back of her mind, leaving campus.

Traveling to Kyansari.

With Ayla.

Serenna slapped a hand over her mouth, releasing a sob before she could smother it. Her heart shattered and eroded to dust. *How did I convince myself this engagement meant nothing?* The prince had danced around her questions. She'd only wanted to discuss what would happen between them with the bond—if he ever intended to fully accept the connection. She needed some type of reassurance—to know *something*.

As her world turned upside down, Serenna's thoughts sank like the descending sun as she entered the Spire's courtyard. She furiously scrubbed away the dampness on her cheeks. *I matter to him. Don't I? Or does everything between us simply exist because of this bond?*

The trees and buildings pressed in against her as she rushed across campus. Cutting through a lawn to avoid one of the patrols, Serenna fled to her residence hall, wishing that Velinya was around. *Maybe I'm taking everything too seriously.* It was obvious that she was still too attached to her human notions of relationships for the elven realm. Velinya would have advice. Her friend frequently entertained a handful of lovers with no broken hearts.

Serenna toyed with the idea of seeking Jassyn out. She could ask him to escort her to the capital's healing grounds. And *not* because she was hoping to run into the prince. *I only want to talk to my friend and see if she's okay.*

Entering her apartment, Serenna stopped in her tracks. The setting sun hooked on a prism on the table, scattering rainbows of light across the walls. With a scoff, she approached the Heart of Stars perched in a decorative box, a jewel on display.

That...that lout!

Serenna had completely forgotten that she'd mentioned to the prince weeks ago that she wanted to inspect the relic again —to see if she'd imagined the strange voice when she'd held it. Vesryn must've dropped off the Heart without her noticing when he retrieved her that morning. He'd *distracted* her enough by putting his mouth all over hers, so Serenna wasn't surprised that she hadn't noticed the container before they'd left.

Snatching the box, Serenna's hands trembled as she glared at the Heart, recalling the time she first met the prince. Vesryn had remembered her request, but it was ridiculous if he thought that she'd be pacified by jewels.

Unable to stop herself, Serenna pointed her awareness toward the east—where Vesryn was in Kyansari. Hurt flashed through her chest like a lightning strike. *I hope he chokes on his dinner.* Serenna slammed the lid shut as her limbs chafed with fury.

Blinking against the fading sun, she focused all of her attention on deciphering the prince's location. Frowning, she perceived a pull, like a fish dragging on a line. But from the west.

Did Vesryn portal somewhere else? The fainter silver cord

weighed on her perception—it never had before, not to any notable degree since the prince's presence was always glaringly bright when he was close. *I thought that thread between us would glow too if we ever accepted the bond, but I'm not sure I want to now.*

Serenna clenched her jaw, drawing the worst conclusions—recalling their visit to the Cerulean Basin where his seduction had led to her manifesting her force ability.

Did he take Ayla there?

A hot slice of jealousy shredded Serenna's chest. She wasn't resentful if Vesryn took Ayla to the waterfall—a place he'd shared with her. That wasn't the twisted feeling in her gut. That wasn't why a sharp breath of bitterness constricted her throat.

A weight of indecision ricocheted against Serenna's ribs, like the wings of a bird battering a cage. *I'll ask him what's going on.* That was the sensible thing to do—lay everything out in the open and avoid this tangled communication.

I'll ask him right now! Serenna squared her shoulders, deciding she'd dwell on it no longer. *I'll shake him until his teeth rattle out an answer!*

Angling her perception toward the twin silver threads, Serenna couldn't make sense of Vesryn's location. *He can't be in two places at once.*

Fingers clenching and unclenching around the box, Serenna paced the sitting room while her thoughts festered. *I shouldn't be spending this much time upset over a male who's making me doubt what's between us.* She yanked the bond's cords in irate frustration. *I deserve better than that.*

Fueled by a desperate need for answers, Serenna seized her power, intent on manifesting her portaling talent. *I'll use the bond to travel to Vesryn.* Reaching through their connection, she strained toward the nexus hovering between them.

Serenna weighed her options, her decision volleying between the east and the west. She couldn't open a portal if he was at the palace—the rift could slice a bystander in half.

Blowing out a breath, she sent her entire awareness toward the cord in the direction of the setting sun.

Diving into her power, Serenna's magic rushed to her like a raging tide. Essence whirled around the room. She ignored the nagging feeling that she might be doing something exceptionally foolish because a male was involved. But she refused to be strung along like some bonded pet.

Recalling a conversation about manifesting portaling with Velinya, Serenna sank into the emotions that she knew would be needed to drag her ability to the surface of her Well—trust and longing. She could snap herself into a talent if she tried. *I don't need the prince prying my magic out for me.*

Serenna tunneled into her Well, searching for her talent. *I'll trust the stars. And I'll trust myself too.* Closing her eyes, she released a frustrated huff, pouring every ounce of emotion into her power. *Fine, I'll use* longing *for the prince but only because I "long" to know what's going on.*

Letting herself drift, magic burst from Serenna. Not a sputter, but a roar, fountaining across the sitting room. Hauling herself away from tumbling into a spiraling pit of emotion, she cleared her mind to rebalance herself.

A rift split the air, opening a dark portal. Serenna gaped, shocked that she'd effortlessly called the talent on her own. *Of course the only time I'm motivated enough is when a male is involved.*

Serenna wasn't sure why she carried the decorative container Vesryn had left behind. It might as well be her own stupid heart in the box. She'd just throw it at his head if she didn't like what he had to say for himself.

Serenna lifted her chin, stalking through the gateway to confront the prince.

CHAPTER 21

SERENNA

Bustling out from the portal, Serenna strode into a wall of shadows. Her body went rigid as she lost control of her limbs to the mob of rending. The box she carried tumbled out of her numb fingers, bouncing to a stone floor. Expecting gravel underneath her boots, she briefly frowned at the silver veins threaded through the polished marble before glaring at the shadows.

Compounding frustration toward the prince had her grinding her teeth. *I portaled for the first time and he's still testing me?*

Serenna couldn't see anything beyond the midnight cloud, but she could perceive Vesryn's presence on the other side. Alarmed and irate.

Irritably drawing on her experience from *practicing* with the prince, Serenna whipped a gale of her own rending. She sliced through the shadowy shackles, incensed enough to summon the destructive talent without a second thought.

Regaining control of her body, Serenna stumbled through the dissipating magic, running into the longest table she'd ever seen. Her fingertips skidded against the grains of ironwood as she righted herself. Scattered papers, maps, and figurines—representing what she assumed were cities or armies—lay arranged before her.

Did I portal to the capital's war room? I thought I was going to the waterfall.

An echo of boots thudded behind her. A deep voice growled something she couldn't understand, sounding like a threat of distant thunder. *I'm sure I disturbed something Vesryn didn't want me to see.* Sensing his furious presence behind her, Serenna whirled to face him.

She met flaming eyes and flashing fangs.

With a shriek, Serenna stumbled backward, hips colliding into the table. Her heart pummeled the inside of her chest as she hauled on her magic, slamming a shield around herself.

Attempting to make sense of this dark-haired stranger who looked impossibly familiar, Serenna's mind whirred with questions. She stared at his half-wraith appearance, analyzing him while her lungs hauled in air.

"Who—who are you?" Serenna stammered, scanning for an escape, searching for the prince. *Vesryn must know him, right?*

Her eyes rolled wildly, taking in the foreign surroundings that could've been carved from a rocky cavern. Sharp golden weapons festooned the stone walls accompanied by flames flickering in strange, spiraled sconces lining the edge of the room. Empty fireplaces somehow emitted rushes of air, heating the space.

The entire wall at the head of the table was glass, curving halfway around the room. The view opened up to a jagged mountain range where the sun crawled below snowy, desolate peaks. Serenna's eyes darted across the frozen expanse, gaping at the unexpected landscape. *I portaled farther than I thought.*

"Where am I?" Serenna asked, her focus hesitantly returning to the elf-like wraith.

Judging from his spiked armor and the cunning look

burning in his eyes, Serenna assumed this male wasn't like the mindless creature the prince had unleashed on her in the dungeons. The seams of his black leathers cut edges even sharper than his jawline. His trousers, the dark color impossible to discern, shimmered with iridescence in the fading sun.

The male peered at her with the same calculating interest that Naru provided the innards of a rabbit. But Serenna sensed that she repulsed him instead, a cockroach to be crushed under his boot.

Her eyes widened, registering that she could perceive his revulsion. Breath hitching on the revelation, the peril of her situation locked every muscle in denial. Covering her mouth, Serenna stifled a wordless gasp, fully identifying him in her mind.

It wasn't Vesryn's presence that had drawn her here. It was this stranger's. The bond that distance must've dimmed, the silver cord now glaringly bright because of his proximity. *It's not possible.* Fear had Serenna refortifying her shield, the violet magic protectively flaring around her.

Flicking a wrist, shadows streaked out from the male's metal gauntlet, effortlessly slicing through her ward. Serenna's body seized, snared in another bind of rending.

The realization of the bond engulfed her in a mute panic, robbing her ability to launch any counter strike. Chest drumming with paralyzed horror, Serenna helplessly watched the elf-wraith approach her, the heavy steps of his boots ominously echoing against the stone.

The stranger's gaze dismissively passed over her before a pressure of force whipped the box she'd dropped into his palm. He flipped open the lid. Scarlet eyes reflecting torchlight thinned, veering to her before glancing back at the displayed Heart. He barked out a sudden laugh, the booming noise jarring Serenna's pulse.

When he rolled his shoulders, it sounded like each vertebrae in his spine cracked in half. Brows forming a severe ridge, his searing gaze riveted on her. "I see this stars-cursed bond proved useful after all."

He knows what's between us too. Struggling to drive air down her lungs, every fiber screamed at Serenna to flee from that intimidating stare.

Touching the relic, five colors sprang from the prism's peak, confirming the obvious fact that this male had Essence. He grunted, jerking his head at the Heart. "How did you come by this?"

Serenna's heart stuttered at his words as shadows continued to billow around her, shackling her in place.

"Speak!"

Her voice fled when she opened her mouth. A burst of Essence had Serenna's body flying toward his outstretched claw, propelled by a blast of force. Colliding with the metal of his gauntlet, he seized her neck like a vise. The grip bit into her skin as sharp canines flashed in front of her face.

"If I have to ask two fucking questions to retrieve one satisfactory answer," he snarled, "then this is going to rapidly deteriorate into an unpleasant experience for you."

A tremor rippled all the way from Serenna's head to her toes as she swallowed the scream coiling in her throat. "I don't see how this day can get any worse," she whimpered, her words hoarse around the fist constricting her air.

His crimson eyes flared like stoked flames, an outpour of his loathing assaulting her.

Serenna's vision blurred.

Agonizing fire blazed through her veins as rending scalded every nerve. Spine arching, Serenna released a strangled howl as the darkness threatened to incinerate her bones. Heart thrashing against her ribs, her limbs contorted, body twisting in excruciating and unnatural ways. Searing anguish raged, the all-consuming torment dragging her toward unconsciousness.

Released from the male's gauntlet but still constrained by the shadowy bindings, Serenna slumped, dazed and panting when the rampant contractions of her muscles finally stopped. Blood flooded her mouth from where she'd bitten her cheek. She stared unblinking at the floor, reclaiming her breath as the memory of pain retreated.

Her power was there, in the crypts of her mind. Waiting. Finally, Serenna's instincts roused. She snatched at her magic. Moments. She only needed moments to spin a portal to somewhere—anywhere—else.

Power erupting, Serenna blasted out a wave of rending from every pore. As if ignited by her outburst, the fires in the lamps flared, casting wavering shadows against the stone. Papers on the table shot in the air, the figurines on the map scattering. The explosion of power crashed around the room, rattling the sconces affixed to the walls.

Her magic bounced uselessly off of the male's shield.

Unfazed by Serenna fighting for her life, he stood with his arms crossed across his leathers, not appearing taxed at all. The arrogance was all too familiar as something about his angled features clawed at her mind.

Gritting her teeth, Serenna channeled her hate along the nexus lurking between them, the second silver cord in her Well connecting her to this…this…*abomination*. His presence soiled her mind, scum clinging to a stagnant pond.

Warring to break out of rending's hold, Serenna hurled shock waves of Essence at the male, her chest heaving from the effort. She threw her entire Well against him, hacking at the darkness constraining her.

His lip curled, shearing her magic with a slash of rending, affording her no more attention than one would a bothersome gnat. Serenna felt just as insignificant. Just as helpless. Recognizing her power was futile against his, she slowly let her shadows dissolve.

"Release me," Serenna demanded through clenched teeth with all the authority she could muster.

The male stepped forward, stooping to growl in her face. "It was *you* who opened a portal and breached *my* fortress." The words he released flayed her cheek with a repulsive heat. Steel edged the low tenor of his voice, promising more pain. "You have no right to make demands."

"I have every right!" Serenna shrieked, her voice shrill with despair. "You wraith brought war to *us*! For no reason!"

As soon as the statement left her mouth, realization clubbed her like a blow. *He must be able to portal.* This...wraith thing had sensed her presence and traveled to Centarya—that was the only explanation. He used the bond to cross the realms, just like she did. She was the reason the wraith were able to attack the academy—the reason so many had died.

It's all my fault. Heart sinking below her ribs, Serenna blinked back tears of guilt. *Have I really been so stupid not realizing I had another bond?*

"You elves—half-elves—whatever you scourge are, forced my hand with your military island." The male's gauntlet squealed as it snapped into a fist. "I can only imagine it will be a matter of time before your kind scours the lands for us. Destroying my people. Hunting us like animals."

Serenna's arms twitched against the restrictive shadows as she battled for her freedom. His words prompted a scathing remark, her chest constricting with a panicked storm. "We wouldn't even have a military academy if it wasn't for you monsters attacking Kyansari!"

The muscles in his jaw flexed as he gritted his fangs. "We have *never* attacked Kyansari."

"You're lying," Serenna seethed.

"Read the bond," he sarcastically taunted, sneering. "You'll find I'm not."

"I don't want to touch your filthy mind." Rage bubbled up in her throat. "Dissolve this connection and you'll never see me again."

"Oh, you're not returning to your elven kin." He straightened, cracking his neck.

The blood drained from Serenna's face. *He can't keep me here...*

"Now, I am going to ask a final time." His eyes burned with an unnatural glow. "Why do you have a Heart of Stars?"

His persistence regarding the relic left Serenna bewildered. Heartbeats stretched in the silence between them. To avoid being on the receiving end of rending again, her stubbornness fractured.

Serenna swallowed and quietly admitted, "It was given to me."

"And who so freely bestowed an Aelfyn artifact to a half-elf grunt?" The male's eyes pinned on her. "The *king?*"

Serenna lifted her chin. "Prince Vesr—"

With no warning, the male ripped off his gauntlet. He shoved a grotesquely clawed hand to her chest, sundering her words. Talons shredded her leathers, gouging into flesh, splitting into skin.

A scream ravaged Serenna's throat when pain like nothing she'd ever known detonated within her Well as he started flaying her power. Agony radiated from the depths of her body as he plucked, slashed, and unraveled the fibers of her magic. White-hot anguish thieved Serenna's sight as her mind caved in on itself, Essence threatening to rip her apart.

Something inside of her shattered and snapped.

Knees buckling, reality disintegrated into splinters as Serenna crashed to the ground. Like a wounded animal whose limb had been cleaved by a trap, she lay panting, unable to process the injury. Unable to comprehend the loss.

The male had taken something. Something that was *hers.*

Mind racing, Serenna frantically dove inward, assessing her power.

There was a hole. A gaping hole in her Well.

Portaling.

Her ability was gone. Serenna's heart careened in fear at the incomprehensible emptiness. Disbelieving, she looked up in horror. The male's concentration focused on a globe of white light hovering above his claw.

Devastated by a thousand warring thoughts, each one more terrifying than the last, Serenna's mind howled, processing that he'd somehow stolen her talent.

"NO!" she screamed as he shoved her ability into his chest. Through the bond, she sensed his exhilaration at the surge of power. "NO!" She stumbled to her feet.

Serenna shook loose hair out of her eyes. Black hair. Trembling, she held up her hands and nearly vomited. The impossible truth pulverized her, crashing into her like a boulder. She didn't have claws, but her fingers had elongated. Gruesomely so.

Her panicked voice rang around the chambers. "What did you do to me?"

With a snarl, he lunged and snatched her leathers. A cloud of rending reared behind him, spreading like dark wings. "Now you will know what it means to be wraith."

Serenna's vision went white when he started plundering the rest of her Well. Thoughts fragmenting, all she knew was pain. Her body convulsed through the endless wave of agony, sanity unraveling. Every nerve on fire, she screamed, calling out for help. For the prince. For Jassyn. For anyone to stop the butchering of her magic.

She distantly heard other voices in the chamber.

"Lykor!" a male yelled. Boots pounded into the room.

Sight blurring, Serenna blinked to see a golden-haired half-wraith dragging the claw away from her chest. He shoved back the male who was raiding her magic.

Blinking again, Serenna discovered she was curled on the ground, having collapsed at some point. She gasped for air as the waves of agony subsided.

"I've got your she-elf," a male voice said behind her.

Serenna flinched when a warm hand touched her shoulder. Gently lifting her under the arms, he hauled her to her feet.

Disoriented, Serenna staggered as a wave of dizziness rocked the ground beneath her boots. Regaining her balance, she went rigid upon seeing the hulking warrior—the only full wraith in the room—restraining her arm with a wicked claw. Torchlight glinting off of the shining rings pierced into his face only intensified his utterly barbaric look.

Eyes swiveling back across the chamber, Serenna watched the half-wraith clench the arms of the one who'd stripped portaling from her. He restrained the one he'd called Lykor, their boots scraping against the floor in a scuffle.

Sensing his frenzy to kill her for reasons she couldn't comprehend, Lykor's gaze was fastened on her. When Serenna instinctively angled her perception toward him, she met a void where she expected his presence to be. He'd gone wild casting out an explosion of Essence, shadows snaking up the walls.

Fear erupted, stealing Serenna's breath as some of that darkness streaked toward her. Forced to include the wraith gripping her arm, Serenna wrenched another shield into place. She channeled her entire strength into the ward, knowing that the rending battering her barrier would obliterate her to blood and bone.

The male wrestling with Lykor gritted his teeth, fangs elongating. "Aesar, now would be the time to take over."

A lance of shock nearly jolted Serenna's power out of her grasp. *What did he say?* Her gaze volleyed between everyone in the room as her confusion compounded.

Serenna's eyes locked for a fraction of a second with the wraith holding her arm. He appeared to be nervously spinning one of the rings in his brow, attention bouncing between her and the surrounding shield.

An icy chill suddenly trickled down Serenna's spine as she sensed a *shift* through the bond. Another entity taking over, a calm that was distinct from Lykor's rage, as different as the moons were from the sun. *He can't be Vesryn's brother. It's impossible.*

Rapidly blinking at the male holding him, Lykor's fangs retracted as the shadows receded. Chest heaving, he slumped, disheveled midnight hair slipping over his face. The elf-wraith helped steady him on his feet, brushing away the strands in front of his eyes.

Lykor trembled as he touched the male's cheek with a tenderness Serenna didn't expect these…beings to possess. His eyes traveled over to her, going round. Serenna sensed his startlement spinning through the bond. His attention whipped to the wraith restraining her. "Fenn, get her out of here. I can't —" he doubled over. The other male lowered Lykor to the ground as he jerked in a fit.

Serenna couldn't begin to guess what was unfolding, but she knew she needed to escape—flee to somewhere safe. If there was anywhere safe. But it wasn't going to be around Lykor, or whatever bedlam she'd foolishly wandered into.

How am I supposed to leave without portaling? She'd have to rely on the prince sensing her location to retrieve her.

Gathering Essence in a rush, Serenna dropped her shield and slammed her palm against the monstrous male holding her. A shock wave of force punched the wraith across the war room. She didn't wait to see if he crashed into the table or a wall. Eyes latching onto the double doors the warriors had entered from, Serenna sensed freedom and ran.

She almost made it.

A shadow unfolded in the entryway, materializing in front of her. Serenna collided with the leviathan's chest. Seizing her, the brute caught her before she fell on her back. As soon as Serenna tried to extricate herself out of his talons, cold metal snapped around her arm.

Essence fled.

A single golden manacle clamped around Serenna's wrist, tethering her magic. A renewed surge of terror at the defenselessness capsized her gut. Writhing against this Fenn creature's hold, Serenna shrieked, resorting to fighting with her fists and feet.

The warrior's claw tightened on her arm, holding her at a distance. "File my fangs," he yelped, dancing out of range of her flailing.

Dashing forward, Serenna snatched the hilt of a long knife at his belt, ripping the dagger out of its sheath. With all of her strength, she lunged with the weapon pointed at his ribs.

"That," the wraith growled, snagging her hand before the blow landed, "was uncalled for." He twisted her wrist, sending the blade clattering to the floor. "I'm not going to harm you."

"Says the red-eyed cretin who tethered me!" Serenna aimed an ineffective kick at his knee.

Fenn spun her around. Serenna's back slammed into his chest, arms pinned to her sides by his.

Knowing she couldn't fight a monster two feet taller than her without her magic, Serenna's focus scurried around the chamber, searching for something else she could use. The wall of windows overlooking the frozen expanse was her next best chance at freedom. She just needed to break out of this restrictive ogre's hold. *But how can I run away if he appears out of thin air?*

Lykor was still on the ground having some type of seizure while the other male hovered over him. Serenna didn't think anymore of it, furiously weighing her options. *I need to get out of here before Lykor steals the rest of my magic.* She'd take her chances jumping out of the window to the snow drifts below and braving the cold. *I'd rather die out there than be torn apart by these wraith.*

Panting out of her nose, reining in her fear, Serenna's mind tumbled over how to escape Fenn's grip. Her eyes latched onto the snow swirling outside the window, caught in a gusty draft. *I know I saw something in the wind when we were flying today even though I don't understand how.*

A second stretched as Serenna caught her breath, stilling in the warrior's hold. She contemplated if she could wield the extinct magic of her shaman ancestors. Without the presence of Essence, she could almost feel vibrations from the air rippling on the other side of the glass, waiting to be called. Like a dracovae finding a warm current to soar on, she cast out her perception.

Serenna's fingertips began to tingle as she reached out with her mind. Snow swirled faster and faster, whipping into a spiraling flurry.

The claws holding her tightened as the weather began to rage outside. "What are you doing, she-elf?" Fenn moved her arm, seeming to confirm that the tether was still touching her skin.

Serenna yanked the wind toward her through the window, bending it to her will.

Glass exploded in a spray of shards. A gale howled as a torrent of snow bombarded the room.

The broken slivers streaked at her like a thousand jagged arrows, propelled by the screaming wind. Serenna gasped, unable to assemble a shield without her magic. Unable to stop the shattered fragments racing toward her.

"*Wind* magics?" Fenn all but groaned behind her. "Stars, slay me."

The mountains in Serenna's vision swam out of view as the warrior whirled her around him. The motion wrenched her feet out from under her legs. Smashed to the ground, Serenna landed on her back, air bursting from her lungs. Before she could draw in a breath, the wraith dove on top of her in a tangle of limbs.

Flogged by strands of his black hair, Serenna's heart stopped as his fangs extended in front of her face. Her thoughts flashed back to the assault on Centarya, memories resurfacing of these creatures nearly ripping her to shreds. *He's going to tear out my throat!*

Fenn's arms wrapped above Serenna's head, body imprisoning hers like a cage. The hailstorm of glass collided into his spiked armor, leathers absorbing the force of the blow. The barrage of razor shards crashed into the floor, sounding like a thousand crystals breaking.

Fenn snarled, sucking in what sounded like a hiss of pain as eddies of snow and the broken window settled around them. His expelled breath strung together a curse of colorful words, uttering exactly what he thought of "she-elves."

Serenna's senses came flooding back a moment after the slap of wind subsided. *I summoned magic without Essence. With the elemental powers that Jassyn said ran through our bloodlines.*

A small mote of hope rose in Serenna's chest. If she could reach the open window, she could… *What? Jump? Run through the snow? To where?* She had no idea where she was and the prince wouldn't either now that she was tethered. Serenna's heart fell at the realization that she was stranded here.

Trapped under this mountain of a warrior's chest, Serenna drew in ragged breaths. She battled to fill her lungs beneath his smothering bulk, assailed by scents of cedar and the frigid air. Fenn's ember eyes burned into hers as the wind subsided, black blood welling from a slice on his cheek.

Serenna blinked, ripping her attention away from his unnerving stare. *Why did he protect me?* Before she untangled that thought, she thrashed wildly like a snake pinned by a spade. "Get off me!"

Fenn's lip curled around his fangs despite his eyes not matching the scorn as they swept over her, like he was *concerned*. Clambering off of her, broken glass slid from the back of his armor, clinking to the stone.

Pushing herself to sit on the floor, Serenna jumped as a boot thudded next to her hand. A bolt of terror shot down her spine, impaling her to the ground.

Lykor.

CHAPTER 22

LYKOR

Lykor burrowed his claw into the elf's armor, yanking her to her feet before dragging her through a portal. On the other side, the volcano's sunless depths swallowed the cavern's dim torchlight. He closed the rift before Kal or Fenn could follow.

As if provoked by the darkness, the elf went rabid, striking out with her limbs. The girl began to fight in earnest, like she wouldn't let him take her alive.

DRACOVAE'S TITS!

Lykor's vision pulsed while she screeched like a strangled bird, the shrill sound bouncing around the stone hallway. He would've used rending to restrain her, but Aesar had restricted his access to that ability.

Again.

Lykor swiped at their Well, attempting to snatch control of his shadows, but to no avail. He resorted to steering the girl ahead of him so that her flailing fists couldn't connect with his face.

I intervened before the coercion did any lasting harm, Aesar said. *You've already done enough damage by stealing her magic.*

YOUR INTERFERENCE WASN'T REQUIRED.

Allowing the elf access to portaling wasn't an option. Not after she knew of their location. Besides, her loss was their gain, but Aesar refused to recognize the benefits. Augmenting an ability they already possessed only strengthened that talent. With her added power, he'd be able to stretch his reach further across the horizon when the time came to portal jump across the Wastes.

But before Lykor could siphon the rest of her Well, the girl had called out for Vesryn, helplessly plunging him into the compulsive magic's nightmare.

You will give portaling back to her, Aesar fumed, irritably cramming a strand of silver hair behind a pointed ear.

Even if the visual of Vesryn in his skull didn't trigger the destructive magic, Lykor still flinched before his irritation began to boil. The increased frequency of the other meddling presence had come with unfortunate side effects.

Instead of being content with simply nagging as a disembodied voice, Aesar had begun appearing in their mind more frequently in his original elf form. He'd become more of a problem—especially now, with this mention of *Vesryn* piquing his interest.

Between the screaming girl flailing in his grip and Aesar battling to seize control of their body, Lykor's frustration was ready to combust. He savagely rammed Aesar back into a crevice, unable to concentrate on fighting them both.

The elf stopped moving her feet, refusing to cooperate. Overriding her pathetic resistance, Lykor dragged her down the stone staircase leading to the dungeons. He briefly considered launching her to the next landing simply out of spite. But any broken bones from the fall would only inconvenience him if he decided to untether her. Not that he planned on letting her have access to his defenseless mind through the accursed bond.

When they reached the bottom level, Lykor towed the

thrashing girl through the cell-lined hallway and into the interrogation room. She stilled under his claw—finally shutting up—as her eyes orbited around the chamber. Flames from the pronged torches glinted off of the instruments of torture. The veins of gold scrawled into the stone walls and ceiling reflected a gleaming, mirrored light.

What are you doing with her? Aesar demanded. Within the shared space of their mind, Aesar recreated his memory of the palace library, appearing in the vaulted atrium.

Lykor ground his fangs at the interfering reemergence and the alarmingly vivid surroundings that Aesar had constructed—a testament to his increasing strength. It was just one fucking thing after another today.

Lykor released the girl's arm. Taking advantage of the freedom, she bolted to the opposite end of the chamber before tearing at the golden shackle clamped around her wrist. The tether had been quick thinking on Fenn's part. Nearly noteworthy.

Before Aesar could nag at him again, Lykor erupted. *WOULD YOU GIVE ME A SCORCHING MINUTE TO GET ANSWERS ABOUT THE HEART? THAT'S WHAT YOU AND KAL WANTED ME TO DO. STARS, I WON'T HARM YOUR BROTHER'S PLAYTHING. THOUGH, CONSIDERING YOUR MEMORIES, I DOUBT HE'D NOTICE IF HE'S MISSING ONE.*

Aesar bristled, shoving his hands into his pockets. In their mind, he paced in front of the expansive windows overlooking the capital. Waiting.

Hauling his attention back to the dungeon, Lykor's ears perked at a whistling, like wind howling around a crag. He frowned, turning to face the noise emanating from the hallway.

Lykor staggered as something bashed him over the head, blotching his sight. He shook the stunned feeling out of his skull before whipping his eyes to the elf, his mind reeling to catch up.

Her mouth was slack for a moment before her face twisted

into a glare. The girl stretched out a hand, forming a fist. The flame from a torch streaked toward him like a fiery arrow. Instinctively, Lykor threw an arm up to protect his face, realizing a moment too late that he should've used a shield. Pain ignited in his palm.

WHAT THE FUCK? Lykor stared at his claw, angry and blistered. Bubbled and burned.

He bared his fangs at the elf, eyes pinning on the tether to confirm that it was still latched to her wrist. Ignoring him, she dashed to the wall of hanging, gold-plated weapons.

Lykor heard chuckling. He tunneled inward to confront that bane in his skull, materializing in their mindspace. Aesar was in his library, doubled over, laughing at *him*.

WHAT? Lykor snarled, keeping half of his attention on the girl, who was jumping to reach a golden mace. She couldn't lift that one anyway.

So Kal's sire curated those human shaman lines with elven blood after all. Aesar wiped at a stray tear, eyes shining with mirth. *What are the odds that we share a bond with one of them?* He flapped a hand and burst into another cackling fit, plopping down onto a reading couch.

YES, FUCKING HILARIOUS. Lykor lingered at the threshold of Aesar's atrium, crossing his arms. *WHAT'S YOUR POINT?*

Elbows perched on his knees, Aesar leaned forward. *What if all of those half-elves have elemental power? That striking male you're obsessed with could too.*

I AM NOT OBSESSED. Aesar's unexpected jab had Lykor's rebuttal more defensive than he'd intended.

Redirecting his thoughts away from that amber-eyed elf, Lykor cycled through the possibilities of having elemental power at his disposal, doubting that he could siphon those powers from the girl and use them himself. Not that Aesar would allow him to attempt it without a fight.

Lykor voiced his conclusion. *SHE COULD USE THAT MAGIC FOR US TO AID IN CROSSING THE WASTES.*

Aesar's amusement faded. *The king has more of a head start than we anticipated if he's already resurrected shaman power.* He stared at the sofa's armrest, tracing a seam. *I wouldn't be surprised if he intends to control the abilities of these half-elves or those with shaman blood. My guess is that he'll attempt to subdue the Maelstrom and brave the sea to reach the Aelfyn homeland.*

Lykor scoffed. *THAT'S ABSURD.*

She might know something. Aesar glanced at him, thumbing his chin. *We have no idea what she could be capable of but you're lucky she appears just as startled as we are by those powers.*

Lykor studied the girl as she finally gave up on reaching for a weapon. His conversation with Aesar occurred in heartbeats while she glowered at him from across the room.

LET ME GUESS. YOU WANT TO BE THE ONE TALKING TO HER?

I could get more answers than you and *not terrify her at the same time.* Aesar folded his arms, kicking an ankle over a knee. *I don't know if the stars finally decided to balance the scales, but we could use the help of her elemental magic. And for the record, I don't agree with keeping her hostage.*

Lykor dug his fists into his eyes, a bone-deep weariness clinging to his marrow. *WOULD YOU LIKE TO RISK HER INFORMING THE ELVES OF OUR LOCATION?*

Fine, Aesar conceded, pursing his lips. *If she's staying, then maybe you can bring yourself to be* civil *and rectify this situation.* Aesar pointed an accusatory finger at him. *How about you start by healing where you sank your talons into her flesh?*

I'M NOT A SAVANT LIKE YOU, Lykor fired back. *I DON'T KNOW HOW TO MEND.*

Stop being such a prick, Aesar reprimanded, his tone withering. *Use my knowledge. You have no qualms about helping yourself to my head with everything else.*

Muttering to himself, Lykor summoned Essence. He sifted through Aesar's mind, curling mending light around his palm. He flung the magic at the girl.

Red threads sailed across the chamber, twisting together like an array of comets. Flinching, the elf stumbled away and gasped when the scarlet tangle collided with her chest, stitching the gashes left by his claw.

So refined. Aesar rolled his eyes. Lykor was surprised that he didn't lose them on their journey into the back of his skull. *Now, try asking her name.*

Closing the distance, Lykor stalked up to the girl and barked, "What's your name, you shaman twat?"

Aesar slumped into the couch, throwing his head back with a frustrated sigh.

The girl's eyes went wide before she scowled, cerulean irises cold enough to frost the room.

ANY OTHER CLEVER SUGGESTIONS?

Don't mind me. Aesar arched his brow. *I'm content with watching you screw this up.* He flapped his hand. *I'll be here when you're ready for me to intervene.*

The girl tilted her chin, folding her arms. "I don't know anything about the Heart if you're going to ask again. Prince Vesr—"

Lykor warped the few remaining feet in front of her. She shrieked, scrambling back to hit the wall before she could finish that damning word. He wrapped his fingers around her mouth and growled through his teeth. "Don't say it."

Lykor yanked his hand away when she bit him. "Don't say his name, you shaman spawn." He seized her leathers, shaking her instead of wringing her neck like he would've preferred. "Do you want to fucking die?"

The girl's nostrils flared, her defiance obviously coalescing. "You're going to kill me anyway, so what does the timing matter?"

"One way or another, you're telling me everything you know about the Heart. It's your choice on how much you'd like to endure first." She shrank back when Lykor elongated his fangs.

Stop scaring her. Aesar scolded, rising to resume his pacing across the library.

"Answer me or I'll start peeling layers off your eyeballs with rending." A bluff since Aesar still had that portion of their Well locked away. But the elf didn't know that.

Do you have to be so needlessly graphic?

Lykor sensed Aesar poised to spring, undoubtedly ready to throw his full strength against him and battle for control if Lykor went any further than intimidation.

Regardless, Lykor flared Essence. The unformed magic glittered like the gold in the stones, billowing around the chamber. The elf stiffened, plastering herself against the wall before her eyes darted to the torches.

Lykor flashed his canines. "Try it," he taunted, fists tightening against her leathers. "I'll play with your fire."

"The Heart spoke to me," she said quickly, apparently thinking better of any more rebellion.

The way she claimed something so asinine dragged an incredulous laugh out of Lykor's throat. She yanked her shredded armor straight when he released her.

"What did the Heart say, then?" Lykor sarcastically mocked. He placated Aesar by releasing his magic before that meddler got any ideas about wrestling their entire Well away. "And don't bother wasting your breath if you're going to say something even more ridiculous."

She faltered, teeth dragging over her lip. "I—I don't remember."

Lykor snorted. "How convenient."

"I'm not lying." The elf straightened, glaring up at him with those unnerving eyes. "Let me hold the relic without this tether and I'll prove it to you."

A wave of uncertainty had Lykor flashing his attention to Aesar before he thought better of seeking his advice. *THIS COULD BE HER ATTEMPT AT MANIPULATING ME INTO TAKING OFF THAT MANACLE.*

Aesar shrugged, apparently not seeing any harm. Obviously, he was more trusting since she had some type of association with his twin. *She doesn't seem to know any more than we do about the Hearts' role in shackling the dragons.*

Cracking the aggravation out of his neck, Lykor entertained the notion. The girl's claim was too bizarre to be a jest. If she was foolish enough to summon her power, he'd finish ripping the talents from her Well and rid himself of this bond's affliction.

Lykor drew out his key and the Heart of Stars from his trouser pocket. He extended the gleaming crystal, dropping the relic into her palms. Seizing her wrist, he unlocked the shackle, letting the metal clatter to the floor.

Unable to barricade from the bond, Lykor braced himself as her awareness flooded into his. The connection's blazing silver cord circled the surface of his Well—threatening like a noose.

Gritting his fangs, Lykor exhaled through his nose before residual dread strangled him. He shoved down memories of the king hacking away the natural defenses of his mind, hoping the elf was too oblivious to take advantage of his vulnerability. Lykor readied himself to react if she ignited her magic.

Frowning, the elf studied the artifact glowing with her talents. Lykor almost thought she wasn't going to speak until she went rigid, her attention fixed on the Heart. The girl's words suddenly flowed out in a rush.

Greetings, young draka, hear our plight,
New hatchlings from earth and starlight.

From distant galaxies did the whelps arrive,

They stole our magic and left us deprived.

They used five Hearts to bind our power in chains:
Earth, Fire, Lightning, Wind, and Rain.

The balance of earth, it must be restored,
The Hearts must be returned to where they were forged.

But the Hearts were hidden by the thieving hands,
The cunning ones from otherworldly lands.

Bring us the Hearts so we can restore,
The harmony as we had before the war.

Young draka, heed our call,
For this balance of nature affects us all.

With a shuddering breath, she snapped out of the trance, meeting his gaze. Silence filled the chamber.

Confusion, then realization, punched through Lykor as he and Aesar processed the spewed words. He glanced inward to see Aesar standing motionless, framed by Kyansari's glass spires.

The dragons are still alive, Aesar said, shaking his head in disbelief. *Or at least an echo of their memory persists.*

Lykor was more concerned about what was in front of them than the speculation about those beasts. *IF THERE ARE ONLY FIVE HEARTS, WHY THE FUCK WOULD GALAERYN LET ONE OUT OF HIS SIGHT?*

Aesar ran his fingers through his silvery hair, talking to himself before including Lykor in his musings. *Maybe she can help locate the Heart within the keep—if one's here.* Lykor sensed him diving into old memories, sifting through any forgotten information that would further explain those uttered words.

Lykor snatched the Heart from the girl and tucked it away.

Snagging the manacle from the floor, he clasped it back around her wrist before she could vocalize a protest. *IF WE COLLECT MORE RELICS, DO YOU AGREE WITH SEARCHING FOR THE DRAGONS ACROSS THE WASTES?*

I see no other option. Aesar flicked his fingers, summoning a tome to his hand. *Assuming the king doesn't already possess all of the Hearts, we have to try locating more before we run out of time. We at least have one to return to the dragons.* Aesar tucked the book under his arm before drawing himself to his full height—a show of his stubbornness fossilizing. *Anyway, about the girl. You're not keeping her in the dungeons.*

Lykor rubbed his forehead. That was exactly what he'd intended. *THEN WHAT DO I DO WITH HER?*

A muscle twitched in Aesar's cheek. *You turned this into a mess and it didn't have to be.* He spun on a heel, retreating deeper into the library. *Clean it up.*

LIKE IT'S MY FAULT SHE'S HERE, Lykor grumbled.

Aesar's words were clipped. *Figure it out. I'm going to think.* He fabricated a door to stars knew where and disappeared, slamming it behind him.

Lykor released a breath. Before he could run through his options, the ground beneath his boots began quaking, like a flight of dracovae charged nearby.

"What are you doing now?" Lykor demanded, ready to shake the elf into submission. Though he had no idea how to stifle elemental power beyond clubbing her over the head.

She stumbled, losing her balance as the chamber rattled and rumbled. "This isn't me!" Her eyes widened as the thundering became more violent.

Fissures raced across the ceiling, dumping rocky debris in a hailstorm of dust and pebbles. Stones from the walls fractured and crashed around them, raining down rubble. Lykor fought to keep his footing while the earth shuddered.

As the prison caved in, Aesar dashed back into his library

mindspace, assessing through their eyes. Reacting, Aesar shoved his awareness fully into their body, like how he would when they brawled for control. An eerie tingle prickled under Lykor's skin, his limbs going numb as Aesar rooted himself into place.

There wasn't a second to think, much less have an endless debate about what they should do. It was either be crushed to death by the volcano or allow Aesar to take over.

For the first time, Lykor willingly let go.

He relinquished his influence without a fight, permitting Aesar unfettered access to their body's motions and their Well. Aesar had always been quick with fabricating shields—a skill that Lykor had never bothered with. Violet light spilled from their fingertips as the chamber crumbled around them.

But even Aesar was too slow.

Something heavy struck their head. The world tilted, pitching to black.

CHAPTER 23

JASSYN

"Wait!" Jassyn yelled as the heels of Vesryn's frayed boots disappeared in a frantic sprint through a portal.

The prince had appeared in Jassyn's chambers earlier that evening, raving about Serenna vanishing through the bond while he was in the capital. It was all Jassyn could do to pry any coherent words out of his cousin.

While Vesryn had paced furiously enough to score trenches in the rugs, Jassyn had eventually pieced together that Serenna must be tethered. The prince had claimed that the bond had winked out instead of shattering as it would've in her death.

A few moments ago, her presence had briefly flashed in Vesryn's mind. The prince snarled something about her disappearing again before he was able to pinpoint her location. By the time Jassyn blinked, Vesryn had slashed open a rift and vanished.

Having no idea what to expect on the other side of the gateway, Jassyn braced himself and dashed after his cousin. He could only hope that Vesryn wasn't transporting them somewhere as perilous as he had with Magister Thalaesyn the night before.

Frigid wind blasted Jassyn on the other side of the portal. He inhaled a shocked breath, his boots churning through snow. The biting air crystallized in his lungs, threatening to freeze him from the inside out. Pursuing the prince, Jassyn tucked his arms against his body. He struggled and lurched, wading through the knee-high drifts.

They were deep in a valley's cradle, surrounded by a mountain range. Jagged, snowcapped peaks stretched up to the canopy of stars, the pinpricks of light as cold as the surrounding tundra. Glinting off the barren landscape, the gibbous moons and spiraling galaxies hovered over the endless white expanse.

Over the blustery gusts, Jassyn called out to his cousin's back, "Vesryn, there's nothing here!"

The prince's breath plumed as he carved a path, blasting away snowy fountains with punches of force. "I need to find her!" he shouted over his shoulder, the sound nearly swept away by the howling wind.

Jassyn wiped away tears that the icy wind ripped from his eyes. He studied the barren landscape, blood chilling along with his limbs. The colorless canvas unfolded in every direction with no end in sight. Attempting to determine how Serenna could be in such a desolate wasteland, Jassyn's thoughts whirled like flakes of snow, but fell short of any explanation.

"We need to go back to Centarya and *plan*, Vesryn." Jassyn trudged after the prince, hindered by the snowy banks. He fought to keep the rising trepidation out of his voice. "You said you didn't sense Serenna's exact location." Curling his arms around his middle, Jassyn shivered, somehow still dozens of paces behind. "You won't find her if you're dead. Stars, we don't even have cloaks!"

Vesryn collapsed to his knees, his anguished words echoing across the valley. "I'm not leaving her here!"

Jassyn halted in place when a pulse of Essence flared from his cousin. *What is he doing now?* Slamming his fists to the snow, Vesryn released a bellow of rage. An ocean of magic exploded from the prince, bursting like a dying star.

The world quaked. A surge of force cracked along the ground, fractures splitting across the ice. Jassyn stumbled as the earth shifted beneath his feet. Snow tumbled down from the surrounding mountain peaks, triggering avalanches across the frozen valley. Straight toward them.

Jassyn yelled for the prince to stop, but the rumbling mountains drowned out his voice. Fear petrified his spine, the frosty air stabbing his lungs as he gasped for a breath that didn't come.

Face now covered with his palms, Vesryn seemed lost to despair as his magic pummeled the land. Essence erupted around him in shimmering waves, knocking the frigid landscape loose. The power flooding from the prince discharged like a vengeful geyser, shaking the foundations of the world.

A freezing landslide rolled down the summits. Horror twisted through Jassyn's gut. If Vesryn didn't open another portal for them to flee, the snow would engulf them within moments.

Jassyn started sprinting. He wouldn't reach his cousin before the tumbling avalanche buried them in a glacial grave. Clutching his magic, Jassyn flared a shield with scant confidence that the ward could withstand a mountain's worth of snow.

Scouring his mind for any way to prevent their rapidly approaching doom, Jassyn recalled the shaman power he'd harnessed the night before. The prince had pressured him to channel the lightning from the clouds. At Vesryn's incessant urging, Jassyn had funneled the sparks from the sky over and over until the proximity of the Maelstrom had splintered his nerves. Hardly possessing a shred of control over the elemental magic, Jassyn had accidentally blasted the prince when his patience snapped.

Shoving away his doubts that his brief practice wouldn't help him now, Jassyn focused on the torrent of snow surging at them. Halting ten paces away from his cousin, Jassyn's heartbeat thundered in his ears, a drum counting down the seconds to their imminent burial.

Snow is water and water is an element—I can do this. At least, that's what he told himself as he decided to unravel his shield, throwing all his strength toward that ancient power. They were dead if he couldn't halt the landslide since Vesryn didn't appear to be in any rational state of thinking to leave. *Stars, this had better work.*

Jassyn branched out his perception, allowing his mind to stray from the familiar embrace of Essence. He grasped at the foreign magic stirring in response. Fingers tingling, a rush of energy ignited in his veins, yanking the world into focus.

The tumbling snow burst into light. Striking out with something unseen—something from the earth—Jassyn shot his arms out like he could physically push back the toppling drifts. Body tensing, legs locking, Jassyn battled an invisible resistance, a colossal heaviness threatening to crush him.

A pocket of space hollowed out, encasing him and the prince. The icy deluge slammed into his control, suspended in the air. Knocked off balance from the impact, Jassyn staggered, sinking into the frosty powder. The remaining snow he hadn't snagged smashed to the ground around them.

With a savage heave against their tomb, he shoved the avalanche away with the sheer force of his will. The snow drift soared through the sky, crashing in the distance.

Jassyn took gulping breaths, bracing his hands on his thighs as he severed his connection to the earth. He brushed snowflakes from his hair and lashes and then flinched. Vesryn's expulsion of power continued to thunder through his chest.

Jassyn swore, numb fingers fumbling as he ripped out a knife from the hidden seams in his armor. *He's really not going to like this.* With the weight of his body, Jassyn whipped the golden blade at Vesryn's back. Screaming through the air, flipping end over end, the dagger impaled his cousin's shoulder.

Vesryn toppled forward, catching himself on his hands, magic snuffed out. He launched to his feet, rounding on Jassyn with rage in his eyes, as if ready to take his fury out on him. Not bothering to remove the lodged weapon, the prince charged across the snow like a rampaging bull.

Jassyn frantically fabricated a shield in his cousin's path. Vesryn crashed into the ward, staggering a few steps back. Baring his teeth, the prince pivoted to skirt around the barrier. Flicking his wrist, Jassyn kenneled him in completely with violet walls. Vesryn clawed over his shoulder to reach the knife while Jassyn stalked up to him.

Snatching another blade from his leathers, Jassyn dropped a portion of the shield, entering the magical cage to confront the prince. Vesryn lunged for him. Jassyn instinctively punched something at his cousin's chest—a wall of air.

The prince stumbled, grunting as the hilt protruding from his shoulder collided with the ward behind him. Jassyn shoved his dagger against Vesryn's throat, the action now practiced and precise. Just to make a point, Jassyn seized his cousin's hair, yanking his head back.

"Stars, are you even thinking?" Jassyn hissed through his chattering teeth, hoping his cousin wouldn't decide to disarm him by breaking his wrist.

He increased the blade's pressure when Vesryn tensed under his fingers, likely plotting to spring. Chest heaving, the prince's skin split around the knife with every breath.

"Serenna is somewhere in these mountains." Jassyn tightened his fist in Vesryn's hair, giving his cousin a shake to rattle some sense back into his skull. "What if you brought one down on her head? You nearly killed us!" The prince's nostrils flared, but Jassyn didn't relent. "You sensed her again. That means she's alive—that's all that matters."

Vesryn's jaw flexed as he panted out of his nose.

A wave of irritation surged through Jassyn from his cousin constantly shoving him to the brink of his patience. He preferred logic and thoughtful discussion, but Vesryn continually forced him to lash out with violence. The prince would only see reason if conquered by aggression. Spending more time in his cousin's company had only made that obvious.

"You are going to take us back," Jassyn said, driving the dagger deeper into Vesryn's throat, fighting his cousin in a battle of wills. The knife trembled against the prince's neck as Jassyn's limbs succumbed to the cold. "Then we can *calmly* discuss what to do next."

Vesryn blinked, the manic fury receding from his eyes. Shoulders slumping in defeat, he hung his head, catching his breath. "I'll need more Essense first to form another gateway," he mumbled. "I doubt I'll be able to regenerate at the moment."

"If you try anything but portaling, I won't hesitate to stab you again," Jassyn gritted out. "Is that clear?"

When Vesryn finally nodded, Jassyn relaxed. Reaching behind the prince, he ripped out the lodged knife and healed the wound. Gripping his daggers in one fist, Jassyn portioned out the barest sliver of power and plunged the magic into his cousin's chest.

Extending a hand, Vesryn opened a gateway and stumbled through. Jassyn followed in time to see the prince igniting globes of illumination in the chambers before collapsing onto a couch in Jassyn's sitting room. Releasing his power, Vesryn gouged his hands through his hair and stared despondently at the floor.

Jassyn sighed, lacking the energy to prevent the blood on Vesryn's leathers from staining his furniture. Since the prince seemed momentarily subdued, he darted into the bathing chambers and tossed the blades into the sink to clean later.

Bracing himself against the porcelain, Jassyn took a moment to compose himself from the unexpected flurry of events. Breathing in through his nose and out through his mouth. Fingers tightening against the polished ceramic, he steeled himself to divulge what he'd withheld since the attack, unsure what reaction he'd evoke from his cousin. *Why did I keep this to myself for so long?* If that elven wraith was somehow responsible for the abductions in the capital and had a hand in Serenna's disappearance...the prince needed to know.

Straightening his leathers, Jassyn grabbed two blankets from a closet before returning to the sitting room. He aimed his thoughts toward the logical conclusion of where the prince had portaled them.

Even though he already assumed the answer, Jassyn initiated what he hoped would be an easy conversation. "That was the Hibernal Wastes, wasn't it?"

Vesryn nodded. "It's the furthest on the western front that I've flown on Naru. I didn't have enough time to detect Serenna's location to portal us any closer." The prince banged the back of his head against the couch, staring at the ceiling. "I don't know why she would be so far away. Or how. There are no settlements anywhere close."

"What if there are?" Jassyn asked, tossing Vesryn a blanket. The prince's brow pinched as Jassyn settled beside him on the sofa, cocooning himself in the other. "The Wastes are the only place your rangers haven't searched for the wraith." Jassyn fortified himself for the admission, his body wracked with shivers. "There's something you need to know." He paused, twisting the fabric beneath his fingers, working up his courage. "There was an elf-like wraith who used Essence during the attack. He—"

Vesryn threw off the blanket and shot up from his slouched position. "*What?*"

Jassyn swallowed, dragging his hand through his curls. Avoiding the prince's demanding stare, he found the rug more interesting to focus on. "I saw that elven wraith portal—he was probably the one who transported their army. But I don't have any guesses on how he traveled to campus in the first place."

"And you're telling me this *now?*" Vesryn snarled. He stood, restlessly pacing a line into the rug, muttering to himself. "I'd assumed an elf was working with the wraith, but that didn't add up." He stopped in his tracks. "What do you mean an elven wraith?"

Gripped by guilt, Jassyn cleared his throat. "I'm not sure how it's possible, but there's more."

Vesryn's fingers twitched. "What else?" he grated out.

"That wraith. He…" Jassyn's voice faltered, a residual chill tingling down his arms. "He was compelled."

Vesryn's jaw went slack. The implications of Jassyn's knowledge caught up to the prince a moment later. "You were close enough to tell?" His eyes widened before narrowing to slits. "You *assessed* him?"

"I—I saved him." Jassyn pulled the blanket tighter around his neck, shame weighing on his shoulders. "I didn't realize the warrior was a wraith. I thought he was an elven-blooded before I saw his eyes and fangs." Jassyn's knees trembled from finally voicing the admission. "I couldn't kill him. But he didn't kill me either—he could have, but he just…left."

Vesryn scoffed, folding his arms. Poised to reprimand. "Your failure to end that wraith puts us at risk." A muscle rippled in his jaw. "What if he returns with that army?"

Jassyn averted his gaze, the accusation landing hard enough to have regret blurring his sight. If he had to do it again, Jassyn still didn't think he'd have the strength to kill. *If Serenna is somehow with that wraith, I hope she's not paying the price for my weakness.*

Vesryn resumed stalking back and forth across the sitting

room. "Do you think that wraith returned this evening and abducted recruits without our knowledge? Like how they raid the capital?" He waved hand in the air. "Relay a message to Nelya and your ring of magus to see if anyone else is missing." The prince halted in his tracks, yanking at the stitching in his rapidly fraying dragon sigil. "Serenna and I captured three wraith today. But the mindless ones. Do you think it's possible those beasts are compelled too?"

Jassyn hesitantly nodded.

Apparently through with the conversation, Vesryn stalked out of Jassyn's sitting room, tearing open the door to the hallway. "I have more questions and you're coming with me to extract the answers from Thalaesyn," he said over his shoulder disappearing down the corridor.

Preparing for another battle with the prince, Jassyn dragged a hand over his face. It was bound to be a long night.

CHAPTER 24

SERENNA

Ripped back into consciousness, Serenna sucked in a startled breath. She hacked on dust and then swallowed, throat raw from her previous screaming.

With a groan, she rolled over onto her back, inventorying her injuries from the fallen rocks. Gingerly feeling the throbbing lump on the side of her head, nothing seemed battered worse than her pounding skull.

Pained tears blurred the edge of her vision as she blinked up at a sheen of violet. Rubbing some life back into her eyes, and then regretting the action when dirt scraped into her skin, Serenna registered a crystalline lattice restraining the ceiling. Lykor had managed to tie off a shield, but there were gaping holes where the gold-laced rocks had disintegrated the magic, breaking through the ward.

With every muscle screaming in protest, Serenna hesitantly pushed herself to a sitting position. Torches now extinguished, the shield was the only source of light, faintly illuminating her domed prison with a purple glow. Her heart catapulted up her throat when she saw Lykor collapsed on his back beside her.

Black blood had congealed on his pale skin, a dried rivulet

descending from underneath his dark hair. Incapacitated—but still breathing—she eyed him for a moment before glancing around the settled dusting of shattered stone. The rubble had reduced Lykor's torture chamber to half its size, the area now smaller than her sitting room.

Serenna shied away from that terrifying fact that he'd stolen portaling from her, wondering if Lykor had included her in the shield so he could steal the rest of her power. Reminded of her defenselessness, Serenna clawed at the golden shackle latched around her wrist.

When the metal didn't budge under her frantic grappling, Serenna reined in her rising panic, reluctantly acknowledging defeat. Glancing over at her captor again, she scrutinized something familiar about his deceptively attractive face. Rather than accepting the simple fact that Lykor might be missing a few spokes in the wheel, Serenna replayed the mayhem in the war room.

The name that other elf-like wraith had mentioned... *I know I sensed another presence taking over through the bond.* Serenna picked at a dry sliver of skin on her lip, combing through the havoc, turning over the events like soil. *If Lykor is truly harboring Aesar...*

A glimmer in the shield's dim light snagged her attention, the hilt of a dagger gleaming at Lykor's belt. Serenna didn't think twice before scrambling over to his prone form.

Eyes riveted on the rise and fall of his chest, she hovered above Lykor's waist, her wild heartbeat blocking her throat. Despite reassuring herself that he was unconscious, apprehension hammered against Serenna's ribs as she considered stealing the knife. *I can't kill Lykor if Vesryn's twin is somewhere in there, but I won't be defenseless.*

Feeling like she was about to disturb a sleeping lion, desperation fueled her determination. In one fluid motion, Serenna yanked the blade from its sheath, clutching the weapon to her chest. With her shred of protection, she scooted back to the edge of their reduced space. Slumping against the rubble, she waited for Lykor to wake.

While Serenna inspected her elongated fingers, she considered working up the courage to probe Lykor's pockets for the key to her tether. Until a sudden intruding thought jabbed her, sharp like the knife she clenched.

This is all Vesryn's fault! Serenna banged her hand on the ground, furious at the prince while hurt carved a hole in her heart. If he hadn't kept her in the dark about whatever was going on with Ayla, she wouldn't have overreacted and portaled to retrieve answers.

Scorched by shame for what had unfolded on Vesryn's balcony, Serenna banished any further thoughts about the prince, knowing it would do no good to wallow in self-pity. There were more pressing matters to worry about now than her wounded feelings.

Serenna jumped when Lykor's eyes snapped open. He sat up, palming his head, dried blood flaking from his face. Swiveling his attention to her, Lykor's fiery gaze narrowed on the blade she held between them.

Without a word, he reached forward for the weapon. Leaning into the wreckage, Serenna tightened her grip, her mind too dulled to consider striking him with the blade. Lykor wordlessly snarled, prying her fingers off the hilt, wrestling the dagger free from her fist.

Serenna wasted a scowl while he absorbed himself in idly tracing the edge of the golden blade. Chills erupted over her skin as she registered the familiar vine-covered handle.

"Where did you get that knife?" she thoughtlessly demanded, forgetting her self-preservation. Lykor's fangs flashed in the shield's violet light but Serenna's curiosity continued to stifle her common sense. "That's not yours—I'd recognize Jassyn's daggers anywhere."

Lykor's eyes snapped to hers so quickly that Serenna flinched, alarm bells clanging in her head to keep silent. His gaze flicked back to the blade.

"Don't be fucking stupid," he said, sheathing the weapon. "I doubt this dagger is the only one of its kind ever crafted."

Suspicion flaring, embers of realization fanned in Serenna's stomach, an accusation combusting from her mouth. "You're the one who attacked Jassyn."

Something that she couldn't decipher flashed across Lykor's face, convincing her to swallow any further remark. He mumbled something inaudible like he was talking to himself before growling, "We need to accept the bond."

Serenna's blood chilled, the unexpected statement stunning her speechless. She clicked her teeth shut, staring at him before a disgusted laugh spilled out of her mouth. "I don't think so. If anything, I want to reject it." Assembling fragments of her confidence, Serenna crossed her arms and lifted her chin. "Tell me how."

Lykor ignored her, seizing her wrist. "I need Essence." He unfolded from the ground, yanking her up with him, his head nearly grazing the collapsed ceiling.

"And *I* need you to let go of me," Serenna bit out, unsuccessfully tugging against him to reclaim her limb.

"I don't have enough magic remaining to suffer your simple-minded objections." Lykor's claw tightened around her arm. "If I don't reinforce this shield, it's going to unravel and dump the remainder of the ceiling on our heads."

"I'm not accepting the bond," Serenna snapped, skin crawling under his feverish fingers. "Portal us out of here."

"If you haven't noticed, we're stuck in a gold-woven prison. I can't portal through." A sneer bracketed his fangs. "Unless you manage to spontaneously manifest illumination and provide me with what's left in your Well, you'll accept the bond." Lykor's shoulders twitched, spine popping. "This is not a request."

How does he know I don't have access to that talent yet? Concealing the flash of panic locking her knees, Serenna battled Lykor's scowl with her own while her mind raced.

What happens if we accept it? A sinking feeling settled in her stomach. Lykor would likely possess even more control over her magic than the prince had exploited during their training. *Bonds go both ways, but I know nothing about them.*

Unable to submit to Lykor's unnerving preternatural stillness, Serenna broke first. "And if I refuse?"

"Your insolence will not be the death of me," Lykor snarled, the unnatural heat from his claw nearly scalding her arm. Serenna shifted her feet, finding some place to anchor her fear while he raged. "I'll obtain your power one way or another. I won't hesitate to drain your remaining talents until you're a wraith." A vein thrashed in Lykor's forehead as he glared at her with fire in his eyes. "Half don't survive the transformation if you wish to gamble with your life."

The crushing silence of the dungeon became too loud. Terror drummed in Serenna's chest while she frantically tried to think of an alternative to either option. *If he turns me into a wraith and I live, my magic will be gone. Would that cause the bond to break with the prince? If so, I'll be stuck here forever.*

Serenna's nails dug into her palms. She hesitantly acknowledged that she'd rather bond to someone like Lykor instead of experiencing the agony of losing more talents. Surely he wouldn't kill her once they were fully bonded.

"I'm going to untether you and you will accept the bond." Lykor jerked her wrist. "If you try anything with your power, or if you reject this abominable connection…" Eyes glazing over, Lykor muttered under his breath, arguing with himself again. His focus pinned back on her. "We'll see if Aesar can stop me. I assure you, his control doesn't extend as far as he believes."

Thoughts circling around explanations, Serenna blinked up at Lykor. "You—you're really the prince?"

"Don't worry, he'll be more than fucking happy to explain." Lykor dug the key from his trouser pocket and unlocked the tether, finally releasing her.

Serenna flinched when the metal dropped, clanging against the stone. Lykor's awareness invaded her mind, his presence overwhelming—a malignant mass of shadows coiling around a bottomless pit of anger and hatred.

But there *was* someone else behind his eyes, obscured and hazy like she was peering through frosted glass. *If my bond is somehow connected to Aesar too...* Serenna bit the inside of her cheek, uncertainty dwindling her resolve to resist. *I need to stay alive long enough to find out more.*

Recoiling from the bond with Lykor, Serenna thought about the one she wanted instead. The connection to the prince was a faint thread, barely there compared to the beacon blazing in her mind. *Vesryn won't be able to portal to me in these dungeons, but could he get close?*

Before Serenna could consider the possibility of the prince appearing, dazzling silver lights suddenly sprang from Lykor. The magic arched to settle on her like hundreds of shooting stars spiraling across the sky.

Serenna's disbelief ignited alongside Lykor's power, the collapsed chambers pulsing with light from the radiant glow. She recognized the magic—the same that Vesryn had spun while half-delirious, wounded by the wraith's arrows.

"No," Serenna whispered, covering her mouth. *Vesryn tried to complete the bond with me.* She squeezed her eyes shut, swallowing a sick feeling burning in her throat. *I didn't even know.*

Lykor's irritation roiled through their connection, wrenching her mind back to the dungeon. "Stop being so fucking dramatic and accept the bond."

"I don't want to be bonded to you," Serenna choked out, eyes welling up. Overwhelmed by dread and a strange sorrow, she brushed away falling tears.

"Are you ready to die then?" Lykor snarled, stooping in her face. "Do you think I want to be shackled any more than you do with this stars-cursed chain of fate? You don't see me weeping about it."

Serenna sniffed and clenched her jaw, meeting his fiery gaze. She straightened, a collision of anger and fear steeling her spine. Attempting to stall for more unfettered moments so that the prince could locate her, Serenna hardened her resolve and asked, "What—what do I do?"

"Will it," Lykor snapped, the bond nearly erupting with his impatience. He crossed his arms, the spikes on his shoulders glinting in the shield's light. "If you keep fucking around, we'll find out how fast Aesar can intervene when I start draining your talents."

Stomach coiling with dread, Serenna shied away from the confinement awaiting her. She hauled on her power, wanting to deny that accepting the bond was this effortless. Her magic swirled, streaking toward Lykor, lashing him with cosmic light.

They both seized as the Essence fossilized between them, solidifying the nexus that linked their Wells. Air evacuated in a rush from Serenna's lungs, swept away by the tide of Lykor's presence crashing into her mind. Their auras twined, braiding together until the beginning and ending of each strand was lost.

The bond's threads solidified between them, strengthening into a bridge of steel, connecting their power. Unrelenting like a metal chain of links.

Binding them completely.

CHAPTER 25

LYKOR

Lykor snatched the girl's arm. Repulsed beyond all belief for solidifying the connection, he burrowed his awareness through the bond. The elf's Well was as much his now, their power linked like an inlet connecting two bays.

Sliding over the nexus to access her magic, Lykor exploited Aesar's knowledge. He rummaged through her abilities, hunting for illumination—another talent he'd witlessly bestowed upon Kal. Sparking the girl's side of their Well, he hauled the ability to the surface, snapping it into place.

"What are you doing?" the elf asked, tensing under his grip. Attempting to pull away, her despair morphed into alarm through the bond.

Lykor's fingers tightened around her arm, gut heaving in unease that his power so effortlessly merged with hers. Exposing him. If she possessed a morsel of knowledge, she'd be able to tap into his magic as freely as he accessed hers.

Lykor ignited four orbs of light in the debris-strewn room, casting shadows on the walls.

The elf's shock crashed against him. "How did you manifest my ability?"

Lykor ignored her, intending to withhold any information related to their connection. He wrenched the entire source of the elf's magic toward himself like an approaching hurricane sucking a shoreline's water out to sea. Compared to the amount of Essence he was capable of holding, her Well of power was a fucking puddle.

The elf gasped as a burst of light erupted from her chest, shimmering around them before rushing into his. From Aesar's recollection, the sudden tapping of Essence was an unpleasant experience of feeling wrung and wicked out. Lykor released her arm after absorbing her magical stores, doubting that the minuscule crumbs would be enough to escape from this tomb.

Still fuming about Lykor's decision, Aesar appeared, pacing the library's atrium. *This could've been avoided if you'd learn to regenerate before nearly depleting our power,* he all but scolded. His heeled boots struck the marble in their shared mindspace, clipping furiously. *Why didn't you have her excavate the rubble instead of completing the bond to pilfer her magic?*

Lykor scoffed. Permitting her access to his mind wasn't an option. He had no intention of depending on this half-elf grunt to deliver them from the wreckage.

Aesar began to chastise him further, but Lykor sensed the girl moving and ripped his attention back to the dungeon.

The girl drove her palms into his chest in an attempt to shove him. "You can't steal my magic!"

Igniting a glittering stream of Essence, Lykor bent the power to refortify the shield. He pushed her away along with her protest. "I can take whatever I want." Retrieving the manacle, he wrestled with her flailing limb to retether her, nearly sighing in relief when her presence vanished from his head.

She balled her hands into fists, looking like she was about to swing one at his face. "Why did you force me to bond if you hate me so much?"

"Since you've failed to manifest illumination on your own,"

Lykor dismissively snapped, harnessing Aesar's chiding tone of offering an explanation, "a fully formed connection was the only way to access your power." He sneered. "And since they clearly teach you nothing at that floating island, I'll enlighten you that the bond doesn't have anything to do with *feelings*."

She glowered, curling her arms around her waist.

Why bother keeping her tethered if you drained her Well? Aesar asked, roaming the library, appearing to contemplate which aisle of bookcases to wander through.

I'M ALREADY FETTERED TO ONE UNWANTED PRESENCE. AT LEAST I CAN STIFLE THE CONNECTION WITH HER. Lykor rolled his shoulders, the attempt at relaxing his spine doing nothing to ease the brain-splitting headache pounding in his skull.

Striding to where the hallway used to be, Lykor inspected the fallen stone barricading them in the collapsed brig, hoping the damage to the rest of the keep was minimal. Their fortress had never quaked before, the volcano centuries extinct.

Lykor extended tendrils of Essence through the rockwork, avoiding the gold-threaded stones. Twisting his magic down the corridor, he analyzed how the ceiling had crumbled, determining the most efficient way to use his limited supply of power to burrow out.

Their predicament would turn dire if he couldn't unearth them before his Well depleted or the shield deteriorated. Lykor plucked a stone from the rubble and flung the rock behind him. He'd resort to manually clearing the debris until he reached the point in the hallway that hadn't collapsed.

Aesar meandered through the shelves in his library. *Perhaps the girl could use her shaman powers to help.*

Lykor rolled his eyes. *YOUR CONFIDENCE IN HER ABILITIES IS CONCERNING.*

Then I guess we'll suffocate if you can't get us out of here, Aesar muttered, extracting a tome from the meticulously filed books.

THAT'S THE PREFERABLE OPTION IF I'M DESTINED TO ENDURE YOUR ETERNAL, INSUFFERABLE COMMENTARY.

Lykor cracked his neck, ignoring the throbbing in his burned palm as he continued to work.

"I want to talk to Aesar," the girl demanded behind him.

Having half-forgotten about the elf, Lykor pivoted toward her. The audacity of this girl. And yet another person preferring Aesar—and she hadn't even spoken to him.

You could be more approachable if you tried, Aesar grumbled, leafing through the book. *You're the one who won't let anyone get close.*

FUCK OFF.

Lykor might've let that slip out loud, judging from the way the elf's eyes flashed in the whirling illumination.

Placing her hands on her hips, she said "Is Aesar also—"

Lykor stalked toward her, cutting her off. She scrambled away until her back collided with the rubble.

"I don't think you understand how this works," he snarled, leaning into her face. "*You* do not make demands of *me*. If I so much as hear a *whisper* of a command, I will sever your fucking tongue." He would do it too, if it brought him a moment of peace.

Aesar slammed the book shut, the crack echoing in Lykor's skull. *You could try.*

The girl's nostrils flared. Her cerulean eyes iced over, but she didn't lower her gaze. Lykor smirked, nearly amused by her stubbornness. That academy should be thanking him for removing this elven brat from their ranks.

Lykor pivoted back to the exit. He continued excavating the gold-laced stones one at a time. The blister from the burn she'd inflicted on him had ripped open, oozing all over the rocks. Suffering through the pain, Lykor gritted his fangs. Discomfort was nothing to him anymore.

"Get over here and do something useful," he barked over his shoulder.

The elf pursed her lips but complied. "What are you going to do with me?" she asked, picking up stones and tossing them behind her. "Just use my magic as your spare Well?"

"Don't flatter yourself. I piss more than your thimbleful of power." Lykor readied a scathing threat, detailing how he could remove her vocal cords and braid them through her flapping mouth if she didn't silence herself, but Aesar confined his words.

Let me talk to her. Aesar squared himself in the library's atrium, apparently ready to bicker over something so trivial. *I'll explain everything. Since you won't.*

Shoulders sagging, Lykor blew out a breath before resting his head against the cool stone wall. If only he could take strength from the rocks.

He was going to die here. He'd survived an eternity of torture, had his magic ripped away over and over, but he was going to die in this vile crypt with an intolerable elf and Aesar's endless prattling for company. It was a wonder Kal hadn't begun talking to him telepathically. All three of them would make a perfect fucking clan, combining their efforts to wear him down like water eroding stone.

Not possessing the will to prevent Aesar from taking over, Lykor slackened his hold on their body. He hadn't disappeared or faded into nothingness—like he'd feared would happen—when he'd relinquished control before.

Drifting toward the sea of unconsciousness, Lykor wondered if he'd ever be free from the king's controlling magic, from Aesar's influence, or from his worry about the future of the wraith.

THAT AMBER-EYED ELF LOOSENED THE MAGIC. THAT MUCH IS OBVIOUS, BUT COULD HE DO MORE?

Unsolicited, Aesar answered his thought. *This girl might know.*

AND I'M SURE YOU'LL DO US BOTH A FAVOR AND FIND OUT.

Perhaps when he resurfaced, this fucking nightmare would be at an end.

CHAPTER 26

JASSYN

"I know Thalaesyn can assist with untangling the coercion if your wraith captives are under telepathic influence," Jassyn said, arguing with Vesryn on their way to the Infirmary—where he suspected the magister would be sleeping.

He'd spent the entire walk reasoning with his cousin before the prince had finally conceded to bring Thalaesyn with them to the Ranger Station. Rather than attempting to extract answers from the magister, Jassyn pleaded his case to involve his mentor with assessing the wraith for coercion.

"Thalaesyn is perhaps the only arch elf we can trust," he continued. "We can't depend on the capital since it's possible that the king has also compelled Elashor's soldiers." Jassyn lowered his voice as they passed a patrol, tracking their vacant stares. "I agree with you, something isn't right with their behavior."

Vesryn grunted a noncommittal noise, shouldering open the Infirmary's doors. Without the use of his power for once, since he'd recklessly exhausted his magic in the Hibernal Wastes.

Jassyn surveyed their surroundings, the late hour leaving the healing wing vacant. "The king locked away something important in the magister's mind." He gently closed the door so that it didn't slam. "We need more allies."

"Stars, fine," Vesryn interjected when Jassyn drew in a breath. "You've made your point."

Even though his cousin was wound more tightly than a coiled rope, Vesryn muttered his assurances to Jassyn that he'd calmed himself enough to regenerate. Leaving Jassyn to explain their intentions to the magister, the prince continued up to the roof to replenish his Well.

Really, the best way Vesryn can help is by making himself scarce, Jassyn thought, knocking before letting himself into his mentor's office.

Despite his cousin's maltreatment of Thalaesyn the prior night, the magister readily agreed to assist with the wraith. Adamantly eager to dive into further study, Thalaesyn seemed to take the potential coercion on Vesryn's prisoners almost personally.

As to not rouse suspicion of the campus patrols, Vesryn fabricated a portal straight from the magister's office when he returned from regenerating his magic. In the dracovae stables on the other side of the gateway, the prince dispatched one of the sentries to collect Flight Captain Zaeryn from her apartments.

The barn's illumination had been extinguished for the evening, allowing the dracovae undisturbed sleep. A glass skylight permitted the light of the moons. Soft, rumbling snores and chirping chuffs escorted them past the stalls.

"You need to find something else to do while we work," Jassyn urged as they strode down the dirt-packed hallway, igniting three globes of soft light to guide their way.

"Absolutely not," Vesryn bit back, steering the three of them toward the end of the corridor.

Jassyn seized the prince's arm, dragging him to a halt.

Thalaesyn raised his brows but ignored their scuffle. A slow-blinking gray dracovae roused to hang its head over the stall door that they stopped in front of. The magister busied himself with stroking its feathery cheeks.

"You are *not* going to rend the coercion if there's any present," Jassyn insisted, tightening his grip around Vesryn's taut muscles. "This needs to be delicate work. What if we manipulate the telepathy improperly and damage their minds?"

Vesryn opened his mouth, presumably to argue that they were feral, but Jassyn interrupted. "The king could've incorporated magic that prohibits anyone from tampering. If we provoke a reaction, we could lose all opportunities to obtain answers—or possible locations of where they came from." The conclusion sounded painfully obvious to him, but Jassyn assumed the prince could benefit from more pointed reasoning. "As unlikely as it seems, what if they're not actually mindless and they're compelled to act in that manner? We know there are higher thinking wraith, so it's possible. We're doing this *my* way or we're not doing it at all."

"Do you even care about getting Serenna back?" Vesryn elbowed his arm out of Jassyn's fingers. "If the wraith are hiding in the Hibernal Wastes like we're suspecting, then that means those beasts likely have her—and who knows how many others who've disappeared over the years." The prince's eyes flashed with what looked like anguish and devastation. "I won't hesitate to flay their minds if it gets me answers."

"I know you're worried. I'm worried too, but you need to trust me on this." Jassyn blew out a breath, releasing his pent-up frustration with his cousin.

With an indecipherable expression chiseled into his features, Vesryn clenched his jaw, looking away. He didn't meet Jassyn's gaze, staring at Thalaesyn petting the dracovae.

Jassyn lowered his voice. "You heard how the magister said everything was his fault. We need to discover how. If we can untangle the coercion on the wraith, I should be able to use the same techniques to dispel the rest of the magic on Thalaesyn's mind. We'll figure out what secrets the king is concealing."

Vesryn's shoulders slumped, like wind vanishing from sails.

"I need his help—this is unfamiliar territory and magic we've never studied before," Jassyn said, sensing he was finally wearing the prince down. "But it *is* possible to unravel the compulsion. Elashor dispelled it on me before I returned to Centarya."

Vesryn yanked a thread off of his uniform. "Elashor should be the one we seize to pry answers out of. He's closer to my sire than anyone else." The prince shook his head, fingers twitching at his sides. "I can't stand here and do nothing."

"Then dispatch your rangers." Jassyn placed a hand on Vesryn's shoulder, knowing he needed to convince the prince to concentrate on something else—so as to not disturb the sensitive work. "You have Serenna's general location. Organize your warriors so they can start patrolling in the morning. Let us handle this part. You focus on what you're good at."

Vesryn blew out a sigh. "Fine." He jerked his chin down the stall-lined corridor. "Our command room is down there. You'll inform me if you discover anything."

Jassyn relaxed, watching the prince hide behind a mask of annoyance to conceal his unease. "Of course."

"I'll leave you to it then." Vesryn pivoted on his heel, prowling down the hallway.

CHAPTER 27

LYKOR

Finally liberated from the gold portion of the dungeons, Lykor punched out a volley of force. The remaining rubble blasted out from the top of the prison stairs, crashing into the caverns. Strangled by a cloud of debris clogging the air, he and the girl both broke into a fit of coughing.

Her name is Serenna, Aesar chided, clearly still furious that Lykor had snatched back control, interrupting the recounting of his complete life story. As if the elf cared about every moment back to the second of his conception.

WHATEVER.

Lykor figured that Aesar had droned on enough that the elf was now sufficiently informed of the wraith. In return, the girl had filled the gaps in their knowledge of what little she knew of the elves' activities these past few decades.

Lykor lifted his eyes when the sting of flying sediment receded, the air hazed from fallen stone. Barnacled to the rocky walls, mushrooms, lichens, and moss shimmered with glowing cyan hues, eliminating the need for illumination. A winding channel flowed ahead, feeding the various underground lakes within the volcano's depths.

Striding toward the crystal water, weariness rippled off Lykor like the waves skimming the surface. Exacerbated by Aesar's prattling and the stars knew how many hours ticking by since the elf had portaled to him, Lykor's throat felt drier than the settling dust.

Staggering, the girl stumbled past him like her life depended on reaching the gravel shore first. She peeled off her boots at the water's edge and glanced back at him. Uncertainty and grime streaked her face.

"Is it safe to drink?" she asked.

Lykor's boots crunched on the shale as he approached the creeping stream. Curious how she'd react, he considered saying no.

In their mindspace, Aesar whirled from a window overlooking Kyansari's spires. *Do you have to be such a prick?*

DO YOU HAVE TO MONITOR MY EVERY MOVE?

What else is there to do? Aesar muttered.

YOU DON'T FIND HER A LITTLE IRRITATING?

Less so than I find you. Aesar flopped to a couch, growing silent as he opened a tome. Lykor nearly asked what the fuck he could possibly be reading, but settled on a different question that had been needling at his mind.

WHY THE LIBRARY?

Aesar's head whipped up.

Lykor vaguely waved around the atrium. OUT OF ALL THE LOCATIONS YOU COULD CREATE, WHY CHOOSE THIS MISERABLE PLACE?

Aesar frowned at the book in his lap before glancing back at Lykor. *I feel like I'm forgetting something. Something important. I don't know where else to look.* His eyes widened, aimed over Lykor's shoulder.

Twisting around, Lykor watched that damning obsidian prison door flicker in and out of existence—likely concealing the answers Aesar sought.

A thud drew Lykor's attention back to Aesar, who had shot to his feet, the tome fallen to the floor. *What is that?* he demanded, storming across the chamber.

Lykor crushed his fist, hurriedly abolishing thoughts of that room. IT'S NOTHING, he said, shoving the memories deep into a recess in his space of their mind. Lykor's heartbeat thrashed in his ears, his fatigue obvious since his control was slipping its leash.

Aesar placed a hand on his hip, flapping his other wrist at the now empty atrium. *That was more than "nothing."* He scrutinized Lykor, jade eyes sweeping over him. Analyzing him. Seeing through him.

Relenting, Lykor bared his fangs. IT'S EVERYTHING I SUFFERED THROUGH SO THAT YOU DIDN'T HAVE TO. Aesar flinched. YOU DON'T WANT TO GO IN THERE.

Blinking, Aesar wilted. *I never thanked you for—*

Lykor ripped his awareness away from their mindspace, thinking better of continuing with a conversation he couldn't care less about.

In front of him, the elf appeared on the verge of crying if the water wasn't potable. Lykor nodded curtly, withholding that snowmelt fed this particular current. His mouth twitched with devious amusement when she sprinted into the stream, the frantic dash soaking her leathers. She resurfaced, gasping and squealing.

Regardless of the near-freezing temperature, the temptation almost swayed Lykor to submerge himself in the same idiotic fashion. His dry skin itched from the plastered grit, the filth unearthing memories of being soiled in the squalor of Kyansari's mountainous dungeons.

Collapsing at the edge of the shore, Lykor cupped the water, greedily drinking and then rinsing his hands and face. The agony in his burned palm had him grinding his fangs into his gums.

Clenching his jaw, Lykor inspected the injury. Rock dust crusted the shredded skin in a mangled, bloody mess. Clearing the rubble had only aggravated the wound, now pulsing with searing pain.

Sensing the girl's attention, he glanced up. Chewing the inside of her cheek, the elf studied his claw—a wraith's talon-tipped hand.

When she didn't peel her prying gaze away, Lykor raised a finger out of his fist. She scowled, apparently registering that he'd silently told her to fuck off.

Giving him a pointed sniff—like that did anything—the girl spun around. She waded through the current toward dangling luminescent moss on a rocky shelf. Idly tracing the leaves on the dagger sheathed at his belt, Lykor considered her shaman powers.

Aside from her peculiar connection to the Heart of Stars, surely there'd be an advantage for the wraith if she could manipulate the frozen elements of the Wastes. And he had just the trifling task in mind to determine her capabilities. Kal had telepathically informed Aesar that one of the volcano's surface lifts was jammed with snow from the quake.

Before Lykor could assign the girl to the chore, he needed to find someone to supervise her—he certainly wasn't inclined to burden *himself* with this dreadful elf. After gaining knowledge of the wraith, the girl seemed agreeable enough with Aesar that Lykor doubted she'd pose any type of threat. But he couldn't say his people—especially the reavers—would take well to this half-elf in their midst.

You could appoint Fenn as her guard.

With reluctance washing over him, Lykor scrubbed more water over his face. Granting the overeager lieutenant yet another assignment he'd interpret as a special privilege already had exhaustion dragging on his limbs. Keeping Kal's enthusiastic son at arm's length required nearly as much energy as dealing with the captain himself, but the pool of reliable options was shallow.

A fragment of intrigue distracted Lykor from his deliberation when the elf pulled down a strand of glowing moss. "What are you doing?" he asked before thinking better of it.

The girl aggressively wrung out the plant. The sharp look suggested she wished she could wring his neck in the same manner.

A mutual feeling.

"That wound will get infected if you don't treat it," she said, words snappy. "This moss will help prevent that. Since I doubt you'll untether me so I can regenerate and mend you." The elf approached him, water swirling around her knees. "Not that I care about your well-being since you're the one who rended me, stole portaling, and then forced—"

Slapping the water, Lykor splashed her, irritation from this whole fucking situation driving him to juvenile actions. "I didn't ask for this accursed connection or to be governed by coercion. And I certainly had no desire for *you* to appear."

She flicked the water off her face, eyes flashing. "Can't we reject the bond?"

"Yes," Lykor growled, disgusted. "And I plan to when I no longer have a use for your magic." Exasperation had him fusing his teeth. "But until then, you're staying tethered."

"I figured my 'thimbleful' of power wouldn't be worth the inconvenience," she said, tossing drenched hair over her shoulder.

"It's really not." Lykor unfolded his legs and rose, ready to move on—both with this conversation and to find a reprieve from this vexing girl.

"Give me your hand," she demanded, extending the moss between hers. When he did nothing beyond narrowing his eyes, she shook the plant at him. "Do you want to lose that claw? Your skin is nearly flayed to the bone and needs to be treated."

"I hadn't noticed." Lykor's lip curled into a sneer. "Does being a half-breed also render you a half-wit?" The agitation knotting in Lykor's shoulders had him cracking his neck. "What do you intend to do with that pile of seaweed?"

The elf scowled. "Like I said, this 'seaweed' will fight infection." She added defensively, "I learned about plants from my friend Jassyn—he's a healer."

Heart thumping in his throat, Lykor cleared his features. "And explain to me how that's relevant?"

"I've watched how you can't keep your fingers away from *his* knife." An angry color flushed up the girl's cheeks as she bit the words off of her remark. "I thought you'd want to know more about him."

Lykor yanked his hand off the dagger as if burned again. Jaw screwed tight, he pivoted and stalked away before he witlessly revealed anything else.

Water sloshed behind him. The elf grabbed his wrist, the contact lifting every one of his hairs in alarm.

"Don't touch me," Lykor snarled, ripping out of her grip.

The girl flinched when he raised his arm, as if expecting a backhand blow. Eying a wild motion of her hands, Lykor realized with an unwelcome jolt that she instinctively attempted to fabricate a shield. Between the tether and her empty Well, the gesture was pointless.

Chest constricting, Lykor's thoughts fled back to his own helplessness in the king's prison—defenseless to Galaeryn's every depraved, torturous whim. He lowered his claw, fingers slowly curling into a fist, pinioning the reactive flash of fury. Like a window slamming against howling wind, his reflexive rage abated. Ribs surrendering his lungs, there was enough space to breathe again.

On second thought... Lykor shoved her.

Shrieking, the elf lost her footing, reeling backward. She

landed with a splash before jumping up, spluttering and swearing.

"Why are you being so stubborn about this?" she spat, wiping water out of her eyes.

Ignoring her, Lykor gestured curtly, a master calling a hound. "Get out so we can leave."

She pointed an accusatory finger at him. "You're the one who pushed me in!"

Lykor's eyes pinned on the water suddenly rippling like a flood of raindrops collided with the surface. The elf glanced at him and then at the roiling stream, obviously considering retaliation.

A torrent of violent words wrestled up Lykor's throat. He bared his fangs. "Don't you *fucking* dare."

Aesar blew an amused snort out of his nose, towing Lykor's attention inward. He lounged on a reading couch, throwing Lykor a satisfied smirk. *She's probably only using that power because you're pissing her off.*

The girl lifted her chin. With a *whoosh*, the channel reared up in a wave behind her. Poised and waiting.

Despite Lykor's mild curiosity to discover how else she could manipulate the water, he pivoted on his heel.

I wouldn't turn—

Before he could make it two paces, water crashed into him, the deluge smashing him like an ocean's swell. Lykor ripped Essence from his Well. *I'M GOING TO KILL HER.*

Aesar had the nerve to wag a finger as rending billowed around him in the library—under his control. Lykor snarled at him and then rounded on the girl.

You know, I think we'd both be able to channel our magic simultaneously if you loosened your grip and didn't oppose me so much.

AND WHY THE FUCK WOULD I WANT TO DO THAT?

Aesar shrugged. He smugly coiled the shadows across his

fingertips, effectively locking that part of their Well away. *The only reason we're alive is because I shielded us during the cave-in.*

WHAT DO YOU WANT? MY THANKS?

Leaning forward on the sofa, Aesar braced his elbows on his knees. *Give me tonight with Kal.*

Lykor's explosive laugh bounced off the damp cavern walls. The girl's eyes widened as she faltered in her furious splashing to the water's edge.

Let me have dinner with his clan. Aesar rose from the couch. Clenching his fists, darkness whirled through the atrium. *It's not like you ever keep company, so I'm not interrupting your plans of lurking in the Aerie alone.*

An icy ball of irritation coalesced in Lykor's chest. HAVE YOU CONSIDERED THAT IF I DIDN'T HAVE TO WAKE UP IN KAL'S BED, I'D BE MORE AMENABLE TO LETTING YOU TWO FUCK AROUND?

Lykor blinked. The elf had made it to the shore, stalking toward him. He swiped sopping hair out of his eyes, now as thoroughly soaked as her.

Aesar's brow furrowed before dipping his head in agreement. *Very well. We'd be more effective if we worked together.*

THAT WASN'T A BARGAIN, Lykor scoffed. I DON'T NEED YOUR HELP. WHY CAN'T YOU HIDE LIKE YOU WERE CONTENT TO DO THESE PAST DECADES?

There's too much at stake now. Aesar squared his shoulders, still ready to quarrel. *We have one Heart, and it's possible another is somewhere in this fortress. I think there could be one in the druid jungle too.*

Lykor crossed his arms. AND YOU'RE SHARING THIS REVELATION WITH ME NOW?

I've been thinking about it. It makes sense, doesn't it? Aesar paced the atrium, shadows billowing around him. *That unnatural pocket of trees in the Hibernal Wastes has to be important. Vesryn and I suspected it was an abandoned druid city when we discovered it.* He traced his lower lip, lost in thought. *Have Serenna help—she's tied to this now. If we could bring more than one Heart to—*

SHUT UP, I GET IT. STARS, I NEED TO DEAL WITH THIS SHAMAN SPAWN BEFORE SHE TRIES STRANGLING ME WITH THAT FUCKING MOSS.

The elf straightened when Lykor's attention focused back on her. He tracked her cautious steps until she stood in front of him.

"If you ruined these leathers," Lykor growled, leaning down to her level, "I'll patch them with your skin."

Lips pursing, she wore an attempt at a brave face before swallowing. Holding out the glowing plant, she asked in a voice pitched with false sweetness, "Would you let me bind your hand?"

Lykor flashed his fangs before glancing over her head at the water receding back into the channel. Fed up with her persistence, he thrust his fist into her chest, knocking her back a step.

She glared at him before taking his claw, roughly coiling the moss around his palm. Lykor clenched his teeth at the pressure, releasing a hiss when she tied the plant into a knot. Tighter than it needed to be.

Torchlight flickering from one of the tunnels drew Lykor's attention away from the elf. Kal's hovering illumination and his band of warriors entered the caverns. Wordlessly leaving the girl behind, Lykor prowled to the group. The soldiers parted around him like a shoal fleeing from a shark. Searching the wraith, he locked eyes with Fenn. Lykor jerked his head for the lieutenant to join him.

Fenn stooped to hear his words. Lykor lowered his voice anyway, so it didn't pitch to the others. "Take the elf to the Aerie and consider yourself elevated to her personal guard. Keep her tethered and away from Mara. I don't want the girl learning of her presence." The last thing he needed was the two females putting their heads together behind his back. Mara already meddled enough on Aesar's behalf.

Lykor provided a brief update of the elf's earthen abilities he suspected—and figured out firsthand—that she possessed. He left Fenn with orders of determining whatever else she could do with those shaman powers along with extracting any information about the elves' military. Fenn rivaled his father at useless driveling—surely his ferreting would get the girl talking.

Retrieving the knife at his belt, Lykor sawed the slimy moss away from his palm, discarding the plant. "Douse the torches in my tower." He didn't glance over his shoulder as he strode away. "I don't want her fucking around with any fire."

CHAPTER 28

SERENNA

Serenna unconsciously retreated a few paces when one of the wraith split away from the gathered ranks. Her back collided with a wall of spongy lichen, knees locking when she recognized the hulking soldier who'd tethered her.

Aesar had assured her that she wouldn't be harmed, but he wasn't exactly present at every moment. Serenna reminded herself that Lykor's wraith hadn't hesitated when they'd attacked Centarya.

The torchlight carried away by the departing warriors flickered against Fenn's sharp cheekbones, highlighting his indigo skin. Rings in his brows, ears, nose, and lower lip shimmered in the fading light, swinging as he swaggered toward her. Serenna cringed at the excessive jewelry, touching her face.

Unwilling to be pinned against the rocks, she swallowed her nervousness and stepped back to the center of the cavern. Serenna eyed the quiver of short arrows at his side and the bandolier of knives crossed over his spiked armor, wondering why he bothered with daggers when his talons were just as sharp.

Anxiously tracing the golden manacle latched around her

wrist, Serenna clung to the hope that the prince would find her if she figured out how to unlock the tether. Stranded in the Wastes, she had no other option without portaling. *Vesryn needs to know what happened to his brother and who the wraith really are.*

The intermittent, thin braids woven through Fenn's hair swayed when he halted in front of her. Crossing his arms, he planted his boots under his shoulders, dominating the space. Serenna's gaze darted down the tunnel as the specks of illumination disappeared around a corner.

Clenching her jaw against his intimidating posture, Serenna lifted her chin, meeting his conflagrating gaze head on. *I can deal with the likes of him.*

As she hunted down a tactic, her stomach dropped instead as he continued to evaluate her with a disturbing intensity. *Well, that is, if he's not like Lykor.* She'd already quickly discovered that she couldn't press her captor in the same defiant ways she had with the prince. *Lykor might actually kill me if I'm too much trouble.*

The steady dripping of water from her soaked leathers was the only sound as Fenn regarded her, his eyes flaring like a flame consuming tinder. Serenna suppressed a shiver, the chill from her plastered clothing seeping into her skin.

As smooth as smoke, Fenn circled around her. Serenna whirled to face him, her boots scuffing against the rocky ground. Hardly able to see, the luminescent plants trailing from the stony walls offered less light than she preferred.

Failing to work up the indignation to endure his unblinking stare, Serenna snapped. "What are you doing?" she demanded, digging her nails into her palms.

"Do all she-elves have eyes the color of the Lagoon?" With a quirky tilt of his lips, Fenn cocked his head. "Or do you simply capture starlight and give it form?"

Serenna blinked, her question coming out breathless with her confusion. "What?" She searched for an answer in his crimson eyes. *Am I missing wraith humor?* "What's the Lagoon?"

The sharp edges of Fenn's fangs peeked out as his grin unfurled. A flash of fear had Serenna stepping backward.

"It would be more appropriate to begin with names before we go to the Lagoon," he practically crooned. Interlocking his talons, Fenn made an unusual bob with his head that she assumed was some sort of bow. "My parents unfortunately upheld the elders' tradition and gave me the elven name 'Fennaeryn.'" His mouth thinned to a tight line before morphing to a smirk. "But, if we're to become intimately acquainted, I'd prefer it if you'd call me Fenn."

Pursing her lips, the knots in Serenna's fingers loosened. She rapidly rearranged how she'd handle this wraith. Deflection would be best. "Why aren't we following the others?"

"I'm escorting you to the Aerie." Adjusting a strap running over his spiked armor that secured a holstered weapon on his back, Fenn surprisingly offered more before she could ask. "It's where you'll be staying with Lykor."

Serenna blustered a scoff. "I don't want to *stay* with Lykor." *I can't even imagine where he spends his time. I'm sure he lives somewhere foul—like this cave.*

The rings in Fenn's ears clinked when he dipped his head again. "I'll ensure your objection is passed along."

Serenna ground her teeth at the sarcasm but ignored it. "Are we going to start moving?" she asked, tucking her hands under her arms to stave off a shiver. She thought better of foolishly risking her only chance at basic necessities if this Aerie possibly had a bath, food, and a bed. "Or do you have other wraith teleportation tricks up your sleeve?"

Frowning, Fenn blinked at his bare arms, each bicep adorned by a single silver band. "I have no sleeves."

Too fatigued to respond, Serenna released a weary sigh.

Fenn pointed at one of the darkened tunnels in the tangle of cavern corridors. "I know a shortcut."

Hesitant to leave the light, Serenna's eyes darted between the luminescent plants, the maw of gaping black, and her wraith warden. Taking it upon himself to override her fear, Fenn condemned her by prodding her toward the entrance of the tunnel.

Spine tingling, Serenna glanced over her shoulder as her feet trudged forward, unsettled at having a stranger looming behind her—and a warrior at that. The last thing she saw was Fenn's eyes, glowing like embers in the vestiges of light before darkness plundered her sight.

Hands outstretched, Serenna blindly stumbled through the dark. Away from the rushing underground stream, the compressed air in the tunnel pressed down with a suffocating weight. Every time she balked, Fenn goaded her with a push, steering her like a herded swine.

Serenna shuffled ahead, attempting to put herself out of his reach. After a few rounds of catching her when she tripped and then propelling her forward again, Fenn apparently had enough.

"File my fangs," he swore beside her, holding her upright with a claw. "We'd be at Lykor's tower by now if you weren't dragging your feet."

Bristling with annoyance, Serenna ripped her arm out of his unnervingly warm grasp. "I can't see in the dark like you…" The remainder of the cruel jab she was about to unleash about his unnatural eyes died on her tongue. The reality of the wraith's origins doused the fire in her gut. *He's not too different from me or any other elf—he just doesn't have Essence.*

"I didn't realize you required sight to move your legs." Fenn snatched her arm when she tripped again.

Before Serenna could retort, something scraped and rapidly clicked against the rocky floor, echoing from every direction.

"Stars, slay me," Fenn all but groaned, fingers tensing against her. "I don't care how much of the sky reflects in those pretty elf eyes of yours—after this, I'm pleading with Lykor for reassignment." His voice sharpened, clipping out an order. "Get behind me."

Fenn didn't give Serenna an option, swinging her around him. The chittering bounced off the walls, traveling closer.

Scalp prickling, Serenna's words were hushed while she blindly searched the dark. "What is it?"

"Cavern scorpion," Fenn muttered. "I'd rather face an ice wolf with my talons shaved off—at least you can keep track of all their legs."

Serenna's heart leaped against her ribs at the sudden glitter of Fenn's scarlet eyes, seeming to glow with their own faint light as he looked back at her.

"Can you see it?" she whispered, the darkness only escalating her fright. "I can't tell—"

Serenna clamped her teeth shut upon hearing the whisper of leather, silently hoping Fenn was unsheathing one of his weapons. She jumped when there was a *click* and the noise of a pulley cranking, like a ship hoisting a sail.

The clacking of the cavern scorpion stilled, the tunnel devouring the sound. Heartbeat thumping in her ears, Serenna strained to hear the creature over her thundering pulse. Biting her cheek in the silence, her breath came fast through her nose. *If I didn't have this tether on, I wouldn't be reliant on Fenn to protect me.*

A burst of hissing split the air. There was a sound like dozens of legs abruptly skittering over stone. Serenna tensed, every muscle coiling. Imagining the creature charging at them in a wild dash had her a moment away from spinning around to flee.

A *twang* ricocheted against the tunnel's walls. The sound of what she assumed was one of those short arrows thudded into...something, drawing out an eerie screech. Cyan light flared with the same dim color of the glowing plants from the cavern, accompanied by an eruption of pungent musk. Serenna nearly gagged, discovering that the foul odor was a pool of the scorpion's blood.

Fenn approached the cat-sized creature, his colossal form casting a faint shadow on the wall. Serenna hesitantly followed, assuming the luminescent scorpion was dead.

Planting a boot on its shelled plates, Fenn yanked the arrow out of a punctured eye. Serenna's stomach turned over at the sickening squelch.

"What's that weapon?" She had an uncomfortable feeling it was the contraption that Vesryn had described when he'd been injured.

"Crossbow," Fenn said, holstering it on his back. "Comes in handy, but it's slow to reload. If there was more than one scorpion, I'd resort to throwing my knives."

Serenna studied the pattern of glowing blue blood, spattered across the rocks. She swallowed, recalling her lacerated peers at the academy during the attack—their deaths now so pointless. *If Aesar spoke true, it's not each other that we should be fighting—it's the king.*

Steering her attention back to the tunnel, she braved to ask, "Why not use your talons?"

"And foul my claws with ichor?" Fenn released a snort. Unraveling a cord braided around his wrist, he dropped to a knee. "I doubt you'd be so inclined to plunge your dainty elf hands inside this vermin."

Point taken, even though my hands aren't exactly 'dainty' anymore. Serenna ran her elongated fingers over her damp hair, pausing to inspect the black color. "Would you teach me how to use it? The crossbow? Or another weapon?" She fidgeted with the end of her braid as he tied a knot under the scorpion's barbed stinger. "Since Lykor is keeping me tethered, I don't want to be…defenseless."

Fenn barked a laugh, making her feel ridiculous for mentioning it. *Why did I ask that?* While she might not technically be at odds with the wraith, it wasn't as if she should expect them to waste time teaching her how to fend for herself. Serenna scowled at Fenn's back, preparing herself for whatever he was about to unleash.

Something that sounded like skepticism pitched Fenn's voice higher. *"Defenseless?"* He cut a look over his shoulder, eyes ablaze with mirth. "I'll have you know, Wind Weaver, that I'm still picking shards of that window out of my ass."

Serenna blinked. Her mouth hinged open with a question but stunned shock deprived her of words.

"What?" Fenn asked, straightening back to his towering height. "You don't believe you dealt my pride a devastating blow?"

Apparently feeling the need to prove his claim, Fenn twisted around. Serenna's eyes popped when he slid the backside of his leather trousers considerably lower than was appropriate, shamelessly revealing much more skin than she was prepared to see. A ridge of white sutures fanned over defined muscles that he was most certainly flexing.

An unexpected laugh spilled passed Serenna's lips before she ripped her eyes back to Fenn's face. Flustered, the points of her ears burned as she battled to keep her eyes on his.

Fenn's crimson gaze smoldered with amusement as he covered himself up. "You're not defenseless. You could snap me in half with a flick of your fingers." He demonstrated with some wild motion of his talons. "I highly doubt my clan has any intention of letting me forget how they sewed my backside together."

Serenna's mouth twitched at the thought. Something about his peculiar behavior dislodged a tiny splinter of fear.

"Is everyone in your clan family?" she asked, curious about the social structure of the wraith.

"It's more of a community—a way of organizing our people. My clan is the largest," Fenn said proudly, returning to the scorpion. "Luckily, we have talented tailors in our district."

Serenna's amusement morphed into guilt from observing his wounds. "Thank you for intervening in the war room." She picked at a nail, chipped from helping Aesar clear the rubble while she assembled her thoughts. "Lykor might've killed me or taken the rest of my power if you and that other warrior hadn't been there."

"That wasn't Lykor's fault," Fenn said quickly. Too defensively. "He's not normally like that."

Serenna remained silent, unconvinced as she mulled over his claim. Aesar had informed her of the compulsive magic on Lykor and how she'd apparently triggered it by calling out for the prince.

Serenna wrinkled her nose as Fenn hacked off the scorpion's legs with a long knife before tying the body to his belt. Fearing it was a culinary conquest, she refrained from asking why he was bringing the creature with them.

Fenn popped his knuckles, each crack of his joints making her cringe. "Let's get back to the light," he said. The spilled blood from the scorpion glowed, dripping as it dangled from his waist. "I'd prefer to leave before the rest of its pod arrives to investigate. I'll carry you, so we're not down here until the next full moons."

Serenna backed away as he approached. "I—I don't need to be—" She released a squawk when Fenn scooped her up, stomach tumbling as he lifted her through the air. Expecting the wind to be knocked out of her when he slung her over a shoulder, Serenna braced herself. Instead, Fenn carried her in front of him in an equally undignified position, like she was an inconvenient bundle of sticks.

Serenna writhed in his arms, trying to put more space between them. An abnormal heat radiated through his armor, melting the chill in her clammy skin.

A sudden sting had Serenna yelping. Her voice bounced

back to her off of the surrounding rock. She rubbed her backside and hissed, "Did you seriously *pinch* me?"

In the faint glow of the scorpion at Fenn's side, she caught his lips twitching. "I'll do it again, she-elf."

"I didn't ask you to carry me like this, you lumbering leviathan." Serenna swatted at him when he attempted to follow through with his threat.

"Then enlighten me as to which position you'd prefer." The rings looped through Fenn's raised brows clinked together. "You're squirming worse than that scorpion and you're about six legs short."

Serenna froze in his arms, imagining a horde of those creatures skittering above them.

Obviously feeding her terror, he continued, "There are beasts fouler than scorpions for those brave enough to venture into the belly of our fortress." Serenna's skin pebbled at the vulnerability, knowing nothing about this area of the world. "You wouldn't want to find yourself alone in the dark with a vulpintera."

Holding her breath, Serenna strained to hear anything beyond her frantic heartbeat and Fenn's boots thudding against the stone. *I can't fathom what kind of creature could be worse.*

"And what is a…vulpintera?" she asked in a hushed voice, as if not to summon one. "Do they have even more legs?"

Fenn flashed his fangs in a nasty smile. "You'll find out soon enough."

Serenna swallowed, picturing an abomination like a giant spider.

"Lykor keeps one as a *pet*," Fenn said, his tone menacing. "I imagine Aiko is quite hungry since she's missed her last few meals."

Serenna stiffened so violently that she feared her spine would crack. She laughably clutched the front of Fenn's leathers, as if she could locate a shred of safety in the wraith warrior.

"See, sitting still wasn't so difficult," Fenn said, shifting her. Serenna didn't appreciate that glimmer in his eyes and his chuckle rumbling through her. "Since you were barely plodding along, I figured you'd prefer being catatonic cargo."

Serenna crossed her arms, hunching like a disgruntled vulture, silently fuming at the arrangement and stubbornly refusing to be grateful for the warmth.

"So what are you? My personal jailer?" She shot a glare up at him, assuming his wraith vision caught the full effect in the dim lichens starting to carpet the walls.

"'Nursemaid' might be a more appropriate term." He ducked under a cluster of hanging stalactites before ascending a narrow staircase, the steps chiseled into the stone. "I have plenty of practice, as the stars saw fit to torment me with eight sisters." Serenna frowned, nearly incapable of imaging someone with so many piercings and weapons entertaining adolescents without frightening them. "But Lykor tasked me with finding out what else you can do with your earthen magics and if you know anything useful."

Serenna scoffed, unsure what to do with the admission. "Doesn't telling me defeat the purpose of you trying to covertly extract that knowledge?"

Fenn's voice mirrored her own bewilderment. "Who said it has to be a secret?" He shrugged, her body moving in his arms with the motion. "Lykor didn't specify."

A flicker of uncertainty sparked and smoldered. No one offered information without a price, a motive, or her prying it out of them. Either Fenn was a brilliant manipulator or he was incredibly straightforward and she'd be wise to figure out which.

Ears perking, Serenna heard water gurgling in the distance. Glowing light crept back into her vision as the tunnel yawned open. She released a relieved sigh that they were about to leave the abysmal darkness—and the scorpions—behind.

At the top of the stairs, Fenn weaved through a dangling curtain of luminous vines, revealing another expansive cavern. Twisted stalactites suspended from the ceiling glistened with frosted blue and green light, casting the surroundings in an ethereal glow.

The humid air encompassed Serenna like a blanket, thawing the chill in her bones. Realizing that she was leaning into Fenn's chest, she jerked in his arms, not letting herself relax. *I'm going to fall asleep if I'm not walking.*

"Put me down," she ordered, simply to see if he would.

Like a dog following a command, Fenn lowered her to the ground with an unexpected gentleness for being a brute.

Serenna sniffed, flinging her hair over a shoulder and smoothing out her damp leathers. Drawn by an enchanting shimmer in a mound of stalagmites, she traced aqua veins similar to frozen waves in an icy sea.

Inspecting more bioluminescence as she wandered around the chamber, Serenna glanced up at her guard, who vigilantly tracked her every move. "Aesar said this place was an ancient druid capital?"

Fenn nodded, leading her toward a rushing stream. A faint layer of fog swirled above the water. "Some unexplained magics preserved this forgotten stronghold over the centuries, leaving it untouched by time." He reached up to trail his talons across low-hanging moss.

It made sense why the elves had no knowledge of such a place if it was hidden in the Wastes. Serenna wondered how Lykor had discovered the keep, though she doubted she'd glean that tale from him. But if Fenn was going to pluck information from her, then she could do the same.

"How many wraith wield Essence?" she asked. "Like that other warrior from the war room?"

"'That other warrior' is my father. You can call him Kal," Fenn said, reaching the water's bank. "And he's the only one—Lykor distributed some of his abilities to him not too long ago." He unsheathed a knife from his bandolier, kneeling by the stream.

That seems a little out of character for Lykor. But the fact that power could be returned momentarily sprouted a seed of hope before it rapidly withered. Serenna nearly laughed at the absurd thought. Lykor returning her power seemed less probable than him setting her free.

Serenna studied Fenn as he busied himself with untying the scorpion from his belt. Cyan blood spilled into the swirling water as he gutted its corpse. *I knew he was going to eat that horrid creature.*

"Wait." Serenna stared at Fenn's back, registering that he hadn't used the elven term 'sire.' "Your father? You have a father?" The wraith must've strayed from elven customs. She couldn't blame them, considering what they'd suffered—and who'd caused it.

Soft plops of water tumbling from the ceiling broke on the stream's surface. Fenn paused, holding the chitin still. Serenna nearly heard him blink before he gaped over his shoulder, clearly taken aback.

He suddenly smirked, revealing the point of a fang. "I was unaware you'd require enlightening as to where wraithlings come from, but if you need a demonstration—"

"No," Serenna quickly interrupted, her cheeks heating. "I meant... Nevermind." The chamber somehow became even hotter. Serenna cleared her throat as Fenn's gaze followed the flush racing up her ears. Mind churning, she strained to think of something to say in order to distract him from finding amusement in her embarrassment. "How is this stream warm when the mountains are frozen?"

Fenn frowned, shaking the scorpion out as the current

carried away its entrails. "Your magics don't tell you?"

Tightening her lips, Serenna shot Fenn a flat look, knowing he was gauging her capabilities so he could report them back to his leader. She'd willed the current to move earlier when she'd dumped it over Lykor, but she hadn't considered what else she could do with that power. *Fine.* She'd entertain him this time—but only because she was curious too.

Like she did with calling the wind outside of the war room, Serenna allowed herself to drift. Eyes unfocusing, she reached out to the world differently than when she heaved Essence from her Well. Instead of wrenching magic toward her, she faded into the surroundings, allowing the world to dissolve.

Ignoring the heavy air and plants creeping into her perception, Serenna aimed her awareness into the stream, the water nearly humming with power. Following the current, mind swimming between the rocks, she delved further into the caverns, detecting the source.

Blinking, Serenna returned her attention back to the chamber. Interested to experiment with her abilities, she cast her magic out like a net. Hauling on the water, Serenna called a tiny orb of liquid to her palm. "The stream flows from a cluster of hot springs," she said, assuming he knew the answer.

Fenn nodded, tying the gutted and washed scorpion back onto his belt. "The Lagoon—our community baths that you were inquiring about—isn't too far from the molten heart of the volcano."

Serenna fumbled with the water. The sphere shattered, splashing to the ground. With an irritated huff, she yanked on the droplets, reassembling them. "For one, I wasn't asking about your Lagoon." Watching the liquid dance above her fingertips, she debated the next question before deciding that she had to know. "And you bathe...together?"

"Oh, we do more than *bathe*," Fenn said, chuckling darkly. "But since you're uninformed as to where wraithlings come from, I'd wager you're not prepared to appreciate the activities that occur." He stretched, scraping his talons along the point of a stalactite. "Though you're welcome to join. I expect the evening will lead me there."

Of course the wraith are promiscuous like the elves. I guess some elements of culture are simply everlasting. Unable to resist the urge, Serenna lobbed the globe at Fenn. He extended a claw to catch it. Releasing her power, the shape burst. The water crashed into his waiting palm, splattering to the ground.

Fenn growled and shook his fingers. "I won't walk into that ruse next time, you water pixie." Choosing another set of stairs at this apparent crossroads, he angled toward a pathway illuminated by lichens.

As she followed, Serenna's legs started to burn from the exertion of climbing upward. Losing count of the steps, she began to desperately hope they neared the end.

When she almost thought about asking to be carried again, a trickle of sunlight poured onto her face. Serenna squinted against the improbable light and then gasped when the tunnel opened up, revealing a massive expanse.

Serenna's mind wrestled with the enormity of the space. The wraith didn't live in a cave. They lived in an underground *city*.

Tilting her head back to marvel from their vantage near the middle level of the stronghold, Serenna's jaw dropped. Thousands of feet above, the crater unfolded to the sky, eclipsed by the setting sun flashing in angled glass. Suspended from the interior mountain slopes, hundreds of mirrors hung, bouncing around shafts of the fading light.

Serenna rushed to a balcony. Leaning over, her eyes greedily absorbed all the city's sights, stretching out in every direction. She couldn't decide where to look first.

Rectangular buildings were carved straight into the rock, lining the walls as far as she could see. Far above, glowing plants in various shades of blues and greens clung to the volcano's sides. The clash between the luminescent hues of the vegetation and the earthen tones of the dwellings was strikingly vivid—a universe of jewels draped like stars in the sky.

Infected with a charge of wonder and fascination, Serenna didn't shy away from watching the multitudes of wraith carrying on with their daily lives. *There's so much life here.* Scores of natural stone bridges arched across the cavern's empty spaces, connecting each winding level of the fortress.

"Where do you live?" Serenna breathlessly asked Fenn as he joined her at the overlook. He kept shooting glances at her like he expected her to sprout wings and fly over the edge.

Waving around the crater, Fenn pointed out the residential districts. Apparently delighted to be her tour guide, he provided her with an extensive recounting of how the wraith had become self-sufficient in this remote section of the world. While reliant on Lykor's portals to collect resources, their citizens were smiths, gardeners, warriors, and nearly all other professions—everyone had a purpose and a place.

"But there were windows in the war room," Serenna said after Fenn told her the entire population lived within the shelter of the volcano. "You said Lykor has a tower? Is it somewhere else?"

Fenn nodded and wandered over to a wall containing a cluster of shimmering blue mushrooms. "There are other dwellings carved into the surrounding mountains. Lykor lives in one of those, above a library." Plucking off a luminous cap, Fenn extended it to her.

Puzzled by the offering, Serenna asked, "What's that for?"

"So you can see in the Aerie after I extinguish the torches." Fenn twirled the stem. "It'll glow for a few hours."

Unsure how to interpret the gesture, Serenna left the overlook to accept the fungus. "And you care about that because...?"

"It is my full intention to prioritize your happiness so we don't have another flying glass debacle." Something like humor tugged at his lips. "Lykor's tower has more windows than the war room."

He expects me to be content as a captive? Instead of mustering irritation, surprise flashed through Serenna, realizing that Fenn inexplicably went out of his way to ensure her comfort.

"Why did you protect me?" Serenna ventured to ask, seeking the motive for his kindness. "From all that flying glass?"

"I owed you a debt," Fenn said, thumbing a lip ring.

Serenna blinked, her fingers tightening around the glowing mushroom. "What debt?"

"You saved me first." Fenn tilted his head. "From Lykor's shadow magics."

Serenna opened her mouth, ready to confess that she had no choice but to include him in her ward, but clicked her teeth shut instead. Fenn didn't seem to notice while he traced the slice a sliver of glass had cut into his cheek. *He's going to poke his eye out with those talons if he isn't careful.*

Fenn jerked his chin toward a corridor, sending his braids swinging. "There aren't too many stairs remaining." Flashing her a fanged grin, he added, "And if you ask nicely, I won't even object to carrying you the rest of the way."

CHAPTER 29

JASSYN

Weariness clung to Jassyn's limbs from spending the small hours of the night meticulously untangling knots of coercion. When he'd begun to sway on his feet, Thalaesyn had shooed him off, urging him to rest. The magister had busied himself with instructing the rangers to prepare more comfortable accommodations for their prisoners.

Well nearly depleted, Jassyn skirted inside the door of the command room to wait for the prince. While exhausted, he was still buzzing with energy, like a lightning storm was caged in his chest. Brimming with new information, Jassyn was eager to share what he and Thalaesyn had discovered. Those three wraith weren't the mindless creatures they used to be—that much was clear.

Finding a place along the wall to observe the meeting, Jassyn swallowed a yawn as the gray dawn snuffed out the setting moons through the windows. It was hard to believe that only a few hours had passed since Vesryn's rampage through the snow.

The prince's eyes flicked to him before returning to the ten assembled officers, arranged around a crescent table. Jassyn scanned Vesryn's handpicked soldiers, a motley group of Alari's elite elven-blooded warriors. He recognized Flight Captain Zaeryn at the far end of the table, angled to face both his position by the door and the prince. Silver-haired and sunbaked like Vesryn, her toned arms bulged from her leathers in a manner equally as intimidating as his cousin's.

Too late, Jassyn realized that he'd inadvertently been staring. They locked eyes across the room. Recalling that Vesryn had mentioned Zaeryn's *interest* in him, he yanked his gaze away.

Shifting his feet, Jassyn briefly considered shuffling to the back of the room—out of her line of sight. The pitching in his gut subsided when he assumed her curiosity had nothing to do with his bloodline—and that was a realm's worth of difference from what he was accustomed to.

Vesryn paced in front of an expansive map draped across a wall's entire length, distracting Jassyn from his unease. In their century-long search for the elusive wraith, the rangers had pinned every location they'd scoured—nearly every corner of all the realms. Jassyn noted the glaring gaps beginning near the foothills of the Hibernal Wastes. No markers extended to the western edge of their known world.

Vesryn cast a circle of illumination over the mountains. "I intend to portal each officer's squad to this location," he said, tapping the highlighted area Jassyn assumed they'd traveled to in search of Serenna. "We'll fan out from here."

The prince drifted to the center of the table, leaning forward on his knuckles. The rangers remained focused, absorbing his orders. "Our advantage is the dracovae, but their safety needs to be prioritized. As you know, they're incapable of journeying far in the glacial air—even if we're using shields. But I still want detailed sweeps of those mountains."

Vesryn pushed around a stack of reports, not glancing at their contents. "I'll leave this to your discretion, but I'd like each of our warriors to seriously consider forming bonds with a trusted comrade."

Jassyn's mouth dried to dust. While obviously not a ranger, the request still struck him like an arrow, piercing him with unease. Zaeryn and the other officers tensed in their chairs, nearly suffocating the room with a collective held breath.

The thought of sharing his magic and a space in his head had Jassyn anxiously twisting a curl dangling in front of his eyes. Some days, he could hardly haul himself out of his own tumultuous thoughts—let alone worry about burdening someone else with the inner turmoil caged in his mind. He could only hope that the prince didn't request the same of the magus at Centarya, even though some of his peers had begun experimenting with the bonding magic on their own.

Vesryn squared his shoulders, looking ready to battle the quiet resistance. "This binding doesn't have to be indefinite, but there are advantages." His hawkish stare roved over the warriors, punctuating the silence. "They'll be able to draw from a shared Well—use each other's abilities if they're lacking in any talents—and communicate without telepathy. Among other benefits I won't waste time spelling out."

Vesryn's jaw tightened to a block of steel. "I know this isn't a common practice, but we need every edge we can get." He fiddled with his uniform's stitching, ripping a thread free, eyes unfocusing on the string in his fist. "I don't want anyone engaging with those beasts if their base is located." The prince blinked, then thoughtfully frowned at Jassyn. "We'll plan our assault and utilize Centarya's forces."

Jassyn gave his cousin an approving nod, respecting that he had enough clarity to keep his warriors safe. After the prince dismissed his officers, Jassyn and Zaeryn joined Vesryn at the map.

The prince clenched his fingers, knuckles blanching before he spoke. "Remind the rangers that those monsters have gold-firing weapons. Their unusual arrows can tear through our shields, so we'll need to avoid fighting them from the air."

"We'll find a way to bolster our weaknesses," Zaeryn confidently said, resting her hand on a short, curved glaive at her side. "In the meantime, I think it's a risk to fly so deep into the Wastes."

"I know." Vesryn raked a hand over his mouth, staring at the illuminated area on the map. "But it needs to be done. We'll have to trust the rangers to not push the dracovae—or themselves—too far before portaling back to safety."

"If the dracovae permit it, we could always assign two to each," Zaeryn offered. One side of her mouth tugged up as her azure eyes pointedly studied Jassyn. "The second rider could be primed with Essence as a reserve."

"We don't have anyone else to train as riders." The prince sighed, shoulders sagging as if burdened by command. "The recruits at Centarya aren't ready. The magus..."

Vesryn joined in Zaeryn's glance toward him. Jassyn's eyes widened as he met the prince's gaze. He stubbornly shook his head, ready to launch into an argument about how his skills were better suited on the *ground* and not thousands of feet in the air.

"You're right," the prince finally said, agreeing with Jassyn's silent objection. "If the wraith return, I need the magus at Centarya."

The clamped pressure released from Jassyn's chest, though he could still feel the weight of Zaeryn's attention.

Vesryn dragged a hand over his face, the dark circles smudged under his eyes betraying his fatigue. "I have little faith that the capital's soldiers on campus will be of any aid. We'll have to work with the numbers we have here."

"Speaking of numbers," Zaeryn said, her eyes finally sliding away from Jassyn. "One of our riders assigned to this coast is a week overdue." She pointed to the northern edge of the map. "Those we've sent on reconnaissance haven't located her or the missing dracovae."

After blowing out a long breath, Vesryn instructed the flight captain to dispatch additional rangers to that area. The location wasn't close to where they'd searched for Serenna in the Wastes, but the prince wouldn't dismiss any potential leads.

Vesryn nodded to Jassyn but spoke to Zaeryn. "We have more to discuss, but Jassyn is going to assess your mind before I can inform you of anything else."

Jassyn straightened. That was news to him, but he couldn't argue with his cousin's unexpected logic. It wasn't beyond belief that some of the rangers might be under the king's control.

After Jassyn verified that the flight captain wasn't coerced and demonstrated to her how to detect the compulsive weaves, the prince divulged their suspicions of the magic influencing Kyansari's soldiers.

"I want every ranger inspected when they return from their patrols," Vesryn ordered. "Send word to me immediately if any of our warriors are coerced."

Crossing his arms, the prince stared at the map. "And there's more—something I have yet to inform the magisters or magus of." A muscle twitched in Vesryn's cheek before he turned his attention back to Jassyn and Zaeryn. "Elashor informed me that the injured Centarya sent to Kyansari's healing grounds have been reassigned. They won't be returning to campus."

"Why?" Jassyn blurted, alarm racing through him. "Where?"

Scoffing, Vesryn shook his head. "The council took it upon themselves to dispatch those initiates somewhere undisclosed on the mortal war front." Rage flashed in his eyes, the harbinger of an impending storm. "I was under the impression that Centarya and the rangers would remain under my command."

"We're on our own then if the capital can't be trusted," Zaeryn said, squinting against a shard of sunlight cascading into the room.

"So it seems." The prince rubbed his temples in a way that seemed to say, *But haven't we been all this time?* "Do you have anything to report from our prisoners?" Vesryn asked, focusing on Jassyn.

Pulling his fidgeting fingers away from his plated earcuffs, Jassyn relayed the information he'd been waiting to divulge. "Magister Thalaesyn and I were able to confirm that the wraith are compelled." Vesryn's nostrils flared at the validation of their assumptions, but he didn't look surprised. "We were able to remove a layer of coercion," Jassyn continued. "And…" he trailed off, eyes darting between the pair of warriors. "The wraith are mute, but they aren't aggressive anymore—you should see for yourself."

The prince left Zaeryn in the command room with instructions to organize the flight squads. Jassyn hesitantly led Vesryn back down the stall-lined corridor to the captive wraith. Stable hands hurried by, starting their morning chores. A handful of dracovae roused, leaning over their doors, curious eyes watching them pass.

Vesryn mumbled something about thinking he'd sensed Serenna's presence flicker in his mind once more when they'd been in the war room.

While it may have been a figment of Vesryn's exhaustion, Jassyn clutched onto the shred of optimism for his cousin's sake. *She's alive,* he assured himself. *Vesryn would know if the bond shattered—he's felt it before.*

Entering the wraith's stall, Jassyn held his breath, waiting for Vesryn's reaction. Eyes stinging, he struggled to swallow past the stench of unwashed bodies. Dust from the straw glowed in the streams of sunlight squeezing in through the open windows.

With the night's work finished, Thalaesyn had unraveled the rending binds he'd previously placed on the wraith. All three sat slumped on the floor, their ragged clothing torn and hanging off their gaunt limbs. Two were still weeping as Thalaesyn stood among them.

"What the bleeding stars is this?" Vesryn demanded, Essence

igniting around him. His eyes ricocheted between the loose wraith and the magister.

"Like I said," Jassyn reiterated, ready to intervene—somehow—if the prince failed to remain calm. "We removed a layer of coercion that apparently made them aggressive. As you can see, they're…" He glanced at the wraith. "Subdued."

"I was able to untangle a few more knots of magic that restricted their speech," Thalaesyn said, kneeling next to a female who was staring at the ground. He cast healing light over her talons, mending the bed of nails she'd injured in her mindless state. "They have awareness of their surroundings now."

"They can talk?" Jassyn asked as confusion wrestled through him. *Thalaesyn made more progress than I anticipated.*

Not giving the magister time to answer, Vesryn stalked to the middle of the stall. "I want to question them." The heat in his voice nearly singed the air. "Now."

"That's not necessary," Thalaesyn said. Rising, he skimmed his fingers through his golden hair. "Velinya here—"

"What?" Jassyn and the prince both snapped in unison. Jassyn's attention flew to the female wraith.

She glanced up at the sound of their voices. Her scarlet eyes widened, meeting his. Faster than Jassyn could blink, she shot to her feet and dashed across the room in a blur, ramming into him. Losing his balance, Jassyn stumbled from the collision, her swift movement stealing time for him to process any alarm.

Vesryn was the first to react, shadows spinning out from his fist. Another pulse of magic rippled across the room. Thalaesyn threw a current of darkness to intercept the prince's power, slicing through the rending before Essence reached the wraith sobbing against Jassyn's chest.

Vesryn snarled, rounding on the magister. "Explain."

"They won't harm us and there's no need to harm them." Shadows churned around Thalaesyn as he combated the prince's rage with a stoic calm. "I fear these three won't be the only recruits your rangers collect from the realms."

Recruits? A beat of silence passed as Jassyn reeled from the named wraith. If she really was Serenna's curly-haired friend, all trace of her was gone. Pulse droning in his ears, Jassyn's thoughts spiraled.

Drawing away, the female sniffed, wiping the back of her claw across damp cheeks. Her crimson eyes searched his, silently begging him to see.

Stomach pitching like he'd toppled forward into empty air, Jassyn loosened the breath barricaded behind his ribs. His voice broke into a hoarse whisper. "Velinya?"

She nodded frantically before bursting into a fresh wave of tears. Grabbing him again in an embrace, she wept into his shoulder.

Shock careened through Jassyn, his reality unraveling as he processed the impossible. Something that went against everything he knew, the inconceivable calcifying into a horrifying dream.

"The wraith were created," he whispered, "with our own people."

Vesryn hit the floor. He leaned against the wall, drawing both palms over his face, his dread a mirror to Jassyn's. The prince didn't even have to ask the question as his eyes flicked to Thalaesyn's.

Nodding, the magister's gaze fell as he dropped down to mend another despondent wraith. He'd been aware the entire time—a prisoner to the knowledge for a century.

The prince's hands muffled his words.

"Fuck."

CHAPTER 30

SERENNA

Serenna's eyes snapped open.

A door had slammed somewhere in the Aerie's lower level. Curled up on a plush sofa in Lykor's sitting room, she turned over, dismissing the commotion.

Long before the sun had faded from the sky, Serenna had been quickly lulled to sleep by the soft hum emanating from the voids set at intervals along the walls. Fenn had explained the vents in excruciating detail. Warm air pleasantly toasted the chamber, collected by a maze of pipes that distributed heat from a fiery lake in the volcano's heart.

Cringing, Serenna scratched her shoulder under her crusty leathers, somewhat regretting that she hadn't hunted down the bathing chambers and a bed on the uppermost floor. All she'd accomplished before sleep had claimed her was gobbling down what Fenn had called "grotto stew."

Serenna hadn't dared to ask what was in it, but unfortunately received an answer while her guard ensured she was stuffed twice over. The proclaimed "staple of every meal" contained anything from morels to lichens to some creature she suspected had too many legs. Serenna would never admit it, but she'd been so famished that she wouldn't have complained if Fenn had prepared and peppered that scorpion dangling from his waist and plopped it on the table.

Despite the extinguished torches and her now-faded mushroom, the frosty stars and the moons slipped in enough light through the windows to see. More than half of the circular chamber was glass, unfolding to the horizon and sky. Tapestries depicting strange winged beings—druids, according to Fenn—adorned the smooth black marble walls. The foreign furnishings could've been crafted from living wood, like roots twisted in on themselves to form tables, chairs, and shelves.

Heavy footsteps clanged against the iron staircase that wound up the center of the tower. Serenna doubted the stomping was from one of Fenn's willowy sisters. He had assigned two of them as her nightly sentinels before sauntering to the Lagoon to *unwind*.

Startling, Serenna concluded the pounding boots most likely belonged to her captor. Her eyes flew to the entryway as the door opened.

Lykor emerged, stalking past Fenn's sisters in the hallway before flicking the door shut with a pulse of force. He was wrapped in a fur-lined cloak and still shrouded in a dark mood—if that permanent ridge between his brows was any sign. He crossed through the sitting room, halting to loom above her.

Curtly motioning to the snow-engulfed balcony, Lykor ordered, "Get outside."

"What?" Rubbing sleep out of her eyes, Serenna sat up and scowled at the rude awakening. "Why?"

Instead of answering, Lykor seized her arm, hauling her to her feet.

"I'm getting tired of everyone dragging me everywhere," Serenna seethed, pointlessly struggling against him as he ignored her.

Not giving Serenna the option of putting on her boots,

Lykor lugged her across the chamber and yanked open the door. A frigid gust howled in, her hair whipped by the blizzard's bite.

Blasting out a wave of force, Lykor cleared the snowy drifts from the terrace. The explosion of frosty powder rained down the mountainside like diamonds shattering to dust.

Lykor shoved her outside, past fanged icicles stretching down from the overhanging roof. Stolen from the sitting room's warmth, Serenna gasped against the sharp air lacerating her lungs. She threw out her arms, stockinged feet sliding over an icy film.

Snatching one of her wheeling wrists, Lykor unlocked the manacle and stowed the restraining metal in a cloak pocket. "Replenish your Well," he growled, breath expelling in an agitated wisp.

Before Serenna could object, the sudden impact of his presence crashed into her mind, momentarily making her forget the glacial cold. Lykor's exhaustion and annoyance—with *her*—rampaged down the bridge of the bond.

Stalking to the parapet, Essence shimmered around Lykor as he planted his palms against the ledge, glaring up at the web of stars. Serenna stared at his stoic profile as he regenerated, skin even paler under the reflection of the moons. The magnitude of his magic churned with the weight of an endless ocean, one that would surely crush her if she tried to channel that amount of power.

Shivering, Serenna shrank back, wrapping her arms across her chest. She'd thought the extent of Vesryn's Well was vast, but the Essence at the prince's disposal was a lake compared to Lykor's sea.

"You should save us both the trouble and infuse me with a *thimbleful* of your power," Serenna snipped through her chattering teeth. "It seemed easy enough when you dragged my magic out through the bond. You wouldn't even notice," she railed on, joining Lykor at the ledge. "I've never felt anyone—"

"And how do you expect to expand your Well if you don't do it yourself?" Lykor snarled, his irritation snapping through their link like a whip. "Maybe if you had to fight for your survival, you'd be able to hold more Essence than a fucking spoon."

Serenna's teeth clicked shut, barricading any retort as her frozen muscles convulsed. Pinching her lips, she turned her back, gazing out across the frozen expanse.

Something heavy crashed onto her shoulders. Stumbling forward, Serenna caught herself on the balcony's icy balustrade. Stunned by bewilderment, she drew Lykor's fur-lined cloak under her chin, stomach turning over from the lingering heat. She risked a glance at her captor, wondering if Aesar had anything to do with her comfort.

"Will you fucking regenerate?" Lykor's patience cracked like ice, the frigid breeze thrashing his unbound hair. "Dawn is approaching."

The mist from Serenna's annoyed huff coiled above her head. Conceding, she acknowledged that the only way to return indoors was to comply. Letting her awareness drift to the galaxies, a foreign array of constellations winked down on their mountainous perch.

Serenna searched for the blue spiral galaxy that Vesryn had pointed out weeks ago, claiming it was the Aelfyn homeworld. Unable to locate that particular celestial light, Serenna focused on the unfamiliar blanket of stars. A strange loneliness from the empty expanse encompassed her like the quiet light from the moons.

"I don't see why I need to restore my magic if you're keeping me tethered," Serenna said, testing the waters as she fished for his intentions.

Lykor clenched his fist, the metal in his gauntlet squealing. Serenna eyed the armor in the corner of her vision, ensuring he wasn't about to lunge for her throat. "I won't squander any advantage—no matter how meager." Seemingly unaffected by the freezing temperature, Lykor rolled his shoulders, the spikes on his black leathers glinting in the moonlight. "Even if your puddle of power is next to useless."

Serenna's cheeks reddened further, the flush rising without the aid of the breeze slapping her face. "So you're simply going to snatch my magic for yourself whenever it suits you?" A new thought wandered through the darkness of night as she curled Lykor's cloak further under her chin. "Why don't you just take my elemental power while you're at it?"

"I can't use that magic. Those abilities are bound to your human blood." He grunted an unamused noise, eyes fixed on the jagged horizon. "But would that I could, and I'd free myself from this shackle to you."

You'd be doing us both a favor, Serenna nearly told him, rubbing her bare wrist. Her heart screeched to a halt and then rallied into a gallop.

I'm untethered. Does Vesryn sense me? Frantic and desperate, Serenna launched her awareness down the dim silver cord. The prince was somewhere to the east, half the world away. *If he realizes where I am, he can come get me!*

Serenna's breath snagged at the sudden realization. *I can't have Vesryn travel here—the coercion would force Lykor to kill him.* Tears pricked the corners of her eyes, freezing to her lashes. Rapidly blinking, Serenna battled the emotions swirling in her chest.

I'm on my own then. How am I going to get out of this? Serenna swallowed her despair, now hoping Vesryn was asleep and didn't notice her abrupt appearance. Another noxious notion rooted like a weed. *And I hope that flame-haired vixen isn't in his bed. He owes me an explanation.*

Serenna hurried to enter a shallow meditative state, somehow replenishing her power with Lykor breathing down her neck. She shoved her wrist at him, anxious to block her location from the prince.

Lykor's eyes suspiciously probed hers. A shard of fear lodged in Serenna's spine—she appeared too compliant. And now he'd probably detected her panic through the bond. Drawing her arm back, she searched for a diversion.

Serenna sensed the agony in the burn she'd given him, even more agitated by his armor. "Will you allow me to mend you yet?" She cleared her throat, hoping that Lykor would interpret the offer as the source of her unease. "It'll be easier to heal your palm before an infection sets in."

Lykor's lip curled around his fangs. His shoulders twitched, a horse irritably dislodging a fly. Muttering under his breath, he removed his gauntlet.

Serenna shoved her shock away, thinking better about making a comment. Her fingers trembled as she hesitantly cupped his claw, the frosty air nearly crystalizing her bones. She flinched when her power leaped in response, slithering through her veins.

At the same time, Lykor's talons snapped closed, digging into the blistered flesh. With an exasperated sigh that bordered a growl, he allowed her to pry his fingers open to inspect the ghastly wound.

Serenna ignited her power. Lykor stiffened. His magic roared to life, shadows rearing behind him, likely ready to strike if she so much as breathed in the wrong direction. Serenna rolled her eyes, weaving a ruby healing lattice around his palm.

Lykor yanked his claw out of her hands as soon as the sores smoothed back to mended skin. He released his magic well after she'd let go of hers.

Serenna speared a sarcastic thought in his direction. *You're welcome.*

Get the fuck out of my mind, Lykor snarled, cramming his gauntlet back on.

Not expecting to hear his voice blasting in her head, Serenna recoiled, rapidly assembling her mental barricades. "Neither of us have telepathy. How could..." Her stomach rolled like a snowball, icing into alarm. *We can communicate through the accepted bond.*

Lykor snatched the manacle out of his cloak—that she was still wearing—and roughly clamped the metal back around her wrist, severing their connection. Serenna rushed indoors and retreated to the far end of the sitting room, away from Lykor and the cold.

Slamming the door shut, Lykor's indiscernible grumble could've been words of gratitude. It sounded more like someone stabbed him in the gut.

Serenna shed the enormous coat, placing the furs on a couch. Pursing her lips, she nearly thanked Lykor for the cloak before deciding to not say anything to him at all. Eager to warm up with a bath and find a bed after, Serenna hurried to the staircase winding up the center of the chamber.

Before she lifted a foot to the first step, something small and dark flew down the stairs straight at her head. Serenna shrieked, tossing her arms up before stumbling backward into a sofa. She spun around as the furry mass sailed over her shoulder.

The creature landed in the middle of Lykor's chest, vocalizing with a strange chirping mewl. The fluffy animal furiously rubbed its fox-like face under Lykor's chin, apparently beyond excited to see him. Leathery wings flapped and rustled frantically as Lykor stroked from the nape of its neck down to its puffy black tail.

Tiny fangs similar to Lykor's peeked out from its long snout while the rumble of its unexpected purr vibrated across the room. With a sneaking suspicion, Serenna shook her head and scoffed. "That's a vulpintera, isn't it?" *Fenn was fooling with me!*

"Aiko comes and goes as she pleases," Lykor muttered, prying the fuzzy-eared bundle off of his chest, perching the vulpintera on his shoulder. The creature contentedly curled behind his neck like a scarf, tail draping to coil around one of his arms. Lykor dropped to a couch, his full attention on scratching Aiko's tufted ears.

Serenna fought back a sad smile as she returned to the staircase. Even though Lykor didn't consider himself Vesryn's twin, they still shared a peculiar similarity when it came to their beasts.

What if I can somehow reunite the prince and Aesar? She'd withheld from informing Aesar of her bond with his brother. If Lykor had awareness of that connection, she couldn't predict what the compulsion would force him to do.

Both anger and fear for the future warred in Serenna's thoughts. If she could somehow unify the elven-blooded and Lykor's exiled people... *We could end this fighting before more innocent lives are lost.*

Hand hovering over the banister, Serenna hesitated before ascending the stairs. "I hope there's a way we can come to an understanding," she said, contemplating how to navigate the precarious ridge she stood on with Lykor and cobble together some type of trust. She skimmed her fingers over the iron railing, thinking of the prince. "I know my people will also want to make the king answer for his crimes once they know the truth about the wraith."

A spark of rage combusted in Lykor's eyes. Serenna rushed on before he cut her off. "Now that the king has an endless supply of magic to drain from the elven-blooded, I'm not sure what will happen to the realms. Don't we—as wraith and elven-blooded—owe it to our people to stop him?"

A sneer razored across Lykor's face. "The wraith 'owe' no one." Hand pausing midway through petting Aiko, he clenched his fist. "And the fate of *your* realms is of no concern to me. There isn't room for *my* people in this world. Not anymore." Lykor bit off his words like ripping meat from a bone. "We're going where the elves can't reach us." Leaning his head back against the sofa, Lykor closed his eyes and dismissively waved her off like a nuisance.

Knowing that he intended to take her with him, Serenna's despair accumulated. *And the truth will disappear with me unless I find a way out.*

CHAPTER 31

SERENNA

Serenna nestled further into the downy blankets, tossing a cover over her face to thwart the sunlight streaming across her eyelids. *Didn't I close the blinds?* she groggily wondered, rolling away from the streak of brightness.

This bed chamber had been one of six in the rounded upper level of the Aerie, carved into the mountain's peak. Evidently, Lykor wasn't concerned with her poking around. Serenna had wandered into a bedroom with a tiny portal permanently opened on a windowsill—a rift she assumed could only be for Aiko. She quickly located different sleeping quarters, selecting one as far away as possible from her captor's.

The edge of Serenna's bed sank before something nudged her shoulder. "She-elf," a low voice crooned.

Flooded with alarm, Serenna's heart exploded against her ribs. Twisted in the blanket wrapped over her head, she yelped, flailing to untangle her limbs. Arms swinging to free herself, Serenna threw the covers off. She slammed her back against the headboard, meeting the gaze of the offending wraith.

"What are you doing in here?" she hissed at Fenn, yanking the sheet up to her chin.

"I feared you'd slumber all day." He glanced out the window that he most certainly had opened.

Serenna rubbed her eyes against the blinding intervention. "That was the idea!" She scowled as he sat there, settled in more comfortably than he had any right to be on *her* bed.

"That's a shame, considering you're more radiant than the sunrise." Pausing for what had to be a dramatic effect, the points of Fenn's fangs flashed in a mischievous grin.

Serenna ignored him with a pointed, disapproving sniff, disregarding the way his lofty words felt like a compliment. The last thing on her mind was encouraging any pathetic attempts at flirtation. *I don't need another problem added to my list.*

Not taking offense, Fenn continued as he turned back to the mountain view. "Daylight is burning across the sky."

"Who cares?" Serenna bundled the covers under her chin, concealing the oversized silken garment she'd found in a dresser—the closest thing to a nightgown. "This is wildly inappropriate. You can't be in here."

Fenn looked around the room as if searching for the meaning of the word "inappropriate," obviously not seeing any issue with his presence. "Someone had to rouse you because it seemed you weren't going to do it yourself. Lykor is already gone for the day and my sisters stationed below were too nervous to come near you." He spun one of the rings in his brows. "So that left me."

Serenna blinked, wading through the unexpectedness of the wraith now being afraid of *her*. *Strange. I spent so much time being afraid of them.*

"That doesn't explain why I *need* to be woken up," she protested.

"We're going to the surface to excavate a lift," Fenn explained, tapping the stack of material next to him. "I brought you some wraithling leathers that I think should fit."

"Right. I'm a captive and yet Lykor expects me to earn my

keep." Still damp from her bath hours before, Serenna untangled her braid, knotted from sleep. "I don't understand why your leader insists on keeping me tethered, but also requires that I use my elemental power."

Is it truly because Lykor doesn't want to sense me through the bond? While thinking she should feel insulted, Serenna couldn't decipher which emotion would be appropriate. Regardless, having her magic forcefully suppressed did conveniently eliminate the risk of Vesryn showing up at an inopportune time.

The spikes on Fenn's armor nearly grazed his cheek when he shrugged. "Lykor thinks those ancient magics might help the wraith."

Serenna shoved a strand of midnight hair out of her face—the same shade as Fenn's. "And why should I help?" She leaned back into the pillows. "I didn't ask to be here."

Fenn frowned, cocking his head. "You're the one who portaled across the realms to be with Lykor."

Serenna gaped before spluttering, "That is not what happened." *Well, it is, but that wasn't my intention and Fenn doesn't need to know that.* "I don't want to be *with* Lykor."

"You're the first to dwell in his tower," Fenn argued, tracing the cut along his cheek. "I thought he decided to keep you here because he intended to pair with you or keep you close as a partner."

Having enough clues to guess what Fenn was implying, Serenna's irritation boiled over. Detesting the assumption—which had to be wraith gossip at this point—she threw a pillow at his head. "Get out!"

Deftly intercepting it, Fenn tossed the cushion back to the headboard beside her, fluffing it after he rose. His lips tightened, but he complied, silently striding to the door.

No longer distracted by the towering wraith seated next to her, an entire host of wafting aromas drew Serenna's attention to the nightstand. Lunch, she suspected, if the intensity of the glaring light was any sign. A perspiring glass of water stood next to a tray featuring steaming breads, meats, and something that smelled earthy.

The considerate gesture smothered the indignant heat in Serenna's chest, making her regret lashing out. She highly doubted Lykor ordered anyone to bring her breakfast in bed.

"Fenn, wait," Serenna quickly pleaded to his retreating back. It wasn't his fault she was upset and stuck in the Hibernal Wastes. Clearing her throat, she asked, "You...brought me something to eat?"

Turning around, Fenn's eyes danced like flames, glowing with their own light. Returning to the nightstand, he plucked a round piece of bread from the tray. "The scorpion-tail pastries are my favorite." Serenna wrinkled her nose even though her stomach rumbled. "You should try them." Fenn's sharp canines pierced the flaky loaf as he chewed with more etiquette than she expected. "I helped myself to the others from the breakfast you slept through."

"Enjoying yourself?" Serenna muttered as he perched back on the bed. *I'm surprised he hasn't made a boast about this food being from his kill.* When Fenn's claw snaked out for another helping, Serenna snatched the remaining piece of spongy bread before he could pilfer it.

He patted her foot through the covers. "I'm simply ensuring the kitchen staff didn't lace your meal with poison."

Serenna froze, the pastry not making it to her mouth. She drew her legs up to her chest. "Why—why would they do that?"

"Your presence makes some of the wraith nervous." Fenn's humor dissolved. "Especially the reavers. They might try to subdue you. Or force you to use your magics for them."

"But I'm tethered!" Serenna flung her shackled wrist in front of Fenn's face, her heart skipping an unsettled beat. Aesar had mentioned there was a fierce faction of younger warriors who clashed with the elders.

"You still have earthen magics." Fenn's gaze flickered to the unlit sconces, almost looking curious. "I imagine by now the clans have heard how you wove the winds and blasted out the windows in the war room."

"And what happens if you're poisoned and they come after me?" Serenna asked, nibbling on the pastry. She almost had herself convinced that it was only grains and dough. It tasted more like the earthiness of mushrooms than anything else.

Fenn reached into the neck of his armor, drawing out a chain. An iron key dangled between them, glinting in the sunlight. "If something unforeseen occurs—hopefully not my demise—I imagine Lykor might forgive me if I need to unlock your tether."

The bread soured in the bottom of Serenna's gut. *Of course my jailer has my freedom dangling around his throat, just out of reach.* Restraining her annoyance as much as she could, Serenna gritted out, "Lykor doesn't seem like the forgiving type."

"Very true. But if any harm comes to you, it'll reflect on me." Fenn plucked a plum off the tray, somehow not scraping the flesh with his razor-sharp talons. "I'd rather take my chances with poison than risk Lykor's ire. Especially since you're claimed by him."

"I do *not* belong to Lykor." Serenna tore the bread in her hands before angrily chewing, biting back any further words. *I don't know why the stars connected my Well to the Falkyn twins, but this link to Lykor has been nothing but an inconvenience.*

"Aesar informed my father that your magics are bound to theirs." Fenn bounced the fruit in his palm before pocketing it. "Are you saying that you only intend on sharing this bond and not Lykor's bed?"

Serenna coughed at the second time he'd insinuated such a thing, nearly choking on her mouthful of food. "If you're so interested in Lykor, you're welcome to take my place," she snapped, pointedly dragging the tray across the table, setting it on the bed next to her when Fenn tried to snatch a sliver of meat. "If you had Essence, you could choose to bond with him. I didn't get that option." She snatched the glass of water from the nightstand, glaring at him as she drank. "Did Aesar fail to mention that Lykor forced me to accept the connection?"

"I'm sure Lykor had his reasons." Fenn's voice grew quiet. "The clans owe him everything and he's often burdened with difficult decisions."

Curling the blankets in her fists, Serenna blew air out of her nose as the wraith in front of her kindled her agitation. She clenched her teeth to restrain her tongue, grinding her anger down. *I won't win any arguments with a zealous soldier.*

Serenna's eyes snagged on Fenn's canines as he opened his mouth—readying further defense for Lykor's actions, she could only assume. Cutting off whatever excuses that he planned to voice, she spoke first. "What's wrong with your fangs?"

Brows pinching together, Fenn straightened, drawing himself up. His response was quicker than she expected. "There's nothing wrong with my fangs."

"You don't keep them extended like Lykor." Sensing she had him on the defensive, a little triumphant thrill had Serenna picking at him further. "Are they stubby or something?" She ignored the firsthand experience of his canines flashing in her face when he'd crashed into her, shielding her from the broken glass in the war room.

Fenn glanced at her sideways before the corners of his eyes lifted with his smirk. "Oh, I assure you, my fangs are longer than Lykor's."

Fenn moved so fast he blurred. Swiveling across the bed, his fangs extended, suddenly flashing in front of Serenna's eyes. Her heart launched into her throat, shoving out a startled squeak. Braced against the mattress, she leaned back, distancing herself from his sharp teeth.

"I thought you required a closer look," Fenn said, chuckling with wry amusement, clearly entertained by pinning her against the headboard with fright. "I'd hate for you to be misinformed."

Serenna's stomach lurched as he lifted a dangerous talon to her foolishly exposed neck. Her entire awareness fastened to the point where his finger hovered above her flesh, prickling where the unnatural heat of his skin lingered over hers.

Serenna cleared the burst of fear clogging her throat. She intended to be sarcastic but her words came out timid. "Consider me well-informed."

Something shifted in Fenn's eyes, like he only now registered her alarm. "However," he said, curling his claw into a fist before pulling away, "we deem it…improper to discuss fangs." He rose, canines retracting with a *click* before busying himself with opening the remaining curtains. "At least in public," he quipped with a wink over his shoulder.

Losing all the ground she thought she'd gained, Serenna huffed, crossing her arms, too embarrassed to voice any witty rebuttal. *Females have fangs too, so I don't know what he's so proud of.*

Drawing on a chain, the strange flat shades covering the domed glass ceiling slid back to the walls, folding closed like a fan. Serenna scowled as more sunlight splashed across her face. Blinking, she directed her glower at Fenn, but her annoyance only seemed to bounce off the spikes of his armor.

"If you show too much interest," Fenn said, glancing at her, "you might discover some wraith all too willing to sink their fangs into that pretty elven neck of yours."

Serenna clapped a hand under her ear, eyes drawn to the markings on Fenn's throat that she'd mistaken for battle scars. She didn't bother tempering the revulsion in her words, now realizing they were punctures left by teeth. "Do you drink each other's blood like bats?"

Fenn blew out a scoff. "Don't be disgusting."

Profoundly curious for reasons she couldn't explain, Serenna asked. "Why did you let someone bite you?"

"Our fangs have venom." Fenn folded his arms, leaning against a dresser. The points of his canines peeked out of his grin, giving Serenna the impression that he was humored by the perplexity plastered on her face. "The paralytic is pleasurable in small doses and enhances the mingling experience."

Serenna's eyes widened. He'd provided her with more information than she'd bargained for. "Oh."

She ripped her gaze away from Fenn's neck, seeing the plentiful evidence of such *mingling* encounters proudly displayed. In the blinding light, she noticed some were fresh. *Probably from last night since he couldn't stop talking about that Lagoon.*

Fenn was obviously taking delight in steering her thoughts in an inappropriate direction. He answered a question she wasn't even going to ask. "I suppose this new assignment as your warden will limit my preferred recreation with my partners."

Serenna rolled her eyes, uninterested in learning any more personal details about this crude wraith. *If he's this forward, I can use that against him.* Maybe it wouldn't be so difficult to wrestle that key from his neck.

Her thoughts circulated, whirling around a plan of reckless hope. If Lykor's habit was disappearing during the day, she might be able to summon the prince with no catastrophic repercussions. Since her key was going to be hovering as close as her bawdy guard, freedom didn't seem so far out of reach.

Fenn unfortunately interpreted her silent reflection for interest. One of his fangs extended, his tongue suggestively circling over the point. "If you're curious and wish to find out—"

Serenna threw another pillow at his head. "Get out!"

CHAPTER 32

SERENNA

For the second time, Serenna found herself on the Aerie's balcony, overlooking the desolate landscape glistening with snow. The chill infiltrated her bundled layers, her new wraithling armor wrapped in heavy furs.

She glanced over at Fenn. Hair lashing, he stood windblown across the parapet, peering over the edge. The cold didn't seem to bother him as his open cloak billowed in the knifing breeze.

"Where are the stairs?" Serenna asked, not seeing how they'd descend the mountain to the base of the fortress.

Fenn slung his crossbow under his furs. "There are no stairs." He arranged the weapon between the long knives strapped to his spine and extended a beckoning claw. "We don't need them."

Not budging, Serenna eyed him suspiciously. "Are you planning on jumping?" She tightened her cloak under her neck, tempted to draw the hood. "I doubt you have wings like those druids, otherwise I'm sure you would've flaunted them by now."

Fenn vanished like a wisp of smoke. Serenna's heart collided with her ribs when he reappeared beside her, lifting her off the ground. Deprived of time to react, she snatched his leathers with a strangled yelp.

"You'll want to hold on, she-elf," he all but purred, clambering up the balustrade to balance on the ledge. "And I'm not picky about where you put your hands." His chest rumbled with a laugh. "The lower the better."

Serenna's protest about his vulgarity and about being carried again morphed into a shriek. An invisible hook grappled her insides, yanking her stomach into her throat. Vision inverting, flipping, and spinning, her sight flashed to black. A rush of wind pounded her ears as everything went weightless.

Serenna gasped for a breath as her feet kissed a soft surface. Snow. Wobbling on unsteady legs, the world trickled back into focus. Fenn chuckled, peeling her fingers off of his armor.

"What—" Head twirling like a tossed coin, Serenna gulped for air, dragging in rapid breaths. "What happened?"

"You survived your first warping." Fenn held her upright as she stumbled. Squinting in the blazing light, Serenna followed his claw, waving around in front of them. "We came from up there."

Serenna's mouth flooded with a sick feeling as her sight soared into the sky. She could hardly distinguish Lykor's balcony from their spot on the ground. The surrounding snow-capped mountains bowed to the druids' ancient volcano, outlining the horizon like jagged teeth.

"We have to see where we're going—we can't travel through walls," Fenn offered, as if reading her bewilderment. He made a shooing motion with his talons, exposed skin shimmering with indigo iridescence in the sun. "If you need to evacuate your stomach, do so a little farther away, if you don't mind. Spin sickness isn't uncommon after the first few jumps."

Breathing heavily out of her nose, Serenna tried to think about *anything* else. Clenching her teeth, she swallowed, wondering if she had any abilities like him. But she was only missing one talent. That hardly made her a wraith.

Once Serenna's middle stopped pitching and she regained her bearings, they started trekking to one of the volcano's ground-level entrances. The tunnels at the base of the fortress burrowed into the stronghold's depths.

A glinting array of light stole Serenna's attention. Head tipping up, she inspected the uppermost point, flat from a previous eruption. Along the rim of the open crater's peak, mirrors arranged like flower petals sparkled in the sun. Fenn described how a system of pulleys swiveled the glass to follow the light, capturing and ricocheting the rays to rows of angled mirrors below.

Chains and lifts crawled up the sides of the fortress like vines dangling from a tree. Windows, balconies, and even landing pads Fenn claimed were for the winged druids had been carved into the slopes.

Serenna blew a breath into her gloves, reviving her frigid fingers. "Why didn't Lykor clear the lift?" Trudging through the icy powder, her boots scuffed, the squeaking noise making her ears twinge. "He could've easily blasted away everything with force."

Fenn shrugged, leading her toward an accumulated pile of snow. "Lykor wanted me to discover what your magics are capable of."

Encouraging me to use my elemental powers seems like a lot of trust on Lykor's part. What's to stop me from trying to escape?

Serenna quickly discovered her answer as the snow became deeper, crumbling beneath her feet. Slowing, she took exaggerated steps to free herself from her boots' sunken imprints. *Right. There's nowhere to escape to.*

"Lykor couldn't be bothered to find out for himself?" Evidently, burning his claw and dousing him with water wasn't enough of a demonstration.

Shortening his strides, Fenn waited for her to catch up. "He had other demands of his time today."

Serenna's question plumed as steam from the exertion. "Like what?"

"Aesar and my father discussed a jungle—one the elders took refuge in after Lykor portaled the wraith from the elven dungeons." Fenn shoved his claws into his cloak pockets, navigating the crunchy surface with ease. "Lykor intends to search for another one of those Starry Hearts there."

"Heart of Stars," Serenna corrected. Brows wrinkling, she wondered why Fenn shared Lykor's plans. *I guess I can't do anything with that information anyway.* "And Kal and Aesar are... involved?"

Nosiness getting the best of her, Serenna's frozen cheeks thawed enough to burn. She didn't want to make any assumptions based on what she'd witnessed in the war room—when Aesar had touched Kal's cheek with a gentleness that she doubted Lykor was capable of.

Her boot snagged on the icy ground.

Fenn's claw shot out, catching Serenna before her face collided with the snow. "Since Aesar has been more present in recent weeks, I suppose they could be considered paired," Fenn said, steadying Serenna on her feet. "I know that's what my father wants. He hasn't mingled since..." Fenn adjusted the crossbow holster strapped across his chest. "Well, I don't keep a tally of who he spends his time with, but he's been alone for many years."

Serenna's heart wrenched at the thought. Mind pirouetting from attempting to dissect wraith culture, she asked, "Is pairing more binding than mingling?"

And she was only asking from a logical standpoint—it made sense to learn more about the wraith. Fenn was clearly willing to discuss the subject and that *wasn't* guilt prickling at her for encouraging him. Surely gaining his trust would be an advantage. Determination settled on her like a dusting of snow. *I'll exploit any edge to wrestle my tether's key away from his neck.*

Fenn glanced at her, tilting his head. "I suppose pairing is similar to...marriage?" Serenna frowned thoughtfully at his interpretation of the word. "The elders wished to make our society more stable than the elves', so they adopted something akin to the mortal practice. I think." Fenn extended a claw. Serenna hesitated for a moment before clasping it, allowing him to assist her over a drift. The heat of his skin bled through her gloves. "Pairing can extend to multiple partners, so long as everyone agrees with committing to one another."

Serenna chewed her chapping lip, mulling over the unexpected cohesiveness of wraith culture—and the fact that they had their own culture at all. She never would've predicted they might have stronger familial ties than the elves.

Nearly panting by the time they reached the buried lift, Serenna's legs ached from the exertion of trudging through the snowy banks. She refrained from voicing her question, deciding it would be rude to ask what Fenn's mother thought of Kal and Aesar. With what he'd shared, anything seemed possible so long as everyone was in agreement. *But Fenn did say his father has been alone for a while, so maybe Kal and his mother had a falling out.*

The punctures in Fenn's neck shamefully summoned Serenna's curiosity. She could only imagine how their venom *enhanced* mingling. Brushing her flustered discomfort aside, she saw no harm in entertaining him by inquiring a little more. He was almost begging for it, if that grin he was giving her was any sign.

Stomach suddenly tumbling with disappointment, Serenna wished the prince had been this forthcoming when she'd wanted to talk. *I did all I could, but it takes two.*

With glove-clumsy hands—the tips of the elongated fingers open to accommodate talons—Serenna swept windblown hair out of her eyes. "Are you...paired with those you mingle with?"

Fenn hardly gave her time to finish the question. "No. I have partners, but I'm free to mingle beyond them." His smirk was annoyingly smug as he traced a fresh bite mark on his neck. "My preferences include anyone willing."

Serenna sniffed disinterestedly. *I don't know why he's flirting with me if he already has multiple partners. Shouldn't they keep him busy enough?* "And am I supposed to gather that those preferences extend beyond the wraith?"

Fenn's crimson eyes glittered in the sunlight. "I'm open to trying new things, if that's what you're asking."

Embarrassment shot through Serenna like an arrow, his teasing words quickening her pulse. "I wasn't asking," she snapped before thinking better of curbing her defensive reaction. *Well, I kind of was.* But only because she was attempting to learn more about his culture. "And for your information, I'm not a *thing* to try."

Fenn's cough was obviously meant to swallow a chuckle. His lips twitched like he wanted to dispute that statement. Instead, he became very interested in toeing a clump of snow, disintegrating the mound into icy pieces.

Serenna shoved her hands into her cloak, a wisp of her expelled breath coiling in the air. *I shouldn't be so harsh and accidently bruise his warrior-sized ego—I'm sure it's as big as those fangs.* Serenna cleared her throat, tempering her tone. "But consider me...enlightened."

As he studied their surroundings, Fenn spun his lip ring before his gaze landed back on her. "Even if I wanted to pair, I'm not of age yet."

Skeptical, Serenna scrutinized his face. He was definitely no youth. "What do you mean you're not of age?"

"I'm still a part of my clan's household until I reach my fifth decade." Fenn stooped to snag a clawful of snow. "It's one topic I actually agree with the reavers on." He grunted humorlessly, balling the flakes into a sphere and bouncing it. "It's absurd that the elders don't consider those of us born as wraith to be mature sooner—I have three decades." With a faraway look, he added, "I've already proven myself as a warrior in battle."

Serenna scoffed, a flare of indignation brewing under her ribs. "I hope that's not a boast about attacking us."

Fangs extending, Fenn suddenly rounded on her with a snarl. "I lost clan there too."

Serenna blanched at his reaction, retreating as he crushed the fistful of snow. She'd never considered the casualties on his side.

"Lykor believed eliminating your military was the only way to keep the wraith safe," Fenn growled, adjusting his bandolier with a yank. "And I'd do my part to protect my people again."

"Then why didn't you finish me off in the war room for your precious leader instead of protecting me?" Serenna bristled. "You've lived in as much fear of us as we have of you." She stepped back into the space she'd abandoned, ignoring her better judgment of antagonizing a soldier. "If those at Centarya knew the truth—"

"I know what you're trying to do, she-elf." Fenn's tone was loaded with a warning that he wouldn't be swayed. "Lykor warned me you'd—"

"And does Lykor not permit you to think for yourself?" Serenna interrupted, planting her hands on her hips.

A two-note horn sounded, breaking off whatever words Fenn was starting to form. Serenna followed his gaze to a mountain pass. Her pulse skipped up her throat upon seeing a group of wraith in the distance, angling toward the stronghold.

"A patrol returns," Fenn announced, alleviating her flash of worry. Shoulders relaxing, he retracted his fangs. "They'll likely have a kill to transport to the kitchens. Let's use your magics to clear this lift."

"Yes, *let's use my magics*," Serenna mimicked under her breath. Blowing out a sigh, she released her frustration. As soon as she started reaching toward the surrounding earth, Fenn stiffened, snatching her arm.

"We're getting out of here," he said, bending down as if to scoop her up.

Uninterested in being carried again, Serenna shook him off. "Why?"

The scouts were much closer now, warping in short jumps to the fortress. A patrol of nearly fifty wraith with red face paint sheared a path through the snow. The sides of their heads were shaved, leaving twin ridges of obsidian braids trailing down the centers of their backs. Crossbows and maces clattered as the soldiers approached.

"We're going back to the Aerie." Fenn caught her wrist. "I didn't expect the reavers to return until nightfall."

Serenna froze when she noticed the smaller beings in front of the warriors. Hands tied, they staggered as the wraith roughly shoved them ahead.

"Humans?" she gasped, seeing the mortals in rags and tattered furs. "What are *humans* doing this far away from the realms?"

One man stumbled and fell into the snow. Laughing, a female warrior punted him in the ribs with a cruel, spiked boot.

Serenna flinched. "Fenn," she whispered, clutching his arm. Fear soaked into her limbs, icier than the surrounding air. "What are the reavers going to do with them?"

Fenn's eyes volleyed around the warriors. The soldiers kicked the remaining humans behind their knees, sending them sprawling face-first to the ground. When a pair of wraith sauntered toward them, Fenn stepped in front of Serenna, concealing her with his towering frame.

"What are you doing with Lykor's elven scum, Lieutenant?" the male sneered, cloak flapping over his armor. Face painted with red streaks, he squared his stance, folding his arms across his chest. The female next to him replicated his pose, flashing her fangs.

Claws flexing, Fenn ignored him and addressed the female warrior, who had a bone pierced through the center of her nose. "Taryn, the humans need to be escorted to Lykor."

The male's snarl cut in, lifting every hair on Serenna's neck. "I'll decide what to do with them. It was the reavers who seized these thieving rats, gorging themselves at our traps. Pilfering our kills like the vermin they are."

"We're starving," one human cried out, eyes smudged with exhaustion. Hands bound behind his back, the man stumbled forward, trying to stand.

Serenna's stomach turned over at their malnourished faces, skin edged in frostbite. The mortal didn't make it far before one of the wraith clubbed him with the butt of a crossbow, sending him crashing to the snow.

"They're defenseless," Serenna said, a swell of anger feathering in her pulse. Fenn snagged her shoulder as she stepped around him.

"I'd keep your new pet on a tighter leash, brother," Taryn said, rolling a braid between her talons.

Attention riveted on the male wraith, Fenn flung his arm toward a tunnel that led into the stronghold. "Get the humans out of the cold and find them something to eat." Eyes on fire, he threw the command like a javelin. "Lykor will want to speak to them."

The male cackled like a crow. "I don't think so. Why would we waste our resources on feeding the elves' fodder? These mangy mutts are as worthless as their bones."

"Larek," Fenn growled, the low rumble from his chest reverberating through the air. His claws clacked, forming fists. "That's an order."

Taking a step forward, Larek broke into a serpentine smile. "You know the funny thing about orders?" His scarlet gaze dismissively slid over Serenna before he stood boot-to-boot with Fenn. "Orders are only respected if you follow the chain of command." Larek's fangs extended. "And I've grown weary of following Lykor's blundering."

Fenn tensed when Larek gave a shrill whistle, like a dracovae on the hunt. A warrior hauled the collapsed human up by his hair. Serenna yanked in a shocked breath as cruel talons sliced across the man's neck. Blood gushed in a spray, drenching the snow.

Fenn lunged, his fist connecting with Larek's face.

The valley erupted into garbled screams as the reavers shredded the remaining humans' throats. Unable to process the fountains of red spouting in waves, Serenna went numb, watching in horror as the slaughter slowed time to a crawl.

Taryn warped beside her, snatching her arm. Wrenched into a nether of darkness, Serenna staggered, reappearing twenty paces away. Positioning Serenna in front of her chest, Taryn's claws dug into her shoulders. Stifling a cry, Serenna inhaled sharply through her nose, recoiling from the slice of pain.

Fenn faced them with Larek on his knees, talons on the reaver's face, threatening to gouge his eye. Twisting the warrior's braids, Fenn yanked Larek's head back.

"Taryn, let her go," Fenn ordered, fangs extending.

A cruel laugh spilled out of the female as weapons rattled and unsheathed. The reavers fanned out, aiming their crossbows at Fenn.

Terror bludgeoned Serenna's chest when Taryn tauntingly skimmed a talon across the front of her neck, scraping skin. Fenn flashed his canines. Claws forming hooks, his nails scored the side of Larek's face, dragging out a hiss and a trickle of black blood.

"The wraith need her magics," Fenn snarled. "You can't harm her."

"Is that you talking or Lykor, brother?" Disdain dripped

from Taryn's fangs like venom. "I don't see how this elven bitch can serve the wraith, but the reavers will discover exactly how far her usefulness extends." Taryn jutted her chin in command. "Run back and inform Lykor that we're taking over her watch. Let Larek go."

Shock from the sudden slaughter fading, tears streamed down Serenna's cheeks, iced over by the wind. *This is just the beginning.* Pulse roaring in her ears, her mind replayed severed throats gushing blood. *The humans will overwhelm the wraith when they come in force, but how many smaller groups will die until they find this fortress?*

Imprisoned in the female's claws, a sense of cold foreboding constricted Serenna's air. Heartbeats passed while scales tilted in her head, weighing her options.

Serenna's eyes locked with Fenn's, the world coming to a stop. Rage honed the rigid lines of his body. If he was trying to communicate something with that fire smoldering in his eyes, Serenna was too panicked to read it. Withdrawing his gaze from hers, Fenn burned his conflagrating stare into his sister.

Sound hushed to a ringing silence as Serenna's breaths came shallow and quick, her terror morphing to fury at the helplessness. She instinctively craved to lash out with rending, to discharge her anger for everything she'd endured since portaling to this wasteland.

Reflexively reaching for her Well, an empty expanse answered her call. Serenna tunneled into the hollow cavern, delving deeper to where she *knew* her power should be. Except there was nothing. A sky devoid of stars. A magic tethered.

Serenna dug her nails into her palms. *I'm not letting these monsters take me.*

Steering her mind away from the horrors that awaited her if she failed, Serenna focused on the snow, falling into the world. Her vision went white, bursts of light exploding around her like a thousand rays of sun. Drifting, gliding across the wintery expanse, a wave of gleaming beams streamed out from every flake, every frozen drop of water.

Serenna heaved on the earth.

Snow exploded, geysering into the sky. Stumbling from the dislodged ground, Taryn released her. Throwing out a hand, Serenna yanked on streams of wind. Summoning the flakes into a blizzard, she aimed the cyclone at the reavers.

A shadow unfolded in front of Serenna, darkening her vision. The world went black as another warp yanked her into a pocket of midnight.

CHAPTER 33

SERENNA

The glass roof filtered in the cavern's mirrored sunlight, brightly lighting the maze of rooms. Serenna didn't register the nauseating mode of transport on the descent to the lower levels of the fortress. Fenn had snagged her from the chaos, warping them through one of the tunnel entrances.

Serenna crumpled onto a stool at the kitchen's center island. Natural stone archways connected the adjacent chambers in the quiet villa. Stairways ascended to open lofted levels in a dwelling that could've rightfully been called a mansion.

Safe within his clan's district, Fenn had shed his cloak and weapons. When he kindled a stove, tongues of flame dashed along the counter's obsidian surfaces in coal-lined channels, encasing the room in warmth. Pulling leaves from bundles of dried herbs hanging in a pantry, Fenn busied himself with boiling water and steeping a brew.

Serenna stared at the grainy patterns in the wooden table in front of her, still frozen by disbelief. She sensed Fenn periodically glancing in her direction, his jewelry clinking together as he worked.

She tensed when he drifted next to her, talons tentatively grazing her shoulder. There was a hesitation to his question. "Do you want to talk about what happened?"

Serenna dug her nails into her palms. The sting of pain hauled her thoughts away from the slashed throats and bloodstained snow. At a loss for words, her vision wavered, blurring when she met Fenn's eyes.

I want to talk about putting an end to this senseless bloodshed. We both know it's for nothing. But she doubted he'd be receptive to that response despite the concern on his face.

Choked by emotion, Serenna swallowed a spectrum of feelings that she wasn't sure how to release. Voice abandoning her, she twisted her boots around the stool's rungs. Brushing his knuckles across her arm, Fenn gave her space, wandering back to the stove.

Crackling from the coals shattered the silence as despondency settled over Serenna like a suffocating fog. Minutes passed before Fenn removed the steeping leaves, returning to the counter.

"I'm sorry you were in danger today," he said, placing steaming porcelain mugs between them before pulling out a seat next to her. "That shouldn't have happened on my watch. If I would've known—"

"I shouldn't need anyone to come to my rescue," Serenna interrupted, a tremor cracking her voice. "I have two types of magic, but I'm still helpless." Her throat closed after the painful admission while she blinked at the curling vapor.

"You held your own, she-elf," Fenn insisted, brows crowding together as he hunched over, peering into his tea. "You commanded the snows and bought us time to flee."

Serenna fanned her gaze toward him. Fenn idly tilted his cup, rotating the liquid around the rim. Seeming to feel her attention, he lifted his eyes, meeting hers.

"If I wasn't scared, if I'd acted sooner, the humans might still be alive." Serenna's hands trembled against the porcelain. "I could've done something."

At odds with all of his piercings, Fenn's face softened. "Regrets will dine on your mind if you invite them in. There's a lesson in sorrow, but don't allow your perceived failures to consume your thoughts." Fenn shook his head, rings glittering in the firelight. "Never would I have expected a display like today." The cup creaked when his claws flexed over the mug, knuckles leeching their color. "The reavers had no reason to slaughter those humans. It...wasn't right."

Serenna chewed her lip, reflecting on his words. He wasn't callous—the reavers' barbarity affected him too. The shared grief cracked open a tiny window of hope that they could somehow work together to prevent more death from occurring. *Maybe Fenn would be willing to talk to Kal and Aesar. Since Lykor refuses to see reason.*

Embracing the cup, Serenna's hands soaked in the only warmth in a world gone cold. Sipping at her tea, lavender and mint bloomed on her tongue, accompanied by an earthy flavor.

"What kind of tea is this?" she asked, interrupting the heavy silence.

Fenn tensed before his gaze fell to the liquid's golden surface. "It's a blend my mother used to brew."

Used to. Serenna's heart twisted, the words hanging between them like the steam coiling above the mugs. Holding the tea to her chest, she inhaled the aroma.

"What..." she hesitated, unsure if he'd want to share something so personal with her. "What happened to your mother?"

Fenn scraped a talon around the rim of his teacup. "She didn't return from your floating island. Along with two of my sisters."

Stomach sinking, Serenna's eyes fell to the counter as she scrubbed away stray tears. *All of this strife is so pointless.*

"I'm so sorry," she whispered, resisting the urge to reach out, clenching her cup instead. *Someone strong like him doesn't need comfort.* Serenna studied him out of the corner of her eye. Fortifying herself with a deep breath, she reconsidered. *That might not be true.*

Pulse ricocheting around her chest, Serenna touched Fenn's arm before questioning the action any further. His skin almost dispensed more heat than the mug. He relaxed, muscles slackening on the table.

"You're not the only one living with guilt," Fenn said, his words softer than snowfall, hardly audible over the popping fire. "I should've fought alongside my clan that night, but I had something to prove, wanting to lead my own squadron." His shoulders curved in, regret shadowing his face. "Taryn and the reavers blame Lykor for the failed assault. For the dead." Fenn's forearm stiffened under Serenna's hand, claws resting on the table curling into fists. "In a way, I lost her that night too, when she joined them. Countless friends—most of my generation—have banded with Larek, forsaking their own clans in favor of his ruthlessness."

"But Lykor has Essence," Serenna pointed out, studying her elongated fingers on Fenn's arm. "The reavers can't do anything to challenge him." Her attention whipped to Fenn when she felt him watching her. Adrift in a sea of awkwardness that she'd inflicted upon herself with her lingering touch, Serenna jerked her hand back.

"One golden crossbow bolt would stifle Lykor's magics," Fenn said, angling toward her. "But the reavers still need him. They're stranded in this fortress without his portals. It would take weeks of travel across the mountains to reach any of the mortal realms—if they even survived the journey. Last night at the Lagoon I heard…" Fenn's eyes flared, glowing like flames. "If the reavers claim you, they'll force you to use your earthen magics to navigate the wilds without Lykor." His mouth twisted into a grimace. "It's my fault they know of it. I let what happened in the war room slip to someone I thought I could trust. I—I'm sorry."

A knot of unease tangled in Serenna's gut as they stared at each other in silence. *That's not exactly what I had in mind for escaping the stronghold.* "Lykor wants the same of me, but I don't see what I could possibly do on such a journey."

"The world bowed to you today, did it not?" Fenn's attention flicked to the smoldering coals, as if only now recalling Lykor's order to keep her away from fire. "I've witnessed you twisting the winds and sundering the snows. If your magics are capable of melting a passage across the tundra or bolstering flames without kindling, that could be the difference between life and death in the Wastes." Extending a claw, Fenn grazed the shackle on her wrist. "You possess a gift that we do not." His words weren't bitter, but they carried a tinge of remorse. "You're not the only one who regrets not saving lives today."

Serenna wondered if those like Fenn—born as wraith instead of transformed by the king—had a Well capable of holding power. Recalling a conversation with Jassyn, she assumed the druids' curse would've prevented Fenn's parents from conceiving if they'd remained pure-blooded elves.

Serenna's heart pinched at the thought. The balance of life restored after so much had been stolen still seemed unjust.

The gloomy reality of the wraith's origins clouded Serenna's mood further. "What if we could bring an end to our people killing each other?" she dared to ask.

Fenn slid a talon into a crack in the counter, plucking at the wood. "I don't see how that would be possible."

Serenna probed, hoping desperation didn't flood her voice. "What if I could tell those at Centarya the truth?"

"And go back to your island with our location?" Fenn grunted, dislodging a splinter. "Lykor wouldn't stand for that—or portal you there." Shoulders sinking, he shook his head. "Would they even believe you?"

Serenna held her tongue, fearing Fenn wouldn't keep her secret if she divulged her bond with Vesryn.

"It would be too much of a risk," Fenn continued more strongly, as if convincing himself. "I think the wraith are destined to brave the world alone. Lykor will find us a safe place. Away from the elves."

"But what if you didn't have to hide?" Serenna swirled the dregs of tea, gently prodding. *As loyal as Fenn is to Lykor, surely he can see that the world doesn't have to be this way.* "The wraith and the elven-blooded could unite and stand against the king. We could stop him from stealing power and put an end to all of this meaningless fighting."

Fenn grew pensive, picking at his claws. "I don't disagree with you, but it's an impossible path."

Deciding against hounding Fenn with her wishful thinking, Serenna grew quiet, saving that battle for another day. Perhaps in time, she could kindle that spark of agreement flickering in his eyes.

Shoving back from the table, Fenn swiveled off his stool and rose. "Come on, she-elf. I want to show you something."

Leaving her empty mug, Serenna sighed. In the meantime, she didn't have anything else to do aside from following him around.

"Is it safe to travel the city?" she wondered out loud.

"We won't leave my clan's district—it's secure here." Fenn's actions didn't align with his words as he shouldered on his bandoliers and strapped his crossbow to his back. "But if anything happens, I'm glad I have your magics by my side."

Serenna flushed as they wound their way around the dwelling. "Where are we going?" she asked, stepping through the door Fenn held open, out to the open brick street.

Fenn gave her a fanged grin, dulling the edge of her sadness. "Have you ever seen a pocket goat?"

CHAPTER 34

LYKOR

Lykor drew to a halt at the top of the iron staircase before descending to his sitting room. Voices. Aiko shifted on his cloaked shoulders with a contented purr, head-butting his cheek. Lykor scratched behind her tufted ears, grumbling his complaint before stomping down the spiral staircase. It was too early in the morning to tolerate whoever decided to lay siege to his dwelling.

He'd roused in his own bed at least. For the first time in weeks. Lykor could only assume that was Aesar's attempt of currying a crumb of favor by executing his "bargain" to earn more control during the day.

Losing a battle to intrigue, Lykor burrowed inward, wondering if there was any other explanation for the change. He blew out an exasperated sigh as he delved into their mind, detesting Aesar's chosen landscape of Kyansari's library. Having endured enough confinement to last a lifetime, Lykor would rather exist somewhere under an open sky.

He materialized in their mindspace. Silent like a wolf on the prowl, Lykor approached the couch containing Aesar's sleeping form and hovered a hand over his silvery hair. Cautiously slipping into Aesar's slumbering awareness, Lykor skimmed through his recollection of the previous evening.

Rummaging backward in time, he passed over flashes of Aesar freeing the snow-buried lift before returning to the Aerie. WHY DIDN'T THE GIRL ACCOMPLISH THAT TASK? Lykor nearly ground his teeth to dust. Fenn had one fucking simple order to follow.

Half of his attention on winding down the stairs to the lower chamber, Lykor continued his search. Sifting through memories, conversations with Kal, Fenn, and Mara filtered in and out. Gathered in Kal's residence, Lykor relistened through Aesar's ears.

Reavers. The younger warriors boiled the blood in his veins. He couldn't control them. The turbulence was beyond repair. Amplified by Aesar's intervention—foolishly withdrawing from the assault.

Aiko pawed at his face. Lykor spared his vulpintera a half-hearted exasperated look before pinning his attention on his sitting room. Staring at him, Kal, Fenn, and the girl had made themselves comfortable, apparently having a communal breakfast in *his* suite.

Rolling his shoulders, Lykor didn't know—or care—how long he'd been standing there, diving through Aesar's mind while the rest of the world drifted by like dust on the wind. Flicking a strand of hair out of his eyes, Lykor strode toward them.

In the middle of the table, the Heart of Stars glittered like some prized, decorative jewel. Lykor swung his glare to his captain, assuming Kal had conceived the brilliant notion to hear for himself what the girl could parrot back. Aesar had deduced that her tether wouldn't interfere with whatever she heard, the relic's secrets tied to her shaman heritage instead of Essence.

Lykor seized an empty chair with his gauntlet. "What the fuck is this?"

Kal waved a hand around their plates. "It's breakfast."

"I can see that, you lackwit," Lykor growled. With a lash of force, he swiped an apple out of a basket, shoving the fruit into one of his cloak pockets. "Is there a malfunction in your clan's quarters that prompted this invasion of mine?"

"We wanted to have a discussion." Kal patted the seat Lykor gripped. An invitation.

"A discussion?" Lykor swept his glower to Fenn and the elf, seated across from Kal. "Like we're some fucking council now?" Agitation rumbled through his throat as he muttered to himself. "I don't think so."

Aiko's leathery wings rustled when Lykor abruptly pivoted on his heel. Intending to leave, he slashed open a portal.

"Lykor."

Screeching to a halt, Lykor twisted around with a snarl. "*What?*" Aiko flew off his shoulders this time, gliding to a sunny spot on her preferred couch.

"Join us." Kal's smile turned brittle, as strained as Lykor's patience. "Please," he added like an afterthought, his jaw latching shut.

Lykor roved his gaze over the other two. Fenn averted his eyes while the elf scowled at him, clenching her fork. Fascinated by an odd kinship with her contempt, Lykor smirked at her.

Kal dragged Lykor's attention back, spewing more of his nonsense. "We need to talk about what happened yesterday."

Releasing his power, Lykor dissolved the gateway. He shed his cloak like a snakeskin, flinging it on a sofa before stalking to the table. "You've already discussed the reavers with Aesar." He ripped out the chair at the end. "What more is there to speak of?" Dropping into the seat, Lykor flared his magic, yanking boiled quail eggs and dried fruit toward his plate. He jabbed his gauntlet at the elf. "She doesn't need to be involved in this."

"She does now since the reavers want her," Kal said, his voice rolling with practiced soothing. "And I wanted to talk to *you*."

Suspicious of the inclusion when Kal had already conferred with Aesar, Lykor thinned his eyes in his captain's direction. So it was brazen manipulation this morning.

"I have nothing more to add to Aesar's blathering about the reavers," Lykor growled, frustration scorching his veins. "Their rabble are the least of our worries with the humans encroaching on our fortress."

A glass slammed on the table, rattling the silverware. Lykor glanced at the girl, folding her arms and sitting straight-backed in her chair. "If those at Centarya knew the truth about your origins, this conflict wouldn't be happening—we'd have no reason to fight."

Lykor deduced her ties to that so-called academy was why Kal wanted her involvement. Another in favor of bleating their secrets to the captain's second-favorite prince.

"The elves will never see the wraith as anything but abominations," Lykor said, steel creaking as he drummed his gauntleted fingers. "We won't be safe so long as they can reach us."

"That's not true," the elf argued. Her gaze dashed to Fenn's before finishing her tirade. "There'd be no need for the wraith to leave if we stop this war."

"Speaking of," Lykor said, turning his attention back to Kal. "Start assembling the clans for departure. If yesterday was any indication of how close the mortals are intruding, it's past time we move on." Lykor cracked his neck, his taut spine twinging with a flash of pain, protesting the motion. "Have Mara assist with the preparations, as I'm sure she'll have opinions about our organization." If he could keep her busy with something trivial, it was likely she'd be too distracted to seek out the girl.

"And what new harborage have you found?" Kal challenged, the corners of his mouth fusing into a frown.

"You only need to concern yourself with my orders, not my undertakings." The metal in Lykor's gauntlet squealed as he ground his hand into a fist. "But if you require an explanation in order to give me a moment's peace," he said through his clenched teeth, "I've had other matters to attend to before I locate another haven for us."

Those "other matters" being that he'd recklessly ventured back to the military island under the cover of darkness in search of the amber-eyed elf. While Aesar was asleep, Lykor had concealed that knowledge from him, caging the memory behind the obsidian prison door.

He knew he should focus on the safety of his people, but Lykor couldn't curb his fixation. If the elf the girl had named as Jassyn could unravel the coercion latched to his mind, he'd be free at last from the king's touch. No longer a helpless passenger, steered by Galaeryn's influence.

Since Aesar had divulged his suspicion of a Heart of Stars hidden in the druids' jungle, Lykor intended to search that vile forest before he began portal jumping across the Wastes. If the wraith could take more than one Heart with them when they departed these wretched realms, that'd be one less relic for the king to possess.

While Kal and Mara were busy organizing the clans for departure, Lykor planned to set Fenn and the girl on the trail for the artifact supposedly in the keep. Then again, if the lieutenant couldn't manage directing the elf to complete one simple task, Lykor would have to do it himself. Like always.

Fenn spoke, bringing Lykor's attention back to why they decided to foul this morning with a fucking intervention. "It doesn't matter where Lykor leads us," he said, spinning one of his brow rings. "The reavers won't remain with the elders."

Lykor shrugged, biting into an egg. "Then let them stay. Their absence would solve more than one problem."

"We can't divide our people," Kal said. "We're stronger together." He reached out, but apparently thought better of resting a hand on Lykor's arm. He'd learned long ago that his touch got him nowhere.

With an irritated blast of breath, Lykor threw his head back. "What would you have me do? Shall I step down and permit that swine Larek to direct the wraith?"

Kal's voice sharpened, cutting like a blade. "There's a way that might appease everyone."

"By letting Aesar take over," Lykor spat, his words hostile. Acting on impulse while his temper threatened to boil over, he added, "How convenient for you."

Kal stared him down. Fenn cracked his knuckles under the table before speaking again. "That's what the *elders* desire." He shook head, piercings swinging with the motion. "Aesar in command won't pacify the reavers."

Kal and the girl swiveled their attention toward Fenn. Curiosity had Lykor listening. The young lieutenant never spoke against his father.

"The reavers want to rule themselves," Fenn claimed. "There's too many warriors aligned with Larek now for you to manage. They've...tried to recruit me over the years." Fenn chewed his lip ring. The same aggravating habit as Kal. "Larek proved that the reavers are going rogue. They won't take orders." He picked at a biscuit on his plate. "They have no intention of crossing the Wastes to the west like you do. Instead, they would travel to the east—to the mortal realms."

Idly tracing the lifted vines on the hilt of the dagger sheathed at his side, Lykor waited for Fenn to run himself out of breath. "Lieutenant, enlighten me as to why we shouldn't let them go."

"The reavers would survive by raiding farms and supply lines to Alari—they have no qualms with harming the humans." Fenn's eyes darted to the girl in a peculiar glance before continuing. "What the reavers did to the mortals yesterday was worse than that raid where they 'practiced' with their crossbows on the farmers."

Tracing a scar on his cheek—courtesy of helping Lykor restore order that day—Fenn studied him, as if weighing his words. "They'll only terrorize the defenseless if they have free rein."

"That behavior was corrected," Lykor growled, crushing his gauntlet to restrain the storm of his temper.

Fenn's face went ashen, likely recalling how Lykor had used Essence to rip out the offenders' fangs and talons. Displays of magic always made the younger generation nervous.

Diving into Fenn's silence, the elf slapped her silverware to the table. "Clearly, you failed to *correct* it."

Lykor's lip curled. "Remind me, who invited you to this conversation?"

The girl glanced at the lieutenant, exposing the blame. Something Lykor couldn't place sparked and then burned in Fenn's gaze.

"Larek tried to seize her yesterday," Fenn growled, fangs extending. "The reavers would force her to use her magics to navigate the Wastes."

Lykor cocked his head, wondering how Fenn had overlooked that he'd require the same of the elf.

"Do you have a suggestion to make, Lieutenant?" Lykor demanded, eyes pinning on Fenn's fangs. "Or do you simply have your father's habit of sucking down air?"

Fenn blinked, abashed, before retracting his teeth.

Lykor continued without permitting him time to answer. "If the reavers cross the frozen expanse, they'll run into that human army." He leaned forward, putting his elbows on the table. "What would it be? A few hundred of them against thousands of mortals? They would be crushed."

Including the captain in his scorn, Lykor swung his gaze to Kal. "Even if the wraith remain united, we wouldn't survive against such a force—those ants would overrun us with their numbers alone. And if the elves portal in their Essence-wielding army, they'd level this entire forsaken wasteland." He raked his attention back toward Fenn. "Or do you not have a head for the obvious, Lieutenant? If that's the case, perhaps I should reconsider those rings in your ears."

Fenn dragged his talons away from the jewelry in his lobes. "The reavers wouldn't focus on the gathered army," he argued, the cords in his arms flexing. "They'd terrorize small farms and villages."

"I'm waiting to hear your point." Lykor scoffed. "The reavers' plans are as witless as they are worthless. They'd draw too much attention to themselves, forcing intervention from the elves. We have the advantage of portaling after raids. They do not. Their ambitions would be their demise." Lykor stretched his shoulders, dispelling his exasperation by popping the joints. "The humans aren't our concern. Let those half-elves like her"— Lykor slid his eyes in the elf's direction, meeting her glare with his own—"busy themselves with pursuing the reavers. The distraction would allow us ample time to relocate to somewhere safer."

"And portaling across the Wastes is still your plan?" Kal countered. He tipped his head at the girl, the bronze in his hair glinting in the sunlight stabbing over the mountains. "You'd have her use that elemental power and risk both of your lives in the process to reach the other side?"

Weary of this circular argument, Lykor beat his gauntlet against the table. "If you disagree, then you can remain here or leave with the reavers."

Kal's plastered congenial look disintegrated. "We don't know if habitable lands even exist to the west. Across the Cerulean Sea it's possible, but anything toward the setting sun could be frozen snow."

"How do you expect us to cross the ocean? By swimming?" Lykor loathed the strain in his voice, but he was forced to argue the obvious facts. "Navigating through the Wastes is our only option, unless you miraculously have Galaeryn's schematics for the Aelfyn galleons stashed up your ass." Earning a glower in response, Lykor flicked the Heart, the metal of his armor *pinging* against the crystal. "You were so star-bent on finding these baubles. But now we have one and you want to sit here instead of searching for the dragons. They're somewhere. And I intend to find them before the king."

"Dragons?" the elf chimed in, a glass of water halfway to her mouth. "I thought they went extinct along with the druids."

"Who else do you think that voice in the Heart belongs to?" Lykor asked, rolling his eyes. "Or do you have another mind leeched onto yours like I do?"

With a calculated deliberation, the girl set her drink down, swallowing what he assumed was a retort. Entertained by the potential imagination of her insult, Lykor nearly goaded her into speaking it.

And to discover if his prodding would lead to the lieutenant flashing his fangs—like Fenn was her self-appointed guardian. *I SHOULD'VE PREDICTED HE'D BECOME POSSESSIVE OVER A CHARGE.*

Lykor expected the girl to back down. Instead, the elf stubbornly held his gaze, making her displeasure known. A wrinkle formed on her upturned nose before she dismissed his question, turning to Kal instead.

"The dragons"—she shot him a glare—"mentioned the Hearts bound their power in chains. So returning the Hearts will free them?"

Lykor released an explosive sigh, interrupting whatever Kal was going to say. At this rate, the girl wouldn't understand if a dragon flew through the trinket and bashed her over the skull. Having their instructions implanted directly into her head apparently wasn't enough.

"There are five Hearts," Lykor clipped, enduring the explanation. He held up his fingers so that she could count. "And those five Hearts," he said, pointing to the tips of his digits, "each have a dragon bound—perhaps the last of their kind." Struck by a ripple of generosity from her rapt attention—well, mostly from her silence—he offered more of Aesar's conclusions. "Your connection to the earth through your shaman blood is likely the reason you can hear the echo of their words."

"Aesar believes these relics are keys," Kal said, before the girl could start bickering back. He rested a hand on top of the Heart, igniting the three colors of his talents.

"And though we only have one," Lykor growled, "surely unbinding the might of a single dragon would be better than nothing."

"But I have elemental power." The elf's brows creased with her furious thinking, looking between them. "Doesn't that mean the dragon's magic has already been freed?"

"Shaman power differs from dragon power," Kal gently explained. "You can't conjure the elements like they could. We don't know the extent of what your human line might be capable of, but it's obvious you can manipulate elements if they're present." The captain nodded at the pitcher of water, and Lykor assumed that the girl had performed her tricks before he'd arrived.

The elf frowned, twirling her hair around a finger. "Then I don't understand why the earthen powers have only now appeared again after all this time."

Lykor dug a fist into his eye, seriously regretting joining this wretched conclave instead of portaling away.

"The druid sterility curse finally going into effect two centuries ago likely triggered the elements to stir—that's what Aesar believes, anyway." Kal glanced at Lykor. "Dragon power slumbered alongside shaman power. Having their magic go dormant was perhaps the only way to protect the mortals. The Aelfyn would've had no reason to target them."

"The king has prepared for the return of elemental magic," Lykor grated out, sneering at the girl. "Aesar presumes

Galaeryn's aspirations extend to controlling shaman spawn like you in order to subdue the Maelstrom. The king will cross the sea and harvest whatever is left of the dragons' ancient magic for himself—or try to." Thinking of Galaeryn accumulating even more power had Lykor's gut twisting into a sour knot. "That's why we need to earn the beasts' favor by freeing them first. If they're alive."

"What about the druids?" Fenn asked, his interest always piquing at the extinct flying shifters. "Could they be guarding the chained dragons?"

"We have no way of knowing since the war took place across the sea," Kal said, twisting a thin braid between his fingers. "If there were any druids left, they wouldn't have permitted the Aelfyn to rule. If the dragons can't stand against Galaeryn, then there's no hope for us." To Lykor's annoyance, his captain had voiced what he was about to say. Kal glanced at him, a residual thunder flashing in his eyes. "Then it won't matter what scorching end Lykor leads us to."

DRACOVAE'S TITS, I DON'T HAVE THE STRENGTH TO DEAL WITH THIS SHIT, Lykor snarled inwardly to Aesar, who he sensed stirring.

Aesar arched a brow, swiveling to hook his knees over an armrest, lounging across a couch in his library. *They're including you.*

NO, THEY WANT SOMETHING FROM ME. I NEED TO—

Yes, yes, Aesar flapped a hand. *I know you want to search that jungle, but you should address what's in front of you too.* He waved a cup of steaming tea into existence on an end table. *There could also be a Heart somewhere in this fortress. Use the resources you have. You don't have to do all of this alone.*

Lykor directed his scowl at Fenn and the girl.

"Lieutenant, you and the elf scour the keep up until the second the wraith are ready to abandon this stronghold. If there's a Heart here, I want you to find it."

Fenn straightened, swelling with apparent pride for being assigned to the task. Lykor knew how to deflate him. "That doesn't mean rousing suspicion by flapping your mouth at the Lagoon."

Fenn flinched, the excited glow in his eyes dimming.

"And what will *you* be doing while we carry out your bidding?" Kal demanded, his unblinking stare conveying his disagreement to trek across the Wastes.

Shoving back from the table, Lykor almost rejected the question as beneath him.

"If I have your *permission*, Captain," Lykor hissed, "I'm going to search that jungle." Shoulders twitching, irritation nearly had Lykor's skin bristling off his spine. "If the druids claimed any Hearts in the war, we prioritize searching their ancient capitals first—that's all we have to go on. We have weeks at best before we need to abandon this place."

Kal crossed his arms, sweeping his gaze over Lykor. "And what about my suggestion of portaling me—"

"No," Lykor snapped. "This is the final time you're bringing that up."

Kal hadn't relinquished his scheme of urging Aesar to transport him back to the military island. The captain intended to spin an illusion and seek Vesryn out, appearing fully as an elf, since his sharper features and skin tone still favored the wraith. Aesar wasn't inclined to put Kal in that danger. Not that Lykor would've permitted the risk anyway.

"What do we do about the reavers in the meantime?" Fenn asked, fiddling with one of his eyebrow rings.

"Let them stay, let them go. It matters not to me." Flaring his power, Lykor snatched his cloak with a whip of force. "If they refuse to follow my lead, then they don't have a place with the wraith. I can only suffer fools for so long." He twisted open a portal, speaking over his shoulder. "Keep a guard on the girl. I don't want her magic falling into their hands."

CHAPTER 35

JASSYN

Shadows swarmed Jassyn like a ballistic beehive. Essence blazing, he spun a renewed flare of violet light, arcing a shield between him and the prince. Doubtful that his crystalline ward would withstand Vesryn's magical assault, Jassyn dodged the barrage of darkness, diving to the ground.

The black sand of the beach cushioned his fall. He rolled over his shoulder, scrambling back to his feet. Curls plastered to his face, Jassyn shook the rain out of his eyes.

A flash of lightning cracked behind the prince, shattering into the turbulent ocean. White-capped waves thrashed, sending the tide surging past their ankles. Forming another fist, Vesryn didn't grant him any time to catch his breath.

Jassyn regained his footing before another volley of darkness bashed against his shield. Thoughts rampant like the storm, he cycled through his limited options. Gritting his teeth, Jassyn tapped into his depleting Well, fortifying his protective barrier before he tried anything else. Aside from blinding his cousin with a burst of illumination—that Vesryn would most likely slash through with rending—he had no talents at his disposal to retaliate against the relentless striking shadows.

A pulse of power billowed out from Vesryn. Before Jassyn could react, a blast of force smashed into him. Ward obliterated, Well completely drained, the punch of magic launched Jassyn into the sky.

Breath clinging to the inside of his throat, he collided with the chilly sea. The water swallowed him. Frantically resurfacing for a gasp of air, a wave crashed over Jassyn's head, plunging him back within the depths.

Vesryn snarled telepathically into Jassyn's mind, tearing past his mental barricades. *I found a storm for you to practice with and you're not even trying to use it.*

Lungs nearly combusting, the ocean finally released Jassyn from its watery grave. Volleying a retort, his simmering grievances against the prince accumulated like the brewing tempest. *My apologies, let me thank you while I'm busy drowning.*

Finding purchase on the coarse sand, Jassyn's hands and knees sank into the shoreline. Disoriented and coughing, he stumbled to his feet before another wave could slap his back.

Jassyn wiped the water off his face, finding no relief from the salt burning his eyes. Sensing the building pressure of Essence, his chest seized on another breath, anticipating the impending attack.

It never came.

The prince stalked up to him, snatching the front of his soaked leathers, towing him up the beach. Jassyn's legs had no choice but to follow as his cousin dragged him to the grass-covered dunes.

Rain showered them, washing off the sticky sand clinging to Jassyn's skin. Gray clouds tumbled past the rim of cliffs bowing over the churning sea. The surf crashed on the rocks, hazing the air with misty spray.

Vesryn finally released him. The prince crossed his arms while blistering displeasure radiated off him, almost hot enough to burn. Buffeted by the breeze, Jassyn lurched in the long grasses before reclaiming his balance. His chest shuddered, drawing in labored breaths to recover his lungs.

Looking anywhere else to avoid his cousin's scorn, Jassyn craned his neck up at the towering craggy bluffs. Squatty black and white birds splayed their webbed feet against the battering wind, clumsily landing with beakfuls of fish before disappearing into burrows.

Vesryn's rebuke was rough like the surf. "I brought you here so you could hone your elemental power."

Tightening his lips, Jassyn hesitantly met the prince's disapproval. "You didn't give me a choice." A glimmer of defiance flickered. "Regardless of what I wanted, you would've tossed me through that portal."

"You agreed to spar with me," Vesryn fired back.

"Not like this," Jassyn grated out. He waited for a peal of thunder to subside. "Have you considered that perhaps I'd like to explore that magic on my own? In a calm environment with a clear mind?"

Vesryn drummed his fingers across his arms. "So what's your excuse for the sloppy way you're wielding Essence?"

"I'm tired," Jassyn snapped, irritably shoving soaked windblown curls out of his eyes. That was an understatement considering that the prince's magical bombardment had exhausted his Well.

Vesryn scoffed. "Then I'll be sure to tell Serenna that we didn't find her sooner because you were 'tired.'" He viciously yanked one of the remaining scraggly threads on his leathers.

"You throwing me all over the beach to release your frustration has nothing to do with finding Serenna," Jassyn argued, tossing his hands up. "I've spent the past week unraveling coercion with Thalaesyn from nearly sunup to sundown."

"And it hasn't been enough," Vesryn growled, a tendon twitching in his neck. He shifted his stance, every muscle in his exposed arms taut.

Jassyn took a calming breath, not rising to meet the prince's hostility. "We're overwhelmed with how many wraith you and your rangers are corralling." He readjusted one of his concealed daggers that was jabbing him in the ribs, cringing as trapped sand scraped between his skin and armor. "And no matter how fast you have us work, we can't extract answers that don't exist."

After spending time consoling Velinya, Jassyn had gathered that her last memories were of a wraith nearly ripping her apart. When Thalaesyn had unraveled the final knots of coercion, she became coherent in the stables—with no recollection of what had happened to her after the attack or how she came to be transformed and magicless.

It was the same story with the other thirty or so wraith the rangers had rounded up from the wilds. Jassyn and his mentor had freed them from their mindless, coerced states, acquiring more questions than answers. The former recruits now secretly lived in dwellings at the Ranger Station while the prince and his warriors determined the next course of action.

This conversation was the closest they'd come all week to discussing the wraith, skirting the truth of the elves devoid of power. The prince had viciously refused to hear any matter pertaining to the wraith or speculate further on Serenna's disappearance.

Dispensing sheets of rain, the wind sawed at the dune's grasses. Water sluiced down their faces in rivulets as Vesryn glared at him. Silence stretched as the tension swelled and thickened, clogging the air. The prince stubbornly clenched his jaw, hinting at words restrained.

Chilled and fatigued, Jassyn's patience with his cousin evaporated. He ruthlessly pointed out the obvious. "If Serenna has already been turned into a wraith, there's nothing we can do."

As soon as the admission slipped past his lips, Jassyn immediately recognized that he couldn't have said anything worse.

He knew they'd both been thinking of the possibility, but neither had given it voice.

Jassyn tensed when Vesryn's retaliation detonated, shadows erupting from the ground. The darkness twisted up the prince's legs, slithering over his arms to pool in his fists. Completely drained of Essence, Jassyn dodged a lash of rending whipped in his direction.

A bludgeon of force slammed into his back, knocking the breath out of his lungs. Sprawling forward, Jassyn's palms shredded on black sand as he caught himself.

"I could be searching for Serenna, but instead I'm wasting my time here with you." Vesryn planted his boots in front of Jassyn's face. "You can't even hold your own with access to ancient magic."

Curls curtaining his eyes, Jassyn glowered up at his cousin. He battled to summon some type of courage to strengthen his spine, but Vesryn ground down his composure with every verbal blow.

"I don't understand why the Vallendes are so fixated on your bloodline." The prince's words turned as dark and destructive as his shadows. "There's nothing special about you if you can't even use that power."

Panting out of his nose, a remnant of icy fear seized Jassyn's mind.

"You're a lost cause," Vesryn growled, looming over him. "A coward who can't even fight to save himself."

"The elves never gave me the chance." Staring at his hands, remembering where the tattoos had been inked into his skin, Jassyn's excuse sounded as pathetic as he felt.

Vesryn would never understand. The prince wasn't the one who'd been shackled to the realm. A captive, catering to every depraved whim.

"I went against the council to claim your contracts. For what? There's nothing to show for it." Vesryn's scathing words rattled around in Jassyn's head, echoing like a gong. "Perhaps I should let Farine have you back."

Pulse thrashing in his ears, Jassyn's racing thoughts went silent. The prince's taunt sent fury barreling through him like a storm. Jassyn's vision flashed to white, the elements in the squall igniting like thousands of fires blazing across the sea and sky.

Fingers curling into the dune, Jassyn snapped. Chest heaving with livid breaths, he disintegrated into all of it. Turning into nothing. Freezing. Burning. Transforming into everything. The world inverted, splintering as time stretched and then stilled, threatening to shatter.

Sensing a fountain of charged air converging, Jassyn lunged to his feet. Lightning flashed, fracturing the sky. Like leaves stretching to the sun, he instinctively reached toward that whispering source of power buzzing in his veins. Jassyn hauled on the crackle of energy, yanking the sparks to his palms.

Vesryn's eyes widened almost imperceptibly as he retreated a few paces. The ground given by the prince spurred Jassyn on.

"Is this what you want from me?" Jassyn raged over the wind, his voice fueled by anger. "You portal us to three different locations to find the biggest storm so I can show off this magic?" He flung his fingers out, hurling a spear of lightning at the prince.

"I want you to stand up for yourself for once," Vesryn snarled, his shadows clashing and tangling with the sizzling blue light. "Stop acting like you're so weak."

Jassyn bared his teeth. "Fine." Tunneling his perception, the surrounding breeze blazed with streamers of light. "Have it your way." Driving out his hands, Jassyn channeled a blast of wind at the prince.

Vesryn stumbled, but his magic flared, darkness exploding around him.

Jassyn snatched another whirlwind of sparks from the sky,

pressing offensively. For the first time, he *could* fight back. While the prince was off balance, Jassyn released a volley of energy. His breath snagged as the charge unexpectedly ripped through Vesryn's cloud of rending.

Now on the defensive, Essence coiled around the prince. He slammed a violet shield between them. Lightning crashed into the ward, showering an explosion of purple and blue light.

"Is that all you're capable of?" Vesryn jeered as rain dripped down his chin. Flicking his wrist, he conjured a tidal wave of force.

Jassyn clenched his jaw so tightly that his teeth creaked in protest. Shoving his hands forward, he met Essence with a rampart of air. Propelled backward by the prince's onslaught, he slid, boots digging trenches into the sand.

Jassyn snatched another crack of light webbing across the sky, twisting it, turning it, aiming it at the prince. Glittering Essence pulsed as Vesryn fortified his shield to absorb the blow.

Sparks spun between Jassyn's fingertips as he released the current. He channeled another surge of energy from the horizon. And another. Slamming a barrage of relentless strikes into his cousin's ward.

Wrenching the wind, Jassyn punched a gale at the prince's chest. Vesryn smirked as his barrier wavered, giving ground as Jassyn pressed ahead. Moving beyond the grassy dunes, waves brewed by the storm splashed over their boots.

Vesryn's amusement only incensed Jassyn further. The anger in his chest was wound too tight, a mooring line stretched too thin. Refusing to relent until he had the prince on his knees, Jassyn channeled chains of lightning, pressing his cousin backward with persistent slaps of air.

His frenzy was a wildfire, fueled by decades of kindling stacked, doused with oil, primed to burn. Losing himself as he drowned on power, Jassyn harnessed the sea. Summoning a colossal fountain, he twisted the water into a cyclone, funneling it into the air.

The flash of fear in Vesryn's eyes broke his cloud of rage, jolting Jassyn back to his senses. His connection to the earth dissipated like fog on the wind. But it was too late to recall the vengeful waters.

The prince disappeared under the crashing swell.

Scorching stars! Jassyn rushed to the shore as the ocean receded, eyes darting along the froth before the next wave knocked into his knees. Clasping his temples, Jassyn's palms shook as he knotted his fingers in his curls.

Breath held, he waited. Moments passed. Each second without sight of the prince only magnified Jassyn's concern.

Swallowing his terror, Jassyn nearly choked on relief when silvery hair bobbed above the waves.

Until he noticed Vesryn was floating. Facedown.

Jassyn dashed into the ocean, snatching the prince's leathers before another wave could claim him. With a burst of panicked energy, he dragged his cousin past the breaking water, cursing Vesryn for his bulk. Hauling the prince all the way to the grassy dunes so the sea wouldn't reach them, Jassyn collapsed next to him.

Vesryn didn't stir.

Floundering, Jassyn fumbled with his depleted Well. *I can't heal without Essence!* Eyes riveted to Vesryn's still chest, Jassyn's hand quivered as he searched for a pulse. *Human lore insists that shamans healed with the earth.*

Slamming his palm to the ground, Jassyn seized the power humming under him. Fingers curling into the grasses, he heaved at the earth's magic.

A ripple streaked out from underneath his touch, beginning with the plants snared in his grip. The circle expanded, racing out in every direction. Seagrass wilted and then shriveled, crumbling into ash. The earth's power rushed into Jassyn, blazing behind his ribs.

Uncertainty churned in Jassyn's gut as he contemplated how to transform the green light spilling from his palms into something he could use to mend. Focusing on the prince, he reached out, resting his fingertips on Vesryn's chest. *I hope this works.*

The prince's eyes popped open. He spit a mouthful of water at Jassyn's face. Before the stream hit his cheek, Jassyn jerked away. Wheezing, Vesryn burst into a cackling fit, choking on water and air.

"I had you there for a minute, didn't I?" Vesryn coughed, sitting up to ruffle Jassyn's soaked curls.

Shoving the prince off, Jassyn scoffed, vacillating between relief and irritation. He slapped his cousin's back harder than necessary, helping him clear his throat.

"I didn't mean it," Vesryn hacked out, rushing through the words. "You're stronger than anyone I know for enduring what you did." An assortment of emotions rotated over the prince's face before guilt anchored in his features. "I just wanted you to believe it for yourself. To *prove* it to yourself." Vesryn directed his attention to the storm drifting further out to sea, a break in the clouds lightening the sky. "I…only meant to help you."

"I'm not like you," Jassyn bit out. His body quivered from too many warring feelings pulling him in every direction. A rope frayed, ready to snap. "Expelling anger in a magical tantrum doesn't exactly help *me*." Pinching the bridge of his nose, Jassyn inhaled deep breaths to calm himself, dispelling the darkness of his mood. "You have no reason to be vicious with cruelty to break me—to get the reaction you want." Adding less forcefully, he added, "I'm already broken enough."

Vesryn averted his eyes, guilt woven into his features. "I'm… sorry. I shouldn't have taken it so far."

Turbulent thoughts settling, Jassyn offered his side of the truce. "We'll find Serenna. She's going to be okay."

A companionable silence unfurled alongside the gentle breeze. Jassyn studied the radius of ash spread out beyond them before drawing his hands to his face. Glowing green light still shimmered from his palms.

The cuts he'd received from skidding in the sand had somehow disappeared, revealing smooth skin. Jassyn's mind raced for any plausible explanation. *I didn't do anything with this power.* He glanced at the prince. Vesryn had his fair share of scrapes from his tumble in the ocean.

Wringing his hair out, Vesryn eyed the foreign magic warily when Jassyn gripped his arm. "Do you know what you're doing with that?" The slight tightness in the prince's voice provided Jassyn with a tinge of twisted satisfaction.

With an honest shrug, Jassyn spooled the earthen magic into his cousin. "You didn't seem to be concerned about that five minutes ago."

"That was *before* you created this"—Vesryn waved around the sandy dunes—"ring of death."

"I'm not sure it's quite 'death.' It feels more like a tipping of scales," Jassyn added after Vesryn's brows rose skeptically. "Or a balance disrupted. I think."

Pursing his lips, Jassyn threaded the strange filaments of light, stitching his cousin like he would with Essence. He couldn't put a finger on the sensation, but something felt unnatural—off in some fundamental way—with stealing energy from the earth.

Driven by instinct more so than intuition, Jassyn hesitantly touched the ground after healing the prince. He sent his awareness tunneling below, attuning himself to the roots of the withered plants. Chest heated with ancient magic that had no place to go, Jassyn shifted the excess power to his fingertips. Dispatching the energy he hadn't used for mending, green light ignited the veins of his arms, the pressure under his ribs flowing back into the earth.

Vesryn's eyes popped along with Jassyn's as tufts of grass broke through the sandy soil, reclaiming the dunes. Redistributing the life he'd borrowed, Jassyn ran his fingers through the scattered blades, comforted by the unexpected equilibrium. The blooming beauty of renewal.

For the first time, he almost felt like something was right.

CHAPTER 36

SERENNA

Three weeks blurred in the search for the Heart of Stars. Serenna and Fenn had explored tunnels darker than pitch, ransacked ancient storerooms, and rummaged through uninhabited dwellings in what felt like every corner of the Frostvault Keep.

They'd managed to avoid entanglements with the reavers while they'd scoured the districts Fenn had deemed safer territory. But more than once, a contingent of his clan's warriors had accompanied them when they'd ventured where the restless wraith had a heavier presence.

A dracovae patrol had been spotted by a scouting group two days prior, stirring the reavers into a frenzied hunt, the bloodthirsty warriors determined to fell the beasts and elves. After the sighting, Kal had surrendered to Lykor's plans of abandoning the fortress, organizing supplies and mobilizing the clans for departure.

Serenna spun the golden tether on her wrist. *I need Vesryn to find me before the reavers harm his rangers. Or before Lykor drags me too far across the Wastes.* The key dangling around Fenn's neck was her best chance at freedom.

But she was well aware Fenn would "file his fangs" before he disobeyed an order and removed her manacle—especially for no apparent reason. *Except...* Serenna studied the lieutenant in his spiked armor. *Today he seems to be toeing a line.*

Fenn had brought her to one of the crossbow firing ranges after they'd spent yet another fruitless morning and afternoon hunting for the Heart. The open caverns at the base of the volcano crawled upwards, the crevices outlined by jagged stone. A sluggish stream of magma bubbled and churned a winding perimeter, shrouding the chamber in a comfortable warmth. Glowing light from hissing flames scrawled shadows across the rocky walls.

Sore from the endless walking in a new pair of wraithling boots provided by Fenn, Serenna shifted her weight. She was tempted to sit on the ground and rub her feet while enduring his long-winded demonstration.

Obviously, fiddling with these contraptions was his favorite hobby. Well, aside from mingling. And Serenna was past tired of hearing about that Lagoon, so she'd suffer through this. Oddly enough, Fenn's infectious excitement sparked her interest as he explained the function of *every* single pin and gear.

"And you crank this lever," Fenn said, his claw working in a circular motion, winding the cords back until it locked with a *click*. He strummed the string with a talon before nodding. "The druids left behind schematics of their weapons and we were able to replicate their craftsmanship to create our own." He placed a gold-tipped bolt into the grooved center channel, aligning the indents in the shaft with the posterior string before offering it to Serenna.

She hesitantly took the loaded mechanism, eyeing the wicked gilded end warily. *This tiny arrow really brought Vesryn down?*

Turning to Fenn, Serenna asked, "What do I do now?"

Fenn yelped. "Don't point it at me!" He shoved the front of the weapon toward the wooden targets.

"That's how you handed it over!" Serenna readjusted her grip. "You're the one who insisted that I learn how to fire it today."

"Because it's past time we did something fun." Fenn jammed his claws into his trouser pockets. "And you owe me a debt for making me swim across that underground lake yesterday."

"I wouldn't consider your floundering to be 'swimming.'" Serenna released a snort at his expense. "You would've drowned if I hadn't displaced the water for you."

Fenn shot her a sizzling glare, the magma's glow catching in his eyes. He scuffed a booted toe on the rippled black ground—dead lava, he'd claimed. "That shoreline was one of the few places we hadn't searched," he mumbled, an attempt to defend what dignity hadn't capsized in the lake.

Serenna's arms strained with the effort of holding the crossbow. "I didn't think a big wraith warrior like you would be scared of a little water." Her gaze glanced off the fang marks on Fenn's neck—a fresh pair that certainly hadn't been there the day before. "I figured you knew how to swim since all you talk about is that Lagoon."

"The Lagoon has me versed in the crafts of *pleasure*, not this" —Fenn made a wild motion with his claws, poorly imitating what she'd tried to teach him—"*swimming*." He smirked. "You would know that if you'd accompany me for once."

Having already warded off multiple invitations to join him and stars knew how many of his partners at the Lagoon, Serenna sniffed her disapproval as an answer. But her thoughts warred.

She was running out of time to get the key away from Fenn's neck. But she couldn't exactly untether herself around so many wraith and have Vesryn appear in the middle of…whatever occurred at the Lagoon.

Aggravation writhed inside of her. On second thought, since the prince probably had the same habits as Fenn, Serenna was sure he'd be delighted to join. *At least Fenn isn't secretive about what he does in his free time.*

Hefting the cool metal on the underside of the bow, Serenna asked, "Are you going to show me how to shoot this?"

Fenn reached around her, his dangerous claws surprisingly gentle as they wrapped over her hands. "First, you'll want to aim it."

Serenna's spine locked when his chest nudged into her back. She smothered the impulse to squirm away from the contact. He was making it a point to fluster her since he'd made a fool of himself at the lake.

Lifting the crossbow to her shoulder, Fenn slid her fingers further down the grip. "Press this lever when you're ready to fire."

Rattled by her racing pulse, Serenna clenched her teeth, resisting the urge to wipe a bead of sweat gathering on her neck. "Do you get this close and personal with everyone you train, *Lieutenant?*"

"If they permit it." Fenn's chuckle rumbled through her shoulders. "But only the wraith I find attractive." He skimmed a talon up her arm. "And apparently feisty she-elves who require intimate instruction on *weapon* handling."

Serenna bristled, refusing to let embarrassment silence her. "And I suppose you're the type of male who thinks the way you handle your 'weapon' is as impressive as the length of your fangs."

"Careful, she-elf." Fenn's claws tightened against her. "You almost sound interested in finding out."

Aware that Fenn would only need the slightest encouragement to press any advance, Serenna's instinct was to skirt away from the dangerous flirtation. *How can I be upset at Vesryn for sneaking around with Ayla if I'm hardly fending off someone else's interest?*

The absence of the bond these past few weeks—and being apart from the prince—had dulled the shock of Ayla's presence. Now Serenna regretted irreparably overreacting. *But I wouldn't have discovered the truth if I didn't accidentally portal here.*

Serenna blew out a breath, calming that flurry of snowballing turmoil. Focusing on the wraith in front of her, curiosity tingled like an incessant itch. She wondered what Fenn found attractive—since his comment implied she was in a different category.

She innocently asked over her shoulder, "So since I'm not a wraith, you don't think I'm pretty?"

Fenn suddenly squeezed Serenna's finger over the trigger, yanking her attention back to the firing range. She gasped as the crossbow jumped, the support of Fenn's chest behind her dampening the recoil. The bolt sailed across the chamber, smacking into a target.

"I think attraction encompasses more than physical features," Fenn said, releasing her hands to spin a ring in his ear. "But since you're inquiring about superficial attributes, I suppose you're not what I'd typically find alluring since I'm more accustomed to wraith." Serenna turned toward him as he drew another arrow from the quiver at his waist. "For one, you have no height or fangs to speak of." His gaze swept over her. "And your breasts and hips are rather...exotically proportioned."

Serenna scoffed, jabbing his ribs with the crossbow. "My figure is simply more human than that of you lanky wraith."

Fenn cleared his throat, quickly correcting himself. "That's not to say I don't appreciate your ample curves."

Doubting he was making a vicious comment about her body, Serenna fought the urge to laugh at his straightforward observation. "Thank you for pointing out how *exotically proportioned* I am," she said while he took the crossbow and then recranked it.

Fenn returned behind her, placing the ready weapon back in her hands. Letting her hold it steady, he loaded another bolt. Serenna glanced back when he remained silent.

He scrutinized her with a serious intensity. "The points of your ears are pleasing."

"Your compliments astound me," Serenna said, hopelessly trying to curb the heat racing up her neck. "Is your skill with words what impels everyone to your bed?"

Inhaling sharply, she nearly dropped the weapon when Fenn glided his claws down her ribs to envelop her waist.

"I have a unique skill set for that." His chuckle was dark, offering no other explanation than suggestively shoving the length of his body against her back, talons scoring into her leathers.

Serenna's fingers seized the trigger. The bolt launched, soaring clear over the target.

Fenn chuckled, pinching one of her ears. "I like how you turn red when you're flustered."

Jolted from the unexpected pressure, a stray nerve shot down Serenna's spine. She swung the crossbow at Fenn like a club, swatting away his pesky talons.

Cackling, Fenn warped to her other side before the blow connected. "It's a shame you have no snow drifts down here to catapult at my head with your magics."

Serenna simmered with irritation. She wouldn't admit it, but he'd bested her this round. Setting the crossbow on the ground, she trapped the stirrup with her boot and copied his previously demonstrated motion, cranking the lever to restring the weapon.

Glaring at Fenn and then scanning the flames spurting from the volcanic stream, Serenna countered, "Maybe I'll try to channel that magma and set your leathers on fire. You can't warp as fast as you think."

Fenn grinned at her empty threat, eyes sparking with challenge. "Allow me to finish admiring you before you descend into pyromania." He drew another quarrel from the holster at his hip, twirling the bolt around his talons.

Serenna pursed her lips, thoughts snagging on the sharp edge of guilt. *I shouldn't have encouraged him.*

"You dismantle me with the skies in your eyes." Fenn's gaze flared as it lingered on hers. "The color reminds me of a glacial waterfall near the outskirts of our fortress. When the moons shine on it just right, it's a sea of starry ice." He fidgeted with the arrow before returning it to his holster. "I'd be happy to show you sometime. But there's more than your features that I—"

"You forgot to mention my fingers," Serenna interrupted, unsure what to do with the compliments she might as well have blatantly asked for. "They're longer now since Lykor stole my magic and wraithed me." Bitterness seeped into her words as she deflected his attraction, brandishing her palm in front of his face. "Do you find them alluring too?"

"*Wraithed* you?" Fenn asked, his mouth twitching, showing the points of his fangs. He snagged her waving hand, inspecting her nails. "Your talons are still stubby."

"I don't have talons yet." Serenna yanked her wrist out of his grip. "Maybe I will if Lykor plans on taking more of my power."

Grin swept away, Fenn's humor faded. "My father said not everyone survives a siphoning of magics..." He twisted one of his braids. "The torture nearly destroyed Aesar. That's why Lykor appeared. He endured years of torment so Aesar and the elders didn't have to."

Heart stilling, Serenna blinked dolefully up at Fenn. *I never wondered how they came to be.*

"But it doesn't make what Lykor did to you right." Fenn's voice softened. He gently rested a claw on her shoulder, the gesture igniting an emotion Serenna couldn't place. "We heard the screams and... I'm sorry my father and I weren't able to stop him." Her pulse skipped when he snarled, fangs shooting down.

"Maybe the magics on Lykor took away his control, but I won't let—"

Fenn's talons abruptly tensed against her. His eyes flashed, a fire in the night, burning a trail across the chamber.

They weren't alone.

CHAPTER 37

SERENNA

"Are you training Lykor's pet with our weapons so she can join your miserable clan, Lieutenant?" Larek asked.

Despite the heat in the chamber, a shiver of foreboding shuddered down Serenna's spine. A band of nearly thirty reavers armed with crossbows, maces, and knives filed in, spreading across the cavern.

Trapping them.

Larek strode to the center of the firing range, crossing his arms over his spiked armor. Breath tight, Serenna glanced around, scanning the wraith. She didn't see Fenn's sister, Taryn, among their number. But that didn't mean another reaver wouldn't try to snatch her this time.

"If you have a problem with her presence," Fenn said, clacking his talons before cracking his knuckles, "you can take it up with Lykor."

"And where has Lykor been these past few weeks?" Larek sneered, the streaks of his face paint glinting red in the magma's light. "Planning his next blunder?"

Fenn ignored him and growled, "What do you want?"

Larek's attention flicked to Serenna. "I'm taking Lykor's elven scum." Serenna flinched when he took a step forward, flashing his fangs. "Hand her over and I'll forgive our previous… disagreement. I'll even let you join us when we abandon this cesspool."

Fenn clasped Serenna's hand, calculating eyes scouring the firing range, likely hunting for any clear path to warp away. Bracing herself, Serenna's stomach clenched in anticipation of the spin.

The weightless feeling never came. There was no way out.

Instead, Fenn's guttural growl lifted every hair on the back of her neck. His extending fangs glinted in the magma's glow. "If any of your clan lays a talon on her again, I will sever every offending claw."

With a twisted smile, Larek's gaze narrowed in a dark promise. He signaled with that eerie whistle through his teeth.

Fenn reacted before any of the reavers, vanishing from her side. He collided with Larek in a clash of talons, his knee jerking upward to smash Larek under the ribs.

Terror strangled Serenna's throat as the other wraith blurred into shadows, converging on Fenn. None of the warriors bothered drawing their weapons.

Disappearing and reappearing around the center of the closing ring, Fenn was a thunderhead of spinning darkness. Distorting into a tempest of smoke, he whirled and dodged the reavers, kicking out, swiping at legs. With brutal bashings of his elbows, Fenn shattered the arms of those daring to get close before ramming them back into the circle of wraith. His lightning fast talons snatched blows, twisting wrists in sickening crunches of bone. Snarls ricocheted across the caverns, punctuated by grunts when fists smacked against flesh.

Despite Fenn's claws flying, jabbing, deflecting, and counterstriking, the reavers caged him in, a cruel vice tightening. Time seemed to slow as Serenna watched in helpless horror, knowing he was going to be overwhelmed by so many.

She gasped as Larek landed a devastating punch square in Fenn's gut.

Off balance, Fenn stumbled, doubling over. The reavers seized him as he struggled to wheeze. Still refusing to surrender, Fenn's motions became choppy and uncontrolled.

Restraining him, the swarm of wraith rained down blows from every direction. A handful of reavers held Fenn up while others beat the resistance out of him. Larek's fist connected with Fenn's face. He sent another rapid hit under Fenn's chin, snapping his head back. A spray of black blood spattered into the air.

Serenna took a step forward, not feeling very brave at all as she faced a pack of ravenous wolves.

Everyone forgot about me. Or rather, they didn't find any point in watching her. Her stomach hollowed out at the helplessness.

Serenna's nails dug into her slick palms as Larek landed repeated strikes against Fenn's middle, depriving his lungs of air. Her eyes ricocheted around the stark chamber, searching for anything to use. Fenn's crossbow lay at her feet, but the weapon was worthless against so many and without the quiver of bolts at his side.

A stir of air brushed past Serenna. She felt like slapping away the useless aid. There were too many reavers to bother with what little she could do by weaving the wind.

Flames spurted from the sluggish magma, tugging on her attention. Chewing a hole into her cheek, Serenna winced at her only option. *Of course Lykor insisted that I practice with everything except fire!*

Desperation to buy time had Serenna's voice ringing out in the caverns, shrill with her panic. "Are you so scared of Fenn that it takes a horde of you to face him? Do the reavers have no honor?"

Every blazing gaze pinned on her, raptors targeting a rabbit. Fear knifed through Serenna's gut as fangs flashed. Fenn sagged in the warriors' clutches, knees giving out as he coughed up a mouthful of blood.

Larek warped to her side. Serenna attempted to scurry back, but he viciously seized her arm.

"What do elven scourge know of *honor?*" Larek asked, his wicked nails scoring into her flesh. "Only the strong survive. Fenn is insignificant without the backing of his pathetic clan."

If Serenna had one foolish tactic she could always rely on, it was running her mouth. "Funny how it takes thirty of *your* pathetic clan to bring him down." She whimpered through her nose as Larek's tightening grip drew more blood in response, feeling as if his talons burrowed down into her bones. Warring against the dizzying pain, Serenna clenched her teeth, fanning the cinders of her defiance. "Did you already forget how fast Fenn outmatched you in front of the fortress?"

Larek's canines flashed in her face. "And for that, your lieutenant is going to take a stroll through the stream." Snatching her shoulders, Larek swung Serenna around as the reavers hauled Fenn back to his feet. They herded him with a barrage of blows, steering him toward the magma.

Gritting his fangs, agony contorted Fenn's bruised features. He struggled, attempting to twist out of their claws, but his opposition only provoked a harsher beating. What air remained in his lungs whooshed out as he folded over, breath bubbling in his throat.

"Stop it!" Serenna shrieked. Terror clanged against her skull the closer the reavers dragged Fenn to the molten shore. *Larek is bluffing,* she told herself. *He just wants to prove he bested Fenn.*

Larek's talons shackled her arms, forcing her to watch. With each passing moment, Serenna doubted more and more that this was merely an act. She thrashed in his grip, as helpless as a fish protesting a hook. "Don't hurt him!"

Larek scoffed against Serenna's back, his claws digging in further. "It would seem the lieutenant is good for more than regurgitating Lykor's drivel. Perhaps we'll keep him around as… motivation for your compliance." He spun Serenna around, lowering his face to hers with a growl. "But he needs a reminder that disrespect comes with a price."

Serenna's lungs pulled in air faster than she could breathe as Larek leaned forward. In a shock of biting pain, she sucked in a hiss as he grazed her neck with his fangs, peeling a layer of skin. The silent threat conveyed that he had the power to effortlessly end her life.

Despair weighed on Serenna like lead, sinking her into an ocean of dismay. *Fenn will only suffer more if I oppose them.*

"I'll do it." Serenna's voice shattered on the agreement. Blood trickled down her chest as she tried to recoil. "Whatever you need to cross the Wastes. Just…don't harm him."

"I'm feeling generous." Larek smirked, releasing her. "I'll let the lieutenant keep half of his toes. This time."

He warped back to the cluster of warriors still wrestling with Fenn. Serenna flinched when Larek seized a fistful of Fenn's braids, shoving him forward to the churning flames.

Mind exploding in terror, Serenna stared across the chamber, every fearful breath straining her lungs. She swallowed her screams as the reavers dragged Fenn closer to the smoldering fire.

Twisting around in the cacophony of the fray, Fenn frantically searched the cavern. Dangerously close to the scorching heat, sweat rolled down his battered face. His eye that wasn't swelling shut met Serenna's with an intensity that pierced through the chaos. A moment stretched as his gaze darted to the trail of blood trickling down her neck and arms.

Outrage washed over Fenn's features before he went truly feral. Claws flying, he somehow connected a blow with Larek, fangs snapping as if he'd rip out his throat.

Something inside of Serenna cracked, carving into her heart. Fenn wasn't battling to escape the magma or the reavers. He was fighting to reach *her*. To protect her, even though he was the one in danger. The one who was hurt.

Hands trembling uncontrollably, Serenna crushed her fingers into knots, fists leeching white. Blood from the gashes Larek had scored into her flesh crept down to her wrists, dripping off her knuckles. Fury crystalized in the fractures of her chest, forging fear into something else. Something stronger.

Forcing a calming breath down her throat, Serenna released her terror.

"Let him go," she commanded, her words echoing across the cavern.

The reavers didn't acknowledge her.

Disbelief punched Serenna in the gut like the blows pummeling Fenn. *They don't see me as a threat.*

She took in another breath.

The world went still.

A gentle breeze stirred, the wind beckoning to her. Flaming plumes pulsed, beacons flaring to life.

Serenna channeled her perception into the stream of magma.

In the space of a heartbeat, the earth answered her call. Magic uncoiled in her chest, singing through her veins as the ancient power rose in response, spreading its wings.

Serenna heaved on the inferno. A burst of flame streaked out of the magma, racing into her palm. Too busy wrestling with Fenn, the reavers didn't notice. She stared at the fire dancing above her fingertips before riveting her focus on Larek, his attention still on beating Fenn half-senseless.

Serenna's fury simmered, boiling over.

Throwing out her hand, she launched the fiery comet across the cavern.

The flaming orb punched into Larek's back. He roared,

stumbling forward. The fire fizzled out, disintegrating into his shoulder in a hiss of burning armor and flesh. Spinning around, Larek's volcanic eyes latched onto her with blood-lusting wrath. Serenna bared her teeth, tearing more of the blaze toward her.

Whipping a column of twisting flame from the magma's depths, Serenna forced the magic to separate. Five. She could manage five flaming spheres. It would have to be enough. She flung the fiery orbs at the reavers.

Dodging the flames, the wraith warped out of the way, evading the smoldering globes before any could land. Serenna wrenched the fire to a halt before the conflagration converged on Fenn, who had collapsed near the fiery river. Whipping her hands around, Serenna searched for her target.

Larek unfolded from a shadow in front of her. Serenna's stomach heaved as the smell of cooked flesh snaked up her nose.

Larek snarled, seizing her throat, forcing Serenna to scramble to her toes. Her control over the fire guttered, the flames snuffing out as they plunged to the floor.

Gasping to fill her lungs, Serenna's vision blurred as Larek's claw tightened. He yanked her off her feet, his superior strength forcing her body into compliance.

Serenna snatched at a jet of fire at the edge of her vision. A blazing whip cleaved the air with a *crack*, wrapping around Larek's neck.

He dropped her. Back arching, Larek clawed at his throat, scorching his hands on the flaming noose as he emitted mindless, strangled screams.

Serenna fell to the ground, catching herself with her palms. Coughing, she panted to catch her breath. Her eyes dashed around the chamber to account for the reavers. Clearly still believing their leader would be the victor, they circled her like a cloud of vultures, waiting for an impending death.

It wouldn't be hers—she wasn't finished.

Swaying to her feet, Serenna riveted her gaze on Larek, reattuning herself with the scorching heat. Greasy fat glistened as it weeped from his seared flesh. Clutching his charred, blistered neck, Larek's eyes widened with a wild terror.

A column of fire reared up behind Serenna, flickering and crackling. Consumed by instinct, her rage flared like a spark igniting oil. With a blast of power, she twisted the inferno into a violent assault.

Larek didn't have time to warp.

Channeling the flaming whirlwind, fire collided with the reaver. The other wraith warped out of the way, scattering like shattered glass. Serenna stoked the torrent with coils of wind, engulfing him in a spinning vortex. Conjuring another gout of flame, she punched out a tidal wave, forcing the other wraith further back with the threat of the same fate.

Howls echoing around the caverns, Larek thrashed like he could throw the flames off. His body smoked and writhed while the cyclone spiraled around him, consuming him, spurting hissing black smoke. The stench of burning leather and flesh invaded the air as his armor charred, skin melting and sloughing off bones.

The flaming funnel of death smothered Larek's screams too soon.

Pulse thrashing frantically in her head, Serenna poured her entire strength into the fire. Her breathing turned ragged as the chamber flickered in her vision, faded slowly, like the beat of Larek's dying heart.

Serenna heard Fenn stumbling to her. He reached out, pulling her away from the flames threatening to lick her boots. The reavers had fled, leaving the caverns as quiet as a tomb.

Fenn grimaced, clutching his ribs, weaving his fingers through hers. With a squeeze, the offered comfort anchored Serenna's senses back to her body, cooling the firestorm in her blood.

The world came back into focus one breath at a time as her

erratic heartbeat settled. Emerging from her trance, Serenna felt no whisper of remorse, no regret for her actions. *I should've ended Larek sooner, before he harmed those starving humans.* His death was bound to give life to others.

Wincing, Fenn wiped the blood away from his broken nose. He glared at Larek's charred corpse, the splashes of fire dying around his blackened bones.

Turning back to her, Fenn retracted his fangs, giving her a crooked smile. Serenna cringed as his lip split further and then lunged forward to steady him as he staggered.

Something like reverent pride and awe glowed in his unswollen eye. Fenn hooked an arm around her shoulder, still grinning, his words mangled in his swollen mouth. "I'm in your debt, she-dragon."

CHAPTER 38

SERENNA

Fenn transported Serenna to the safety of the Aerie with a handful of sickening warps. She wasted no time steering him upstairs to the bathing chambers to tend to his wounds.

When they reached the obsidian marble tile, Fenn stumbled, luckily catching himself on a standing towel rack. Serenna would've undoubtedly been crushed under his towering form if she tried to support him.

Sleet pelted the icy windows while humidity clung to the black walls. Heat from the vents whistled softly through the room, the temperature balmy like the shores next to the castle she'd once called home.

Serenna selected the rectangular tub instead of the central rain shower. Both were large enough to accommodate a druid's unfolded wings. Or so Fenn had claimed.

This had better not become routine. I've had my fill of stitching males back together. The memory of the prince's blood splattered over his bathing chambers in the Spire resurrected a rising tide of concern. Serenna recalled fumbling over Vesryn's injuries—

Jassyn wouldn't be saving the day this time. She forcibly anchored those unhelpful thoughts away.

Turning a series of valves, Serenna filled the bottom of the marble bath. Steaming water spouted from the pipes, ushered in from hot springs within the depths of the keep.

"Sit on the edge," Serenna ordered, grabbing a few cloths to submerge. "I can't reach you when you're hovering like that."

Arm braced around his ribs, Fenn gritted his teeth. "We're dressing your wounds first."

"I'll be fine." Serenna raised her brows as he nearly lost his balance. "I'm not the one about to fall on my face."

Clenching his jaw, Fenn's unswollen eye flared as he focused on the gashes in her arms.

Serenna irritably huffed but humored him with the bare minimum of compliance, making a show of washing out her wounds in the sink. Pursing her lips to conceal a wince from the stings, she toweled off and pointed at the filled tub.

Fenn obediently shuffled over, sucking in a sharp breath as he unclasped his armor's buckles and straps. The spiked leather tunic dropped to the ground in a clatter. Unable to fully lift his arms, Fenn swore, struggling to peel off his loose undershirt.

I'll never get that leviathan up if he crashes to the floor. Serenna rushed to him. "Here, let me help." Before Fenn could irreparably entangle himself in his braids and clothes, she guided him to the marble ledge of the bath.

He grimaced, lowering to sit. As gently as she could, Serenna rolled the fabric over his head, exposing lean muscles bisected with countless scars. Glittering rings—pierced into his nipples of all places—drew her attention straight to his chest like a crow transfixed by a shiny coin.

Fingers tightening around his shed shirt, Serenna ripped her gaze away from his carved flesh to assess his wounds. Worry began to crowd back into her thoughts. A collage of wicked bruises bloomed even darker than his skin, black veins distending and branching out like an infected web.

At the sight of the vicious damage, Serenna's stomach lurched, his injuries more severe than she'd anticipated. *He needs to be mended.*

"File my fangs," Fenn hissed, betraying his pain as he shifted on the tub. "I think they shattered a few ribs."

Serenna swallowed back that he'd stated the obvious. "Let's get your nose cleaned up first." She tossed his shirt beside him. "I think I can set it. At least, I've done it with Essence. Your ribs…" Serenna's words slipped along with her traitorous eyes.

This would be easier with magic. She studied the iron key swinging from its chain on Fenn's bare chest, gears whirling in her mind. As far as she knew, Lykor had left that morning and wasn't anywhere in the keep. If she could convince Fenn to unlock her shackle under the guise of healing, it might not be catastrophic if the prince appeared. Unless Vesryn rended Fenn on sight.

"She-elf, my nose is up here."

Serenna yanked her gaze back up to a smirking Fenn and blabbered a response. "I was thinking about what to do for your ribs. You'll have to instruct me on how to bind them." She cleared her throat, her voice coming out embarrassingly hoarse. "You know…" Serenna trailed off, kneeling beside Fenn to reach over the tub. "I could mend you if you'd untether me." She concentrated on wringing out a cloth, trying her best to look indifferent before glancing up to read his response.

Claw locked around the key, Fenn's reply sounded automatic. "Lykor doesn't want you using your elf magics."

Serenna's correction was a little too defensive. "No, Lykor said he doesn't want to sense me in his head." She aggressively wrung out the towel with an unnecessary twist. "He's been having you *encourage* me to use my elemental power, so it's not about magic." Serenna probed the boundary, wondering how far she could push him, hoping his current state would make him easier to prod. "It would only be for a moment—Lykor might not even perceive me if he's in that remote jungle. You're hurt and most likely bleeding inside." Leaning forward, she rested a hand on his leg. "I could—"

Fenn tensed, grabbing her fingers. "Please do not ask of me what I cannot give, she-elf."

Serenna opened her mouth to argue, but the regret weighing in Fenn's eye cut her short. He gave her a squeeze as she tugged out of his grip.

Serenna rose to her feet, hope falling along with her heart. *If saving himself from pain isn't enough of a reason to remove my tether, what is?*

As gently as she could, Serenna wiped the dried blood from Fenn's face. "When do you think the reavers will retaliate after...what happened today?"

"That depends on how long they fight among themselves to choose another leader." Fenn winced as she cleaned his split lip, working around his piercings. "But I'm sure they'll think twice about crossing you again."

His words were a crutch for a confidence Serenna had never quite developed in her abilities before. Heart lodged in her throat, her words came out as a whisper. "I would kill Larek again." She nearly questioned her lack of guilt. "If I didn't agree to use my power how he wanted, the reavers would've tortured you."

"Thanks to you, I only wound up with a broken nose and a few cracked ribs instead of being burned to a crisp." Fenn popped his knuckles. Serenna grabbed his wrist with an exasperated sigh when the motion ripped open his scabs. His mouth twitched as Serenna wiped the fresh blood off his hands. "Do you think our difference in height will be an issue?"

Serenna leaned over the tub to rinse the rag, the black blood swirling in the water like dumped ink. "That's why you're sitting—so I can reach you."

Checking if his pupil had blown wide, Serenna peered into his good eye. If Fenn couldn't remember why she had him perched, it was possible the reavers had rattled his skull more than she thought.

"No," Fenn chuckled. "I mean when I bed you."

Startled, Serenna blinked. The cloth slipped through her numb fingers, plopping into the water. He'd never been so blatant before, beyond inviting her to the Lagoon. Her surprise must've been the reaction he wanted, because Fenn burst into laughter and then swore through his teeth, grabbing his ribs.

It served him right. Serenna sniffed, wiping her hands on her leathers.

"I've gathered from the elders," Fenn gritted out with a wheeze, "that elven-kind aren't shy." He struggled to straighten. "And because for some unfathomable reason you have no interest in Lykor…" he faltered when Serenna scoffed. "Well, since you say he's failed to make a claim on you, I have a hundred different ways I'd like to show my appreciation."

Fenn frowned, as if considering how effective his battered body would be at following through with those boasts. Or he could've been counting out each imagined pleasure—Serenna couldn't tell.

In either case, her cheeks burned. The offer both thrilled and abhorrently enticed her as his insinuation steered her thoughts down an inappropriately curious path. Serenna's mind conjured countless assumptions of just how thorough Fenn could be. If the frequent fanged marks of passion on his neck were any sign, he had to be true to his word.

It sounds like he dallies with anyone who blinks at him. I shouldn't feel special just because he's showing interest. He obviously had no shortage of partners and she wasn't inclined to be added to that list.

Skin feeling unusually tight, embarrassment won out. Serenna snipped a response, her time with this wraith influencing her to be crass. "You must have a high opinion of yourself, *Lieutenant*, if you think your member is magical enough to cancel out a life debt."

"You're right," Fenn said, his voice pitched low with implication, tongue suggestively circling along the point of a fang. "In that case, I'd owe you multiple joinings."

Serenna's nostrils flared, beyond irritated that a flush of heat sparked between her thighs. *I just like the attention he's giving me.* That was completely normal. Something about him was straightforward. Easy. And it wasn't like she had anyone else to interact with.

Rising to her feet, Serenna pointedly herded her gaze away from his bare chest. "That's…unnecessary."

Hoping Fenn's one good eye didn't catch the flush racing to her ears, she rinsed the remaining cuts on his face. Serenna's attention kept flitting to her tether's key. *But if he's offering…* A sourness pooled in her gut as she considered exploiting his interest to snatch the iron freedom away from his neck. A tiny, nasty voice in her head asked why she should care if she used him.

Even if he was only around because she was his assigned duty, he was the closest thing she had to a friend among the wraith. Serenna couldn't justify such a deception, especially to someone so kind and thoughtful. He always made it a point to bring her a blend of his mother's tea in the mornings. And more than once, he'd taken her to see those comical miniature goats.

Sleet pattered against the windows, filling the silence. Serenna's heart tripped over a beat when Fenn captured her hand.

His voice was somber as he searched her face. "I failed to protect you today." He skimmed his talons up her arm, skating around the trenches left by Larek's claws. "And because of that, you were hurt." Fenn's brow furrowed, tearing open another scab. "If I had magics like you, maybe..." he shook his head.

Fenn doesn't shy away from power like the other wraith. Serenna stared at his claw gently circling her fingers, considering if one talent would've made a difference. Even against so many, he might've warded off the brutal beating.

"You were in danger again on my watch," Fenn said, drawing back and setting his trembling fists in his lap. "I'll have to inform Lykor that I'm not fit to be your guard."

"That's not true." Serenna cupped his cheek, wiping away the fresh streak of blood from his temple. "You should keep those thoughts to yourself."

Fenn's unswollen eye whipped to hers. "I have to report this. I—"

"I know Lykor needs to hear what happened," Serenna gently interrupted. "My actions might've worsened the tension between the elders and the reavers. But Larek initiated it." Anger flared like the fires that had incinerated Larek's bones. "You didn't run or balk. You met them head on—outnumbered." A realization doused the flash of fury. "You could've died putting yourself in harm's way. You could've let the reavers have me instead."

Fenn averted his gaze to stare out the icy window. "That never crossed my mind."

Something gentle in Serenna's heart fluttered, but she caged it, clipping its wings. Instead, her mind anxiously darted around the idea of Fenn *not* being the one assigned as her guard. Her captivity could be much worse. The thought of being locked alone in the Aerie until Lykor had a use for her wasn't comforting.

"You're the only one who actually talks to me," Serenna said, cleaning a gash on Fenn's collarbone. "When you station your sisters here, they just stare at me. The other wraith in your clan hardly acknowledge me. And let's not forget to mention how

Lykor has fewer conversational skills than Aiko—not that he makes a habit of being in the same room as me. Please don't have someone else assigned—"

Fenn winced. Serenna realized she'd abandoned the cloth to grab his face in her escalating, frantic tirade. She hurriedly dropped her hands. Pulse hammering her ears, she couldn't—wouldn't—identify what occupied the space between them aside from the awkward silence.

As if summoned, Aiko broke the tension, soaring into the chambers with a chattering mewl. Serenna pursed her lips when the dainty vulpintera landed at Fenn's feet in a flurry of flapping leathery wings. Prancing on her paws, Aiko rubbed against his boots.

Serenna scowled at the vulpintera. "That furry bat never gets excited to see *me*. And I'm here more than Lykor."

Fenn clutched his ribs, leaning forward to scratch Aiko's fuzzy ears. "She knows who has a better touch." His widening grin had Serenna yanking her mind's improper imagination straight.

After receiving what Serenna deemed was an excessive amount of attention, Aiko curled up in front of a vent with a contented purr. Tail coiling in front of her fox-like face, she squinted at Serenna over her fur.

Determining the best angle to straighten Fenn's nose, Serenna slipped in between his knees. She could feel Aiko's disapproval burning into her spine. *I wouldn't put it past her to scratch out my eyes while I'm sleeping.*

As light as a hummingbird, Serenna settled her hands along the planes of Fenn's face. Releasing a hiss of pain, his fangs snapped out.

"Just remember, you're the one who refused healing," Serenna chided, adjusting her fingertips across his nose, feeling for the break.

"I'm thinking that decision might've been misguided now."

Fenn cinched his talons around her waist, obviously intending to hold on to her for support.

Serenna narrowed her eyes on him. "Claws on the tub."

Fenn's ridiculous, fanged grin split his lip even further. "Are you giving me an order, she-elf?" Instead of listening, his grip tightened around Serenna's hips, pulling her closer to his chest.

"Those talons are going to shred these leathers." Serenna resisted the urge to snatch one of his rings—the jewelry pierced into his nipples—to shake some sense into him. "You'll snap me in half when you flinch."

"I wouldn't hurt you." Fenn pursed his lips but complied, gripping the stony rim. "Don't tell me when—"

With a twist of her wrists, Serenna snapped the cartilage back into place.

Fenn growled a string of obscenities through his clenched fangs, claws scraping channels into the marble. He panted through his mouth, face paling to ash. Eyes glazing over, he teetered on the edge of the tub.

Serenna snatched his shoulders, but he tumbled forward, crashing to the floor in a heap.

CHAPTER 39

JASSYN

Bracing his hands on his knees, Jassyn yanked in gasping breaths, unable to haul in enough air. Through the white pulsing across his vision, he shot Vesryn a scowl, mustering all of his scant energy to form the glare.

After spending another evening sparring together in the secluded mountain vale, Jassyn had humored the prince by agreeing to a "cool down." *I didn't realize that meant Vesryn intended to kill me.*

For no apparent reason, his cousin had kicked into a sprint. They ran for what felt like miles, up and down and across the grassy hills before finally halting near a lake.

"I'll be back," Vesryn said, unbinding his hair from a topknot. The stars-cursed menace didn't even sound the least bit out of breath. With a wave of his hand, the prince opened a portal, disappearing before Jassyn could react, closing it behind him.

He'd better not strand me here with only his dracovae for company. Through his strained breathing, Jassyn heard the thunderous wingbeats of Trella and Naru flying off in the distance. Vesryn had said the pair preferred roosting in a mountain plateau in the evenings.

A flock of ravens screaming their croaking caws followed shortly after. In a flurry of rustling feathers, the raucous birds dive-bombed their objections as the dracovae disturbed the valley's peace.

Jassyn silently apologized to his battered body, regretting that he hadn't propelled himself forward with the wind. In the past month since his liberation from Stardust, voluntarily being brutalized by the prince had gotten no easier. Vesryn possessed a frustratingly keen way of gauging when he began to adapt to the exercise, consistently heightening the difficulty in response.

Lacing his fingers behind his head, Jassyn stretched one of his cramped legs, straining to find some relief. The sun vanished behind the rim of mountain peaks while his heartbeat slowly settled back into place.

A few paces away, a gurgling stream spilled into the lake, carving a route through the rolling landscape. The serenity of the untamed vale offered a brief respite from the exhausting weeks spent untangling coercion at the Ranger Station.

Now spending more time at the stables than on campus, Jassyn had glued himself to his cousin's side when Vesryn wasn't out wrangling wraith in the wilds or flying on Naru in search of Serenna—despite still not sensing her presence through the bond.

He'd become all too familiar with his cousin's routine—beating his body to a pulp to fill every idle moment. Jassyn had a nagging feeling that grief would consume the prince if he stopped long enough to dwell on Serenna's absence and how many wraith he'd slaughtered over the years.

But none of us knew the truth until a few weeks ago. Vesryn can't blame himself for doing what he thought was right.

Jassyn turned around when he sensed the pulse of a portal opening. The prince lumbered through the rift, interrupting the quiet chirping of crickets.

"This isn't quite how I pictured spending the Lunar Solstice,"

Vesryn announced, dissolving his gateway. "But I suppose your company will do."

The prince hefted a basket, bursting to the brim with food that Jassyn assumed was looted from Centarya's kitchens. With his usual cavalier front, the prince sauntered to the edge of the stream with his spoils, dropping to a patch of grassy ground.

Jassyn wasn't fooled by the act, but he didn't have the heart to call Vesryn out on his performance. Not tonight.

Untying the cloth the prince had given him to restrain his curls, Jassyn shook his hair out. He folded himself across from his cousin, leaning against a boulder. While it was summer's eve, the mountains hadn't yet relinquished their hold of the chilly evening air—for which he was grateful.

Vesryn unpacked the basket, arranging the food between them. Jassyn buried his dismay, noting the prince had only pilfered cured meats, nuts, and cheeses—no fruit or anything sweet, of course. Grabbing a canteen, he gulped water down while watching a low wall of fog roll into the lower part of the valley.

Letting his awareness drift, streams of air ignited before Jassyn's eyes. Snatching one, he whirled it around them to *actually* cool down until his drying skin pebbled in the vigorous breeze.

Vesryn took a pull from a silver flask, capped it, then lobbed the vessel at him. Snagging it before it collided with his head—a reflex now, thanks to the prince forcing him to catch *knives*—Jassyn inspected the liquid.

Nostrils burning from the alcohol wafting up to assault him, Jassyn rubbed his nose. "You're not going to tell me what this is, are you?"

"It's not the fine wine you're accustomed to." Vesryn shrugged. "The rangers trade farmers dracovae feathers and scales for it. The humans claim the drink will have elves sprouting chest hairs like them." Vesryn pulled down his loose tunic, inspecting the scarred patch of bare skin. "I, unfortunately, have yet to experience that effect."

Jassyn took a hesitant sip. The drink seared his throat like a swallowed coal. He spluttered, abandoning any semblance of manners by spitting the liquid on the ground.

"Scorching stars," he hacked, as some of the alcohol slid past his tongue. "You might as well drink fire."

Vesryn smirked. "I never pass up the opportunity to watch someone try it for the first time."

"I'm glad I didn't disappoint," Jassyn coughed, flinging the flask back.

The prince retrieved a bottle of Jassyn's preferred sweet red blend. Flaring Essence, Vesryn popped the cork with a tug of force. Apparently not having packed glasses either, he floated Jassyn the entire bottle. With a sigh, Jassyn grabbed the wine, taking a drink before placing it in the grass. Frowning, he glanced toward the prince.

"Aren't you supposed to..." Jassyn trailed off, pursing his lips as Vesryn shoveled slices of beef into his mouth. "Aren't you supposed to be in Kyansari?"

"Probably," Vesryn said around the food.

Napkins and utensils were absent, not surprising Jassyn in the least that the prince had also deemed those unnecessary. Succumbing to getting his hands dirty, he folded a sliver of cured veal in half, wedging a cheese square into the pocket.

Jassyn gazed out over the rolling expanse as the first stars bloomed across the sky. He hesitantly asked, "I thought you had to attend your engagement ceremony tonight?"

"Fuck that." The prince scoffed, peeling off his boots and socks. "I've already done enough where that *obligation* is concerned."

Jassyn cringed as his cousin took more than one continuous swallow from the flask without even flinching. *Vesryn has already crossed the line for decades. Open defiance like this...*

Worry still nagged at him, preventing Jassyn from dropping the matter. "But surely the king won't tolerate it if you disregard the royal pairing."

"Do you think I care?" Vesryn glared a challenge at him, halting Jassyn's counter. "What do you think he'll do? Coerce me to his will? Turn me into a wraith? I don't know what to do about the capital yet, but I'm not going back." Vesryn idly picked at a sliver of wood on the basket, studying the adjacent stream shattering against the rocks. "If he's responsible for the deaths of my mother and brother…"

A sharp sting of sorrow collided with Jassyn's chest. Dulling himself, he took another sip of the sweet raspberry vintage. Neither of them had any guesses as to what had truly transpired during the first attack on the palace—if "attack" was even the right word.

A victim of curiosity, Jassyn asked, "Do you think the king is somehow absorbing Essence if he's the one turning elves into wraiths?" He swallowed more wine. "You've also noticed how his strength has increased over the years. That shouldn't be possible."

Vesryn dodged the question, growling, "I'm tired of this pointless speculation." His knuckles blanched around the flask. "We won't know anything else until you can unravel the rest of the coercion on Thalaesyn."

Jassyn had nearly untangled the web of magic on his mentor, unlocking the answers in the magister's head. Thalaesyn had insisted that Jassyn spend more time focusing on the wraith, rather than on him—what he knew wouldn't change anything anyway.

"But how do you think all of this started?" Jassyn pushed. "Magister Thalaesyn said it was his fault, but surely he didn't set out to create monsters."

"Can we talk about something else?" The prince scowled, jabbing a finger at Jassyn, railing on. "How about we discuss why *you* aren't at the palace tonight. I figured you would've received no less than fifty invitations."

Jassyn clicked his teeth shut, the reminder cutting like a blade. The nobles apparently hadn't abandoned the notion that he'd be amenable to joining the courts.

"I stopped counting after seventy-three," he mumbled, scoring his boot heels into the ground, not appreciating Vesryn flipping the uncomfortable topic onto him.

Vesryn fiddled with the laces on his tunic, eyes fixed on the western horizon. "Speaking of the capital, I want to transfer Thalaesyn and the wraith somewhere else. Somewhere hidden. If any of the rangers are compromised and alert my sire..." Vesryn clenched his jaw, picking stones out of the ground. "I want the entire story first before we even consider what comes next."

"Where are you thinking?" Jassyn took a sip of wine, contemplating the prince's uncharacteristic logic. "Between Elashor's soldiers and the possibility of that wraith army returning, I'm not sure Centarya is much safer."

"I know a place. I'm confident in its security." Drawing his arm back, Vesryn skipped a pebble out onto the lake. "There's an unusual jungle in the Hibernal Wastes—an ancient city, long abandoned." He bounced another rock in his palm before tossing it into the water. "Aesar and I discovered it. As far as I know, no one else knows about it."

Jassyn frowned, unsure how a *jungle* could exist in the middle of the endless frozen mountains, but he had more pressing concerns to address. "I worry those with shaman blood might be in danger as well."

Anticipating Vesryn would insist that he practice with his elemental power now that he'd brought it up—even in the middle of their makeshift dinner—Jassyn cast his awareness out to his surroundings. An ocean of energy hummed under his skin, a sensation that still wasn't quite familiar. Attuning himself to the stream, a pressure of power blossomed in Jassyn's chest. He twisted his wrist, hauling out a globe of water.

"Maybe we could bring those from Centarya to the jungle at some point," Vesryn said. With a pulse of Essence, he ignited dim illumination, sending the lights whirling around them. "Do you have any theories on why you're the only one who's manifested those elemental powers?"

It was a question Jassyn had reflected on multiple times. "I think it was because of the Stardust." The admission didn't gut him like it used to. Curling his fingers, he shifted the shape of the water, stretching the liquid out like a serpent. "I couldn't channel Essence effectively because of the dust's interference. And I sensed the earth's magic when…" When he'd thought someone was going to die. Jassyn blinked at the water spinning around his hands, guilt furrowing his brow. "When I was desperate and out of options."

"Maybe those with Essence haven't noticed that the other power is there waiting." Vesryn tracked the liquid winding around Jassyn's hands. "But we have no way of knowing who might share the same abilities as you—Nelya and your ring of magus haven't noticed anything unusual on campus."

I could be the only person aside from the king and the Vallendes who are aware of the others. Jassyn glanced away, dragging his hand through his curls. He sighed, knowing he shouldn't have kept the knowledge to himself this long. He still hadn't informed the prince of Serenna's shaman ancestry—but that was her secret to tell.

"I…may have some insight on that," Jassyn admitted. Flattening his palm, he formed the water into an orb again before pitching it all the way to the lake. "There are books in Farine's estate." He blinked, realizing his words were slurred. Surely that was only hesitation thickening in his throat. Jassyn squinted, examining the empty bottle against Vesryn's illumination, unable to recall drinking every last drop.

"Books?" Vesryn thumbed his lower lip. "I can get you books. My mother's library has been sealed off since... Well since she's been gone, but there isn't a finer collection." He idly plucked at the grasses near his feet, shucking seeds from tassels. "The archivists were able to restore most of the volumes my sire destroyed."

Jassyn shook his head. "No, I need Fynlas' research—he tracked shaman bloodlines and his notes might shed light on what the king intends."

Vesryn's face hardened like the surrounding boulders. "And it would tell us who could be in danger." He drank again from the flask before scowling up at the rising moons.

Jassyn's fingers tightened around the empty wine bottle. "Farine presented me with an offer after my last summoning." Stomach churning, his mind veered away from what that next visit would entail. "She indicated I could have another tome if I—"

Choking on his drink, Vesryn spluttered a flurry of coughs. "You can't be serious about returning to that hag's estate."

Now wishing there was more wine, Jassyn set the bottle aside before scrubbing a hand over his face. "It's the only way." He nearly asked Vesryn for a sip of that vile firewater. "I thought...if I had Stardust—"

"Absolutely not," Vesryn said, pounding the ground with his fist. "You're obviously drunk. Where are these books? Somewhere in that mansion?"

Jassyn nodded, the dregs of wine souring on his tongue. "Fynlas had a study."

Unfolding himself, Vesryn rose and tipped his head back, emptying the flask before tossing it into the basket. Straightening his tunic, he opened a portal. Gaping between the gateway and his cousin, Jassyn's mouth worked in a silent question.

"It's been a while," Vesryn said, rebinding his hair. "But I can probably still find my way around."

Jassyn scrambled to his feet, primed to argue now that his mind had caught up with the prince's plan. "You can't barge into the Vallende estate and demand that research."

Vesryn scoffed, offended. "I *could*. But where's the fun in that?" A frenzied glint shone in his eyes—a precursor Jassyn recognized all too well of the prince plotting something exceptionally maniacal. Vesryn interlaced his fingers, flexing his palms outward. Turquoise light warped around him. "I'm going to *steal* it."

Surrendering his height—not by much—the illusion shortened Vesryn a few inches, adding a stockiness to his frame and a darker hue to his hair. Jassyn's eyes popped when the prince's clothes disappeared. A diaphanous curtain replaced his trousers, his chest left bare.

"Is this what the servants still wear?" Vesryn asked, morphed into a passable elven-blooded.

Jassyn stifled a nervous laugh at how ridiculous—and accurate—the illusion looked. "White now, instead of silver."

Vesryn flicked his wrist, changing the color. Jassyn's gaze shot back to his cousin's face. The sheet of fabric was utterly miserable at concealing skin and Vesryn had no qualms about displaying what was underneath. Though Jassyn had a suspicion the prince had *enhanced* himself as part of the illusion.

"You're the one who's drunk," Jassyn argued. "I don't think this is a good idea." Somehow losing his balance, he stumbled, catching himself on a boulder.

Vesryn arched a brow. "Everyone of note is at the palace tonight—it's the perfect opportunity. And from what I remember, some type of inebriation is the usual state of the servants. I doubt it'll take me five minutes."

Intrigue waged war with the anxiety slinking through the dark corners of Jassyn's mind. His shiver had nothing to do with the mountain's chilly air. *Stars, I can't believe I'm considering this.*

"I'll go with you," he said in a rush, before indecision could constrict him.

Alarm prickled the back of his neck as Vesryn's grin morphed into genuine excitement. The last time Jassyn had seen such a delighted look was seventy years ago when the prince had spun illusions of wraith to chase him down the corridors of the palace.

Pinching the bridge of his nose, Jassyn momentarily wrestled with Essence before his power sparked and ignited. Squeezing his eyes shut, he wrapped himself in a similar scandalous illusion.

CHAPTER 40

SERENNA

Serenna busied herself with poring over one of Aesar's tomes. Even though he would've already gleaned anything important, she had nothing better to do than to search for any clues as to where one of the remaining Hearts of Stars might be.

A few hours had passed since Fenn had peeled himself off the bathing chamber's floor and shambled out of the Aerie for the evening. *With those injuries, he'll need weeks before returning to the—*

A heavy cloak dropped onto the table. Serenna reared back in her seat. Having been so absorbed in skimming Aesar's translations, she hadn't heard anyone enter the sitting room.

Across from her, Fenn loomed with folded arms. Uncharacteristically out of his armor, his dark trousers glittered like scales, catching the light from the moons. His own cloak enveloped a loose tunic, unlaced halfway down his chest. Flaunting her tether's key.

"What's this for?" Serenna asked, touching the garment's furry hood.

"We're going outside." Fenn crouched to indulge Aiko, who

padded over from a sofa to reap his attention—which she'd refused to tolerate from Serenna earlier with a flick of her tail. "Bundle up."

Evading reminders of what the eclipsing moons' glaring light meant for tonight, Serenna had selected a seat facing away from the open sky. She twisted around, looking out a window. "But the sun just set. I can't imagine it's pleasant out. And besides, you're…" She frowned, examining Fenn's completely healed face more closely. Her question was beyond skeptical. "Did *Lykor* mend you?"

"Aesar did. We discussed what happened." Fenn engrossed himself in scratching Aiko's tufted ear, coaxing out a purr that vibrated throughout the room. "In an unrelated matter, he thought you might enjoy watching the elven eclipse with company."

Fenn's comment was a flaming arrow punched into her gut. Serenna's heart tumbled, thinking about the prince performing his *duty* in Kyansari. Aesar's books had been an escape, a way of avoiding thinking about what the Summer Lunar Solstice meant.

Serenna closed the tome in front of her, intending to decline. "And I suppose you volunteered because you have nothing better to do tonight?"

"I certainly didn't imply that." Fenn rose, his unbound hair spilling over his shoulders, softening the planes of his cheekbones. He tilted his head, earrings clinking. "As I'm still indebted to you, I was hoping this service would be repayment enough."

When Serenna narrowed her eyes to see through his flimsy motivation, Fenn suggestively raised his brows. His painfully obvious gaze drifted to the center stairs, leading up to the sleeping quarters before he said, "Unless you had an impulse to engage in a different activity this evening."

The insinuation kindled a cursed, molten thread of intrigue.

Scowling, Serenna crossed her legs and shoved her arms into a knot. Unamused by the spark of hope glowing in Fenn's eyes, she battled his smoldering stare.

She could remember when this warrior had intimidated her just because he was a wraith, but now... Now she wrestled with a shameful thrill heating her blood. Unsure how to navigate this straightforward, relentless interest she'd never received before, skirting the fringes of flirtation was Serenna's only defense.

Knuckles braced on the table, Fenn extended his fangs—likely to intimidate her—leaning forward to combat her defiance. "I *had* planned on spending the evening at the Lagoon, but now, rather than getting my—"

"Put those fangs away," Serenna snapped, her exasperation coming out more forcefully than she intended.

Rising, Serenna decided that she wouldn't squander this presented opportunity to annoy Fenn. She shouldered on the cloak, since her guard seemed determined to drag her outdoors. It seemed pointless to mention that they could watch the moons more comfortably from inside the Aerie.

"For your information," Serenna said, tugging on her boots, "I didn't ask for you to sacrifice your time at the Lagoon."

"It's a chilly night." Fenn shrugged. "I'm open to warming up there afterward."

Serenna's heart banged against her ribs while she made every effort to avoid envisioning what that entailed. She yanked her hair out from under the cloak, tossing the strands over her shoulders. "I wouldn't want to intrude."

"Hard to intrude when I'm inviting you." Fenn had retracted his canines by the time he opened the sliding glass door leading to the balcony. He stretched, scraping the obsidian stone of the doorway before waving her through. His eyes locked on hers before she passed the threshold. "Perhaps I have an interest in spending time with a particular she-elf."

Serenna's pulse stilled from his claim, any clever response

she hoped to form crumbling to dust. *He's shameless. But I like that about him.*

Pointedly ignoring him as she sidestepped outside, Serenna surrendered her arguments about how they spent nearly every waking moment together as it was. Fenn's low chuckle said that she'd only lose whatever ground she hoped to gain.

Light streamed down from the full moons, hovering over the jagged mountains, drenching the valley like beacons in the night. "Should we move some of the furniture out here?" Serenna asked, drawing the furred hood around her neck.

An errant gust swirled a flurry of powdery snow, flakes gliding aimlessly through the icy air once the draft subsided. Fenn brushed the stirred hair out of his face, smirking too smugly. "I have a more secluded place in mind."

"Naturally," Serenna said, nervously laughing as her heart picked up speed. *So it'll be just the two of us. Alone somewhere.*

Placing his palms on the balustrade, Fenn leaned over the edge to inspect stars knew what. Safe from his view, Serenna studied him. From his towering height and wraith lankiness, to the way his indigo skin glinted with shimmering iridescence, highlighted by moons. When he turned back before she could get any further, Serenna whipped her eyes up to the sky.

Realizing how they were going to get there, she emitted a defeated sigh. "And I suppose you'll be jumping off the balcony and warping us to this mysterious place."

Fenn tilted his head. "Do you not trust me?"

"Of course I do," Serenna answered automatically, grasping the claw he extended.

Eyes dancing like the stars, his slanted, cocky grin was irritatingly charming. Serenna pinched her lips and flushed.

She squeaked when Fenn suddenly swept her off her feet, cradling her across his chest.

He pulled himself up to stand on the parapet, teetering on the ledge. Serenna's stomach clenched. Knowing her objection was futile, she still asked, "Can't you simply hold my hand when we do this?"

"I could." The chilly gale whistled past, yanking at Fenn's unbound hair. "But I like this position better."

"I figured," Serenna muttered, clutching his cloak. The precarious height and the blustering breeze snagged the breath in her lungs. Anticipating the whirl of his teleportation, she squeezed her eyes shut.

Fenn's chest rumbled when he spoke. "I think I can make it there in ten warps."

Serenna jerked in his arms, squawking with alarm. "*Ten!*" Her eyes flew open to see Fenn scanning the horizon. "Wait—"

They disintegrated into a twisting nether of darkness, her protest snatched away by the wind.

CHAPTER 41

SERENNA

Finally brave enough to open her eyes, Serenna's tangled stomach untwisted itself when Fenn placed her back on her feet.

"That...was...definitely more than ten," she panted, gripping his arm to steady herself. Miles away, the ancient volcano towered over the mountains, the snowy outlines glowing with the light of the moons.

Fenn chuckled. "It seems I miscalculated."

Serenna brushed disheveled hair out of her face while her brain slowly stopped spinning. Readjusting her cloak, she nearly slipped, finding ice beneath her feet. The glassy surface reflected turquoise hues in the celestial light before rolling over the ledge in front of her. Fenn must've ferried her to that frozen waterfall he'd mentioned.

From their vantage at the top, a rocky overhang sheltered the crest from the howling wind. Serenna's gaze drifted down to the valley below, then soared above to the expanse of glimmering stars. Steam curled in wisps around their legs, permeating from a tunnel behind them.

"There's a hot spring back there if you follow the ice," Fenn said, waving a claw at the cavern's depths and the ripples of frozen water disappearing into the darkness. Along the stony walls, lichens and mosses twinkled with cyan luminescence, casting pinpricks of light deeper into the cave.

Spreading his cloak on top of the frozen stream, Fenn folded himself onto the ground, patting the space beside him. "So, what do the elves find so extraordinary about these moons kissing?"

Serenna settled next to him, tucking her knees up to her chest. "The eclipse marks a new half-year, I suppose." Not being a natural furnace like Fenn, she needed more than a single layer to keep warm. Staving off the chill, she tucked the furs of the hood under her chin. "I never saw how the solstice was celebrated in Alari, but I..." Dwelling on where she might've been if she hadn't portaled away, Serenna faltered. Her voice lost its strength, fraying to a whisper. "I was invited to the celebration at the palace tonight." *I think I was, anyway.* She wasn't sure why she brought it up to Fenn.

"The palace?" Fenn's brows rose, lifting his piercings. His surprised expression shifted to uncertainty. "You know someone important back in your realm?"

Serenna coiled the ends of her hair around a finger. She wavered like a flame in the wind, considering how much to reveal. Fenn's eyes flared with genuine interest, his quiet attention all the encouragement she needed to discharge the ruminations that had festered the past few weeks.

"I used to live in a castle in the human realms..." With a deep breath, Serenna released the torrent of her pent-up frustrations. She recounted everything she hadn't shared with Fenn yet—beginning with Jassyn's arrival in Vaelyn and ending when she'd portaled away. The only fact she withheld was her bond with Vesryn.

With a guilty sting needling her for the lie, Serenna twisted the ending of her tale. She claimed to have accidentally portaled to Lykor, pulled by his presence, skirting the truth of how she'd meant to confront the prince.

"Vesryn's engagement will be announced during the eclipse tonight," Serenna continued, wrapping her arms around her legs. Fenn remained silent, attentively listening to her tirade as she ran out of words.

Unable to ward off her heartache, a raw pang of sadness sank Serenna's spirits as she told Fenn of running into the prince's betrothed traipsing to his quarters. *And right after we... on his balcony...* Indignant anger welled like a tide. *Vesryn must've known she was on her way since he tried to rush me out.*

Serenna could acknowledge that it was her fault for letting everything go so far when she knew the prince was promised. *I was too caught up in the bond and should've anticipated what it meant to be the other female in all of this.*

"Your prince is dishonorable for tangling your heart," Fenn said, dragging his talons across the ice. Scraping trenches, he dislodged a mound of frozen crystals. "He shouldn't have cultivated doubt by partnering with another while paired with you —unless you both had discussed it and agreed."

A lump swelled in Serenna's throat as Fenn's words echoed in the hollow cavern of her chest. "We're not paired," she said, defending the prince. "We never discussed any level of commitment."

"If I were your elven prince," Fenn continued softly, talking up to the moons, "I wouldn't shy away from claiming the she-elf with eyes like the universe, burning with stars and fire."

Serenna's pulse skipped up her chest to thunder in her ears. "But—but you have partners already," she stuttered, unsure how to accept Fenn's admission. "What about them?"

"I'm committed to them, but I wouldn't deny myself from another who harmonizes with my heart." Fenn turned to face her, eyes flaring like comets blazing across the sky. "I find love to be like a tapestry, with each partner weaving their own unique thread into my life."

"You want me..." Serenna blinked as his gaze lingered on hers, mind working through his poetic words. "...As one of your partners?"

Fenn shrugged and plucked at his hair, shifting on the ice. "I understand if you find me distasteful because I'm a wraith and you're a pretty little elf."

Serenna's response tumbled out, her bruised heart soothed by his straightforward honesty. "You're not distasteful." That didn't really answer the question he'd hidden in those words, but she hadn't exactly had a conversation discussing such an arrangement before. "I appreciate how open you are." Which still skated around what he was after.

Serenna's attention roved over his sky-high cheekbones and dancing eyes, always shining with a light of their own. She pried her stare away from the low cut of his tunic, the memory of his sculpted chest still burning in her mind.

"It doesn't matter that you're a wraith," she insisted. "I think you're attractive." That was the only answer she could provide with her thoughts still dwelling on the prince.

Fenn smirked, leaning back on his claws. Kicking one ankle over the other, he circled his tongue along the point of a canine as it elongated. "It's the fangs, isn't it?"

Serenna cursed herself for stroking his inflated ego, attempting to recover. "It's impossible to ignore your fangs when you flash them at me all the time."

Fenn glanced away, his canines retreating with a *click*. "It is rather...embarrassing when they extend on their own."

Serenna hardly restrained a disbelieving snort. "I thought they appeared when you were angry or when you feel the need to assert your dominance."

"When you phrase it like that, it doesn't sound like an attribute to be proud of," Fenn mumbled, folding his arms across his chest, apparently insulted. He cleared his throat. "It is *typically* an uncontrolled, aggressive response." Serenna almost swore the points of Fenn's ears colored darker with a rush of his charcoal blood. "But you've made a habit of challenging me, and I seem to lose control of them when I'm aroused by that." Fenn's incinerating stare slid back to hers. "Sometimes, all I can think about is about how much I'd like to sink my fangs into that ravishing neck."

Serenna's hand leaped to clap the skin under her ear—the same spot on his flesh bearing puncture marks.

"And not to harm you," Fenn hurried to say, lifting a claw as if to offer a comforting touch. He formed a fist instead, withdrawing. A volcanic storm swirled in his eyes, flicking to the scabs where Larek's teeth had scraped into her skin. "Quite the opposite, actually."

Heart whirling like a tempest, Serenna's breath hitched on a riot of sensations. The confession evoked a tingle of fear fused with indecent excitement as she recalled Fenn's claim about the effects of wraith venom. Heat scorched Serenna's cheeks as a flurry of improper thoughts had her imagining what that experience would entail.

Fenn grinned in a way that seemed to outshine the stars. "I don't bite without permission," he reassured her with a salacious wink. "But I do hope you'll ask."

A brief smile curved Serenna's lips before slipping off her face. Shame churned in her gut for finding amusement in his flirtations. She couldn't help but feel like she was betraying the prince in some way. *But it's not like I need to deny myself friends if my life is heading beyond the realms. And Fenn just teases me, nothing more.*

With a sigh, Serenna burrowed her hands into her pockets. Mainly so she wouldn't fidget and pick at her nails. "Would you..." She cleared her throat, reclaiming her voice. "Would you tell me about your partners?"

Fenn's spine snapped straight, glancing at her sideways. "Really?"

"I want to know more about you." Serenna conjured courage, resisting the urge to squirm. She couldn't deny her simmering curiosity, but she gave him the option to deflect. "Unless you have too many to list in one night."

Fenn barked a laugh, stretching his arms above his head like a cat languishing in the sun. "If you believe that, then I suppose I gave you the wrong impression."

Serenna pursed her lips, pointedly staring at the punctures on his neck. The bite marks were blatant evidence that he kept himself as entertained in the evenings as he made it seem. Unoffended, Fenn all but preened under her accusing look, tossing his cascading hair over his shoulder, providing her a better view.

"My first partnering was with Koln—we're still together," Fenn said, carving a talon into the frozen stream. "We didn't always see eye to eye—still don't." He chuckled to himself, plucking out a sliver of ice. "I might've been to blame. I was jealous that Lykor spent more time training him instead of me."

Fenn's eyes flashed back to the past. "Lykor wanted nothing to do with me because of my father." He curled his fist and water dripped from his palm as he melted the ice. "I can't number the times Koln and I thrashed each other to a pulp. But I discovered later that he gives it as good as he takes it." Fenn lifted the side of his tunic, pointing to an old, wicked injury wrapping around his ribs, reaching back to his spine. "I took his eye for this."

Speechless, Serenna gaped, jaw dropping open as she studied the puckered blemishes, a roadway of brutal scars. Settling his shirt back, Fenn barreled on, forgetting to mention how they'd reconciled their differences before what was between them developed into…more. Letting him speak, Serenna tucked that skipped story away, saving it to ask about another day.

"Koln is a lieutenant now too, so we're not on the same patrols anymore." Fenn idly swirled his talons across the frozen water. "But we still manage to see each other every few days at the Lagoon."

An expression Serenna nearly considered dreamy spanned over Fenn's face as his eyes unfocused. "And then there's Liah. She has the most stunning—" Fenn coughed, quickly catching whatever he was going to say. He dashed a glance at her. "She and Koln hardly tolerate each other though. It's of no help that Koln doesn't favor females. And..." The light in Fenn's eyes faded like a star vanishing from the sky. "I guess I don't really see her anymore."

Serenna bit the inside of her cheek before daring to ask, "Is she with the reavers?"

Fenn nodded. "She was there that day with the humans on the snows."

A bleak sadness smothered Serenna, constricting her ribs for his loss. She expected insecure jealousy to ricochet around her chest for each partner named—for each person more important than her. Instead, something empathetic unfurled, her turmoil relaxed by the open truth.

She quietly said, "I'm sorry you lost both Liah and your sister Taryn to the reavers."

As they silently watched the moons drift closer toward each other, Serenna's heart extinguished like an ember, growing cold like the stars. *Why does knowing that Fenn has an interest in me while he carries affections for others not hurt like Vesryn's secrets? I was so jealous of Ayla.*

When Fenn didn't speak further, Serenna prompted him, if only to distract herself from her spiraling thoughts. "And what about your other partners?"

Fenn shrugged, eyes bright with mischievous guilt. "That's it."

Serenna sputtered, "That's—that's *it?*"

"I've been with others," Fenn said almost defensively,

rubbing the back of his neck. "But I've come to prefer something more...consistent."

Serenna laughed, shaking her head. "Thank you for spending your evening here with me." She placed her hand on top of his, the heat from his skin radiating into hers. "If someone had told me a few weeks ago that I'd be watching the solstice with a wraith who I consider a friend, I wouldn't have believed them."

Turning his claw over, Fenn's fingers enveloped hers. Serenna studied their intertwined hands, searching for her next words.

"In a way, I'm glad I'm here because I learned the truth about your people. I only wish everyone else could too." Each of her blinks became a battle to hold his gaze, steady like stone. The wind outside the cavern seemed to still like her heart. "But I need to be honest, like you've been with me. Regardless of what happens in the capital tonight..."

Losing her nerve, Serenna glanced away, wishing the frosty stars provided solace. "I think my broken heart is still with the prince. Even if I'll never see him again." Brushing a stray tear away, her voice cracked, strained by the vulnerability of her words. "I wouldn't want to give those pieces to someone else."

Serenna's pulse leaped when Fenn leaned closer, consuming everything in her sight until all she saw was him. "I'd gladly accept just a piece if only to protect it." He squeezed her hand, an offered comfort. "If you trusted me with a shard of your heart, I wouldn't break it further." His gaze dropped to her tether peeking out from her cloak, glinting between them in the starlight. "I'm sorry Lykor gave you no choice but to be with the wraith and separated you from your prince." His fingers tightened around hers, eyes brimming with an apology that wasn't his responsibility to give. "But you could have a life with us."

"A life shackled to Lykor?" Serenna whispered, her voice barely audible. "A life where I'm simply used for my magic? Where I'm locked in a tower or dragged around the world?"

Dejection flashed across Fenn's face before he withdrew. "Of course you'd wish for freedom and to have your magics back. I don't fault you for that." He looked on the verge of saying more.

"Would you want magic?" Serenna blurted, an idea suddenly wheeling like a swirling of snow. Fenn had mentioned it before, musing that he could use the power to help others. She couldn't put him in a position that compromised his loyalty to Lykor, but... *If I could offer him something to provide aid...*

Fenn spun a ring in his brow, frowning as he watched a streak of cosmic light dart across the sky.

"What if..." Serenna began. Her voice tapered out, the pirouetting of her mind stealing her words.

She glanced over the frosty expanse, wondering if Vesryn would open a portal in the valley below. *Even if he's in Kyansari tonight, he'd travel here if he sensed me. He wouldn't abandon me.* She clung to a sliver of hope that she'd be able to inform the prince of his brother and the truth of the wraith. *Vesryn would tear the capital down with his bare hands if he knew about Aesar. We could change everything.*

"What if I gave you one of my abilities?" Serenna couldn't think of a stronger incentive to encourage Fenn to remove the tether. "Like Lykor did for your father?"

Fenn's eyes went as round as the moons.

"You could have defended yourself today," Serenna rushed on, finding his claw to squeeze. "You could have defended me."

She hated herself as soon those words flew from her mouth. Fenn flinched, tugging his fingers out of hers.

Heart wrenching for exploiting his protective nature, Serenna clutched Fenn's arm. "I—I didn't mean... I only meant..." Waging an inner war, nausea burned her stomach for leveraging his guilt, for being the cause of that shame curving his shoulders. "Magic would've made a difference."

Fenn tensed, like he was ready to shake off the weight of her hand. His gaze blazed through the sleeve of her cloak, to where

Larek's claws had scraped into her skin. A whirlwind of emotions flared in Fenn's eyes when they slowly lifted to meet hers. Serenna wondered if he could hear the deception in her words—wondered if he could hear the pounding of her guilty heart.

Fenn's voice was quiet. Disbelieving. "Why would you offer me such a thing?" He scanned her face, seeming to scour for what she withheld.

Because I'm manipulating you to get this tether off. Serenna tightened her fingers around his strained muscles, staring so deeply into the flaming depths of his eyes. *This is the only way I know how. We could save lives by uniting Centarya and the wraith. We could end this war before it gets worse.*

Conflict split Serenna's chest, but she pushed forward, abusing Fenn's devotion to his leader. "Can't you see the advantages of helping Lykor protect the wraith or subduing the reavers if they rise? My power isn't useful locked away." She frantically considered which ability she could sacrifice and manage without. "I could give you my force talent and you could be the one who clears the snow from the lifts." The joke hung in the air, silent like the moons, as hollow as her heart.

"I don't even know if it's possible," Fenn eventually said. He retreated out of her grip, clasping the key hanging around his neck.

"There's a way to find out." Serenna hesitated before slowly presenting her wrist. "If Aesar is still out tonight, I can ask him how to draw out my power. And if he doesn't agree or if he's of the same mind as Lykor and doesn't want me untethered, you can put it back on."

"But what about you?" Fenn's fingers curled around hers, searching Serenna's eyes with a deep-rooted concern that tightened her chest. "You'd become more wraith if we do this."

Serenna's smile was fragile, threatening to shatter, her throat too tight to form anything but hoarse words. "We're not so different."

Letting go, Fenn drew the chain over his neck, turning the key over and over in his palm. His brows pulled together, studying the tether on her arm. "Are you sure?"

Heart tumbling down her ribs, Serenna battled the raging hurricane of her doubt, tempted to tell him everything. *I'm scared you'll inform Lykor of the bond. So I'm taking that choice away from you and hoping I can live with myself after the prince appears.*

Serenna managed a nod. Despite finally coming so close to having the gold removed, the expected excitement was nowhere to be found. *If Vesryn portals to the base of the waterfall, I have to make sure he doesn't rend Fenn.*

Heart clenching with her deceit, Serenna trembled as Fenn unlocked the shackle. The manacle dropped between them, thudding against the ice, the sound clanging against her choice.

Serenna tensed as Aesar's alarmed awareness flooded into her mind, his proximity shining like the sun. Breathing a sigh of relief for being spared from Lykor, Serenna hurriedly shoved thoughts down their bridge. *After what happened with the reavers, I want to give Fenn one of my abilities. Can you show me how through the bond?*

Aesar relaxed, but Serenna perceived his confusion. She hoped he assumed her nervousness was for surrendering a talent. Her attention flitted toward the dim connection to the prince, assuring herself that Vesryn was searching for her.

Conferring with Aesar while Fenn worriedly chewed on a lip ring, Serenna eventually convinced him that she'd made up her mind. Nerves buzzing like bees in a jar, she brought her focus back to Fenn.

Inhaling a shaky breath, she dove into her Well. Serenna's fingers shook as she lifted them to her chest, stomach tipping like she stood at the edge of a cliff. Aesar informed her that the voluntary extraction of power wouldn't be painful as he guided her. Serenna plucked the fibers of her force talent, severing a portion of her magic.

Power surged, each loosened string firing a falling spark through Serenna's body. Her skin prickled, tinting from sun-kissed bronze to a deeper shade. Mouth tingling, she had a suspicion her teeth might've altered too. Serenna didn't bother cataloging the changes, now committed to the course.

Freed Essence flew into Serenna's palm, an orb of radiant light. Hoping her offering to Fenn would be worth the time she'd bought, Serenna's attention darted down the bond toward the prince. Realms still separated them.

Thoughts scattering in every direction, she pulled herself back to the frozen waterfall. Serenna met Fenn's eyes as her ability hovered between them.

"Wait." Fenn captured her wrist before she dispensed the shimmering globe of power into his chest. "If I lose my fangs, can you retrieve your magics?"

Fighting the tide of her jumbled emotions, Serenna forced a smile, unsurprised that he'd joke at a time like this.

Holding her breath in anticipation, Serenna spiraled Essence into him. Fenn went rigid, every muscle taut. Fingers seizing, he clasped her hand over his stampeding heart.

Fenn's features shifted ever so slightly, his gaunt angles softening—nearly impossible to discern if Serenna hadn't been staring. Still undeniably wraith, his scarlet eyes focused on her. Fenn's chest heaved as he gulped in air, catching his breath.

Reclaiming her hand, Serenna glanced out to the snowy valley. Her heart plummeted, still sensing the prince a world away. *He'll be here.*

Serenna's pulse skipped when Fenn lightly touched the side of her face, silencing her fretting thoughts. His fingertips pressed a warm blaze against her chilly cheeks, a delicate flame melting frost. Tracing the edge of her jaw, his talons skimmed along her neck, sliding through her hair to cradle the base of her head.

A shiver rippled through Serenna when their eyes collided.

"Thank you for this gift." Fenn blinked, the closest she'd seen him to startled. "Your eyes." Peering further, his gaze danced across hers. "There's a halo of red surrounding the blue. It's beautiful," he breathed. "Like fire enveloping ice. I…" The look of his usual confidence ebbed as his gaze trailed down to her lips.

Serenna shied away from the way her stomach fluttered. Fenn must've felt her stiffening because he cleared his throat and untangled himself from her hair.

"How do I use the magics?" he asked, holding his claw above his chest like he could haul Essence out. "It's force magics, you said?" He cocked his head. "Is it like weaving the winds?"

Torn between emotions, Serenna somehow wanted to burst into tears at the prince's absence and laugh at Fenn's antics at the same time.

Opening her mouth to explain how he could use emotions to facilitate channeling his talent, Serenna flushed. Her teeth clicked shut at the memory of Vesryn seducing her into power with desire. She refused to do that to Fenn.

"It might take a little time to perceive your Essence," Serenna said, sweeping her attention out for one final glance over the rolling snow. *He's not coming.* "I can teach you what I know, but your father or Aesar would probably be better instructors." She focused back on Fenn, guilt souring her gut. "You're technically a pure-blooded elf, so maybe you'll manifest your power more easily than I did."

Fenn inspected his talons. "Sometimes I wonder if the Aelfyn were wraith before they captured the magics of the stars." He curled his claw into a fist, studying his scarred knuckles in the moonlight. "Why else would we change?"

"That…" Serenna frowned, grabbing the tether. "That is an

interesting thought."

She clasped the gold around her wrist, extinguishing her hope. *Vesryn didn't come. He didn't...* Ribs caving in, a piece of her heart shook loose, tumbling into the depths of her chest. *I used Fenn and he thanked me for it.*

Not sensing her inner war, Fenn looked up at the sky as he spoke. "I didn't think you'd be the one inside of me first, but here we are."

Serenna's throat clogged as she choked on a laugh. Fenn beamed, brighter than the moons' light. He snapped his fangs out and then retracted them, as if assuring himself they were still there.

"They're still longer than Lykor's," Serenna heard herself saying, not wanting to ruin his evening just because hers was. She carefully touched the points of her canines with the pad of her thumb, inspecting the change.

Fenn cackled and said, "Now who has the stubby fangs?" He bumped his shoulder into hers. "Are we going to watch these moons kiss or what?"

Heart twisting, something in the way Fenn was looking at her had Serenna convinced that he'd try to pluck a shooting star out of the sky if she asked. Wrapping an arm behind her back, he braced his claw next to her hip, close enough to dispense his radiating heat. All she had to do was lean a fraction to be absorbed by his offered embrace.

Serenna allowed herself to imagine doing it. Falling into him, melting into the cradle of his arms. Letting him distract her, sweep her thoughts away from this night. It would be so easy to crumble her defenses and drown in his lofty boasts.

Fenn doesn't deserve pieces. He deserves a whole heart. And I've already used him enough.

Tucking her shame and sadness away, Serenna bleakly returned Fenn's smile before gazing up to the eclipsing moons.

There isn't a way out. My future is with the wraith.

CHAPTER 42

JASSYN

Regretting every foolish decision he'd made the night before, Jassyn's body shook as he gripped the edges of the porcelain sink. He studied his bleary reflection in the bathing chamber mirror before digging his palms into his eyes.

Reminded of the dreadful experience of withdrawing from Stardust, Jassyn massaged his pounding head. Since dawn, he'd been yielding his stomach, thoroughly convinced that what he was going through now was worse. Much worse.

Why in the bleeding stars did I let Vesryn convince me to drink so much? They had no reason to help themselves to the Vallendes' wine stores. And that certainly hadn't been his idea—no matter what the prince had claimed when they were drowning themselves in the spoils.

Opening the door out to his sitting room, Jassyn halted in his tracks. On his hands and knees, Vesryn was retching through a portal in front of the couch. Gut clenching with another wave of nausea, Jassyn clamped his teeth, fighting the urge to dive back into the bathing chambers to do the same. *At least he opened a rift.*

Every rain drop pelting the windows resounded like a gong in his skull. Dodging mountains of tomes and scrolls stacked on the floor, the sitting room spun as Jassyn stumbled to a water pitcher perched on an end table. Wispy memories of Vesryn shoving Fynlas' research through a gateway faster than a squirrel stashing a horde of nuts floated through his mind.

But there was more than books and scattered parchments. The prince had stolen nearly *everything* that had been in Fynlas' study. The easels with human family trees tracing the shaman lines, every single paper, inkpot, and quill—Vesryn had pilfered it all. They'd even filched a *chair*. But it was a nice chair. White oak, intricately carved, with a lovely cushion as soft as a downy pillow. *Maybe I grabbed the chair, I don't remember. Stars, my scorching head.*

Jassyn swayed as he poured them both glasses of water. Somehow still holding Essence, Vesryn crawled up the couch, struggling more than someone pulling themselves over a ledge. Jassyn collapsed on the sofa next to his cousin, offering a cup.

The prince waved him off. "Don't worry, I threw up…" Vesryn frowned at the portal by his feet before releasing his magic. He drew a hand over his face. "I actually have no idea where I opened that." Bracing his elbows on his knees, the prince groaned, gripping fistfuls of hair. "Can you"—he tapped his head, wincing as his throat bobbed—"use your healies?"

Jassyn swallowed hard before attempting to grapple with his power. He blinked against a streak of lightning flashing through the windows, eyes throbbing in protest at the cruel slash of light. By the time Essence swirled around him, darting in and out of his control, Jassyn was panting.

Vesryn chuckled and then cringed. "Stars, you're still drunk."

"We are *never* doing that again," Jassyn gritted out. Threads of mending light unraveled, slipping through his fingers. "And you're healing me after I'm finished with you."

Vesryn clutched his middle with a groan. "You're suddenly very trusting of my healing."

"The way I see it," Jassyn said as he regathered Essence slowly, like clouds rolling in ahead of a storm. He shrouded Vesryn with a curtain of power, easing his stomach and dispelling the inflammation in his skull. "You can't do any more damage to me than you've already done."

"You have me there," Vesryn said, sagging in relief.

After the prince returned the favor of setting his body back to working order, Jassyn frowned at the books scattered across his sitting room floor. "Did we really…"

"Yup," Vesryn said, eyes now bright and alert. He plucked a tattered tome from the top of a pile on the floor. "We raided the Vallende estate."

Jassyn snatched the volume, swatting away his cousin's wandering fingers. The prince grinned, reaching over to ruffle his curls. When Vesryn leaned down to rifle through a stack of family trees, Jassyn gave up on trying to defend the fragile research.

"What can we do for those with shaman blood?" Jassyn asked, leafing through a text so ancient that he feared the pages would disintegrate.

Vesryn gnawed on a thumbnail, frowning as he studied the parchment in his hands. "It's likely the king has plans to compel those like you."

Jassyn's thoughts darkened, twisting like the clouds outside. "To what end?" He scowled when the prince flicked his severed nail to the floor. "To somehow use us as a conduit to control the elements?"

Vesryn shrugged. "It's obvious now that coercion does more than restrict speech. If that compelled guard we ambushed at the Vallende estate was any sign, that magic can dictate someone's actions."

Jassyn blinked. "What guar—" His eyes widened as the

isolated memory rematerialized. Stomach rolling over, bile crept back up his throat. "You had me untangle coercion. While drunk."

Jassyn tugged at the surrounding air, corralling the smallest breeze. Directing the delicate zephyr, he gathered the disgusting growing pile of Vesryn's shed nails and hurtled them into a wastebasket. "Stars, that was a senseless thing to do. I could have destroyed his mind!"

"But you didn't," Vesryn argued. "I knew you were capable if you had a little encouragement." The prince jabbed him in the arm. "And thanks to the information from our new friend, we now know that Elashor has the skill to compel—at least to some degree. So it's not just my sire like we previously thought."

"Which is alarming." Jassyn set the tome aside. "That coercion wasn't as extensive as the magic on Thalaesyn or the wraith we've worked on." *Or that mysterious elven wraith I saved.* "But it's an understatement to say it's disturbing that we're seeing magic govern actions now." After Jassyn had restored that guard's faculties, the prince had portaled the warrior to the safety of the Ranger Station.

Ignoring his apprehension, Vesryn traced the names on the family tree. His mouth worked silently before he glanced at Jassyn and then back to the parchment. And then back at Jassyn.

"What?" Jassyn finally asked.

"Are these…" Vesryn trailed off, rapidly blinking before scrutinizing the paper again. "*All* of these are your offspring?"

If he was still drunk, Jassyn immediately sobered up from the verbal punch. He began tumbling. Falling. No, *drowning*. Suddenly there wasn't any air. He couldn't think, couldn't remember how to breathe as a weight like an anvil settled on his chest.

Sound swam away while memories came flooding in, throwing Jassyn back in time. The sleepless nights. The way his skin had crawled, feeling the weight of someone else's body on his. Head spinning, spots flecked across his vision. Everything was going dark. No, it was too bright. The only thing he saw was the parchment in Vesryn's hand.

Jassyn lunged for it, tearing it into pieces. If he could destroy it, erase the evidence, he could—

He couldn't move. Panting, Jassyn struggled against the shadows that had shackled him. Vesryn was in his face, gripping his shoulders, wrestling him back into the couch. The prince's mouth was moving, but Jassyn heard nothing beyond the ringing in his ears.

Breathe. Vesryn shoved the command into his mind. *Breathe. You're safe. Just. Breathe.*

Jassyn latched onto the phrase as an anchor, using it as a mantra as he hauled in gasping breaths. Breathing in through his nose and releasing the air out of his mouth.

Breathe.

Minutes slipped by, the splashing of rain against the windows filling the silence between Jassyn's struggle for air. Another ragged inhale. Another unsteady exhale.

Assembling the remnants of his broken composure, Jassyn began reconstructing himself. It felt more like he was fumbling, scraping, shoving the shattered fragments back at all the wrong angles, lacking enough pieces to make himself whole. *I'll never get over this.*

Vesryn stood at his side, keeping a silent vigil. Fingers twitching, he reached out more than once only to retreat before finally touching Jassyn's shoulder.

"What can I do?" the prince asked, voice soft with concern. He released his hold on Jassyn, letting the shadows dissipate.

Jassyn's focus slid to his family tree, torn on the floor. "Get rid of it. I don't want to know."

Vesryn gathered the shredded paper. He folded the scraps, tucking them into his leathers before hesitantly meeting Jassyn's eyes with something that looked like pity.

"We need to know who they are," the prince said quietly. He glanced at the other scattered parchments detailing the lines with shaman ancestry before touching his tunic. "I'll keep this one safe. They're my kin too."

Jassyn buried his face in his hands, craving Stardust. He longed to take enough to forget everything—to forget how he'd been forced to play his part like a puppet on a string.

"The capital likely has copies of these lists," Vesryn said. The section of couch next to Jassyn dipped and he felt the prince scoot closer. "We'll start keeping track of those identified on these trees. That's all we can do for now. They'll need our help someday."

Mustering the strength to pull himself out of his misery, Jassyn studied the rain outside the windows and the wind chasing the clouds across the sky. *How am I supposed to help anyone else when I can't even help myself?*

Vesryn drained a glass of water. "We'll begin moving our wraith to the jungle for their safety. And Thalaesyn. Elashor's soldiers have already noticed his absence." The prince crossed his arms, drumming his fingers. "I'll assign a few rangers to keep the group protected and provisioned. We'll need to keep a close eye on the recruits here to make sure no one goes missing. We simply don't have the resources yet to relocate everyone."

Thankful for the distraction of Vesryn developing a course of action, Jassyn clung to the conversation. "I imagine it'll only be a matter of time before the elemental powers begin manifesting in others. We don't know—"

Jassyn's spine stiffened. Too scattered to have his mental barricades in place, a telepathic link coiled around his mind. Upon registering it was Nelya's presence, he relaxed. She'd been directing their ring of trusted magus, managing the network of watchers and relaying anything peculiar back to him.

Jassyn, the portal attendants sent a missive that General Elashor is bringing additional soldiers to campus—more than the prince permits.

Alarmed, Jassyn tensed at her words. This was more than a routine report. *How many?*

I'm not sure, but a hundred have already come through the gateways. The general is ordering the entire island to gather at the Spire.

Towed into a riptide of dread, Jassyn's eyes darted to his cousin. Vesryn's brows rose, reading his anxiety.

Do you know why? Jassyn asked.

They're looking for the prince.

Jassyn swore in the solitude of own mind, wondering if the Vallendes knew he and Vesryn were the ones who'd plundered their estate.

"What's going on?" Vesryn asked.

Jassyn flapped a hand, gesturing for his cousin's silence. *Make sure the magus in our circle join those gathering so their presence isn't missed. I'll...inform the prince.*

Swallowing back a tide of uncertainty, Jassyn ran his fingers through his curls, delivering the message.

Vesryn scoffed, gaze roving around the room, landing on his boots. With a pull of force, he ripped them toward himself. "Elashor goes too far if he thinks he has any say over me or our operations at Centarya." Stomping into his shoes, the prince aggressively tied the laces.

"What do you want the magus to do?" Jassyn asked, rising to retrieve his own footwear. His mind immediately began inventing increasingly alarming scenarios of what would unfold.

"Nothing." Vesryn pushed off from the couch, yanking his wrinkled leathers straight. "I don't want this secret coalition you've cultivated to commit a blatant act of treason. Not yet." He grunted. "I have a better idea." He patted Jassyn's cheek, but his grin looked forced. "I'll simply to tell Elashor to fuck off." And with that, the prince pivoted on a heel and prowled out of Jassyn's apartment.

"Wait!" Charging out of his quarters, Jassyn hurried to catch up to Vesryn in the hallway. "If the capital is here in force, I don't think it'll be that easy. I have a bad feeling about this."

"I won't be returning to Kyansari if that's what they're here for," Vesryn growled, tying his hair back.

"Then shouldn't we portal away now?" Jassyn's pulse began to race as he kept pace with the prince, descending the stairs two at a time.

"I need to make an appearance so Elashor doesn't interrogate the magus about my location." Vesryn flared a ward, shielding both of them from the shower of rain as they left the residence hall.

That's oddly logical of him. Gusts tore at the manicured trees edging the cobblestone pathway, whipping leaves into the air.

Vesryn scanned the courtyard, taking in every magus and recruit on their way to assemble at the Spire. "I'll need you here on the inside. As my silent watcher, working from the shadows."

Feeling backed into a corner, Jassyn didn't know which direction to dart. Campus certainly didn't feel like the safe option if Vesryn wasn't going to be around. *I can do more good helping Thalaesyn and freeing those already coerced.*

Jassyn's words broke past the clump of worry beginning to clog his throat. "I'm coming with you."

Vesryn glanced at him as they hastened down the stone pathway, the island hazy with rain. "Are you sure? We won't be able to return to Centarya after this. Or maybe anywhere civilized."

Fear began to tangle in Jassyn's chest, but he nodded. A crack of lightning in the distance lifted the hairs on his arms. He swallowed, knowing the choice would be irreversible, a blind step off a cliff. "We're in this together."

The prince gave him a conspiratorial grin. "I was hoping you'd say that."

The watery assault from the sky had Jassyn's awareness of the earth sharpening. The last thing he needed was for sparks to jump into his hands again and reveal that his powers had manifested. *I have to stay in control.*

"What if we make our stand now?" Jassyn's heart quickened even further when Centarya's population came into view, organized into lines across the Spire's lawn.

Vesryn shook his head, the breeze lashing the fringes of his hair. "This is between me and the general. If Elashor's soldiers are compelled, then they're innocent."

"There's more of us," Jassyn said, unsure why he was insisting beyond knowing that the king would transform more elven-blooded into wraith if no one put an end to it. He studied Kyansari's white-armored force as they surrounded the initiates, stationing themselves like bars on a cage. "We're supposed to be the capital's army. What if we turn against them?"

Vesryn kept his attention pinned on Elashor, positioned at the base of the Spire. "I'm not putting our half-trained recruits at risk by initiating a bloodbath." He switched to sending a telepathic thought once they approached the edge of the gathering. *Relay to your peers to keep silent and let me handle this.*

Breaking away from the prince, Jassyn encompassed himself in his own shield, warding off the rain. He reached out to Nelya's mind, communicating Vesryn's orders. His boots sloshed through the sodden grass as he found a place to stand among the magus assembled twenty paces away from Elashor—much closer than he wanted to be if a confrontation was about to unfold. He nearly reached out to Vesryn, realizing that they hadn't discussed exactly how they were going to stage their departure.

Rain bounced off of the prince's shield as he sauntered through the ranks, proceeding like everyone standing at attention was gathered in his honor. Lightning sheared across the sky and an accompanying clap of thunder rumbled through the air. Vesryn stalked across the courtyard to face Elashor, a panther ready to taunt a bear.

Elashor's hand rested on the hilt of the longsword at his waist, barring entry to the Spire. "The king requires your presence at the capital."

Roving his gaze over Kyansari's small army, the prince ignored the general. He addressed the assembled magus and recruits. "Return to your classes and duties. This doesn't concern you."

The slant of Elashor's jaw tightened as his surrounding shield flared. He opened his mouth, but Vesryn cut him off. "Unless my sire demands the entire population of Centarya to accompany me to Kyansari, they have other responsibilities."

Elashor clicked his tongue in annoyance, but made no further objection as everyone dispersed.

Unsure where to position himself as his peers departed, Jassyn's chest constricted before he decided to join Vesryn in his solitary stand. He tried to ignore the way Elashor's eyes slid to him. Always calculating.

Vesryn snarled, dropping all semblance of civility. "My sire sends his favorite hound to retrieve me?"

The general pulled his shoulders back. "The king found your absence at the Lunar Solstice to be unacceptable. You've left him no choice but to strip Centarya from your command." Elashor crossed his arms, a humorless chuckle shaking his chest. "Perhaps once you return to the capital, you'll be reminded of your duties to the realm."

Jassyn tensed, gauging that the unstated threat was that the king would compel Vesryn into compliance.

The prince's fingers twitched at his sides. "If my sire desires a succession beyond me, then he can be the one who ensures it." His lip curled. "But let's do ourselves a favor and stop pretending like he'll ever relinquish power."

Elashor smirked, smiling cooly. "The king has taken matters into his own hands, but I assure you, your insolence will not go unpunished. Too long have you openly defied him." The general lazily stroked the hilt of his sword. "His orders are to retrieve you. You can come willingly or as a prisoner." With a sneer, he jabbed, "So what will it be, *Prince?*"

Vesryn's jade eyes glittered in a flash of lightning, his ire appearing to gather like the storm. His attention roamed over the surrounding soldiers, edging closer. They didn't seem to breathe as they waited for Elashor's command.

"What I want," the prince said, his focus pinning on the general, a hunting falcon honing in on its prey, "is to know what magic you two are fucking with. Care to explain how my sire's power has increased or how the years have slipped from his bones? I have a feeling it has something to do with our 'reassigned' recruits." Silence loomed like the clouds, the rain continuing its steady drumming. "This campus is under my protection. You've overstayed your welcome."

Face devoid of expression, Elashor unsheathed his sword. In unison, Essence pulsed, shimmering around the capital's warriors as they readied their weapons.

Fists clenching at his sides, Vesryn scoffed dismissively. "I have no interest in killing your thralls."

Elashor shrugged, unbothered. "There's more where they came from."

A muscle rippled in the prince's cheek as he went still. Jassyn swore even the wind held its breath.

His eyes flicked toward his cousin. Vesryn's ticked toward him. As something unspoken passed between them, the prince formed a telepathic link, wrapping around Jassyn's mind. They rapidly fabricated a plan while Elashor undoubtedly waited for them to submit.

Vesryn spoke first. *Elashor will be an issue. I haven't gone toe-to-toe against him, but even I'm not stupid enough to underestimate him. I'd prefer not to kill any of the soldiers if we can avoid it.*

Stomach roiling, Jassyn's knees locked. *If we're taken to Kyansari, you know they'll compel us—or worse.*

That won't happen. I don't think these mind-controlled warriors will be any match if Elashor has to direct them.

The general took a step forward. Magic flared from every direction—shields flexing, shadows rising, force strengthening. The air warped with a hum of energy.

Hold the soldiers back with your shields, Vesryn ordered. *I'll subdue Elashor and assist you after. Then we'll—*

One amendment, Jassyn interjected before the prince became too carried away with a complicated plan that would fall apart as soon as anyone blinked.

Vesryn arched a questioning brow at him. Before Jassyn even realized he'd made the decision, something inside of him snapped.

Elashor is mine.

CHAPTER 43

JASSYN

In a burst of irrationality, Jassyn sprinted toward the general. He disregarded Vesryn's frantic telepathic protest, ordering him to stop.

Watching Elashor stand there with entitlement radiating off of him had something dark rearing its head in Jassyn's chest. For too long he'd cowered under the general's imposing will, shrank under his scorn, withered under his gaze.

This was his chance to defy those who had the power to deem others lesser in this cruel world. Incensed by the revelation about the wraith, the elven-blooded bred for a darker purpose, and the dead-eyed, compelled warriors surrounding them, Jassyn saw red.

He streaked toward Elashor, boots splashing across the soggy earth. The closest soldiers collapsed to the ground before they could react, trussed by the prince's shadows. Sights fixed ahead, Jassyn couldn't sacrifice his focus to observe Vesryn's fight.

The past few weeks of training with his cousin had increased his speed, instilling more confidence in his stride. Jassyn rolled one of his hidden blades into his fingers, flinging the golden dagger directly at the center of Elashor's shield to buy a moment of distraction.

The knife ripped through the ward. Steel screaming through the air, the general effortlessly deflected the blade with a vicious swing of his longsword.

Jassyn faltered, his mind catching up with his legs. Elashor likely rivaled Vesryn in combat and he was recklessly charging at the arch elf warrior armed only with his throwing knives.

Midnight tendrils of rending lashed out from the general, a hundred striking vipers. Flaring Essence, Jassyn shelled himself in a protective wall, wearing the violet shield like a second set of armor. The shadows mercilessly flogged his ward, accompanied by the pounding rain and wind whipping from the storm.

Hilt sliding in his sweaty palm, Jassyn snatched another dagger from inside his armor and threw the knife.

Slapping aside the blade in a clang of metal, Elashor's lip peeled away from his teeth. "Are you the prince's pet now, you ineffective half-breed?" he spat. "Tell me, what do you think will happen to *you* when I return Vesryn to the capital in chains?"

Elashor tossed out a hand. A punch of force ripped away the ground at Jassyn's feet. The impact sent him stumbling along the shredded earth, halting his advance.

A lake of shadows spilled from the general's palms as he conjured another wave of rending. The darkness engulfed Jassyn, threatening to splinter his shield as magic converged on him like a surging tide.

"Surely you don't believe the prince will retain exclusive ownership of your contracts. This temporary *protection* of his will be revoked." The general barked a mirthless laugh, reeling in his shadows. "I'll see that you're permanently assigned to *me*."

Jassyn floundered to shove away his fear as Elashor's words repaved an old path. But the added shock from facing the reality of his descendants was too fresh. A wound unhealed.

Helpless, the dark crevices of Jassyn's mind resurrected the horrors he'd endured at the hands of so many. His anxiety spun into a vortex of terror, imagining Elashor dragging him back to the Vallende estate.

Amidst the rising panic of being returned his contracts, Jassyn's magic fled. Abandoning him. The illusion of his freedom crumbled to ash. Jassyn's shield disintegrated, leaving him unprotected from the pelting rain.

Elashor lunged with a whip of rending. The restrictive power coiled Jassyn in a bind, effortlessly forcing him to his knees. As he lost control of his body, Jassyn's heart staggered through a mire of dread. Closing the distance, the general approached him with slow, predatory steps.

Smirking, Elashor loomed over him. "I'll send you to my mother for safekeeping, since you've proven you need a firm hand." A crack of lightning sharpened the general's features against the darkened sky. He grunted in amusement as if a thought occurred to him. "I think your neck would look better tethered with that golden collar she's so fond of. She does relish a short leash." Elashor's sneer razored across his face. "But you already know that."

Not again. Jassyn's distraught thoughts devoured him. His chest compressed with panic, throat tightening around his breath. He believed the general, that certainty in his voice. The finality of the sentencing.

Essence was nowhere in sight. Shoulders rising and falling rapidly, Jassyn flailed against the rending but remained kneeling, a prisoner to the shadows.

"And this little stunt you pulled with the prince?" The general rested his sword over his shoulder. His eyes flicked above Jassyn to the commotion of battle as fountains of power erupted around them. "Unacceptable."

Fear clawed out of Jassyn's gut. *What was I thinking?* He flinched when the general reached for him.

Elashor shoved Jassyn's rain-soaked curls away from his

eyes. Twisting threads of darkness across his fingertips, he said, "I see you wasted no time shedding the Vallende sigil." A streak of midnight knifed straight for Jassyn's head. Sharper than a blade, the rending sliced into his skin.

A hiss of pain escaped through Jassyn's clenched teeth as Elashor started splitting his flesh. He refused to give the general the satisfaction of crying out.

"My mother will have to fix this, of course." Elashor tilted his head, lips thinning as he concentrated on peeling Jassyn's skin. "A shame I don't have the skill to draw her trillium as well the capital's tattoo artists, but she'll appreciate the sentiment." He flicked his fingers, weaving his magic. "I wasn't asking for much, you know. But you've forced my hand."

Retreating into himself, Jassyn squeezed his eyes shut. A gust of wind rammed into him.

"I'll still get what I want," Elashor growled, carving deeper. "I think I'll have my soldiers bring Serenna back with us—she's been as resistant as you. We'll see how long you'll continue this act of rebellion with...*motivations* to spur you into action."

Jassyn's eyes snapped open. He blinked away the blood and rain pouring into his vision. *Now he's threatening Serenna?* A breeze thrashed him, sharper than the last. Beckoning. *Elashor must not know she's gone.* He had to believe that wherever Serenna was couldn't be as perilous as in her sire's hands.

Jassyn's fear began to crack, fracturing as it transformed. A flicker of defiance sparked, flashing through him like the lightning cleaving the sky. *I'll die before I let him take me.*

As if he'd heard the thought, Vesryn's reassurance rippled through their telepathic link. *Hang on, I'll be right there.*

No. The ferocity of the word Jassyn pushed back at his cousin ripped something free that he didn't recognize. Something Vesryn had been poking and prodding. Through their training, the prince had hauled Jassyn up to his feet in the only way he knew how—relentlessly pushing Jassyn to his limits.

Blood and rain sluiced down his face, dripping off his chin to the grass. Driving away the general's familiar harassment and taunting, Jassyn mentally steeled himself, ready to rely on his strength to stand on his own.

I'm handling this, he told the prince.

Heart thrashing against his ribs, Jassyn slowed his apprehensive breaths. He silently pleaded to the stars that revealing his magic wouldn't put others like him in danger. But he'd had enough.

Jassyn called the storm.

A primal fury consumed him as he cast out his perception, reaching past the torrent of whirling rain. Sensing a surging pulse of power, Jassyn yanked on a flash of lightning fissuring across the sky. The tempest answered with a roar, infusing him with a charge of energy that raced through his veins like liquid fire.

A streak of light spun from the clouds, harmlessly crashing into him, arcing and dancing over his skin. Elashor's eyes widened. Jassyn bared his teeth, channeling the barrage at him.

Elashor staggered back from the volley, muscles twitching and seizing from the shock. Jassyn didn't temper the lightning's might. The general's flesh charred, mauled by the searing sparks.

The rending that was wrapped around Jassyn unraveled. Body back under his control, Jassyn swayed to his feet, lightning spitting from his palms. The purple sparks hissed in the rain, tangling in his fists, dancing over his knuckles. Punching the power out, Jassyn threw another charged web straight at Elashor.

The general choked on a scream. Bands of lightning twisted across his armor and skin, burning red streaks into his flesh. He spasmed as the energy stole control of his limbs. Jassyn spooled sparks with a flick of his fingers, twisting the magic, forcing Elashor to his knees.

Unleashed rage fueling his actions, Jassyn assaulted Elashor with telepathy, a talent he'd thought useless beyond communicating. But he now knew the ability was capable of more. Weeks of studying and untangling coercion had flung open a window to its secrets.

Compulsive magic had nothing to do with strength, like everyone had been led to believe. Knowledge was the source of power.

Vengeful and wild, Essence and lightning poured into Jassyn as he hauled on both sources of power. His breaths came fast, vision spotting as he funneled a cataclysmic whirlwind of each magic.

Channeling Essence, he threw the entire might of his telepathy talent against the general. *I'll pry out everything the king intends.*

A breath of time unfolded between them.

Jassyn's awareness invaded Elashor's oily mind, lurching and slipping through the maze of his thoughts. Sensing the general marshaling his strength to pummel him like a mob of swinging fists, Jassyn's Essence surged. He impaled a spear of telepathy into Elashor's consciousness, latching on, a leech preparing to dine.

Any attempt Elashor made to erect a mental barrier was too slow. Too flimsy. Jassyn ravaged those fragile defenses, rampaging like a bull. He charged further into the general's awareness, blocking Elashor's power before he could assemble a counterstrike.

Twisting his wrist, Jassyn stripped control from Elashor, taking over his body. Jassyn bent the general's limbs with his mind, forcing him to hold his sword to his throat.

"I should make you do it," Jassyn whispered through his disbelief, his voice snatched away by the wind. Forming a fist, lightning flared and slithered across his skin.

Jassyn stalked up to Elashor, chaining the general's legs to the ground with sparks. A swell of anger barreled through him, imbuing his words. "I can see inside your feeble mind."

Body trembling, veins thrashing in his forehead, Elashor snarled as he fought the sword. But the general's physical strength was no match for the magic at Jassyn's command.

He could control everything.

He could *end* everything.

"It seems so simple now." Something vengeful had Jassyn tilting his head, a predator for once, cornering defenseless prey. "I can snap my fingers and make you sever your own throat." He snapped. Elashor gritted his teeth in response, pushing the sword deeper into his neck, skimming skin to draw a thin stream of blood. "But you already know that, don't you?" Jassyn spun sparks in his palm. "What else do you know?"

Show me what the king is planning, Jassyn seethed into Elashor's mind.

Images unfolded, incomplete thoughts Elashor battled to withhold, discussions with—

Someone snatched his shoulder, startling Jassyn out of the telepathic assault. Blinking rapidly, the prince came into focus.

"Easy, Slayer," Vesryn said, squeezing Jassyn's arm, anchoring him back into his own mind.

Jassyn's eyes whipped to the soldiers. A blanket of rending enveloped them like fog, shackling them to the ground. Clarity returned slowly as he caught his breath. *Stars, what was I doing?*

He refortified the telepathy and lightning constraints on Elashor, restricting access to his magic and body. Despite his defeat, the general sneered, lips opening to speak. Jassyn yanked the words out of his throat, silencing him.

Vesryn tugged Jassyn's elbow. "We're leaving."

The prince spared Elashor a dismissive glance before his eyes sharpened on Jassyn's forehead. Reaching out, he cautiously brushed Jassyn's curls aside. Jassyn winced when Vesryn's fingers trailed over the bloody cuts.

The prince's confusion quickly morphed into realization. His attention ricocheted to Elashor and then back to Jassyn, face twisting with fury. Shadows exploded, mirroring the roiling tempest, encompassing the three of them in a raging gale.

Vesryn faced the general, still fettered with sparks, kneeling on the ground. Jassyn dashed to seize the prince's elbow when he stalked forward, shadows churning in his wake.

"I'll kill him," Vesryn snarled, ripping out of Jassyn's grip.

"He's not worth it," Jassyn urged. "If we do anything to him, someone else will just take his place."

Nostrils flaring, Vesryn wavered, fists clenching and unclenching at his sides. The shadows receded around them as the prince calmed his magic, but embers of anger burned in his eyes.

A muscle feathered in Vesryn's jaw. "Let me mend you, at least."

"I'm fine—you can heal me later." Jassyn shook out his arms, releasing the sparks from his fingers. "Like you said, we need to leave."

The liberating strength left behind an irrational aftermath, an intoxicating residue corroding Jassyn's thoughts. *I should destroy Elashor's mind and harvest the king's secrets.* Warring to halt that wild urge, a shred of control had him yanking on the reins.

No. I'm not finished.

Faster than his lightning, Jassyn planted a foot, pivoted, and twisted. His fist smashed into Elashor's face with a satisfying crunch of cartilage and bone. The general crumbled to the ground in a heap, sword clattering beside him.

Vesryn's nod was more than approving as he opened a portal.

Jassyn's knees threatened to give out as exhaustion caught up to him. He wiped blood and rain-soaked curls away from his eyes and asked, "Where are we going?"

The prince lowered his voice, scanning the battalion shrouded in rending. "We're portaling all of that research in your rooms to the jungle."

"We're really fleeing," Jassyn said, accepting that he was about to leave behind the only home he'd ever known.

But it's not safe here anymore. Glancing around, they were the only ones from Centarya in the courtyard, but he knew the residents must've observed the displays of power. His eyes shied away from Elashor, collapsed on the ground. Word would spread. *I hope this didn't sentence the others like me.*

"There's something I want you to consider," Vesryn said, one boot through the portal. "You won't like it, but if today was any sign, the benefits would outweigh your distaste." The prince idly scavenged the front of his bare uniform for a thread that wasn't there. "We'll need an edge since it's just the two of us now."

"And that would be...?" Resignation pooled in Jassyn's stomach. The quiet rain droned, pattering in the growing puddles. He already knew the answer before Vesryn spoke.

"I think we should bond."

CHAPTER 44

SERENNA

The Aerie's sitting room door slammed open. Serenna jerked upright from lounging across a couch, eyes whipping to the entryway. Lykor stalked into the chambers.

With an irritated huff, she readjusted on the sofa, cradling a glowing mushroom. Already thoroughly bored with the evening, she stared out the windows, watching the sun flee from the sky.

A week had passed since the Lunar Solstice. Disappointment from the prince's absence had waned like the twin crescents rising over the mountains. *I'll try to get my tether off again. Maybe Vesryn was busy in Kyansari.*

Serenna ground her teeth. That circular thought offered no comfort. With Lykor readying the wraith to leave, time was the more pressing issue rather than her bruised feelings.

Upon hearing Lykor shed his cloak and seeming to settle in for the evening, Serenna's quizzical gaze cut back to him. He tossed the snow-covered furs onto a chair. Snatching his gauntlet from the table—where Aesar had left it that morning—he shoved it onto his claw.

"Is your dramatic entrance necessary?" Serenna griped, secretly relieved that he hadn't portaled directly into the sitting room. "Take off your shoes if you insist on stomping all over the place."

Predictably, Lykor responded with a sizzling glare. He strode through the room, unexpectedly dropping to the other end of her couch. Serenna squawked, barely yanking her legs to her chest before he crushed her feet.

"What are you doing?" she snapped, swiveling to sit up.

Lykor grunted. "I'm sitting in my spot." His gauntlet creaked as he unlaced his boots, the leather glossy like a crow's plumage.

"You couldn't have picked, I don't know, one of the other four couches?" Serenna scoffed when he ignored her. Leaning back into the sofa, she idly traced the mushroom's glowing gills.

A rustle of wings gliding down the spiral stairs announced Aiko's arrival. Landing on Lykor, the vulpintera curled around his neck with a contented purr, rubbing her head under his chin. From her perch on Lykor's shoulders, Aiko fastened her beady gaze on Serenna.

I didn't want to pet you anyway, you vile bat. Serenna had settled onto the same sofa as Aiko earlier, earning a hiss before the vulpintera had retreated to Lykor's bedroom. She pinched her lips at the pair of them, tossing the luminescent fungus to an end table with the others.

Fenn had been supplying caches of mushrooms before departing in the evenings. The delivery had turned into a game of sorts—even after Serenna insisted that she didn't need them. Since giving him a talent, she'd gained some measure of enhanced wraith sight. The stars trickling in through the windows provided sufficient light.

To humor Fenn, Serenna had begun asking for more obscure colors. She smirked at the cluster he'd collected today. One was *nearly* violet. Fenn had claimed *his* wraith eyes could see more hues than hers and argued it was the color she'd requested, refusing to hear otherwise.

Serenna turned her attention back to Lykor. "Why are you here?"

Lykor rolled his shoulders, reclining back into the couch. "I live here."

"And what?" She hardly ever saw Lykor in the evenings. Usually Aesar spent his time with Kal. But Serenna didn't voice her observation. "You're blessing me with your presence tonight?" She sniffed. "I'd rather be alone."

Lykor's lip curled, the tips of his fangs capturing the final shards of sunlight. Serenna considered throwing a mushroom at his head, annoyed with him for being as irritating as he was attractive. *At least he looks different enough from Vesryn. I couldn't live with him if he looked like the prince and...* Serenna let the reflection die. *That's terrible for me to think of considering what happened to him.*

Lykor scratched Aiko behind her fluffy ears, drawing out a purr. Her eyes glittered in Serenna's direction. Like she'd defend *her* roost if Serenna so much as dreamed of staking a claim on Lykor.

On the same end table as Serenna's mushrooms, Lykor's attention hooked on the Heart of Stars she'd been listening to earlier. His gaze flicked back to study the shimmering fungus. Serenna didn't need to be untethered to sense him reaching conclusions about where her collection had come from.

"Fenn's making progress with his ability," Lykor commented. *Conversationally.*

"You're chatty this evening." Serenna's voice dripped with false sweetness. "Shall I make tea while you tell me about your day?"

"Aesar was out today," Lykor muttered. *Elaborating.*

As easy as it would've been for Serenna to despise her captor, something inside of her still softened. Fenn had mentioned that Aesar and Lykor were attempting to divide their time. *I can't imagine sharing my life with another like they do.*

Serenna decided against being snide, carrying on with Lykor's previous comment. "Fenn is..." *How do I describe him?* She grabbed a mushroom, twirling it by the stem. "Fenn has made a habit of using force for *everything*."

A more accurate way to define how he wielded Essence would be "annoying." That afternoon, he was the one to launch a snow drift on *her* head before she could summon the elements to halt the freezing tide of flakes. Though Serenna assumed Fenn would figure out maddening ways to utilize even an innocent talent such as mending.

It wasn't fair how he'd manifested his magic so fast. "I'm almost regretting giving him that power now," Serenna mumbled, staring out the window as the tranquil stars blossomed across the sky.

Lykor's eyes thinned in Serenna's direction. Assessing. "Why did you?" he asked, unbinding his hair, shaking the fringes away from his face. Aiko batted at a stray strand like a cat pawing a string.

Guilt from deceiving Fenn still clung to Serenna like the hoarfrost on the windows. She shrugged, withholding the truth. "It seemed like a better use for Essence since..." She waved her golden shackle between them.

Lykor's jaw clenched, the ticking in his cheek suggesting she'd struck a nerve. He barked and bit out every word. "Do you want to take the tether off?"

"No." Serenna lifted her chin, despite feeling like it was practically an offer, rather than a challenge. She set the fungus back on the table, crossing her arms. "I don't want you in my head."

Lykor made a show of rolling his eyes.

And wouldn't it be fitting if he forced me to ditch the gold and Vesryn finally appeared? Serenna reached for an easy escape, picking up the Heart of Stars. She hoped it was enough to keep

Lykor away from contemplating her power and the tether. For all of his browbeating to find another relic, he'd all but abandoned this one on the dining table like it was nothing more than a decoration.

"What are you doing fiddling with that trinket?" Lykor asked, right on cue.

The topic change had the tension in Serenna's arms dissolving. "You've been away in that jungle while Fenn and I have been searching the fortress for weeks." She relaxed into the couch. "If there are any clues about where the other artifacts might be, couldn't the Heart tell us?"

"And has it blessed you with some miraculous insight?" Lykor sarcastically asked. Aiko stretched, flapping her wings before winding down the front of Lykor's chest to curl up on his lap. "Or have you picked up the habit of prattling like your lieutenant companion?"

Serenna scowled. "You're the one who asked."

"What is it saying then?" Lykor prompted, apparently lowering himself to engaging.

Sighing as if he'd demanded a tedious favor, Serenna held the relic to her ear. She frowned, acting like she heard something aside from the poem.

Lykor leaned closer, burning her with his stare. "What is it saying?" he repeated with increasing interest.

Serenna shushed him, eyes darting, like she was absorbing every word. Letting her jaw go slack, she met Lykor's gaze with awe.

"It says you're a prick."

Lykor barked out an explosive laugh. Serenna glared at him, slouching into the sofa. *I should've known he'd be amused.*

Attention wholly on scratching Aiko under the chin, Lykor asked, "Have you tried *asking* the Heart where the others are?"

"Of course I've tried," Serenna snapped. A blatant lie. And Lykor knew it, judging by his arching brow, the action pinching her chest as it reminded her of Vesryn. "What would *you* ask the dragons?" she volleyed back.

"Ask it, *specifically*, if there are Hearts hidden in the ancient druid capitals." Lykor cracked his neck. "Start with the jungle and the volcano."

Serenna studied the artifact, chewing on her lip as the repeating verses droned on in her head. "How would I do that?"

"I don't know," Lykor growled. "That's a voice I'm not privileged to hear inside of my skull." He waved his gauntlet. "Send a thought into it. Surely you can manage that."

Serenna pursed her lips, focusing on the crystal's depths. The riddle floated over her like snowflakes on the wind.

Greetings, young draka, hear our plight,
New hatchlings from earth and starlight.

Feeling absolutely ridiculous, Serenna interrupted the words. *Greetings great dragon, master of skies...* She faltered, having no clever rhyme.

Serenna sucked in a breath when the Heart ceased its chanting. Whispers lingered at the corners of her mind, giving her the impression of a silent beast rearing its head at a whiff of prey.

Scalp prickling, Serenna hurried on with Lykor's questions. *Do you know what happened to the Hearts? You spoke of the galaxy whelps hiding the relics after binding your power. Did the druids steal any back in the war?*

An unfamiliar voice uncoiled in her thoughts, a snake stretching in the sun. The lilt was higher, but no less guttural than the one that had been intoning before. Pulse thundering, Serenna went rigid, fingers blanching from clenching the artifact.

Hatchling of earth and starlight, we do not know what has passed while chained to dreams, blind to the events of time's tapestry.

Serenna ripped her eyes away from the depths of the crystal as a shadow formed and shimmered into an outline—a great serpent unfolding its wings. She glanced at Lykor, receiving his expectant stare. Turning her attention back to the relic, she asked, *Would the druids have hidden the Hearts in the volcano or jungle cities?*

If the druid tribes subdued the whelps from the stars, it is possible they concealed the Hearts in their domains. A shadow darted in Serenna's mind, a reflection of a reflection, almost giving her the impression of a dragon's form as it spoke. *Search in tempest's eye, where fury reigns; nature's roots, the shade of a glade; or volcano's core, where flames cascade.*

The presence dimmed, like one returning to the soft embrace of sleep.

Do you have more information? Where can we find you? Serenna hurried to ask.

Our places of slumber are scattered like the stars. Young draka, return the Hearts—unbind...

Hands shaking, Serenna blew out a held breath as the voice faded. Bracing herself, she turned to Lykor, repeating what she'd heard.

"That fucking glade," Lykor muttered to himself along with a string of entertaining words that Serenna tucked away for later use. Aiko crawled up his armor, settling on the rim of the sofa. Watching her. "You're going to search the Slag," he ordered, rubbing his temples.

"Right now?" She and Fenn hadn't ventured there. For obvious reasons, not feeling the need to explore the volcano's magma chambers.

"Yes, right now." Lykor sat up, suddenly stern. "What else are you doing? Staring at your thumbs?"

Glaring since she didn't have a rebuttal, Serenna flung a finger in the gesture she'd learned from him.

"Where's Fenn?" Lykor glanced around, as if only now noticing her guard's absence.

Serenna shrugged, telling herself she couldn't be bothered to care. *Probably the Lagoon.*

She rolled her eyes when Lykor ripped open the sitting room door with a burst of force. Two of Fenn's sisters hesitantly peeked in from their post.

"Where's the lieutenant?" Lykor barked, stomping his boots on as Essence vibrated off of him.

Fenn's sisters shared a nervous glance at Lykor's magic. Rank silently elected the one wearing more earrings to speak. "He's typically at the Lagoon at this hour."

Lykor rose and opened a portal. He gently petted Aiko a final time, the gesture so at odds with his acidic command. "Take the elf and tell that oaf to stop fucking around. He's back on duty until they locate the Heart."

Serenna scoffed, folding her arms. "And where are you running off to, *dearly bonded?*"

"I'm returning to that fucking jungle." Lykor cinched his shoulders. "Find the Heart here. Swim through that lake of fire if you have to. As soon as we retrieve the relics, we're crossing the Wastes and leaving this stars-forsaken place."

CHAPTER 45

SERENNA

At the base of the fortress, not too far from the residential district, Fenn's sisters shuffled Serenna into a tunnel. Swaying like curtains in a breeze, glowing vines dangled from the cave's yawning mouth. Serenna ducked under a pair of low-hanging stalactites looming like fangs—fitting for the wraith. Dim teal light emanated from shimmering lichens anchored to the walls, illuminating the way.

Steady drumbeats pulsed through the rocks, nearly pounding in time with Serenna's thudding heart. *This absurd idea of Lykor's could've waited until the morning.* She hadn't intended to ever visit the Lagoon. And that wasn't curiosity creeping into her thoughts about what occurred here—she'd already gleaned enough from Fenn to know.

Wading through steam, wispy tendrils coiled up to Serenna's waist. Fenn's sisters herded her into a cavern, opening up like a gaping maw. Assaulted by activity, Serenna's eyes couldn't go any wider. Dragging her feet in protest was pointless—one of her guards hauled her steadily along by the arm.

Serenna began sweating, smothered by the trapped humidity. Brighter than Vaelyn's turquoise beaches, chalky hot springs twisted around stalagmites, flowing as streams.

Nerves firing, Serenna's attention ricocheted across the gathered wraith. Heat scorched her cheeks, and it had nothing to do with the stifling temperature.

She didn't know where to look. No location was safe. Everywhere her eyes skipped, her gaze bounced off scantily clad or *completely naked* bodies, barely obscured by the cyan waters.

Some of the pools contained groups of raucous wraith, puffing and passing thin, smoking sticks. The sweet floral aromas twined with the cavern's earthy moisture. Wobbling, Serenna's pulse quickened as her breaths became erratic. She suddenly felt weightless—obviously addled by the fumes.

Most of the couples and clusters of wraith were engaged in *mingling*. The writhing bodies and animated moans of pleasure only burgeoned Serenna's embarrassment into a flustered tangle.

Ripping her astonished stare away from a position that she didn't even know was possible, Serenna felt the heat of Fenn's gaze burning into her before her eyes landed on him in an adjacent pool. He had an arm thrown around a male wearing an eye patch, who could only be his partner Koln. Serenna spun to her escorts before she witnessed anything else.

"Can't you bring Fenn to the entrance?" she squeaked. A pathetic plea. "I—I doubt I'm welcome here." While no face-painted reavers were in sight, her presence would surely be unwanted—regardless of what Fenn had claimed.

Fenn's elder sister tightened her claw on Serenna's arm, denying her retreat. Her eyes glittered, reflecting light from the luminous plants dotted on the ceiling. "Lykor was very explicit about bringing you *to* our brother." Neither of her guards had the right to look so pleased by following the order.

Serenna pulled against Fenn's sister and said, "Well I'm here, so retrieve the lieutenant." She staggered, not expecting to actually be released. "I'll be in the tunnel." Recovering herself, Serenna fled from the erotic chambers before they forced her to go any further.

Or rather, she tried.

Serenna slammed into a solid and wet shadow materializing in front of her. Stumbling back a step, she registered Fenn. Shock nearly punched all the air from Serenna's lungs. He scarcely wore anything beyond her tether's key, dangling between the gleaming rings pierced in his chest.

A pillar of carved muscle that could've been chiseled from midnight granite, Fenn's sinewy form would've put a sculpted statue to shame. Serenna's heart thrashed against her ribs like it was the first time she saw him without a shirt. Sharp muscles cut with an excessive number of dips and curves drew her traitorous eyes over the length of his stomach, sweeping over the proudly displayed network of scars.

Mind jumbling into a chaotic knot, Serenna inhaled sharply as the angles of his body yanked her awareness further down. His soaked undergarments were useless at concealing—

Ears on fire, Serenna whirled away before she even braved meeting Fenn's gaze. She couldn't decide if it was more distressing to witness the wraith in various stages of passion or to know that Fenn was essentially naked and aroused behind her. *Well, what did I expect to see in an obscene environment like this?*

She'd beg Fenn's sisters to return her to the Aerie. That's what she'd do. Serenna didn't spare any worry if that made her seem frantic. Looking up at the females, she winced, a petition of desperation. Caging her discomfort between them, Serenna's unhelpful escorts provided her with wicked grins.

The older sister rolled a braid in between her talons. "You're back on duty, Fenny." She shot her brother a smirk over Serenna's head. "Lykor's orders are no rest until you find the Heart."

"Wait!" Serenna pleaded, but her guards vanished, warping away. Eyes wildly searching, running around the steamy chamber like a mouse trapped in a grain bin, she found them shedding their armor, apparently intending to take Fenn's place in the pools.

Serenna crunched her hands into fists, deciding she'd draw on the entire Lagoon and spout all the water into the air to stage her escape. She jerkily revolved in a turn, a marionette on a frayed string. *Keep your eyes on his face, you stargazer.* The exit was behind Fenn. She simply had to dodge around him. And past—

Fenn's scarlet eyes shimmered in a firestorm of roguish delight. "This is an unexpected but welcome surprise." His carnal stare extended through the space between them, clutching Serenna like a vice.

Her stomach swooped from that predatory look. Clever plans dissolving, Serenna battled the urge to run, shamefully wondering what would happen if she were caught.

Excruciatingly confused by what she wanted, Serenna's voice cracked over a hoarse protest. "Lykor made me come."

Grin spreading wider, Fenn tilted his head. His loose hair dripped at the ends, leaving droplets of water sparkling on his waist. He stepped closer, the smolder in his eyes pinning her in place. The room started to spin as he pulled Serenna into his gravity.

"And since you're here…" Fenn grazed her wrist, skating his talons up her arm. "Perhaps you have an interest in *coming* again?"

Serenna sucked in a broken breath, her heart pounding significantly faster than the beating drums. She shuddered when Fenn's claw curled around her shoulder, encompassing her with his unnatural warmth.

The flush from Serenna's cheeks raced down her spine, kindling coals far too low in her belly to be unease. Her wandering eyes drank in the beads of water glistening on the rippled planes of Fenn's abdomen like they were parched. And then lower.

Serenna gouged her nails into her palms, anchoring her stupid fingers to her hands so that she wouldn't reach out. She swallowed, focus riveted on the scraps of clothing plastered to Fenn's hardened body. The temptation to touch him had her clenching her thighs, a futile attempt to smother the heat stoking in her core. The outline of his arousal twitched, as if preening under her attention.

Head emptying faster than water discharging from an open dam, Serenna's eyes flew back to Fenn's face. "What?" she breathlessly asked, thinking he must've said something.

Fenn gave an amused chuckle, jutting his chin toward the cavern's depths. "Do you want to take a dip in the pools?" He slid a claw across her shoulder, fingers wrapping around the base of her neck. "If you'd prefer privacy," he said, his deep cadence strumming a wild chord in her chest, "I know a place."

Serenna was nodding before even processing his words. Her heart nearly burst through her ribs when Fenn extended his fangs. She blinked. "No! I mean…" Serenna cleared her throat, the pause not providing enough time to recover her wits. "Lykor wants us to go to the Slag."

"So…not a no." Fenn's palm swept down her back, a distracting pressure guiding her closer to him, a gentle ebb tugged by the sea. "I don't think the lake of fire will be as pleasurable as the location I have in mind."

Ignited by his blazing fingers, Serenna felt primed to combust. She forced herself to stare straight into the flames dancing in his eyes. "We're supposed to search for the Heart," she whispered, trembling under his touch.

They were having a perfectly normal conversation. That's all they were doing. Her skin was so hot because of the proximity to the thermal pools. Not because Fenn had circled his claws around her waist. They were discussing their orders. Though Lykor could choke on his commands for all she cared.

For whatever reason, Serenna's hand developed a mind of its own, planting against Fenn's chest. Obviously, she couldn't think clearly—the fumes from those smoking sticks were muddling her thoughts.

As his heart beat against her fingertips, Serenna's attention tumbled down the length of Fenn's body again, determined to catalog every inch. *He was concerned about our height difference? I'd be more worried that he wouldn't fit—* Serenna ruthlessly sundered those dangerous thoughts. Something primal—something she refused to consider—sent the blood roaring in her veins.

It was just the atmosphere with everyone engaged in this lascivious activity. She interrupted Fenn and that's why he was so worked up. And now she was too, but that wasn't her fault.

It took more strength than she cared to admit, but Serenna forced herself to peel her hand away. Fenn's fingers cinched tighter around her hips, drawing her gaze back to his. Her insufferable guard smirked, like he knew his exposed body was making her brainless.

Fenn leaned in, skimming his fangs along the shell of her ear. Serenna quivered, warring with every urge to grab him again. His voice rumbled through her, his breath fanning against her neck. "So, you want to go to the volcano's core instead of..." he trailed off, allowing her to choose.

Lykor wouldn't know if we didn't hunt for the Heart tonight. Serenna's inhalations came fast and shallow as reckless desire clouded her thoughts. Some part of her scattered mind broke through the circulating haze of lust.

"I—I didn't mean to interfere with your evening," Serenna whispered, feeling like she was tumbling through open air. "We can start our search in the morning."

Releasing her, Fenn cleared his throat and straightened. "Well, since we have orders, let me retrieve my clothes."

Essence shimmered and pulsed around him. Stretching out a claw, a blue tendril exploded from his palm, streaking behind her. Fenn's clothing flew into his fingers, hauled by force.

Holding Serenna's gaze in that wraith way of his, he didn't blink as he dressed. She lost their silent standoff, her traitorous eyes diving to his middle as soon as he slipped a leg into his trousers. Fenn gave her a fanged grin before retracting his teeth, crouching to tie his boots.

"Come on she-elf, we'd better leave if you're going to insist on looking at me like that." Rising, he bound his hair into a tail at the base of his skull. "Otherwise, I might be tempted to defy that order of Lykor's and discover just how loudly I can get you to scream."

CHAPTER 46

SERENNA

Serenna screamed.

At her expense, Fenn had warped them with more jumps than she assumed were necessary to avoid the reavers' presence—just to hear her squeal. From the Lagoon, they teleported through twists and turns of various tunnels and caverns, traveling deeper into the heart of the fortress.

In the pauses between sending Serenna's stomach catapulting up her throat with his warps, Fenn rattled off the names of the different locations. From the weapons ranges, to the smithies, past furnaces collecting heat and distributing the warmth, he followed one current of magma like a fish swimming upstream.

Fenn finally placed Serenna back on her feet. Bright light exploded around her when she opened her eyes. Teetering on the edge of a craggy precipice, she locked her knees with a gasp.

Serenna looked out over a vast lake of fire at least the size of one of Centarya's training rings. Magma churned below in bubbles of blacks, yellows, and oranges, popping like tar. Channels of sluggish, molten rock webbed out like veins, feeding various rivulets before disappearing through underground tunnels.

A wave of heat rose over the surface, shimmering like liquid metal poured from a forge. Fed from a source somewhere deeper in the volcano's dying heart, the Slag slowly cooled as the centuries wore on, solidifying into stone.

Scaling a path along the cavern walls like one of those pocket goats, Fenn wound up a carved trail hugging the rocky ledge. He angled toward a slender natural bridge, stretched across the length of the chamber.

Serenna balked, placing her hand against the stony wall. "That can't hold us," she protested, wiping her back as a trickle of sweat snaked down her spine.

Completely showing off, Fenn warped to the middle of the suspended rock. Sitting on the edge, he swung his legs over the simmering flames a hundred feet below.

To delay joining Fenn in his precarious position over the magma, Serenna surveyed the domed cavern reaching hundreds of feet above. Pitted cavities reminding her of dips in coral sporadically dotted the rocky walls. Whips of snowy air danced through the chamber like streamers in the wind, ushering in minimal relief through holes honeycombed into the rock.

Serenna reached her perception up to snatch at a coil of air, drawing on a whirlwind of snow. The flakes briefly danced around her before melting, the frosty breeze a fleeting reprieve.

When Fenn beckoned to her from his perch, Serenna tentatively followed his route—minus the warp. She paused, placing a foot on the archway. Narrow, and no more than eight feet across, she was skeptical of the bridge's ability to support their weight.

I'm sure the druids have magic in place holding it up. Fenn had mentioned that something they couldn't perceive preserved the entire fortress. *We'd be boiling alive in this cavern if that wasn't the case.* Serenna almost had herself convinced as she scurried forward to reach him.

Head swimming, she settled next to Fenn. Serenna tucked her legs up to her chest, reluctant to dangle her feet over the ledge like him. "What now?" she asked, surrounding them in a steady swirling of icy wind.

Fenn shrugged. "You moved water in that lake with your magics." He shot her a scowl, evidently still touchy about that shared experience. "Why not shove this magma around in the same way?"

"And the Heart will conveniently be sitting underneath the fire?" Serenna raised her brows. "I doubt it's that simple."

"Well that's not the right attitude to have." Fenn reached out, catching a drifting snowflake. "Lykor wanted us to search here."

"Lykor is also the one who didn't want me practicing with fire." Serenna scoffed at her captor's absurd expectations, binding her hair away from her neck with a leather tie. "All I've ever managed was pulling flames from magma—and that was under stress."

"I think you can do anything she-elf," Fenn said, his certainty making something in Serenna's chest catch. "You're twice as fierce as any warrior, even though you're practically half our size. I don't know anyone more terrifying than you." Spinning his lip ring, Fenn backtracked with a considering frown. "Well, aside from Lykor. But you always grumble about how I—"

"Always state the obvious," she finished for him.

The heat broiling upward had Serenna wiping beads of perspiration away from her face. She abandoned her efforts of hauling in the outside air—it was a losing battle anyway. Wobbling to her feet, Fenn rose to join her.

Teetering on their rocky perch, Serenna suppressed a shudder—open air was the only thing separating them from plunging to a flaming death. She glanced at Fenn. *He can warp us to safety if this bridge collapses. Probably.*

Turning back to study the expanse of roiling molten rock, Serenna drew in a deep breath, sending her focus below. This shouldn't be any different than pushing with force or manipulating water. She simply had to move the burning sludge instead.

Scattering her perception like pollen on the wind, Serenna dissolved into the heartbeat of the earth. Enveloped by her surroundings, the elements thrashed in time with her pulse.

Serenna snatched at the fire, bending the flames to her will. Using her hands to direct the pressure building in her chest, she parted the magma clear across to the edge of the lake. A hissing blaze fountained like a miniature geyser, bubbling faster. Small, disturbed swells rolled, slapping against the rocky wall.

Gritting her teeth, Serenna wrestled with the inferno to keep the laughably narrow channel clear. She and Fenn both scanned the now-exposed steaming floor, observing nothing but bare black rock, solidified into wavy ridges.

Serenna released her grip on the earth. The sluggish flames retraced their disrupted path, crawling back to consume the empty space.

"This seems ridiculous," she protested, wiping a fresh sheen of perspiration from her brow. "What if the Heart is buried beneath that layer of rock? I don't think I can move stone."

"You would surrender so easily? I know you possess more determination than that." Fenn waved a claw, as if trying to cut through her doubt. "Lykor won't permit us to rest until we find the Starry Heart." Like that was supposed to be motivation for her.

"I doubt that," Serenna insisted. "Lykor isn't painfully literal like you." She scowled up at Fenn. "You could help, you know."

"I fear I need to regenerate first." He tugged at his lip ring, shifting his weight. "My magics are running low."

Serenna rolled her eyes. "You found enough time to go to the Lagoon."

To speed up this mission of theirs, she nearly offered to replenish his Well with her reserves. But persuading him to unlock her tether felt like a battle she didn't have the energy for. Serenna decided to appeal to his vices instead. "Lykor said we have to *start* searching tonight—and we did. He didn't say we have to finish. We can continue tomorrow. If we leave now, you can return to your…activities before the night is over."

"Maybe I'm right where I want to be," Fenn all but growled at her, snagging her hand, fingers tightening over hers. "I find it difficult to believe that the druids would bury the relics in unreachable locations."

"But they also wouldn't make it easy for the Aelfyn to reclaim them." Serenna pursed her lips. "And we're only chasing Lykor's interpretation of *possible* locations." Out of principle, she wouldn't allow herself to be swayed by Fenn's logic.

Rings swinging in his ears, Fenn jerked his head toward the lake of fire, ordering her like he would his subordinates. "Keep trying, she-elf. If you need an incentive, I promise to take you back to the Lagoon once we find the Starry Heart."

Serenna huffed but swallowed her protest, letting the retort die in her throat. When Fenn stubbornly shoved his talons into a pocket, she knew there'd be no swaying him.

With a defeated sigh, Serenna extended her hands again, shifting the bubbling magma one sliver at a time. Working around the chamber, rotating like the stars wheeling across the sky, she drove away the flames in sections, revealing the rock underneath.

While Serenna funneled all of her focus on manipulating the fire, Fenn searched the exposed slabs. When he found nothing of note, he'd give her arm a squeeze, signaling for her to move on to the next segment.

Exhaustion began to tug on Serenna's limbs as she maintained a steady connection with the earth. Sweat poured down her face from the exertion while the chamber's heat threatened to singe every pore. Never having tested the limits of her endurance, she was uncertain how long she could channel her shaman power.

"Wait," Fenn finally said nearly a half hour later, fingers tensing against her. "Right there." He pointed with a talon almost directly below, frowning as he peered over the edge of the bridge. "Is that a hatch?"

Fighting against a weary haze, Serenna blinked the chamber back into focus. Gulping in breaths, she swayed, a flickering flame on the cusp of being snuffed out.

Steam coiled above the exposed rocky surface. Smooth, flat metal as large as a door gleamed like a silver mirror in the sun, somehow unharmed from the magma.

"How am I supposed to move that?" Serenna asked, arms shaking as she held the flaming tide away from the revealed strip of earth.

In answer, a burst of Essence whirled around Fenn—a sight Serenna still wasn't accustomed to seeing from a wraith. He punched out a claw, casting down a blue stream of force. Forehead furrowing in concentration, the pressure of his magic hummed in the air. On silent hinges, the metal trapdoor swung open, revealing a darkened cavity burrowing further into the ground.

Fenn's eyes widened, glancing between her and the pit of darkness disappearing below. He asked, "If I warp down there, can you keep the magma back?"

A strike of unease flashed in Serenna's chest. "Take me with you. What if there's more fire down there?"

She bit her cheek, restraining her worry that he'd be charging into the unknown alone—that line of thinking would only encourage him to prove that he could.

Fenn chewed his lip ring, studying her and then the open hatch—weighing the risks to her safety, she had no doubt.

"I might lose my control for a moment after we jump," she

admitted, trembling from the strain of holding the magma back. "But I should be able to keep the flames away from us if we go down that entrance."

Taking matters into her own hands when Fenn continued to hesitate, Serenna clasped his claw. Pulse thrashing in anticipation, she met his apprehensive gaze with an encouraging nod.

His fingers curled around hers, the pressure providing a familiar warning. Bracing herself, Serenna sucked in a breath as he hauled her into shadows.

The world tilted on its axis before her feet hit the ground next to the open hatch. Vision swimming, Serenna reoriented herself, throwing her palms forward. A burst of energy streamed from her fingertips as she drove away the magma sloshing toward the tunnel's mouth.

"Let's hurry," Serenna gritted through her teeth, preventing the fire's advance by flinging a steady pressure against it. Wrestling the heat of the swell for much longer would surely stretch her to her limit.

Compulsively scraping his talons against the lip of the entryway, Fenn stooped as they walked down a set of stairs into the tunnel's darkened depths. Guided by him as they disappeared below the lake, Serenna walked backward down the steps to keep the fire at bay.

Focusing on the magma's dim light when they reached the bottom, Serenna talked over her shoulder. "Do you see anything?" She didn't dare break her wavering concentration by glancing around the dark cavern that had opened up around them.

Fenn's voice came from beside her. "There's a pedestal at the center of the chamber crowned with the Starry Heart."

Serenna's head whipped toward Fenn to gauge his sincerity. His eyes flared, glowing as he peered into the darkness. Fires slipping out of her control, Serenna riveted her attention back toward the entrance, redoubling her efforts. She thrust back the creeping magma from the steps, expelling it from the tunnel.

"Well, go get it," she excitedly urged, waving him on. *It was that simple?* Brimming with a swell of smug triumph, Serenna couldn't wait to rub in Lykor's face that he'd been sitting on top of a relic this entire time.

Fenn's grin matched her own before he melted into the shadows. A breath later, he warped back to her side. Proudly holding the retrieved Heart, blue light from his talent blazed from the crystal.

The ceiling groaned, the only warning before it caved in.

Dropping the relic, Essence exploded from Fenn. A fountain of force erupted, aimed straight up at the falling stone. He collapsed to his knees, punched down by the weight of the chamber.

Boulders crashed to the ground outside of his dome of power, entombing everything but a small pocket of space around them and the stairs leading out. Stony chips crumbled to the floor, streaming in a rush of pebbles. The surrounding rocks quivered, held back by his magic.

Terror spiked through Serenna's ribs when magma seeped in through the shattered roof, dripping like flaming honey. Whirling her hands, she shoved away the fire's slithering advance.

"It must've been rigged with magics." Fenn's body shook as he waged a war, wrestling his power against the disintegrating earth. "I didn't know." An arc of blue light surrounded them, holding back the bottom of the fiery lake. "She-elf, grab the Heart and travel up that staircase before more collapses."

"What are you talking about?" Serenna looked frantically at him, then back toward the cavern's exit.

"That's an order," Fenn barked, palms up, magic billowing out from him in waves. "Return the Heart to Lykor."

Serenna bristled at his sharpened tone. "I don't take orders from you. Get up before more fire comes in and the rest of these boulders fall on our heads."

Fenn's voice was strained. "I can't move. You have to go before my magics deplete."

The blood drained from Serenna's face. Her eyes bounced around the cavern, now lit by Essence and the fire oozing along the rocks.

"I won't be able to return to that bridge without you," she whispered, silently meaning that she wouldn't abandon him to a gruesome death.

Fenn growled matter-of-factly, "Move the flames, walk across the bared stone, and scale the walls." His chest heaved, muscles wracking in waves. "There are enough ledges to climb out of the Slag."

Serenna shook her head, unable to form any words, clenching her fists to clamp down her fear.

More magma seeped in through the cracks in the ceiling as the weight of the lake trickled through. Splitting her focus, Serenna rushed to block the fresh wave of fire from raining down.

"This is not a debate," Fenn snarled. "Lykor needs that Heart. Go."

"Let me untether myself and call him through the bond." Fear festering, Serenna's mind darted around a way out. "Lykor can come retrieve his precious relic and portal us out."

"Are you even capable of mind-speaking across such a distance?" Fenn's fangs extended from the strain, held immobile as if chains wrenched him down. "My Well is draining while we're arguing. Move those flames from the entrance and leave."

Serenna gasped as the roof caved in further, sending another cascade of small rocks tumbling to the ground. Magma hissed, splashing onto stone. Nearly on the verge of her own collapse,

Serenna moved the lurking fiery sludge away from the exit, clearing the path up to the lake.

Ensuring she had a grip on her power, Serenna crumpled next to Fenn and grasped his arm. "Warp us out of here."

"She-elf," he said as an exhaled plea, an attempt to reason with her. "I can't hold the boulders back and shadow walk at the same time."

"You haven't even tried!"

"Some things aren't possible for magics."

"Says the person who's had Essence for a week!"

The fear in Fenn's eyes mirrored her own. "I won't risk you being crushed."

"I'm not leaving you!" Serenna shrieked, her voice echoing against the silent squeeze of stone. Horror twisted through her gut, breaths coming in too fast as her panic spiraled out of control. "I'm not moving until you make me." She swallowed against the tightness in her throat, choked by everything she'd left unsaid—the truth. "And you're only going to do *that* if you warp us away."

Fenn released a dark chuckle through his clenched fangs, clearly at the end of his battle. "Take the key around my neck and release yourself. Don't you have shield magics? Wrap one around yourself and get out of here."

Serenna snatched the Heart from the ground, clutching it to her chest. "I don't know if I can tap into both powers at the same time—it's something I've never tried before."

"And yet you're asking the same of me," Fenn growled, a rightful accusation.

"I've seen Lykor warp and wield Essence." Serenna chewed at her lip, considering Fenn's argument while his body strained under her fingertips. "So you're capable too."

Fenn's eyes dashed around the cavern, searching for another option.

"Warp us, Lieutenant," Serenna hissed, on the verge of tears, her voice clogged with emotion. "I'm going to lose my hold on the magma as soon as you jump us, but you have time before the fire floods this chamber." Her fingers tightened against his arm. "Use it."

The cavern shook. Fenn's power faltered, rocks slipping past his wavering control of force. "I've told you before to not ask of me—"

"I'm not asking. I'm telling," Serenna snapped, struggling to see through the burning in her eyes. "Two jumps," she said, squeezing him tight. "One to the top of the stairs. And one up to the bridge." A tear fell and she angrily wiped it away. "Fenn," she whispered. "Please."

Something broke in his gaze, and it shattered her heart. Serenna knew she had him. This was her fault, manipulating him to the point where he'd accepted her power. And now she was pressuring him beyond what his capabilities might be.

Serenna moved her palm to cradle Fenn's cheek. Her chest caved in as his eyes searched hers, silently pleading. Unable to speak, too scared to put her thoughts into words, she did the only thing that made any sense in the chaos of her confusion. It could fracture his concentration. But if she was going to die here, she wouldn't do it without—

Serenna kissed him.

Fenn sharply inhaled sharply against her mouth. A part of her almost wished that he'd push her away. Scorn her. She didn't deserve his feelings for her. Not after selfishly using him to twist together a plan that failed to unfold.

But his lips pressed back into hers, stealing the air from her lungs. The way their mouths met was soft. Sweet and tender, soothing like a spring rain. It was easy. Carefree. Just like everything else about him.

Somehow, despite the peril, Serenna felt safe in a way that

430

she never had before. And those complicated thoughts she'd kept buried—denied all these weeks—bubbled up in her chest like the magma threatening to envelop them.

Serenna flinched as she heard the chamber crash in around them.

CHAPTER 47

SERENNA

Fenn seized Serenna's waist, hauling her into a whirlwind of darkness. Her knees buckled as the world spun. Vision swimming, Serenna tumbled through open air until she landed on a hard surface—spared from the magma.

Through the haze of her panic, she slowly blinked her surroundings into focus. Chest heaving, splayed on her back across the stone archway, Serenna reflexively reached out, searching for Fenn.

Finding him sprawled out beside her, no sooner than their eyes met, they both burst into laughter. Whether it be from the brush with death or simply joy from still being alive, she couldn't say.

Feet nearly dangling off the edge of the bridge, Fenn dragged his claw over his face, still chuckling. Panic lifting from her chest, Serenna salvaged her breath, staring up at the cavern ceiling. A swirl of snow spiraled in through the natural openings, melting before it reached them. The magma hissed below, settling back against the stony floor.

Serenna uncoiled her fingers from around the Heart still

clutched to her chest, setting the relic aside. Glancing over at Fenn, he'd propped himself up on an elbow, angled toward her. The corner of his lip lifted in that quirky way she found endearing, eyes catching the flames below.

With the back of his finger, he brushed a stray strand of hair away from her cheek. "There's my she-elf."

Something settled in Serenna's heart as it ceased belonging just to her. It was a gentle claiming, like a butterfly landing on a flower. Her mouth automatically curved in response as her gaze roamed over the face of a courageous warrior. Her friend, one who didn't hesitate to throw himself in danger. A fearless protector—almost to a fault.

The chamber faded while what she wanted came into focus. Serenna's eyes must've given away the rest. She didn't know who moved first, but her mouth crashed into Fenn's at the same time as his crashed into hers.

This kiss wasn't delicate like the one moments ago, below the magma. This was bruising. Thoughtless with need. Explosive with want.

The stone archway scraped into Serenna's side as she wrapped her arms around Fenn's shoulders, but all she could feel was him. Drawing her against his chest, Fenn enveloped her like he had the day he'd shielded her in the war room.

Gripping his face, Serenna tugged him closer, trailing her fingers up to the points of his ears, his jewelry gliding under her skin.

"Stars, slay me," Fenn growled against her lips. His body lurched against hers when Serenna made a second teasing pass over the peaks of his ears before weaving her fingers into his hair.

Tongue sweeping past her teeth, Fenn pressed further into her mouth, deepening the kiss. Warmth that had nothing to do with the heated chamber kindled low in Serenna's belly. She released a whimper as his tongue caressed hers. Fenn's claws stiffened against her back when she arched into him, seeking out his hungry lips, loosening another breathy noise.

That was all the permission he needed before he began exploring her body. His fingers began roving—threading in her hair, gliding down her spine, circling around her hips as he pulled her closer to him. His touch was fierce but gentle. Urgent but not demanding.

Serenna melted into Fenn, inhaling scents of pine, fresh snow, and the smoky floral aromas of the Lagoon. She grabbed his lip ring between her teeth and sucked the metal into her mouth. Sparks flew down her spine when Fenn's growl thundered through her chest, the ache between her legs beginning to pulse ruthlessly in response.

Needing to be closer, Serenna hooked a knee over his waist. Fenn swiveled to sit up, cradling her in his lap. Straddling his hips, Serenna anchored him between her thighs. She skimmed her hands over the planes of his chest, flowing over every ripple of muscle through the thin fabric. The shadows they cast from the stony bridge danced across the cavern walls, suspended above the churning magma below.

Fenn tugged at her hair, angling her head to sweep his lips along the edge of her jaw before sucking gently at the slope of her neck. Heart pounding mercilessly, Serenna ground her hips into his. Fenn's fingers tightened where they were resting against her curves, his body hardening between them. Head kicking back, he snarled a curse, sliding his length against her center.

Serenna chased after that sound rumbling from his throat, wanting to hear more of it. Demanding to hear more of it. Grabbing his face, she hauled his mouth back to hers. Fenn met her with the same reckless abandon, their tongues and teeth colliding.

The bridge scraped into Serenna's knees as she began steadily rolling that aching part of herself across the length of him, sweeping like waves flowing onto a shore. Fenn moved with her as she selfishly rode against his rigid hardness, vaulting herself to the brink.

But she didn't want to be the only one taking pleasure—didn't want to go over the edge alone.

Panting, Serenna stilled and broke the kiss, fighting every urge to grind her hips against his. Her entire body was on fire, throbbing for more. Loosening her nails from where they dug into Fenn's scalp, she untangled her fingers from his hair. He reclaimed his breathing with her, resting his forehead against hers while their heartbeats evened out.

Returning to her senses, Serenna pulled back to meet Fenn's gaze. His fangs had extended. He averted his eyes, cheeks flushing a darker shade. Clenching his jaw, she watched him fight a losing battle to retract them.

"Keep them out," Serenna whispered.

She didn't want him to feel like he needed to hide what he was for her sake. He was beautiful, the way the fire shimmered against his skin breathtaking like a trail of stardust draped against the deep indigo of night.

Fenn's claws tightened against her waist, a carnal desire burning in his eyes. He leaned forward, brushing his lips against hers cautiously, as if careful to work around his fangs. Serenna ran her tongue along the point of one. Fenn's hips bucked, seemingly of their own volition.

His kiss turned wild. Meeting his frantic mouth, Serenna sucked in a gasp as he cupped her rear, grinding every inch of his arousal against her. His snarls of pleasure reverberated throughout her body, bouncing off the cavern walls.

The sounds tearing out of his throat had Serenna ripping his shirt off.

Fenn raced her. By the time she unweaved the ties on his trousers—thanking the stars he wasn't in armor—he somehow already had her chest bare and boots off. He used his talons to slice through the last few laces of her pants after growling some obscenities about his claws slowing him down.

They broke apart to shed the rest of their clothing. Fenn hastily arranged the discarded scraps under them, offering some protection from the rugged stone. With an effortless wave of power that had Serenna wondering if he channeled desire to fuel his punch of force, Fenn cast the Heart away from the bridge to a safer location on a rocky shelf.

With nothing between them this time, Fenn sat up and Serenna climbed back into his lap, straddling him. Her eyes drank in every inch of his body, every unveiled ridge and plane, the desire to touch him swiftly turning into a need.

Serenna ran her fingers through his cascading hair, sailing down the taut muscles of his back. Moving to his chest, she glided her palms down over the chiseled ripples of his stomach. She swallowed hard before reaching for his length between them.

"Wait."

Serenna's heart staggered to a halt when Fenn seized one of her hands, preventing her from exploring further. Stopping her before she could reach for that rigid, tempting flesh wedged between them, so close to her aching core.

A protest nearly flew from her tongue as she met his eyes. Instead, Serenna's thighs tightened, drowning in his consuming look. Holding her gaze, Fenn lifted the chain over his neck, pressing the key to her tether into her palm. Serenna's breath caught as he wrapped her fingers over the iron, offering the tiny piece of metal—her freedom.

Fenn searched her face. "You should have the choice to be free like the wind."

Heart squeezing at the gesture, Serenna couldn't even deliver a quip about Fenn defying Lykor. Perhaps she was already free, but in a different way. A reckless impulse nearly had her flinging the key over the bridge.

When she didn't move, Fenn settled the chain over her neck. He traced a talon over the key after it slipped from her hand, nestling between her breasts.

And then lower.

His eyes followed the path his fingers traveled down her stomach before skimming back up her body. Fenn swallowed, throat tensing as his voice came out unsteady. "Stop me if I harm you."

"I think you're the last person who'd harm me." Serenna touched his face, his expression full of concern. "I want you," she breathed, heart twisting, conflicted with what she felt for the prince. She hadn't yet abandoned all hope that he'd find her.

The heat flaring in Fenn's eyes returned Serenna's focus to him. She swiped her thumb over the angles of his cheek. "I…" she began, unsure how to finish the thought.

Everything about him confused her, making her question what she thought she wanted. But there was something about him—something about Fenn's honesty and friendship that had filled a void she hadn't been aware of until he'd entered her life. He'd made her feel special, like she was the center of his universe, even though she wasn't the only one who he shared his heart with. Guilt carved a path through Serenna's chest— similar circumstances had inflicted jealousy before, polluting what she felt toward the prince.

"I want you," she repeated, falling into the fire in his eyes. It was all she had the courage to admit.

Fenn's knuckles grazed the swell of her chest. "You have me, she-elf."

Breath hitching, Serenna's pulse skipped from excited fear as Fenn's wicked claw gently cupped her breast. The danger he controlled sent her heart hammering, knowing he could effortlessly cleave her in two. A moan escaped her as his thumb drifted over her nipple, rolling the bud under the safety of his talons.

Fenn's innocent fascination with surveying her body sent heat blazing out in waves from everywhere he caressed. His talons and eyes trailed a fiery wake across her chest, down her ribcage and over her stomach, across her hips, skimming all the way to her soaking core.

When Fenn tucked his claws away into a fist, Serenna arched into the pressure he offered against her center. Rocking against him, she frantically met his mouth, ready to ignite as he coiled her pleasure into bliss.

Fenn shivered, swearing something nonsensical when Serenna slid her palms between them to return his touch. She couldn't help but stare, the elongation of her fingers the only reason they met as she enveloped his girth. A brief flicker of doubt had her wondering if he was right to be nervous about harming her. Some primal desire overrode that concern—she intended to find out.

Stroking the steel length of him progressively more vigorously with every pass from root to tip earned Serenna approving growls. As they both quivered with desire, she didn't feel the need to wait any longer.

Steadying herself with a hand braced against his chest, Serenna lifted herself, lining her center up with the point of him. Fenn pulled back, going preternaturally still, unblinking as he tracked her motions.

Taut like a pulled bowstring, the wall of his abdomen trembled when Serenna lowered herself a fraction. They shared a sharp inhale as the broad head of his arousal skated through the wetness pooling between her thighs.

Fenn's eyes went feral, chest rising more rapidly than her own as she aligned him, angling to guide him in. He released a guttural groan, throwing his head to the ceiling as her slick folds enveloped the first inch. Talons anchoring on her hips, his mouth returned to claim hers.

Fenn's arousal twitched in her entrance, his lips tilting in response. "Be gentle with me," he said against her, muscles shuddering with restraint. Holding something back. Their gazes locked, his eyes flaring brighter than the magma below.

Serenna's breath hitched as she slowly lowered, taking him in, adjusting to his girth. She gasped from the smallest sting of pain, overtaken by a shock of pleasure as her walls clenched around him. Fenn somehow seemed to have a harder time than her, gritting his fangs, breathing harshly through his nose.

Serenna took her time absorbing every inch, spurred on by Fenn's growling curses. The way his body stretched hers, molding her to him, was bliss and devastation, ecstasy and annihilation. She threw her arms around Fenn's neck, panting against him when there was no space left between them.

Impatient for more, she circled her hips into his, grinding their bodies together. Serenna kissed him as they moved together, sliding back and forth to meet every thrust. His arousal hit every inner wall, every nerve, striking chords deep in her body that she wasn't aware she'd possessed.

"Fenn," Serenna whispered as she rocked against him, riding every wave. Legs clenching against his waist, her movements became erratic as the pressure inside of her spiraled. Fenn's eyes met hers, ruby gaze blazing with a conflagration of lust. "Bite me," she breathed.

He didn't need to be told twice. If anything, he'd been waiting for her to ask. Fenn dove to the slope of her throat, his fingers tightening against her waist. Serenna shuddered as his canines skimmed the sensitive skin below her ear.

She seized the muscles on his back with a gasp, body jolting when his fangs pierced her, sinking into her flesh. A soothing flood of ice chased away the brief prick of pain.

Serenna's eyelids fluttered as the coolness raced down her neck. Reaching her heart, the venom transformed into a warmth, trickling through her veins, limbs going weightless as they relaxed.

Fenn withdrew, his mouth brushing against the punctures. He trailed a kiss, moving across her jaw, returning to her lips. Claiming the rhythm, Fenn clutched Serenna tightly to his chest, guiding each stroke. She collapsed into him feeling more buoyant than intoxicated, elated rather than hazy.

His body drove exactly where she needed, rekindling a molten fire in her core. Every sweeping roll struck her inner walls, the angle of him providing friction against that sensitive spot between her thighs.

The sparks igniting between them had Serenna peaking toward combustion as she rode the motion of his hips. Every thrust, every retreat, threatened to cast her over the precipice of release. She sensed Fenn reading her writhing body, the change in her ragged breathing.

He answered her unspoken question. "I'm right with you, she-elf."

Serenna clutched his shoulders as his movements became frantic, more urgent, driving a faster tempo, steering them toward oblivion. Vision splintering, Fenn's name was on her lips as she shattered. Her center clamped against him as she detonated and dissolved, disintegrating into a thousand stars.

Arms wrapping around her back, Fenn crested the same wave. He seized and shuddered, tumbling off the cliff alongside her. His arousal swelled, stretching Serenna further, throbbing as he spilled his warmth deep into her body. Clutching her, he shivered and groaned her name, resting his head against the space between her neck and shoulder.

The world faded as they held each other, hearts beating in time, recovering their broken breathing as the tremors of pleasure subsided. Still buried in her, Fenn drew back to meet her eyes, his warm breath fanning across her skin. Serenna returned his smile, slowly piecing herself together with every lungful of air.

Fenn cupped her face, thumb stroking her cheek. "Serenna,"

he began, his voice barely there. He searched her eyes with a gentle intensity that had her blood surging for a different reason. "I...I think I'm falling—"

Serenna took the coward's way out before he could say anything else, kissing him to smother what would undoubtedly be flowery words. She wasn't ready to give the feelings a name —to twist her heart further into a knot. Not yet.

Before the kiss turned into anything else, Fenn lifted her in a fluid motion, pulling himself out. Serenna gasped, unprepared for the sudden emptiness.

With laughable ease, he flipped her over, pressing her stomach against their shed clothing on the stone bridge. Spreading her knees with his, the heat from his torso pressed into her spine.

Fenn's mouth swept across her neck, his tongue brushing the tender spot where he'd lodged his fangs. The heartbeat in his chest drummed against her back, his weight on top of her a pleasure of its own.

Hooking an arm around her waist, Fenn jerked her hips up to his. His canines grazed her shoulder, the primal threat of his fangs pinning her down. Serenna inhaled sharply, forgetting to breathe as his arousal nudged against her entrance, still slick with both of them. He apparently didn't need time to recover.

Claws curling against the rocky bridge, Fenn's talons scraped out chips of stone in front of her eyes. "Grab my wrists."

Serenna's pulse lurched. His order had her going liquid all over again, this time without his venom. She'd comply with any command, so long as he didn't plan to stop. Reaching forward, her fingers shook in anticipation, obediently clamping down.

A ricochet of pleasure blazed straight through her as Fenn's body slipped back into hers. Moaning, Serenna writhed against him as he dove into her slowly—torturously slowly—stretching her, letting her body readjust to every inch of his girth.

When he extracted himself, she released a breathy protest.

Her objection quickly became a shriek of pleasure in a voice that definitely wasn't her own as he seated himself fully with one smooth, brutal plunge.

Fenn's words morphed into a growl. "Hang on, she-elf."

Setting a vicious pace, his body slammed into hers over and over, building speed faster and faster, the restraint he'd displayed earlier completely gone. "We're going to see stars."

CHAPTER 48

LYKOR

With a slash of rending, Lykor hacked through a vine in the wretched jungle. The infernal heat in the humid forest only intensified his deteriorating mood. Despite the overwhelming desire to eradicate this unnatural pocket of life in the Hibernal Wastes, he refrained—such destruction might endanger the Heart of Stars.

The clearing he sought was where the wraith had taken refuge after fleeing from the prisons. His muscles spasmed in protest. Those whispering grasses harbored too many torturous memories.

After Kal and Mara had excavated the golden spikes from his spine in the squalor of the dungeons, an infection had ravaged and burned his body. In those days, when the fire in his back became unbearable, Lykor would collapse in a stream near that fucking glade. His shoulders had never fully recovered—the flesh around his bones a gnarled mess like the knobs on the surrounding trees.

Hauling his mind away from the past, Lykor scowled at the darkening night stretching through the endless forest. In hindsight, he should've dumped the elf and Fenn off here and remained in the keep.

Water dripped from monstrous leaves, splashing into his face. Swiping the obnoxious moisture away from his eyes, Lykor's boot snagged on a root. He cursed as he lost his balance, stumbling forward. Spinning around, he blasted the offending plant into the next realm with a punch of force.

The spray of soil showered Lykor's armor as he strode off through the vile jungle, aiming for the clearing that he'd ironically avoided all these years. It was the only "shade of a glade" that he could think of—assuming what the girl had heard through the Heart was correct. He and Aesar had been scouring this forest for weeks without a clear sense of what they should be looking for.

Lykor doubted his luck would have another relic gallivanting into his lap like it had with that shaman spawn. He could only hope the elf and the lieutenant's fucking around would finally lead to something productive—ideally locating the artifact that might be in the keep. Between the encroaching humans, the elven patrols, and the restless reavers, the wraith were overdue to abandon this side of the world.

A dim glow from the moons bled through the canopy of leaves, scattering splotched pools of light across on the loamy forest floor. Flashing glowbugs whirled around Lykor like overbearing chaperones. He slapped the audacious insects away from his face, staining his gauntlet with streaks of their luminous entrails.

An unexpected pulse of magic flared to his left. Alarmed, Lykor pivoted, wrenching on his entire sea of Essence. Darkness exploded from him, a veil of death, ready to defend.

Lykor's heart impaled itself on a rib. Power slipping from the shock, he ruthlessly refortified his control. Shadows churned like a raging whirlpool while he gaped.

It was him.

The elf who'd saved him, the one haunting his dreams. The one he'd recklessly been visiting the military island in search of during the dark hours of the night when Aesar was deep in slumber. The elf that the girl had insisted was called Jassyn. If the blade in Lykor's possession had actually belonged to her friend.

Exiting a colossal tree that was presumably an ancient dwelling, the elf skidded to a halt. He dropped the tome that he was carrying before a violet shield slammed around him.

Aesar had insisted that this location was secure—his twin being the only other with knowledge of this place. Searching the jungle was a risk they'd both agreed to take—surely Vesryn would have no reason to venture here.

But much could change in the century they'd been absent from the realms. The king could very well be dispatching his soldiers to every corner of the world to hunt for the Hearts—or the wraith.

Lykor stalked forward. "How did you get here?" he demanded. A witless question wasting words. Of course the elf had portaled to this miserable jungle. "Are there others with you?"

Surrounded by floating globes of illumination, the elf glanced around and backed away. Raven curls skipped over his forehead as he silently shook his head in response.

Lykor's shadows thrashed, ready to flay the elf if he so much as moved a hand too quickly. He didn't temper the growl in his voice. "Did the king send you?"

The elf's eyes widened before hardening. "This is the only place I could hide from those like him."

He wasn't here for the Heart then.

Still on his guard, Lykor's shoulders marginally relaxed from the reassurance. He retracted the threatening darkness along with his fangs. There wasn't any reason to act like a feral beast. Judging from the elf's shifting gaze, he was already nervous enough.

When Lykor stepped forward, the elf retreated another step. Something Lykor didn't have a name for twisted through his chest like one of the accursed vines strangling the trees. A strange uncertainty needled at him for being the source of fear. He'd never thought twice about intimidating others before—it was all he knew, birthed from the necessity to instill order when the wraith had turned savage in the prisons.

Cautiously stepping forward to retrieve the dropped tome, Lykor resisted the impulse to leaf through the pages to see what the elf was reading. He extended the volume, offering it back. The elf hesitated, his attention hooking on Lykor's gauntlet clamped around the book.

Detesting the constant reminder of what he'd endured, Lykor was seized with the temptation to hide the clawed monstrosity behind his back.

The elf's gaze swept over him, appraising the rest of his armor, flicking over the raw Essence blazing around him. Lykor felt systematically deconstructed, analyzed, and then assembled again. His breath hitched as those fascinating amber eyes lingered on his, the surrounding illumination highlighting flecks of greens and golds. Ears burning with an unfamiliar warmth, the unusual attention made Lykor feel seen for once instead of seen through.

The elf dropped his shield to claim the presented tome. "What can I call you?" he asked.

Lykor blinked, the question slashing through his guard. No one had ever asked him that before. He couldn't number the years he'd spent raging that he wasn't Aesar.

"Lykor," he said, shifting his feet. His spiked boots suddenly felt distractingly heavy.

Following the elf's lead, Lykor reluctantly released his magic and fumbled for something else to say, drawing on what guidance he assumed Aesar would offer if he were awake. He doubted there were any normal questions to ask a stranger in a forgotten jungle.

Lykor settled on stealing the elf's words. That had to be an acceptable response, but his pulse raced faster as he fretted that it might not be. "And…what can I call you?"

"Jassyn," the elf said, his long fingers tightening around the book.

So the girl was right. Lykor unclenched his fists, not knowing when they'd snapped shut.

"I'm going to the glade." The statement sounded like a pathetic attempt at engaging in a conversation—uncharted territory. "Were you…heading in that direction?" A stupid query to fill the silence.

"Are you searching for something?" Jassyn asked, rather than answering the question. A considering frown flashed over his face before he set the volume near the entrance of the tree.

Despite his bewilderment at the elf's presence, Lykor retained enough sense to avoid prattling everything to this stranger. It was unknown where his loyalties truly lay—or how he'd gained knowledge of this jungle.

Lykor cracked his neck and admitted, "Yes—something for the wraith."

Twisting on his heel, Lykor picked his way along a stone path that wound from the ancient dwellings to the clearing. The rocks encased glimmering gems, carrying a luminescent glow of their own as they shimmered against the forest floor like stars in the sky.

While feigning a scan of the jungle, Lykor stole a glance at Jassyn. He'd followed, long strides keeping pace at his side. Height exceeding his own by a hand, Jassyn was much taller than Lykor expected of an elf—let alone one with mortal blood.

Feeling oddly aware of his body's every unwieldy movement,

Lykor focused on the ground so he wouldn't trip over his own fucking feet. The moss-carpeted floor spread out like a blanket beyond the stones, glittering with hues of lustrous cyans and verdant greens.

They silently snaked their way around an undergrowth of ferns and various gargantuan leaves before the foliage opened up, spitting them out at the edge of the glade. A gurgling stream carved a path through the clearing, mirroring the cold radiance of the stars.

"I've been thinking about you—" Lykor drew to a halt, jaw screwing tight as he severed those words. His statement sounded absolutely ridiculous, that of a blathering simpleton like Kal.

Swallowing what he hoped were the last remnants of any further idiotic remarks, Lykor corrected himself. "I've been thinking about what you said. That you could…help me?" He searched Jassyn's eyes for something. For hope, even if it was foolish. "You could release me from the king's power?"

Lykor's pulse droned in his ears, louder than the collective chorus of the jungle's insects. He turned away sharply, his desperate words lingering between them for far too long. A feeling that had to be mortification nearly drove him to slash open a portal and flee—anything to avoid this uncomfortable silence tightening the skin over his bones.

He must've misremembered what Jassyn had said that night, fabricating this delusion in his head. After all, Lykor was the one who'd attacked his home, the wraith most likely killing his comrades. Why would Jassyn want to help him? A barricaded breath loosened from Lykor's lungs when the elf finally spoke.

"It's a slow process," Jassyn said. Lykor turned back hesitantly, watching him drag a hand through his curls, twisting one that was determined to land in front of his eyes. "It depends on how extensive the web of coercion is. I…" he trailed off, eyes ticking around the clearing before orbiting back to Lykor. "I have reason to believe the king had a hand in creating the wraith."

Lykor flinched at the memory of Galaeryn mutilating his mind, experimenting with the compulsive magic. His reaction must've been all the confirmation Jassyn needed.

Jassyn folded his arms across his white leathers, shoulders slumping like he was trying to occupy less space. He glanced away when he spoke. "I'll help you if you're willing to tell me everything you know."

Despite being the one who'd asked for aid, a wave of indecision rippled through Lykor like water disturbed. If he permitted Jassyn to delve into his awareness, he'd be defenseless—at Jassyn's mercy.

The king had ensured Lykor would never be able to form mental barriers again by utterly eviscerating his mind. Everything would be on display, ripe for the taking—Aesar, the wraith's location, and his future plans.

An icy fear crawled out of Lykor's chest at the potential exposure, the armor around his ribcage constricting his air. Steadying himself with the grating of steel, Lykor crushed his gauntlet into a fist at his side.

They both had their secrets, but the offer was one Lykor didn't think he could refuse. He wasn't sure what business Jassyn truly had in the jungle, but the elf hadn't demanded an explanation for his presence either.

"If…if you can assure me that all you will do is unravel the coercion," Lykor finally said, his spine tensing from the risk, "I'll tell you all I know of how the wraith came to be."

Jassyn's eyes examined his with a clever intensity. "But you're not wholly wraith." His arms abandoned their defensive, folded position as he hovered an orb of illumination over his fingertips.

Lykor decided to offer a fraction of his knowledge, to bridge some sort of trust. "Galaeryn returned a handful of my talents." Voice wavering, he focused on digging the toe of his boot into the grass. "I was among the first transformed into a wraith." Not quite the truth since he'd emerged after the king had tortured Aesar, but unpacking everything concerning his other half was a tedious tale for a different day.

Another moment stretched too long. Lykor glanced up, the scars down his back twinging from the motion. Those fascinating eyes trapped him like a fly in honey, prolonging the awkward silence.

Breaking free and rolling the tension out of his cramped muscles, Lykor said, "In the dungeons, I learned what Galaeryn intends to do with the magic he's plundering. He'll redistribute Essence—if he hasn't already. To the pure-bloods, creating arch elves of those who aren't, augmenting the powers of those who are."

Aesar's residual anger roiled in his gut at what his people had endured. Innocent citizens who'd been in the wrong place the night Galaeryn had become drunk on power.

As Jassyn's calculating eyes absorbed every word, Lykor nearly felt compelled to mindlessly spew more. "I think the king encouraged the breeding of half-elves to exploit as a source of magic." Lykor gripped the blade at his side—the one he'd stolen. "Collecting enough Essence will grant him immortality—"

"And he either hasn't harvested enough yet or it requires replenishment over time," Jassyn finished. Tilting his head, he idly trailed his fingers over a vine dangling from a tree. "What if we could work together? Our people could unite against the elves' oppression."

Now he sounded like the girl. "The wraith can't stand against the king as we are." Lykor tightened his grip around the dagger's hilt. "We need an edge. Our own source of power." He glanced at the surrounding jungle as it suddenly became eerily still. "I'm taking my people away—hopefully to a place the elves can't reach. You could come with us."

The words slipped past Lykor's flapping tongue before the thinking part of his brain had any hope of catching up. Heat stained his cheeks. He couldn't believe he'd suggested something so absurd. To someone he didn't even know.

Lykor averted his gaze, attempting to recover with an explanation. "As an Essence wielder, you could help the wraith." Still wildly unbalanced, another inadvertent admission skidded out. "I was going to take your friend Serenna—"

Jassyn moved so fast that Lykor had no time to react. Pain streaked through his shoulder as Jassyn shoved him, crashing his back into a tree.

Instincts flaring from the impact, Lykor ripped Essence to his command. Except...there was nothing there. His attention flew to a golden blade—a sister to the stolen one at his side—protruding from a weak point in his armor. Black blood spilled over the hilt. Before he could tear the weapon out, vines erupted from the ground, wrapping around his wrists, legs, and torso, rooting him in place.

Shock mauled Lykor's chest as he sucked in a broken breath. Jassyn had shaman powers too. Of course he fucking did. Lykor nearly laughed at his own sheer stupidity for not predicting this.

Jassyn drew himself to his full height. "Have you harmed her?" he demanded, towering over Lykor. "Where did you take her?"

This was about the girl? Lykor scoffed. "She came to *me*," he hissed, writhing against the restricting plants. His agitation and fear careened into anger. "Release me."

Lykor flinched when Jassyn's hands rose to the sides of his face. His skin buzzed in alarm from the proximity. The vulnerability. Essence churned around them, a riot of whirling magic.

"Don't fucking touch me," Lykor snarled, extending his

fangs. Every muscle strained as he struggled against the vines. Yanking in progressively more panicked breaths at the constriction, the jungle's oppressive air threatened to smother him.

Jassyn hesitated, fingers hovering next to Lykor's temples before he grabbed him. A thought assaulted Lykor, diving into his mind. A command. Coercion. *Show me where she is.*

Lykor's spine went rigid as telepathic power penetrated his skull. The past repeated itself, drowning him in a whirlpool of horrific memories. Galaeryn invading his mind. Breaking him. Shattering him. Reforging him. Binding him with orders. Rendering him powerless. Tethered and shackled to a cold stone table. Alone. Left for dead time and time again after every transformation from elf to wraith and wraith to elf.

Recoiling from the flashbacks, Lykor furiously wrenched his awareness back to the glade. Jassyn clutched his face, impaling telepathy further into his brain, lodging the magic like a spike.

Lykor snapped his fangs in an attempt to reach him. To stop him. He had no other defense now than to tear out the elf's throat. His pulse thrashed in his head as the coercion tunneled into him, burrowing into his thoughts.

"Get out!" Lykor barked, grappling the restraining plants with all his might.

Disregarding him, Jassyn's fingers tightened around his face. *Where is she?* His eyes glazed over as he delved further, invading the depths of Lykor's mind. *What else do you know?*

Lykor was a fool, believing this elf had wanted to help him. Jassyn's true intentions were clear now—exploiting him to discover what the king had tucked away, concealed from the world.

"I am not a curiosity for you to poke and prod," Lykor snarled.

An animalistic rage erupted at the helplessness. Lykor went wild ripping at the vines—a rabid beast chained, fighting for freedom. He was unable to toss Jassyn out, unable to assemble a mental barricade, unable to do anything but stand there as the elf rifled through *everything*.

Jassyn barreled through those obsidian doors where Lykor kept his memories concealed from Aesar. Nothing was hidden. Everything was on display. Aesar, the wraith, their stronghold's location, the girl, the compulsion to kill Vesryn. Everything.

Jassyn released him, staggering back with a gasp. The surrounding plants wilted, slackening their hold on Lykor.

HE KNOWS. HE KNOWS EVERYTHING ABOUT US. WHAT HAVE I DONE?

"You..." Jassyn trailed off, face frozen in disbelief. Rapidly blinking, comprehension of all he'd reaped spun in those amber eyes that Lykor was going to rip out of his skull. "You're—"

Lykor bared his fangs. Lunging forward, he tore free from the vines, sinking his canines into Jassyn's neck. An explosion of coppery blood curled Lykor's tongue, hauling bile up his throat.

Ice slithered out of his teeth. Lykor didn't hold the toxins back—didn't know how—didn't care if the venom stopped Jassyn's heart.

Lykor dodged to the side as Jassyn stumbled forward and collapsed, a boneless fish flopping to the ground.

Lykor spit profusely before yanking in a breath, inflamed by the assault. The violation. He savagely scrubbed his mouth as an uncomfortable swarm of emotions crawled over his skin like a horde of fleas.

The wraith would have to leave immediately. There was no more time. Not now. Not when he'd foolishly allowed this elf to get so close.

Wild with rage, Lykor's chest heaved as he stared at the elf's crumpled form, paralyzed by the venom. He ripped the blade out of his shoulder, flinging it to the ground.

Clarity returned to Lykor, one breath at a time. The elf

wouldn't be able to inform anyone of his secrets if he was dead...

No, Aesar answered, panicked and alarmed. And now, inconveniently, awake. He hauled rending away before Lykor could obliterate the elf, greedily clutching the talent. Withholding retribution.

IT'S A RISK KEEPING HIM ALIVE, Lykor snarled. DON'T TRY TO STOP ME. Lykor wrestled with Aesar, forcibly shoving him into his precious library, locking him behind the atrium doors. *HE WILL DIE FOR INVADING MY MIND.*

Like scruffing a pup, Lykor seized the back of the elf's white leathers. Dragging his limp body across the glade, Lykor dumped him face down into the stream. Bubbles broke the surface as he floated along the water, releasing his last lungful of air.

As an afterthought, Lykor plucked the stolen dagger from his belt. Whipping it through the air, he impaled the elf's shoulder, lest he try to use Essence to save himself.

Which reminded him... Lykor stepped forward, intending to siphon his power.

Aesar remerged, warring to reassert his control over their body to aid the drowning elf. But Lykor's grip was too strong, his fury too bright. *You're no better than the king if you do that.* Aesar's accusation was quiet, but his words sliced deep.

AND HE'S NO BETTER THAN THE KING FOR RAVAGING MY MIND. IT'S A WASTE NOT HARVESTING HIS MAGIC FOR THE WRAITH.

Sensing Aesar rallying, Lykor pivoted, cleaving the air to tear open a portal. Uninterested in a battle of wills, he retreated to the Aerie, abandoning the search for the Heart.

He'd foolishly put the wraith at risk, but he wouldn't make the same mistake again. And as punishment for stupidly seeking help, Lykor had endured another breach of his mind. It was no less than he deserved for having such an idiotic weakness.

For putting his trust in a stranger. Believing that he could be saved.

It was too late for that.

CHAPTER 49

SERENNA

Swaggering with an arm flung around Serenna's shoulders, Fenn was still marveling at the Heart of Stars, shimmering with a soft blue glow. Gentle starlight trickled down the cavern mirrors, illuminating the empty streets as they journeyed back to the Aerie.

Fenn drew to a halt after they crossed a stony bridge, finally tucking the relic away. Chewing on a lip ring, he cradled Serenna's hands in his claws.

"What?" she prompted while he hesitated.

"After we give the Heart to Lykor..." Fenn's fingers tightened around hers. "Would you be interested in staying with me tonight?" The rest of his words tumbled out in a rush. "You don't have to. I only thought... Perhaps I could tempt you to surrender more sleep?"

The hopeful look smoldering in his eyes heated Serenna's chest. "Are you always this insatiable?" Her voice held more interest than she'd intended. "I can hardly wal—"

Fenn smirked before she had a chance to finish. Cheeks flushing, Serenna wasn't about to stroke his ego by asking if all wraith had the same stamina.

"I'll always be ravenous for you, she-elf." A storm of desire brewed in Fenn's gaze. "I fear I'll perish if I don't have you again."

Serenna released an undignified snort, raising her brows at his dramatics. But his offer tugged at something deeper and thoughts of the prince bubbled to the forefront of her mind.

Guilt still weighed heavily on her chest, now accompanied by her tether's key. Fenn had refused to accept it back, insisting that he'd have a discussion with Lykor about her captivity.

He made it sound so easy. No one simply "had a discussion" with Lykor. But maybe this was different since Lykor had already offered to untether her. *He was being sincere. I think.*

Serenna's hands trembled in Fenn's. It was past time to share her bond with the prince. Fenn had saved her life more than once—surely she could trust him with this. She'd ask him to not inform Lykor and plead with Fenn again to push for uniting their peoples.

It would be better if Fenn could warp us somewhere secluded when I take the tether off. I can't risk Vesryn portaling to the keep.

"I need to tell you something," Serenna began, heart racing. Reclaiming one of her hands, she clutched the iron key dangling on its chain. Her stomach clenched against the secrets she'd kept locked away. Swallowing, she gathered her courage, hoping what she said next wouldn't douse the fire in Fenn's eyes. "It's about a bond—"

So absorbed in her confession, Serenna didn't register the whistle, a sundering of wind. White-hot agony exploded through her shoulder, the impact of something ripping through her body knocking her forward.

Fenn grunted as he caught her, a sickening thud smacking into his side. Dizzy with the lance of pain, Serenna couldn't breathe. Spots flecked her vision when she looked down, uncomprehending of the quarrel driven between them. A crossbow bolt had impaled her from the back, the point now embedded in between Fenn's ribs.

Fenn's eyes ignited with a feral light as he searched behind her. He snarled, an animalistic challenge, fangs aggressively shooting down.

"Eyes on me, she-elf," Fenn gritted out as she tried to look over her shoulder.

Serenna clutched at him as he jostled her wound. Whimpering, she flinched when he grabbed the shaft lodged between them.

"I've got you," Fenn said, holding her in place with his other claw. He stepped back.

A scream Serenna couldn't restrain pierced her ears as the bolt tore the rest of the way through her.

Black blood spilling through his tunic, Fenn yanked the quarrel out of his side, throwing it to the ground. He spun Serenna behind him as he faced the threat.

Taryn led a horde of what must've been the entire clan of reavers. The warriors converged on them, descending from the upper levels of the fortress, stalking across bridges, warping through the streets. Face-painted soldiers had their crossbows loaded and aimed, others had knives and maces drawn.

Serenna's mind splintered in terror. There was nowhere to flee—they wouldn't be able to escape from a group so large even if Fenn tried to warp. She clasped her injury, hot blood streaming down her arm.

"The elven bitch and I have a debt to settle," Taryn snarled at Fenn. She whipped her braids over a shoulder, pointing her crossbow at him. "Stand aside, brother."

Weaponless, Essence surged around Fenn. The magic sputtered, his Well nearly drained. He cast a quick glance back at Serenna, as if ensuring she was still safe behind him. Like either of them could be safe while opposed by hundreds of bloodthirsty reavers.

Taryn only hesitated long enough to scoff before firing.

Fenn punched out a shockwave of force, knocking his sister and the front line of reavers back. Serenna didn't have time to cry out as crossbows twanged. Clearly confident, they didn't bother wasting their supply of gold-tipped bolts. Her hands flew up, quickly blasting a lash of wind to meet the volley of quarrels hurtling toward them.

Serenna's power fell short.

The summoned breeze tossed a handful of the fired arrows off course, pattering onto the stony street. Her wind slowed the others. But not enough. Time stopped along with Serenna's heart as the rest of the barrage struck Fenn.

Heavy thumps sounded. One after the other. Serenna's entire body went numb. Each blow was a smack to his chest, a punch to her gut. Fenn staggered into her before the world tipped and spun as they toppled to the ground.

Serenna suppressed a shriek as her injured shoulder slammed to the stones. Scrambling out from under Fenn, she protectively crouched over him as the reavers converged on them.

They were going to kill him. If they hadn't already. And then they were going to kill her.

Serenna's mind froze with disbelief, unable to process the blood gushing from Fenn's body, peppered with so many bolts. Each breath came faster than the last as panic compressed her ribs. She clutched at Fenn, powerless to prevent his life force from draining out.

She had to mend him.

A hopeless, broken sob escaped from Serenna's throat before she sawed on the reins of her terror. Lungs hauling in air, she whipped her head up, scanning the reavers.

She didn't have time to struggle with her elemental magic against so many before they overwhelmed her. She needed something familiar. Something destructive.

Serenna snatched the key away from her neck. Fingers shaking uncontrollably, palms slippery with Fenn's blood, it took her three tries to unlock her tether. The shackle finally fell off, clattering to the stones.

Essence slammed into her and Serenna seized the torrent of power.

A beacon blazed in her mind.

Lykor.

He was close. Somewhere in the keep—maybe the Aerie—his proximity glaringly bright through the bond.

Hope dared to swell in Serenna's chest, her eyes darting between Fenn and the reavers. She couldn't manage both mending and fighting off an army alone.

Serenna *screamed* for help down the bridge of their bond, desperately hauling on the silver chain connecting them.

Shoving her panic into a dark corner—a place where emotion and feeling didn't exist—Serenna riveted her attention on the reavers brave enough to stalk closer.

She silently vowed that it would be their last mistake.

Gritting her teeth, Serenna lurched to her feet. Shadows streamed from her fists, swirling around her, coiling like vipers before a strike.

Snarling, the wraith fanning across from her hefted their weapons. Knowing a shield would be useless if they loaded golden bolts, Serenna didn't squander her magic on weaving a ward.

Throwing her hands forward, shadows streaked out from her fingertips in a wave of ebony wrath. The closest reavers ruptured, bursting from the inside out. An explosion of blood showered down, splattering against the cobblestone street.

More wraith warped in front of her. Heart pummeling her chest, Serenna spooled the lake of rending, recalling her magic. Lashing out like a cracking whip, she snapped shadowy tendrils around the reavers' throats. Yanking on the cords of power, heads flew off of necks in a spray of blood.

Ripping at Essence, Serenna spun a mantle of midnight over the next wave of wraith materializing, lacerating them in fountains of viscera and bone. Shadows raced across her hands. Channeling webs of darkness, Serenna shrieked, demanding more of her power.

Her vision started to haze as terror rooted. A handful of weeks tethered had reduced the capacity of her Well by an alarming amount.

She was going to be overwhelmed.

A burst of pressure rent the air beside her. A portal opened.

Lykor raged through like a storm, Essence combusting with the intensity of a sun. He'd answered her call. If Serenna wasn't so numb with shock, she would've wept in relief.

With a flash of fury, Lykor bared his fangs at her, stalking forward. Serenna stumbled back at his sudden motion, holding her bloody palms out like she could stop him. Panic climbed back into her throat. She hadn't anticipated that he'd be so vengeful for her reaching out through the bond.

Lykor's attention flicked to Fenn on the ground, gurgling blood.

His rage toward her dissipated. Serenna didn't need to tell him anything. Noticing the reavers, Lykor's crimson gaze pinned on the horde, the fires of retribution flaring in his eyes.

Lykor's focus shifted back to her. An unspoken understanding passed between them—one Serenna would've never expected. He gave her the most subtle dipping of his chin, the barest of nods.

He'd handle it.

Only seconds had ticked by since Lykor had appeared. Serenna's stomach bottomed out as the next surge of wraith approached with golden bolts in their crossbows. She cried out as they aimed the weapons, tossing her hands to frantically reassemble scraps of wind. *Lykor can't stand against—*

The *twang* of crossbows echoed along the streets. He was going to be impaled. Just like Fenn. In her desperation, she'd called Lykor to his death without even realizing it.

The cobblestone street exploded.

Losing her balance, Serenna staggered from the foundations quaking. Lykor whipped force in a hurricane of wrath. Crushing his gauntlet into a fist, he demolished the closest bridge, sending reavers falling to the lower depths. Ripping down a building, bricks flew through the air, forming a shield of solid stone.

Serenna coughed, hacking on the dust clogging the streets while Lykor continued hauling on the fortress. He prowled down the pathway straight for the rebellious wraith, his makeshift barrier moving and rippling around him. The reavers' bolts ineffectively clanged into his impenetrable wall, deflected.

Shadows detonated, the movement of Lykor's magic rapid and violent. The closest reavers erupted into geysers of gore. With a punch of force, the rocks of his shield blasted out, colliding with the horde. Robbed of time to warp, the wraith fell, having no defense against the barrage of bricks ripping holes through their bodies.

Lykor snarled down the bond into Serenna's mind. *Stop fucking staring and mend the lieutenant!*

Serenna wrenched her gaze away from Lykor wreaking havoc. She all but slipped in the pool of Fenn's blood, collapsing to his side.

"Hang on," Serenna said, hands shaking while she corralled her power. Her own speck of pain was forgotten, infinitesimal compared to Fenn's horrific wounds.

Gritting his fangs, blood trickled past the corners of Fenn's mouth. Serenna grabbed a bolt, his torso spurting a black stream of blood when she yanked the shaft free. Too many had impaled him. More than she was willing to count.

Fighting back her welling fear, Serenna's mind began replaying the memory of when Vesryn had been on death's doorstep. But this was worse. So much worse. She was alone, with no hope of any menders coming to her aid.

Serenna frantically set healing lattices to work, cocooning Fenn with scarlet light. His injuries were too severe. He was hemorrhaging too much blood. Panic lacerated Serenna's chest, threatening to cleave her apart. She couldn't do this. She didn't have enough skill or Essence.

Fenn convulsed. He clutched one of her hands where it hovered above his chest. "Take…take your magics back." Voice hoarse and labored with the effort, blood bubbled over his lips as he gasped for a breath. "Take…it."

Serenna's vision swam as she shook her head in denial, tears spilling free. Weaving healing light, she threaded mending over Fenn's body, faster than she'd ever channeled Essence before. She wasn't even stitching him completely closed. Desperate to stop his life force from draining out, she was merely patching his gaping wounds.

Serenna ripped out another bolt, drawing a pained hiss from behind Fenn's fangs. "You're going to need your power when we help Lykor finish off the reavers," she told him with more confidence than she felt. Power rushed through her as she cast a tangle of healing into the wound.

"I won't…" Fenn coughed and Serenna gripped his claw tighter. "I won't need it…where I'm going."

"Don't say that," Serenna hissed, her throat closing around her words. "You're going to be fine." She heard the lie. "I'm mending you." She was trying. "These are hardly scratches for a big brute like you."

"Do it for me, she-elf." Fenn squeezed her fingers weakly, a frail farewell. "I have"—he drew in a labored gasp—"I have nothing else...to give you." His eyes started to glaze, the red flames dimming. "You already have"—his chest shuddered as he strained for another wheezing breath—"a key to my heart."

Serenna's hand tensed against Fenn's claw as he went limp. She snatched his face, bloody hands slipping over his skin.

"Fenn!" Serenna shrieked, her voice breaking with emotion as his eyelids fluttered. "Look at me! You're going to live!"

Silver streamers of light sailed away from him, settling over her like a scattering of starry snow. Devastated by grief, Serenna sobbed. Fenn didn't know what he was doing. He was fumbling, attempting to return her talent.

Serenna's thoughts flashed back to Vesryn in his delirium. But now, she recognized the magic of the connection. A soul reaching out. The fibers of a bond straining to form.

Spasming, a breath rattled from Fenn's chest. This wouldn't be his end. It couldn't be.

Before the faint silver lights winked out, Serenna lashed back with her Essence, the strength of her will. She twined her magic with Fenn's, knotting her power to his. Completing the bond, a bridge solidified between their Wells.

I need you here with me, she pleaded, the words slipping down the bridge of their link. She clutched Fenn's claws as if she could anchor her body to his. He was fading. She could sense it. Hardly able to perceive his awareness, Serenna latched onto his wavering aura.

Find me, she-elf. The echo of his thought brushed her mind, a gentle caress. *When it's your time to soar the skies. Find me, and our dust can dance between the stars.*

A helpless observer to her own sorrow, Serenna couldn't breathe. She choked on her tears, dragging her focus back to mending Fenn's mangled body. Healing light cascaded from her palms, but it wouldn't be enough. It wasn't going to be enough.

Serenna screamed, shattering from the desolation of her heart. She tore out another bolt from the scattering across

Fenn's chest, blanketing him with a wave of crimson light, loosely stitching a single wound.

You're staying with me, she told him. Begged him. *Do you hear me? You're staying right here.*

Silence answered through their flickering bond.

Power discharged next to her, another portal opening. Serenna's first thought—her hope—was that Lykor had sensed her distress and would help heal Fenn.

She blinked, her connection with Lykor telling her that rage still devoured him as he focused on his own battle. She had no idea how he fared against the horde of reavers. But he was alive and unharmed, beyond a minor pain in his shoulder.

Serenna's heart lurched when a familiar pair of ragged boots stepped through the rift.

Time stopped and then tripped. Her breath abandoned her as she locked eyes with a sea of jade.

"Vesryn," she whispered, a fresh sob swelling, breaking from her throat.

The prince was here, standing in front of her in his black leathers, glaives glinting over his shoulders. Essence whirled around him, a halo of light. A renewed wave of tears streamed down Serenna's face as he shone like the sun. In that moment, he was the most breathtaking thing she'd ever seen—a sight she hadn't expected.

And he was *here*. He'd come for her.

Serenna's voice cracked through the storm of her tears. "You're here."

Vesryn kneeled beside her, resting a hand on her back. His brow furrowed with concern and then confusion, eyes darting as he processed her clutching Fenn's twitching body.

Serenna's bond with the prince overflowed with more emotions from him than she could track. A tempest of rage, a shower of surprise, a riot of relief.

And he... Serenna's breath caught, sensing an emotion so strong, so bright—one she'd never discerned from him before.

"You came for me," she repeated, convincing herself that Vesryn was real, struggling to force air back into her lungs. Serenna pried her gaze away from his, sending another web of mending into Fenn's broken body. "You..." She squeezed her eyes shut, the scalding tears too much to bear. *You love me.* She felt it, undeniable warmth from the prince blooming in her chest.

Her head whipped back to Vesryn. He could portal Fenn to a mender. Better yet, he could bring one here. Jassyn could heal Fenn. Everything would be okay.

Serenna's bursting heart screeched to a halt as reality smacked her in the face.

"You're—you're *here.*" She frantically glanced around, searching for Lykor.

Vesryn's mouth opened, but she interrupted him with a shriek. "Get out of here!"

He recoiled. Serenna sensed his alarm and hurt through the bond. He hadn't had time to analyze the mayhem he'd portaled into—he'd been so focused on her.

"Leave!" Serenna pushed him away, desperate to make him understand. "You're in danger. Lykor is going to—"

What felt like a wave of lightning seared Serenna, frying her from the inside out. Body seizing, her perception flew down the bridge with Lykor.

His awareness had vanished. Aesar was nowhere in sight. A void met her, the iron fist of the coercion pulverizing his mind.

Serenna searched the streets, finding Lykor across the wreckage. Countless portals were open, the reavers... Every single one was gone.

Lykor's rabid sight was aimed at Vesryn. Rending spilled out of him—a geyser, an uncontrolled tidal wave of a never-ending night.

Essence exploded through the cavern, chaotic like a dying star.

Serenna didn't even have time to scream as a cataclysm of shadows erupted through the volcano, plunging the world into darkness.

THANK YOU FOR READING!

The story will continue in the Shadows of Stars, releasing in 2025.

If you enjoyed The Chains of Fate, please consider helping other readers discover this series by leaving a review or a rating on Amazon or Goodreads. Independent authors appreciate word of mouth recommendations—we couldn't spread awareness of our books without your help! Thank you again!

ACKNOWLEDGMENTS

A huge thank you to every reader who has picked up an unfinished series from a debut author. Your support means the world and I'm so grateful for the time you've taken to read this story. I truly couldn't do this without your support.

To Michael, who has spent countless hours listening to me brainstorm. Thank you for reading my manuscript multiple times and going above and beyond helping shape this story into what it is today (and thinking of better banter).

To my author friends Roxie, Lacey, K.L, K.C., and Amarah. I love our group chats and you all have taught me so much about publishing! I wouldn't know what to do without all of you! Your friendship means the word.

To my alpha readers Craig and Pieter, thank you so much for reading a messy early draft and helping me mold this into a story. Both of you had input that changed the direction for the better!

To my beta readers Kaitlyn, Brooke, Michaele, and Eden, thank you for taking the time to comb through the early stages of the story and offer your feedback. I definitely was able to work out some wrinkles from all of your help!

To my ARC team and everyone who has shared my story, thank you being my biggest fans and cheerleaders! I'm so grateful to have you all on board.

The series is starting to gain plot momentum and I can't wait to share what's next!

ABOUT THE AUTHOR

Samantha Amstutz is the author of the Aelfyn Archives and is inspired by Wheel of Time, World of Warcraft, Star Wars, Lord of the Rings, the entire romantasy genre.

In her novels, you can expect immersive magic systems, different races, plot and intrigue, slow-burn romance, diversity and inclusion, and believable characters with flaws.

She is honored and beyond thrilled you're reading her work and she hopes something in her created world resonates with yours.

Printed in Great Britain
by Amazon

45557649R00280